At last I held a picture of a young Flo, a snapshot turning white at the edges. It was taken outside a ramshackle building with 'Fritz's Laundry' above the door. A man in a dark suit and wire-rimmed glasses – Fritz? – stood in the middle of six women all wearing aprons and turbans. Flo was recognisable immediately because she was so like me, except that she was smiling and I had never smiled like that in all my life. She looked about eighteen, and seemed to be bursting with happiness, you could see it in her eyes, her dimples, and the curve of her lovely wide mouth.

As I replaced the silver-framed photo on the table, I sighed and was turning away with the intention of getting on with what I'd come for, when I noticed a studio portrait, in sepia tones, of a woman with a baby. There was something familiar about her grim yet good-looking face. I knew nothing about babies and couldn't tell the child's age – it was a boy in an old-fashioned romper suit with a sailor collar – but he was adorable. I looked at the back, and read, 'Elsa Cameron with Norman (Martha's godson), on his first birthday, May, 1939'.

The baby was my father!

Have you read them all?
Curl up with a

Maureen Lee

STEPPING STONES

Lizzie O'Brien escapes her dark Liverpool childhood when she runs away to London – towards freedom and a new life. But the past is catching up with her, threatening to destroy her dreams . . .

LIGHTS OUT LIVERPOOL

There's a party on Pearl Street, but a shadow hangs over the festivities: Britain is on the brink of war. The community must face hardship and heartbreak with courage and humour.

PUT OUT THE FIRES

1940 – the cruellest year of war for Britain's civilians. In Pearl Street, near Liverpool's docks, families struggle to cope the best they can.

THROUGH THE STORM

War has taken a terrible toll on Pearl Street, and changed the lives of all who live there. The German bombers have left rubble in their wake and everyone pulls together to come to terms with the loss of loved ones.

LIVERPOOL ANNIE

Just as Annie Harrison settles down to marriage and motherhood, fate deals an unexpected blow. As she struggles to cope, a chance meeting leads to events she has no control over. Could this be Annie's shot at happiness?

DANCING IN THE DARK

When Millie Cameron is asked to sort through her late aunt's possessions, she finds buried among the photographs, letters and newspaper clippings, a shocking secret . . .

THE GIRL FROM BAREFOOT HOUSE

War tears Josie Flynn from all she knows. Life takes her to Barefoot House as the companion of an elderly woman, and to New York with a new love. But she's soon back in Liverpool, and embarks upon an unlikely career . . .

LACEYS OF LIVERPOOL

Sisters-in-law Alice and Cora Lacey both give birth to boys on one chaotic night in 1940. But Cora's jealousy and resentment prompt her to commit a terrible act with devastating consequences . . .

THE HOUSE BY PRINCES PARK

Ruby O'Hagan's life is transformed when she's asked to look after a large house. It becomes a refuge – not just for Ruby and her family, but for many others, as loves, triumphs, sorrows and friendships are played out.

LIME STREET BLUES

1960s' Liverpool, and three families are linked by music. The girls form a successful group, only to split up soon after: Rita to find success as a singer; Marcia to become a mother; and Jeannie to deceive her husband, with far-reaching consequences . . .

QUEEN OF THE MERSEY

Queenie Todd is evacuated to a small town on the Welsh coast with two others when the war begins. At first, the girls have a wonderful time until something happens, so terrifying, that it will haunt them for the rest of their lives . . .

THE OLD HOUSE ON THE CORNER

Victoria lives in the old house on the corner. When the land is sold, she finds herself surrounded by new properties. Soon Victoria is drawn into the lives of her neighbours – their loves, lies and secrets.

THE SEPTEMBER GIRLS

Cara and Sybil are both born in the same house on one rainy September night. Years later, at the outbreak of war, they are thrown together when they enlist and are stationed in Malta. It's a time of live-changing repercussions for them both . . .

KITTY AND HER SISTERS

Kitty McCarthy wants a life less ordinary – she doesn't want to get married and raise children in Liverpool like her sisters. An impetuous decision and a chance meeting twenty years later are to have momentous repercussions that will stay with her for ever . . .

THE LEAVING OF LIVERPOOL

Escaping their abusive home in Ireland, sisters Mollie and Annemarie head to Liverpool – and a ship bound for New York. But fate deals a cruel blow and they are separated. Soon, World War II looms – with surprising consequences for the sisters.

MOTHER OF PEARL

Amy Curran was sent to prison for killing her husband. Twenty years later, she's released and reunited with her daughter, Pearl. But Amy is hiding a terrible secret – a tragedy that could tear the family apart . . .

Dancing in the Dark

MAUREEN LEE

An Orion paperback

First published in Great Britain in 1999
by Orion
This paperback edition published in 2000
by Orion Books,
an imprint of The Orion Publishing Group Ltd,
Carmelite House, 50 Victoria Embankment,
London EC4Y 0DZ

An Hachette UK company

4

Reissued 1999

Copyright © Maureen Lee 2009

A CIP catalogue record for this book
is available from the British Library.

ISBN 978-0-7528-3443-6

Printed and bound in Great Britain by
Clays Ltd, St Ives plc

The Orion Publishing Group's policy is to use papers that
are natural, renewable and recyclable products and
made from wood grown in sustainable forests. The logging
and manufacturing processes are expected to conform to
the environmental regulations of the country of origin.

www.orionbooks.co.uk

For Yvette Goulden

I am grateful to the authors of the following books which were of great assistance when writing *Dancing in the Dark*. *The Admiralty Regrets* by C. E. T. Warren and James Benson, published by White Lion Publishers, provided a thorough and detailed description of the *Thetis* tragedy. David M. Whale's fascinating series, *Lost Villages of Liverpool*, published by T. Stephenson & Sons, told me all I needed to know about old Toxteth.

Prologue

It always began with the sound of the footsteps, the soft, slithering footsteps on the stairs, the unshod feet in their well-darned socks lifting steadily from one step to the next. He wasn't the sort of man to wear slippers. Listening, I would picture him in my mind's eye, just his feet, coming up the narrow beige carpet with the red border, the cheapest you could buy, worn away to threads in the middle and secured to the stairs with triangular-shaped varnished rods that slid into bronze brackets at the side. I saw everything very, very clearly, in precise detail.

Even on the nights when there were no footsteps, I never went asleep before Mam came home from work at ten o'clock. Then I would feel relatively safe, but not completely. Mam had never been able to offer much protection. But even he must have realised that a child's screams at dead of night might have alerted someone; a neighbour, a passer-by.

I still dream about it frequently, always the footsteps, never the violence, the terror that was to come. Because in my dreams I am not there when he enters the room. My bed is empty. Yet I can see him, as though an invisible me is present, the tall figure of my father, an expression on his dark, handsome face and in his dark eyes that I could never quite fathom. Was it excitement? Anticipation? Behind the glitter of the main emotion, whatever it might have been, I sensed something else, mysterious, sad, as if deep within him he regretted what he was about to do. But he couldn't help it. The excitement, the anticipation, gripped him like a drug, stifling any other, kinder, feelings he might have had.

In my dream I would watch him slowly undo his belt

buckle, hear its tiny click, the feathery smooth sound the leather made as he pulled it through the loops of his trousers until it dangled from his hand like a snake.

Then he would reach down to drag me out of bed, but this was a dream *and I wasn't there!*

Oh, the look on his face then! I savoured it. I felt triumphant.

At this point, I usually woke up bathed in perspiration, my heart beating fiercely, still triumphant, but at the same time slightly sick.

I'd escaped!

Sometimes, though, the dream continued, just as life had continued in the days when the dream wasn't a dream but real.

I knew that when he came back from the pub, always drunk, he would scratch around downstairs, poking here and there, in the dirty washing, through the toys, searching for something that would give him an excuse to let rip with a thrashing. He liked to have an excuse. He'd find the mark of a felt-tipped pen on a tablecloth that Mam hadn't had time to wash, paint dropped on a frock at school, the arm off a doll, or toys not put away properly. Anything could trigger the sound of those slithering footsteps on the stairs.

There were other nights, the best ones, when he would fall asleep in the chair – according to Mam, he worked hard – or he might watch television. Looking back, my memory softened slightly by time, this probably happened more often than I used to think.

In the extended dream I still wasn't there, but now my little sister was in the other bed, and it was she who bore the brunt of our father's anger, or frustration, or excitement, or self-loathing, or whatever it was that made him want to beat the life out of his wife and children, so that his dark shadow lay heavily over our house, even when he wasn't there.

There would be no feeling of triumph when I woke up, just desolation and despair. Would the dreams never end? Would I ever forget? For the rest of my life, would I, Millie Cameron, never stop wishing that I was invisible?

Millie

I

The sun spilled under the curtains, seeping on to the polished window-sill like thick cream. The wine bottle that Trudy had painted and given me for Christmas dazzled, a brilliant flame of light.

Sunday!

I sat up and stretched my arms. I was free to do whatsoever I pleased. In the bed beside me, James grunted and turned over. I slid carefully from under the bedclothes so as not to disturb him, put on a towelling robe and went into the living room, closing the door quietly behind me.

With a sigh of satisfaction at the thought that it was all mine and mine alone, I surveyed the room, its dark pink walls and off-white upholstered sofa, old pine furniture and glass-shaded lamps. Then, I switched on the computer and the television and reversed the answering-machine. In the kitchen, I paused momentarily to admire the effect of the sun on the Aztec-patterned tiles before filling the kettle. Back in the living room, I opened the door to the balcony and stepped outside.

What a glorious day, unseasonably hot for late September. The roses bordering the communal garden were overblown red and yellow cabbages, the dew-drenched grass glistened like wet silk. In the furthest corner, the biggest tree had already begun to shed its tiny, almost white leaves, which scattered the lawn like snow.

I loved my flat, but the thing I loved most was the balcony. It was tiny, just big enough for two black wrought-iron chairs and a large plant-pot in between. I knew nothing about gardening and had been thrilled when the squiggly green things I'd been given last spring had turned out to be geraniums. I enjoyed sitting outside early in the morning with a cup of tea, savouring the salty Liverpool air; the river Mersey was less than a mile away. Occasionally, just before bed on warm evenings, I would sit with the light from the living room falling on to the darkness of the garden, reliving the day.

Most of the curtains in the three-storey block of flats that ran at right angles to my own were still drawn. I glanced at my watch – just gone seven. From the corner of my eye, I became aware of activity in a kitchen on the ground floor. The old lady who lived there was opening a window. I kept my head turned away. If she saw me looking she would wave, I would feel obliged to wave back, and one day I might find myself invited in for coffee, which I would hate. I was glad I'd managed to get a top-floor corner flat. It meant I was cut off from the other residents.

The kettle clicked and I went to make the tea. There was a political programme on television, so I switched it off and turned up the sound on the answering-machine. I nearly turned it down again when I heard my mother's voice. A shadow fell over the day when I remembered it was the last Sunday of the month; my family would be expecting me for lunch.

'. . . this is the third time I've called, Millicent,' my mother was saying shrilly. 'Don't you ever listen to that machine of yours? Ring back straight away, there's bad news. And I don't see why I should always have to remind you about dinner . . .'

I groaned. I could tell from the tone of my mother's voice that the news wasn't seriously bad. Possibly Scotty had been on one of his regular sexual rampages and other dog owners had complained, or Declan, my brother, had lost his twentieth job.

Just as I was about to take my tea on to the balcony, the bedroom door opened and James came out. He wore a

6

pair of dark blue boxer shorts and his straw blond hair was tousled. He grinned. 'Hi!'

'Hi, yourself.' I eyed his tanned body enviously and wished I could turn such a lovely golden brown in the sun.

'Been up long?'

'Fifteen, twenty minutes. It's a lovely day.'

'The best.' He enveloped me in his muscular arms and nuzzled my neck. 'Know what today is?'

'Sunday?'

'True, but it's also our anniversary. It's a year today since we met.' He kissed me softly on the lips. 'I went into a wine bar in Castle Street and there was this gorgeous leggy ash-blonde with the most amazing green eyes – who was that guy you were with? I knew him slightly – that's how I managed to get introduced.'

'I forget.' I felt uneasy. Remembering anniversaries seemed a sign of . . . well, that the relationship *meant* something, when we had always maintained stoutly that it didn't.

'Rodney!' he said triumphantly. 'Rod. I met him at a Young Conservatives' do.'

I moved out of his arms and went to the computer. 'I didn't think you were interested in politics.'

'I'm not, but Pa maintains it's good for business. He makes lots of useful contacts in the Party. Is there more tea?'

'The pot's full. Don't forget to put the cosy back on.'

He saluted. 'No, ma'am.'

When he came back, I was seated at my desk. He stood behind me, his arm resting lightly on my shoulder. 'This your report?'

'Uh-huh.' I pressed the mouse and the words rolled down the screen. I read them quickly. Despite night school and the subsequent A level in English, I worried that my terrible education might be obvious when I wrote at length. I hoped I hadn't split any infinitives or put an apostrophe in the wrong place.

7

'You've spelt "feasible" wrong,' James said. 'It's "-ible" not "-able".'

'I did that bit when I was tired. I probably wasn't thinking straight.' He'd gone to one of the best public schools in the country, followed by a good university.

'Shall we go somewhere special for lunch to celebrate? How about that new place in Formby?'

'Sorry, duty calls. Today I'm lunching with my parents.' I wished I had a more pleasant excuse.

'Of course, the last Sunday . . .' To my irritation, he knelt down and twisted the chair round until we were facing each other. 'When am I going to meet your folks?'

'What point is there in you meeting them?' I said coldly.

'You've met mine.'

'You invited me, I didn't ask.' I disliked going to see his family in the converted, centuries-old farmhouse in its own grounds three miles from Southport. I felt out of place, uncomfortably aware of the stark contrast between it and my own family's home on a council estate in Kirkby. His mother, with her expensive clothes and beautifully coiffured hair, was always patronising. His father was polite, but in the main ignored me. A business-man to the core, he spent most of the time on the phone or ensconced in his study plying fellow businessmen with drink. Phillip Atherton owned three garages on Mersey-side, which sold high-class sports cars to 'fools who've got more money than sense', according to my own father. Atherton's rarely dealt in cars worth less than twenty thousand pounds. James was nominally in charge of the Southport garage, but his father kept a close eye on all three.

The phone went. James was still kneeling, his arms around my waist. After three rings, the answering-machine came on, with the sound still turned up. My mother again. 'Millicent. You've not been out all night, surely. Why don't you call back?'

8

James's eyes sparkled. 'Millicent! I thought it was Mildred.'

'I would have hated being Mildred even more.' I got up quickly to pick up the receiver. I didn't want him hearing any more of the whining voice with its strong, adenoidal Liverpool accent, one of the reasons I'd told my mother never to call me at the office. 'Hello, Mum.'

'There you are!' She sounded relieved. 'Can we expect to see you today?'

'Of course.'

'Sometimes I worry you'll forget.'

I rolled my eyes. 'As if!'

'Don't be sarcastic, Millicent. After all, it's only once a month you visit. You'd never think you only lived a few miles away in Blundellsands. Mrs Mole's Sybil comes every week from Manchester to see her mam.'

'Perhaps Mrs Mole's Sybil's got nothing else to do.'

'You might like to know she's got two kids and a husband.' There was a pause. 'You've become awfully hard, luv.'

'Don't be silly, Mum.' With an effort, I made my voice softer. Mum set great store by the regular family gatherings now that only Declan was left at home. 'What's the bad news?' I enquired.

'Eh? Oh, I nearly forgot. Your auntie Flo's dead. The poor old soul was knocked down by a car or something. But the thing is, luv,' her voice throbbed with indignation, 'she was already six feet under by the time some woman rang to let your gran know.'

'Why should Gran care? She had nothing to do with Flo.' Auntie Flo had, in fact, been a great-aunt, and the black sheep of the family, I had no idea why. Gran never mentioned her name. It was only when Auntie Sally had died ten years ago that I first set eyes on Flo, at the funeral. She was the youngest of the three Clancy sisters, then in her sixties, had never married, and seemed to me an exceptionally mild old woman.

9

'Blood's thicker than water,' my mother said meaninglessly.

'What did Auntie Flo do that was so awful?' I asked curiously.

'I think there was a row, but I've no idea what it was about. Your gran would never talk about it.'

I was about to ring off, when Mum said, 'Have you been to Mass?'

To save an argument, I told her I was going to the eleven o'clock. I had no intention of going to Mass.

I replaced the receiver and looked at James. There was a strange, intense expression in his light blue eyes, and I realised he'd been watching me like that throughout the entire conversation with my mother. 'You're very beautiful,' he said.

'You're not so bad yourself.' I tried to sound jokey. Something about his expression disturbed me.

'You know, marriage isn't such a bad thing.'

Alarm bells sounded in my head. Was this a roundabout way of proposing? 'That's not what you've said before.'

'I've changed my mind.'

'Well, I haven't.' He came towards me, but I avoided him by going on to the balcony. 'I've tried it before, remember?'

James was standing just inside the window. 'You didn't keep his name. Were things really so awful?'

'I didn't want his name once we were no longer a couple. And it wasn't awful with Gary, just deadly dull.'

'It wouldn't be dull with me.'

So it *was* a proposal. I stuffed my hands in my dressing-gown pockets to hide my agitation and sat down. Why did he have to spoil things? We'd made it plain to each other from the start that there was to be no commitment. I liked him – no, more than that, I was very fond of him. He was good to be with, extraordinarily handsome in a rugged open-air way. We got on famously, always had loads to talk about, and were great together in bed. But I didn't want to spend the rest of my life with him or with anybody else. I'd struggled hard to get where I was and wanted to get further, without having a husband questioning my every decision, interfering.

I remembered Gary's astonishment when I said I wanted to take an A level. We'd been married two years. 'What on earth d'you want that for?' I recalled his round pleasant face, his round moist eyes. We'd first gone out together at school and had married at eighteen. I'd realised, far too late, that he'd been my escape route from home.

Why did I want an A level? Perhaps to prove to myself that I wasn't as stupid as my teachers had claimed, for self-respect, to gain the enjoyment from books that I'd only briefly experienced before my father had put a brutal stop to it.

'I'd like to get a better job,' is what I said to Gary. I was bored rigid working at Peterssen's packing chocolates. 'I'd like to learn to type as well, use a computer.'

Gary had laughed. 'What good will all that stuff be when we have kids?'

We were living in Kirkby with his widowed mother, not far from my parents. Although we'd put our name down for a council house, one would not be forthcoming until we had a family – not just one child but two or three. I visualised the future, trailing to the shops with a baby, more kids hanging on to the pram, getting a part-time job in another factory because Gary's wages as a storeman would never be enough to live on. It was why we'd never even considered buying a place of our own.

Two years later we were divorced. A bewildered Gary wanted to know what he'd done wrong. 'Nothing,' I told him. I regretted hurting him, but he was devoid of ambition, content to spend the rest of his life in a dead-end job wondering where the next penny would come from.

My father was disgusted, my mother horrified: a Catholic, getting divorced! Even so, Mum did her utmost to persuade me to come back home. My younger sister, Trudy, had found her own escape route via Colin Daley and had also married at eighteen, though Colin had been a better bet than Gary. After ten years they were still happily together.

Wild horses couldn't have dragged me back to Kirkby and my family. Instead, I rented a bedsit. I had my English A level by then, and until I bought my flat, nothing in life had given me more pleasure than the certificate to say I'd achieved a grade C. Armed with a dictionary, I'd *made* myself read the books I'd been set, struggled for hours to understand them in the bedroom at my mother-in-law's, while downstairs Gary watched football and game-shows on television. It seemed no time before the words started to make sense, as if I'd always known them, as if they'd been stored in my head waiting to be used. I shall never forget the day I finished reading *Pride and Prejudice*. I'd understood it. I'd enjoyed it. It was like discovering you could sing or play the piano.

Once settled in the bedsit, I took courses in typing and computing at night school, left Peterssen's, and began to wonder if it had all been worth it as I drifted from one dead-end office job to another – until three years ago, when I became a receptionist/typist with Stock Masterton, an estate agent's in the city centre. Of course, I had to tell George Masterton I'd worked in a factory until I was twenty-four, but he had been impressed. 'Ah, a self-made woman. I like that.'

George and I hit it off immediately. I was promoted to 'property negotiator'. Me! Now George was contemplating opening a branch in Woolton, a relatively middle-class area of Liverpool, and I was determined to be appointed manager, which was why I was writing the report. I'd driven round Woolton, taking in the number of superior properties, the roads of substantial semi-detacheds, the terraced period cottages that could be hyped and sold for a bomb. I'd noted how often the buses ran to town, listed the schools, the supermarkets . . . The report would help George make up his mind and show him how keen I was to have the job.

It was through Stock Masterton that I'd found my flat. The builders had gone bankrupt and the units were being sold for a song, which was unfair on the people already there who'd paid thousands more but the bank wanted its money and wasn't prepared to wait.

'I've not done bad for someone not quite thirty,' I murmured to myself. 'I've got my own place, a job with prospects and a car. I earn twice as much as Gary.'

No, I'd not done badly at all.

Yet I wasn't happy.

I leaned on the iron rail and rested my chin on my arms. Somewhere deep within I felt a deadness, and I wondered if I would ever be happy. There were times when I felt like a skater going across the thinnest of ice. It was bound to crack some time, and I would disappear for ever into the freezing, murky water beneath. I shook myself. It was too lovely a morning for such morbid thoughts.

I'd forgotten about James. He appeared on the balcony tucking a black shirt into his jeans. Even in casual clothes, he always looked crisp, neat, tidy. I turned away when he fastened the buckle of his wide leather belt.

He frowned. 'What's the matter?'

'Nothing. Why?'

'You shuddered. Have you gone off me all of a sudden?'

'Don't be silly!' I laughed.

James sat in the other chair. I swung up my bare feet so they rested between his legs and wriggled my toes.

'Cor!' he gasped.

'Don't look like that. People will realise what I'm doing.'

'Would you like to do it inside where no one can see?'

'In a minute. I want to take a shower.'

13

He smacked his lips. 'I'll take it with you.'

'You've just got dressed!'

'I can get undressed pretty damn quick.' He looked at me quizzically. 'Does this mean I'm forgiven?'

'For what?' I was being deliberately vague.

'For proposing. I'd forgotten you modern women take an offer of marriage as an insult.' He took my feet in his hands. I was conscious of how large and warm and comforting they felt. 'As an alternative, how about if I moved in with you?'

I tried to pull away my feet, but he held them firmly. 'The flat's only small,' I muttered. 'There's only one bedroom.'

'I wasn't contemplating occupying the other if there were two.'

No! I valued my privacy as much as my independence. I didn't want someone suggesting it was time I went to bed or asking why I was late home – and did I really want the living room painted such a dark pink? I wished I could start the day again and stop him proposing. I had been quite enjoying things as they were.

James put my feet down carefully on the balcony floor. 'Between us we could get somewhere bigger.'

'You've changed the rules,' I said.

He sighed. 'I know, but it's not the rules that have changed, it's me. I think I'm in love with you, Millie Cameron. In fact, I know I am.' He tried to catch my eyes. 'I take it the feeling isn't reciprocated?'

I bit my lip and shook my head. James turned away and I contemplated his perfect profile: straight nose, broad mouth, pale, stubby lashes. His hair lay in a flattering corn-coloured quiff on his broad, tanned forehead. He didn't look as if it was the end of the world that I'd turned him down. According to his mother, who never failed to mention it, there'd been an army of girls before me. How many had he fallen in love with? On reflection, I didn't know him all that well. True, we talked a lot, but never about anything serious; the conversation rarely strayed from films, plays, mutual acquaintances and clothes. Oh, and football. I sensed he was shallow and also rather weak, always anxious still to do his father's bidding, even though he, too, was twenty-nine. I felt irritated again that he'd spoiled things: I didn't want to give him up. Nor did I want to hurt him, but I couldn't be expected to fall in love with him just because he had decided he was in love with me.

'Perhaps we can talk about it some other time?' I ventured. In a year, two years, ten.

He closed his eyes briefly and gave a sigh of relief. 'I was worried you might dump me.'

'I wouldn't dream of it!' I jumped to my feet and ran inside. James followed. Outside the bathroom, I removed my dressing-gown and posed tauntingly before opening the door and going in. I stepped into the shower and turned on the water. It felt freezing . . . but it had warmed up nicely by the time James drew the curtain back and joined me.

2

'Hello, luv. You look pale.'

'Hi, Mum.' I made a kissing noise two inches from my mother's plump, sagging cheek. Whenever I turned up in Kirkby, she claimed I looked pale or tired or on the verge of coming down with something.

'Say hello to your dad. He's in the garden with his tomaters.'

My father – I couldn't even *think* of him as Dad – had always been a keen if unimaginative gardener. Dutifully, I opened the kitchen door and called, 'Hello.'

The greenhouse was just beyond the neat lawn, the door open. 'Hello there, luv.' My father was inside, a cigarette hanging from his bottom lip. His dark, sombre expression brightened at the sound of my voice. He threw away the cigarette, wiped his hands on the hips of his trousers and came inside. 'How's the estate-agency business?'

'Okay.' I managed to keep the loathing out of my voice. He told everyone I was a property negotiator. Nowadays he claimed to be proud of his girls. 'Where's Declan?'

'Gone to the pub.' Mum couldn't have looked more harassed if she had been preparing a meal for royalty. She took a casserole out of the oven, then put it back. 'What have I done with the spuds? Oh, I know, they're in the top oven. Declan's promised to be back by one.'

'Will the grub be ready on time, luv?'

'Yes, Norman. Oh, yes.' Mum jumped at her husband's apparently mild question, though it was years since he'd beaten her. 'It'll be ready the minute our Trudy and Declan come.'

'Good. I'll have another ciggie while I'm waiting.' He disappeared into the lounge.

'Why don't you have a talk with your dad and I'll get on with this?' Mum said, as she stirred something in a pan.

As if I would! She'd always tried to pretend we were a perfectly normal family. 'I'd sooner stay and talk to you.'

She flushed with pleasure. 'What have you been up to lately?'

I shrugged. 'Nothing much. Went to a club last night, the theatre on Wednesday. I'm going out to dinner tonight.'

'With that James chap?'

'Yes,' I said shortly. I regretted telling them about James. It was when Declan had jokingly remarked he was thinking of trading in his bike for a Ferrari that I'd told him about Atherton Cars where several could be had. The following Sunday, my father had driven over to Southport to take a look and I was terrified that one day he'd introduce himself to James.

Mum was poised anxiously over the ancient cooker, which had been there when we moved into the council house in 1969. I was three and Trudy just a baby; Declan and Alison had yet to arrive. These days, Mum wasn't just stout but shapelessly stout. Her shabby skirt, with no waist to fix on, was down at the front and up at the rear, revealing the backs of her surprisingly well-shaped but heavily veined legs. I always thought it would have been better if they had grown fat with the rest of her. As it was, she looked like some sort of strange insect: a huge, round body stuck on pins. Her worried, good-natured face was colourless, her skin the texture of putty. The once beautiful hair, the same ash-blonde as her children's, she cut herself with no regard for fashion. She wore no makeup, hadn't for years, as if she was going out of her way to make herself unattractive, or perhaps she just didn't care any more. She was fifty-five but looked ten years older.

Yet she'd been so lovely! I recalled the wedding photo on the mantelpiece in the lounge, the bride tall, willowy and girlish, the fitted lace dress clinging to her slim, perfect figure, though her face was wistful, rather sad, as if she'd been able to see into the future and knew what fate had in store for her. Her hair was long and straight, gleaming in the sunshine of her wedding day, turning under slightly at the ends as mine and Trudy's did. Declan and Alison had curly hair. None of us had taken after our father, with his swarthy good looks and bitter chocolate eyes. Perhaps that's why he'd never liked us much; four children and not one in his image.

The back door opened and my brother came in. 'Hi, Sis. Long time no see.' He aimed a pretend punch at my stomach and I aimed one back. 'That's a nice frock. Dark colours suit you.' He fingered the material. 'What would you call that green?'

Declan had always been interested in his sisters' clothes, which infuriated our father who called him a cissy, and had done his brutal best to make a man out of him.

'Olive, I think. It was terribly cheap.'

' "It was terribly cheap!" ' Declan repeated, with an

17

impish grin. 'You don't half talk posh these days, Mill. I'd be ashamed to take you to the pub.'

A shout came from the lounge. 'Is that you, Declan?'

'Yes, Dad.'

'You're only just in time,' the voice said pointedly.

Declan winked at me. He was twenty, a tall, lanky boy with a sensitive face and an infectious smile, always cheerful. He was currently working as a labourer on a demolition site, which seemed an entirely unsuitable job for someone who looked as if a feather would knock him down. I often wondered why he still lived at home and assumed it was for Mum's sake. He shouted, 'Scotty met this smashing bitch. I had a job getting him home. I forgot to take his lead.'

'Where is Scotty?'

'In the garden.'

I went outside to say hello to the little black dog that vaguely resembled a Scotch terrier. 'You're an oversexed ruffian.' I laughed as the rough hairy body bounced up and down to greet me.

A car stopped outside, and seconds later two small children came hurtling down the side of the house. I picked up Scotty and held him like a shield as Melanie and Jake launched themselves at me.

'Leave your aunt Millie alone!' Trudy shouted. 'I've told you before, she doesn't like kids.' She beamed. 'Hi, Sis. I've painted you another bottle.'

'Hi, Trude. I'd love another bottle. Hello, Colin.'

Colin Daley was a stocky, quiet man, who worked long into the night six days a week in his one-man engineering company. He was doing well: he and Trudy had already sold their first house and bought a bigger one in Orrell Park. I sensed he didn't like me much. He'd got on well with Gary and perhaps he thought I neglected my family, left too much to Trudy. During the week, she often came over to Kirkby with the children. He nodded in my direction. 'Hello, there.'

'Do you really not like kids?' Jake enquired gravely.

18

He was six, two years older than his sister, a happy little boy with Colin's blue eyes. Both Trudy's children were happy – she'd made sure of that.

'I like you two,' I lied. As kids went they weren't bad, but talking to them got on my nerves. I hugged Scotty, who was licking my ear. I would have had a dog of my own if I hadn't spent so much time at work.

Jake looked at me doubtfully. 'Honest?'

'Cross my heart.'

We all went indoors. Mum shrieked, 'C'mon, you little rascals, and give your gran a hug.' The children allowed themselves to be kissed, then they cried, 'Where's Grandad?'

'In the lounge.'

Mum looked wistful as Melanie and Jake whooped their way into the other room. She said, 'They've got a thing about their grandad.'

'I know.' It was strange that Trudy's children adored the man who'd once nearly killed their mother. She still bore a scar from his belt buckle above her left eyebrow.

When I went in Trudy was standing in the lounge, hovering near her children who were sitting on their grandad's knee. I noticed her eyes flicker to the big hands, one resting on each child's waist. We looked at each other in mutual understanding.

As usual, the meal was revolting. The mound of mashed potatoes, watery cabbage and stewing steak on my plate made me feel nauseous. 'I'll never eat all this, Mum,' I protested. 'I asked you not to give me much.'

'You look as if you need a decent meal, luv. There's a nice apple charlotte for afters.'

'It's a sin to waste good food,' my father said jovially.

I caught Trudy's eye and Declan hid a grin. The final Sunday of the month was a day for catching eyes and making faces. Odd phrases brought back bitter memories: 'It's a sin to waste good food,' was not said so lightly in those days.

On the surface, it was a civilised gathering, occasionally merry, a family united for Sunday lunch, except for Alison, of course. But I always felt on tenterhooks, as if I were watching someone blowing up a balloon, bigger and bigger until it was about to burst. Perhaps it was just me. Perhaps no one else remembered how Colin detested his father-in-law, how nervous Mum was, what Sunday dinner used to be like when we were little. Even now, I was still terrified that I would drop food on the tablecloth and that a nicotine-stained hand would reach across and slap my face, so hard that tears would come to my eyes, even though I'd sworn at an early age never to let him see me cry.

The conversation had turned to Auntie Flo. 'We were friendly for a while before I married your dad,' Mum said. 'I went to her flat in Toxteth a few times, though your gran never knew.' She turned to me. 'Actually, Millicent, that's where you come in.'

'What's Auntie Flo got to do with me?'

'Your gran wants her place cleared before the rent runs out, otherwise the landlord might chuck everything away.'

'Why ask me?' I could think of few less welcome things to do than clear out the belongings of an old lady I hadn't known. 'Why not you or Gran or Trudy? What about that woman you mentioned, the one who rang?'

Mum looked hurt. 'It's not much to ask, luv. I can't do it because . . .' she paused uncomfortably '. . . well, your dad's not very keen on the idea. Gran's too upset, she's taken Flo's death hard. Anyroad, she never goes out nowadays.'

'And Trudy's already got enough to do,' Colin growled.

'As for the woman who rang, she's just someone who lives upstairs. We don't want a stranger going through Auntie Flo's precious things, do we?'

'What precious things?' I noticed my father's fists clench. I reminded myself that he could do nothing to me now. I could say what I liked. 'I don't know what she did for a living, but I can't imagine Auntie Flo having acquired many precious things.'

'She worked in a launderette till she retired.' For a moment, Mum looked nonplussed. Then she went on eagerly, 'But there'll be papers, luv, letters perhaps, odds and ends of jewellery your gran would like. The clothes can go to one of those charity shops, Oxfam. I'm sure you'll find someone to take the furniture, and if there's anything nice, I wouldn't mind it meself. Declan knows a lad who has a van.'

I tried to think of a way of getting out of it. My mother was looking at me pleadingly, her pasty face slightly moist. *She* would probably thoroughly enjoy going through the flat, but Dad had put his foot down for some reason, not that he'd ever needed a reason in the past. The mere fact that Mum *wanted* to do something was enough. Maybe I could get it done in a few hours if I went armed with several cardboard boxes. I had one last try. 'I've always avoided Toxteth like the plague. It's full of drugs and crime. People get murdered there, shot.'

Mum looked concerned. 'Oh, well, if that's —' she began, but my father butted in, 'Your auntie Flo lived there for over fifty years without coming to any harm.'

It seemed I had no choice. 'Oh, all right,' I said reluctantly. 'When's the rent due?'

'I've no idea.' Mum looked relieved. 'The woman upstairs will know. Mrs Smith, her name is, Charmian Smith.'

'Don't forget to give me the address before I go.'

'I won't, luv. I'll ring and tell Gran later. She'll be pleased.'

After the meal was over and the dishes washed, Trudy produced the bottle she'd painted for me. It was exquisite, an empty wine bottle transformed into a work of art. The glass was covered with roses and dark green leaves edged with gold.

'It's beautiful!' I breathed, holding it up to the light.

'I'm not sure where to put it. The other one's in the bedroom.'

'I'll do you another,' Trudy offered. 'I'm running out of people to give them to.'

'I suggested she have a stall in a craft market,' Colin said proudly. 'I could look after the kids if it was a Sunday.'

I waved the bottle in support. 'That's a great idea, Trude. You'd pay ten pounds for this in a shop.'

'Millicent.' Mum came sidling up. 'Have you got much to do this afternoon?'

I was immediately wary. 'I'm in the middle of a report.'

'It's just I'd like to go and see Alison.'

'Can't you go yourself?' The only reason she'd learned to drive was so she could visit Alison in the home.

'There's something wrong with the car. Your dad promised to get it fixed but he never got round to it.'

He'd probably not got round to it deliberately. He would prefer to think his youngest child didn't exist. 'Sorry, Mum. As I said, I've got this report to write.'

'We'll take you, luv.' Colin must have overheard. 'It's a couple of weeks since we saw Alison.'

Mum looked grateful. 'That's nice of you, Colin, but there's nothing for Melanie and Jake to do. They get fed up within the first five minutes.'

'You can leave the kids here with me,' my father offered.

'No, thanks,' Trudy said, much too quickly.

'I'll take them for a walk once we get there, and you and Trudy can stay with Alison,' Colin said.

In the midst of this discussion, I went upstairs to the lavatory. The bathroom, like everywhere else in the house, reeked of poverty, the linoleum cracked and crumbling, the plastic curtains faded. I was well into my teens before I discovered we were relatively well-off – or should have been. My father's wages as a toolmaker were high, but the family saw little of the money. He'd been a betting man all his life and a consistent loser.

As usual, I couldn't wait to be back in my own place. I felt guilty for refusing to visit Alison, pity for my mother, angry that the pity made me turn up for the monthly get-togethers then guilty again, knowing that I would get out of coming if I could. When Stock Masterton had begun to open on Sundays, I'd hoped that would provide a good excuse, but George, a workaholic, insisted on looking after the office himself with the help of a part-timer.

After saying goodbye, I went outside to the car. Several boys were playing football in the road, and someone had written 'Fuck off' in black felt pen on the side of my yellow Polo. I was rubbing it off with my handkerchief when Trudy came out with the children. She ushered them into the back of the family's old Sierra and came over to me. 'Thank the Lord that's over for another month.'

'You can say that again!'

'I can't get me head round this kindly old grandfather shit.' Absent-mindedly she rubbed the scar over her left eyebrow.

'I suppose we should be thankful for small mercies.'

Trudy regarded me keenly. 'You okay, Sis? You look a bit pale.'

'Mum said that. I'm fine, been working hard, that's all.' I eyed the car. I'd got most of it off and what was left wasn't legible. 'Look, Sis, I'm sorry about Alison,' I said in a rush, 'but I really have got work to do.'

Trudy pressed my arm. She glanced at the house where we'd grown up. 'I feel as if I'd like to drive away and never have to see another member of me family again, but we're trapped, aren't we? I don't know if I could bear it without Colin.'

As I started the car, I noticed that the house opposite had been boarded up, although children had broken down the door and were playing in the hallway. There was a rusty car without wheels in the front garden. As I drove away, the sun seemed to darken, although there wasn't a cloud to be seen. Unexpectedly, I felt overwhelmed by a sense of alienation. Where do I belong? I wondered, frightened. Not here, please not here! Yet I'd been born in a tower block less than a mile from this spot, where nowadays Gran lived like a prisoner: Martha Colquitt rarely left home since she'd been mugged for her pension five years ago. My own flat in Blundellsands was a pretence, more like a stage set than a proper home, and I was a fake. I couldn't understand what James saw in me, or why George Masterton was my friend. I was putting on an act, I wasn't real.

And what would James think if he met my slovenly mother and chain-smoking father, and if I told him about my brutal childhood? What would he say if he knew I had a sister with severe learning difficulties who'd been in a home since she was three, safely out of my father's way? A scene flashed through my mind, of my father slapping Alison, knocking her pretty little face first one way then the other, trying to make her stop saying that same word over and over again. 'Slippers,' Alison would mutter, in her dull monotone. 'Slippers, slippers, slippers.' She said it still, when agitated, although she was seventeen now.

Even if I were in love with James, we could never marry, not with all the family baggage I had in tow. I reminded myself that I didn't want to get married again, that I wasn't capable of falling in love. I belonged nowhere and to nobody.

Nevertheless, I had an urgent desire to see James. He was calling for me at seven. I looked forward to losing myself in empty talk, good food, wine. He would bring me home and we would make love and all that business with my family would be forgotten, until the time came for me to go again. Except, that is, for the dreams, from which I would never escape.

It wasn't until Thursday that I managed to get to
Toxteth. James had tickets for a jazz concert at the
Philharmonic Hall on Monday night, which I had forgotten about. Tuesday, I'd promised to go to dinner with
Diana Riddick, a colleague from the office whom I'd
never particularly got on with, but then few people did.
Diana was thirty-five, single, and lived with her elderly
father, who was a 'pain', she claimed, particularly now
that his health was failing. She was a small, slight woman,
permanently discontented, with a garishly painted face, a
degree in land and property management, and an eye on
the position of manager of the Woolton office. She didn't
realise that I nursed the same ambition and when we
were alone together she openly discussed it. I'd suspected
she had an ulterior motive in inviting me that evening
and it turned out she wanted to pump me about George's
plans.

'Has he ever talked to you about it?' she asked, over the
Italian meal. There were red and white gingham cloths
on the tables and candles in green bottles dripping wax.
The walls were hung with plastic vines.

'Hardly ever,' I replied truthfully.

'I bet you anything he gives the job to Oliver.' She
pouted. Oliver Brett, solid and dependable, was the
assistant manager, in charge when George was away,
which was rare.

'I doubt it. Oliver's nice, but he's proved more than
once he couldn't handle the responsibility.' I sipped my
wine. On nights like this, Kirkby seemed a million miles
away. 'Remember last Christmas when he rang George
in the Seychelles to ask his advice?'

'Hmm!' Diana looked dubious. 'Yes, but he's a man.
The world is prejudiced in favour of men. I shall be very
cross if it's Tweedledum or Tweedledee.'

'That's most unlikely.' I laughed. Apart from June,

who'd taken my old job as receptionist, the only other permanent members of staff were two young men in their mid-twenties, Darren and Elliot, startlingly alike in looks and manner, which accounted for their nicknames. Both were too immature for promotion. 'George has never struck me as being prejudiced against women,' I added.

'I might do a survey of Woolton, see how the land lies.' Diana's rather heavy eyebrows drew together in a frown and the discontented lines between her eyes deepened further. 'I'll type up some notes for George.'

'What a good idea,' I murmured. I hadn't added to my own report since last week.

It was late on Wednesday when I returned to the office in Castle Street. I'd taken a couple, the Naughtons, to see a property in Lydiate. It was the sixth house they'd viewed. As usual, they walked round several times, wondering aloud whether their present furniture would fit, asking if I would measure the windows so they could check if the curtains they had now would do. George insisted that keys were returned, no matter how late, and it was almost eight when I hung them on the rack. George was still working in his glass-partitioned office and Oliver was about to go home. His good-natured face creased into a smile as he said, 'Goodnight.'

I was wondering if there was time to drive to Blundellsands, collect the cardboard boxes I'd acquired from a supermarket, return to town and start on Auntie Flo's flat. I couldn't bring the car to work with boxes on the back seat when I had to take clients to view.

Before I'd made up my mind George came out of his cubicle. 'Millie! Please say you're not doing anything special tonight. I'm longing for a drink and desperately in need of company.'

'I'm not, doing anything special that is.' I would have said the same whatever the case. At the moment it was essential to keep in George's good books.

We went to a wine bar, the one where I'd met James.

George ordered a roast-beef sandwich and a bottle of Chablis. I refused anything to eat. 'You should get some food down you.' He patted my hand in a fatherly way. 'You look pale.'

'That's what everyone keeps telling me. I'll wear blusher tomorrow.'

'You mean rouge. My old mother used to go to town with the rouge.' His mother had died only a year ago and he missed her badly, just as he missed the children his ex-wife and her new husband had taken to live in France. He was alone, hated it, and buried himself in work to compensate. George Masterton was fifty, tall and thin to the point of emaciation although he ate like a horse. He wore expensive suits that hung badly from his narrow, stooped shoulders. Despite this, he had an air of drooping elegance, enhanced by his deceptively laid-back, languid manner. Only those who knew him well were aware that behind the lazy charm George was an irascible, unpredictable man, who suffered from severe bouts of depression and panic attacks.

'Why the desperate need for company?' I asked lightly. I always felt at my oddest with George, as if one day he would see what a fake I was, and never speak to me again.

'Oh, I dunno.' He shrugged. 'It was Annabel's birthday on Monday. She was sixteen. Thought about whizzing over to France on Eurostar but told myself Stock Masterton would collapse without me. Really, I was scared I wouldn't be welcome. I'm supposed to be having her and Bill for Christmas, but I shan't be at all surprised if they don't come.'

It was my turn to pat his hand. 'I bet Annabel would have been thrilled to see you. As for Christmas, it's months off. Try not to start worrying yet.'

'Families, eh!' He chuckled. 'They're a pain in the arse when you've got them, and a pain when they're not there. Diana calls her old dad everything but now he's ill she's terrified he'll die. Poor chap, it sounds like cancer. Anyway, how's your lot over in Kirkby?'

'Same as usual.' I told him about Auntie Flo's flat, and he said bring the boxes in tomorrow and put them in the stationery cupboard until I found time to go. He asked where the flat was.

'Toxteth, William Square. I don't know round there all that well.'

His sandwich arrived. Between mouthfuls, he explained that William Square had once been very beautiful. 'They're five-storeyed properties, including the basement where the skivvies used to work. Lovely stately houses, massive pillars, intricate wrought-iron balconies like bloody lace, bay windows at least twelve feet high. It's where the nobs used to live at the turn of the century, though it's gone seriously downhill since the war.' He paused over the last of the sandwich. 'Sure you'll be safe? Wasn't there a chap shot in that area a few weeks ago?'

'I'll go in daylight. Trouble is, finding the time. Things keep coming up.'

George grinned. 'Such as me demanding your company! Sorry about that. Look, take tomorrow afternoon off. I'd feel happier about you going then. Don't forget to take your mobile and you can call for help if you get in trouble.'

'For goodness sake, George, you'd think I was going to a war zone!'

'Toxteth's been compared to one before now. As far as I'm concerned, it's as bad as Bosnia used to be.'

At two o'clock on a brilliantly sunny afternoon, William Square still looked beautiful when I drove in. I found an empty parking space some distance past the house I wanted, number one, and sat in the car for several minutes, taking in the big, gracious houses on all four sides. On close inspection, they appeared anything but beautiful. The elaborate stucco decorating the fronts had dropped off leaving bare patches like sores. Most of the front doors were a mass of peeling paint, and some houses were without a knocker, the letterbox a gaping hole. Several windows were broken and had been repaired with cardboard.

The big oblong garden in the centre of the square was now, according to George, maintained by the council. Evergreen trees with thick rubbery leaves were clumped densely behind high black railings. I thought it gloomy, and the square depressed me.

With a sigh, I got out of the car, collected some boxes and trudged along to number one. Two small boys, playing cricket on the pavement, watched me curiously.

The house looked clean, but shabby. Someone had brushed the wide steps leading up to the front door recently. There was a row of four buzzers with a name beside each, so faded they were unreadable. I ignored these and used the knocker – Charmian Smith lived on the ground floor.

A few seconds later the door was opened by a statuesque black woman not much older than me, wearing a lime green T-shirt and a wrap-round skirt patterned with tropical fruit. Her midriff was bare, revealing satin smooth skin. She held a baby in one arm. Two small children, a boy and a girl, stood either side of her, clutching her skirt. They stared at me shyly, and the little girl began audibly to suck her thumb.

'Mrs Smith?'

'Yes?' The woman regarded me aggressively.

'I've come for the key to Flo Clancy's flat.'

Her expression changed. 'I thought you were selling something! I should have known from the boxes. Not only that, you're awful like Flo. Come in, luv, and I'll get the key.'

The magnificent hallway had a black-and-white mosaic tiled floor and a broad, sweeping staircase with an intricately carved balustrade. The ornate ceiling was at least fourteen feet high. But whatever grand effect the architect had planned was spoilt by crumbling plaster on the coving and cornices, hanging cobwebs and bare

29

wooden stairs worn to a curve. Several sections of balustrade were missing.

I stayed in the hall when Charmian Smith went into the ground-floor room, the children still clinging to her skirt. Through the open door, I could see that her flat was comfortably furnished, the walls covered with maroon flock paper. Everywhere was very clean, even the massive bay window, which must have taken hours to polish.

'Here you are, girl.'

'Thanks.' I took the proffered key and wondered if the children stayed attached to their mother like that all day. 'Which floor is it?'

'Basement. Give us a shout if you need anything.'

'Thanks.' I returned outside. The basement was situated behind railings down a narrow well of steep concrete steps. Little light reached the small window. I struggled down with the boxes to a tiny area full of old chip papers and other debris. To my consternation, there were several used condoms. I wondered what on earth I'd let myself in for.

A plastic mac and an umbrella were hanging from a hook inside the tiny lobby, and a brass horseshoe was attached to the inner door, which opened when I turned the knob.

The first thing I noticed when I stepped inside was the smell of musty dampness, and the cold, which made me shiver. Although it was broad daylight, I could see nothing. I fumbled for a light switch just inside the door and turned it on. My heart sank. The room was crammed with furniture, and every surface was equally crammed with ornaments. There were two sideboards, one very old and huge, six feet high at least, with little cupboards in the upper half. The other was more modern, but still large. Beneath the window was a chest covered with a red fringed shawl and a pretty lace cloth. On top of that a vase stood filled with silk flowers; poppies. I touched them. The effect was striking, as if they'd been bought to echo the colour of the shawl. It was the sort of thing I might have done myself.

I walked slowly down the room, which ran the length of the house. Halfway along, two massive beams had been built into the walls to support an equally massive lintel, all painted black, and covered with little brass plaques. An elderly gas fire was fitted in the green-tiled fireplace, and on each side of it, more cupboards reached to the ceiling, one of which I opened. Every shelf was stuffed to capacity: clothes, crockery, books, bedding, more ornaments stored in boxes . . .

'I can't do this all on my own,' I said aloud. I had no idea where to start, and I would need more like a hundred cardboard boxes than ten.

A window at the far end overlooked a tiny yard, which was level with the rear of the flat. It contained a wooden bench, a table and plant-holders full of limp pansies. The wall had been painted almost the same pink as my lounge – another indication that Auntie Flo and I had shared similar taste. The woman upstairs had said I was like Flo, and I wondered if there was a photograph somewhere.

I turned and surveyed the room, and supposed that, in its way, it had charm. Very little matched, yet everything seemed to gel together nicely. There was a large brown plush settee and a matching chair with crocheted patch-work covers on the backs and arms. Obviously Flo hadn't believed in leaving an inch of space bare. There were numerous pictures and several tiny tables, all with bowls of silk flowers. Linoleum, with a pattern of blue and red tiles, covered the floor, and there was a handmade rag rug on the hearth. A large-screen television stood next to an up-to-date music centre, a record visible on the turntable beneath the smoky plastic lid.

If only it wasn't so cold! On the hearth next to the fire I saw a box of matches. I struck one, shoved it between the bars and turned the knob at the side. There was a mini explosion and the gas jets roared briefly before settling down into a steady flame.

31

I held out my hands to warm them and remembered I'd been looking for a photo of Flo. After a while, I got up and moved round the room again until I found some on a gate-leg table, which had been folded to its narrowest against the wall. The photos, about a dozen in all, were spread each side of a glass jar of anemones.

The first was a coloured snap of two women taken in what looked like a fairground. I recognised Flo from Auntie Sally's funeral. Despite her age, it was obvious that she'd once been pretty. She was smiling at the camera, a calm, sweet smile. Her companion wore a leopardskin coat and black leggings, and her hair was a violent unnatural red. I turned the photo over: 'Me and Bel at Blackpool Lights, October 1993'.

There was a picture of Auntie Sally's wartime wedding, which I'd seen before at Gran's. The bride, in her pin-striped suit and white felt hat, looked like a character out of *Guys and Dolls*. Another wedding photo, the couple in Army uniform. Despite the unflattering clothes, the woman was startlingly lovely. On the back was written, 'Bel & Bob's wedding, December, 1940'. Flo and Bel must have been friends all their lives.

I found two more photos of Bel getting married; 'Bel & Ivor's wedding, 1945,' in what looked like a foreign setting, and 'Bel & Edward's wedding, 1974' showed a glamorous Bel with a decrepit-looking old man.

At last I held a picture of a young Flo, a snapshot turning white at the edges. It was taken outside a ramshackle building with 'Fritz's Laundry' above the door. A man in a dark suit and wire-rimmed glasses – Fritz? – stood in the middle of six women all wearing aprons and turbans. Flo was recognisable immediately because she was so like me, except that she was smiling and I had never smiled like that in all my life. She looked about eighteen, and seemed to be bursting with happiness, you could see it in her eyes, her dimples, and the curve of her lovely wide mouth.

As I replaced the silver-framed photo on the table, I

sighed. More than half a century spanned the images of my great-aunt, the one in Blackpool, the other outside Fritz's Laundry, yet little seemed to have happened over the years to make her expression change.

I was turning away with the intention of getting on with what I'd come for, when I noticed a studio portrait, in sepia tones, of a woman with a baby. There was something familiar about her grim yet good-looking face. I knew nothing about babies and couldn't tell the child's age – it was a boy in an old-fashioned romper suit with a sailor collar – but he was adorable. I looked at the back, and read, 'Elsa Cameron with Norman (Martha's godson), on his first birthday, May, 1939'.

The baby was my father! His mother had died long before I was born.

I slammed the photo face down on the table. I was shivering again. I was about to kneel in front of the fire once more, when I saw the sherry on the sideboard, the modern one. My jangling nerves needed calming. In the cupboard underneath, where I looked for a glass, I found five more bottles of sherry, and several glasses hanging by their stems from a circular wooden stand. I filled a glass, drank the sherry, filled it again, took it over to the settee, and sank into the cushions. My head was buzzing. How could such a beautiful child grow up to become such a *monster*?

The sherry took effect quickly and I began to relax. There seemed to be a sagging hole in the middle cushion of the settee into which my bottom fitted perfectly. Perhaps it was where Flo had always sat. Outside, cars drove past occasionally and I could hear children playing in the square. People walked by, heels clicking on the pavement, only their legs visible from the knees down through the small window by the door.

I put down the empty glass and promptly fell asleep.

When I woke up it was nearly half past five. There was a throbbing between my eyes, which I supposed was the result of the sherry, though it didn't feel particularly unpleasant. I would have given anything for a cup of tea or coffee and remembered I hadn't seen the kitchen yet, or the bedroom.

I got to my feet, and staggered towards the door at the back of the room, where I found myself in a little dark inner hall with a tiled floor and two more doors, left and right. The left led to a tiny Spartan kitchen with a deep porcelain sink, a cooker older than Mum's, a digitally operated microwave oven but no fridge. In the wall cupboard, behind several packets of biscuits, there was coffee and, to my relief, a jar of Coffeemate. I put a spoonful of each with water in a flowered mug and stuck it in the microwave to heat.

Whilst I was waiting, I went back to the inner hall, opened the other door, and switched on the light. The bedroom was mainly white, curtains, walls, bedspread. A pair of pink furry slippers were set neatly side by side under the bed. A large crucifix hung from the wall and there was a statue of Our Lord on the six-drawer chest, surrounded by smaller statues. The walls were covered with holy pictures: Our Lord again, Baby Jesus, the Virgin Mary, and an assortment of saints. Otherwise, the room was sparsely furnished: apart from the chest, there was only a matching wardrobe with a narrow, full-length mirror on the door, and a little cane bedside table, which held an old-fashioned alarm clock, a white-shaded lamp, and a Mills & Boon novel with an embroidered bookmark. An old brown foolscap envelope was propped against the lamp. I picked it up and put it in the pocket of my linen jacket. It might contain Flo's pension book, which would need to be cancelled.

I admired the wardrobe and the chest-of-drawers. They looked like stained oak and had been polished to satin smoothness. They'd look lovely in my flat, I thought. I wouldn't have minded the brass bedstead either. My own bedroom furniture had been bought in kits and had taken weeks to put together.

In the kitchen, the microwave beeped. I sat on the bed, which was like sitting on a cloud it felt so soft, and bounced up and down, but stopped when I caught sight of my reflection in the mirror. I saw a tall, graceful young woman who looked years younger than her age, dressed in white and pink, with long slim legs and hair that shone like silver under Auntie Flo's bedroom light. Her wide, generous mouth was turned up slightly — she'd been childishly enjoying bouncing on the bed. At school, she had been regarded as stuck up because of her straight, slightly patrician nose, but James's mother had said once, 'What fine bone structure you have, Millie. Some women would pay a plastic surgeon a fortune for cheek-bones like that.'

The young woman had forgotten to use blusher and she *did* look pale, as everyone had been saying, but it was the deadness in the green eyes that shocked me.

I took the coffee and a packet of custard creams into the lounge, switched on the television and watched *Neighbours*, then an old cowboy film on BBC2.

Just as the film was finishing, I glimpsed through the window the majestic figure of Charmian Smith descending the concrete stairs. I kicked the boxes aside and opened the door, feeling slightly uncomfortable when she gave me a warm smile, as if we were the greatest friends.

'I'd forgotten all about you until our Minola, that's me daughter, collected her kids and said there was a light on in Flo's flat. Me feller's just got home and I wondered if you'd like a bite to eat with us.' She came into the room without waiting to be asked, as if it was something she was used to doing.

'What does your daughter do?' I was astonished to learn that Charmian was grandmother to the children I'd seen earlier.

'She's learning to use a computer. It was when Jay, that's me son, went to university last year, she decided it was time she used her brain.' Charmian's brown eyes danced. 'I told her she'd regret getting married at sixteen. I said, "There's more things to life than a husband and a family, luv," but kids never listen, do they? I didn't listen to me own mam when I got married at the same age.'

'I suppose not.'

'Are you married? Y'know, I don't know your name.'

'Millie Cameron, and no, I'm not married.' I wished the woman would leave so I could get down to work. It seemed imperative suddenly that I take at least half a dozen boxes of stuff to Oxfam tomorrow. To my dismay, she sank gracefully into the armchair, her long bead earrings swinging against her gleaming neck.

'I didn't know Flo had any relatives left after her sister Sally died,' she said, 'apart from Sally's daughter who went to live in Australia. It wasn't until Bel gave me a number to ring after the funeral that I knew there was another sister.'

Bel, the woman in the photographs. '*After* the funeral?'

'That's right, Martha Colquitt. Is she your gran?' I nodded. 'I felt terrible when the poor woman burst into tears, but Bel said that was the way Flo wanted it.' Charmian glanced sadly round the room. 'I can't get used to her not being here. I used to come and see her several times a day over the last year when she was stuck indoors with her terrible headaches.'

'That was very kind of you,' I said stiffly.

'Lord, girl, it was nothing to do with kindness. It was no more than she deserved. Flo was there for me when I needed her – she got me a job in the launderette when me kids were little. It changed me life.' She leaned against the crocheted cover and, for a moment, looked as if she might cry. Then, once again, her eyes swept the room. 'It's like a museum, isn't it? Such a shame everything's got to go. People always fetched her ornaments back from their holidays.' She indicated the brass plaques on the beams. 'We brought her the key and the little dog from Clacton. This was Flo's favourite, though – and mine.' She eased herself smoothly out of the chair and switched on the lamp on top of the television.

I had already noticed the cut-out parchment lamp with its wooden base and thought it tasteless. It reminded me of a cheap Christmas card: a line of laughing children dressed as they might have been in this very square a hundred years ago, fur hats, fur muffs, lace-up boots.

'I'll switch the main light off so you can see the effect once the bulb warms up,' Charmian said.

To my surprise, the shade slowly began to revolve. I hadn't realised there was another behind it that turned in the opposite direction. The children passed a toyshop, a sweetshop, a church, a Christmas tree decorated with coloured lights. Shadows flitted across the ceiling of the long, low room. Hazy, almost lifesize figures passed over my head.

'Tom brought her that from Austria of all places.'

I felt almost hypnotised by the moving lamp. 'Tom?'

'Flo's friend. She loved sitting watching her lamp and listening to her record. The lamp was still on when I came down the day they found her dead in the park. Did you know she got run over?'

'My mother said.'

'They never found who did it. Oh dear!' Now Charmian did begin to cry. 'I don't half miss her. I hate the thought of her dying all alone.'

'I'm terribly sorry.' I went over and awkwardly touched the woman's arm. I hadn't the faintest notion how you were supposed to comfort a stranger. Perhaps another person, someone who didn't have dead eyes, might have taken the weeping woman in their arms, but I could no more have done that than I could have sprouted wings and flown.

Charmian sniffed and wiped her eyes. 'Anyroad, I'd better go. Herbie's waiting for his tea – which reminds me, luv, would you care to join us?'

'Thanks all the same, but I'd better not. There's so

37

much to do.' I gestured at the room, which was exactly the same as when I'd come six hours before.

Charmian squeezed my hand. 'Perhaps next time, eh? It'll take you weeks to sort this lot out. I'd offer to help, but I couldn't bear to see Flo's lovely stuff being packed away.'

I watched her climb the steps outside. I had meant to ask when the rent was due, so that I could pay a few weeks if necessary. I hadn't realised that dusk had fallen and it was rapidly growing dark. The streetlights were on, and it was time to draw the curtains. It was then that I noticed someone standing motionless outside. I pressed my face against the glass and peered upwards. It was a girl of about sixteen, wearing a tight red mini-dress that barely covered her behind and emphasised the curves of her slight body. There was something about her stance, the way she leaned against the railings, one foot slightly in front of the other, the way she held her cigarette, left hand supporting the right elbow, that made me guess immediately what she was. I pressed my face the other way, and saw two more girls outside the house next door.

'Oh, lord!' I felt scared. Perhaps I should let someone know where I was – James or my mother – but I couldn't recall seeing a phone in the flat and, despite what George had said, I'd left my mobile in the office. As soon as I'd had another cup of coffee, I'd go home and come back on Sunday to start packing.

The kitchen was like a fridge. No wonder Flo didn't have one – she didn't need it. I returned, shivering, to the settee, my hands wrapped round a mug of coffee. It was odd, but the room seemed even more cosy and charming now I knew about the girl outside. I no longer felt scared, but safe and secure, as if there was no chance of coming to any harm inside Auntie Flo's four walls.

I became aware of something stiff against my hip and remembered the envelope that I'd found in the bedroom. It didn't contain a pension book, but several newspaper cuttings, yellow and crisp with age, held together with a paper clip. They'd mainly been taken from the *Liverpool Daily Post* and the *Echo*. I looked at the top one for a date – Friday, 2 June 1939 – then skimmed through the words underneath.

THETIS TRAPPED UNDERWATER was the main headline, followed by a sub-heading. *Submarine Fails to Resurface in Liverpool Bay – Admiralty Assures Relatives All Those On Board Will Be Rescued.*

I turned to the next cutting dated the following day. *Hope Fading For Men Trapped On The Thetis. Stunned Relatives Wait Outside Cammell Laird Offices in Birkenhead.* The news had been worse when the *Echo* came out that afternoon: *Hope Virtually Abandoned for 99 men on Thetis*, and by Sunday, *All Hope Abandoned . . .*

Why had Flo kept them?

On the television, the lamp swirled and the children did their Christmas shopping. I found myself waiting for a girl in a red coat and brown fur bonnet to come round. She was waving at someone, but the someone never appeared.

Flo had sat in this very spot hundreds, no, thousands of times, watching the girl in red, listening to her record. Curious, I went over to the record player and studied the controls. I pressed Play, and beneath the plastic lid, the arm lifted and swung across to the record.

There was crackling, then the strains of a vaguely familiar tune filled the room, silent until then except for the hiss of the gas fire. After a while, a man's voice, also vaguely familiar, began to sing. He'd been in a film on television recently – Bing Crosby. 'Dancing in the dark,' a voice like melting chocolate crooned.

What had Flo Clancy done to make her the black sheep of the family? Why had Gran refused to mention her name? Bel, Flo's old friend, had asked Charmian Smith to ring Gran *after* the funeral because 'that's the way Flo wanted it'. What had happened between the sisters to make them dislike each other so much? And

39

why had Flo kept cuttings of a submarine disaster beside her bed?

I would almost certainly never know the truth about Auntie Flo, but what did it matter? As the lamp slowly turned and dark shadows swept the ceiling of the room and the music reached a crescendo, filling every nook and corner, I took a long, deep breath and allowed myself to be sucked into the enchantment of it all. A quite unexpected thing had happened, something quite wonderful. I had never felt so much at peace with myself before.

Flo

I

Flo Clancy opened her eyes, saw that the fingers on the brass alarm clock on the tallboy were pointing to half past seven, and nearly screamed. She'd be late for work! She was about to leap out of bed when she remembered it was Whit Monday and she could lie in.

Whew! She peeped over the covers at her sisters, both fast asleep in the double bed only a few feet away. Martha would have done her nut if she'd been woken early. Flo pursed her lips and blew gently at Sally who was sleeping on the outside, but Sal's brown eyelashes merely flickered before she turned over, dead to the world.

But Flo was wide awake and it was a sin to stay in bed on such a lovely morning. She sat up carefully – the springs of the single bed creaked like blazes – and stretched her arms. The sun streamed through the thin curtains making the roses on the floorcloth seem almost real. She poked her feet out and wriggled her white toes. As usual, the bedclothes were a mess – her sisters refused to sleep with her, claiming she fidgeted non-stop the whole night long.

Shall I get up and risk disturbing our Martha? Flo mused. She'd have to get dressed in the little space between the wardrobe and the tallboy. Since their dear dad, a railwayman, had died two years ago – struck by a train on the lines near Edge Hill station – and they'd had to take in a lodger, the girls could no longer wander round the little house in Burnett Street half dressed.

The frock Martha had worn last night when she'd gone

with Albert Colquitt, their lodger, to see Bette Davis in *The Little Foxes* was hanging outside the wardrobe. Flo glared at it. What a miserable garment, dark grey with grey buttons, more suitable for a funeral than a night out with the man you hoped to marry. She transferred her gaze to her sister's head, which could just be seen above the green eiderdown. How on earth could she sleep with her hair screwed up in a million metal curlers? And did someone of only twenty-two *really* need to smear her face with layers of cold cream so she looked as if she'd been carved out of a block of lard?

Oh dear! She was having nasty thoughts about Martha again and she loved her just as much as she loved Mam and Sally and Mr Fritz who owned the laundry where she worked. But since dear Dad died, what with Mam not feeling too well, Martha seemed to think it was her job as the eldest to be In Charge and keep her sisters in line. Not that Dad had ever been strict – he'd been a soft ould thing. Flo's eyes prickled with tears. It was still hard to get used to him not being there.

She couldn't stand being in bed a minute longer. She eased herself out and got dressed quickly in her best pink frock with white piping on the collar and the cuffs of the short puffed sleeves. That afternoon, she and Sal were off to New Brighton on the ferry.

As she crept downstairs, she could hear Mam snoring in the front bedroom. There was no sound from the parlour. Mr Colquitt must have gone to work, poor man. Flo felt for him. As a ticket inspector on the trams, he had to work on days most people had off.

In the living room, she automatically kissed the feet of the porcelain figure of Christ on the crucifix over the mantelpiece, then skipped into the back kitchen where she washed her face and cleaned her teeth. She combed her silvery blonde hair before the mirror over the sink. As an experiment, she twisted it into two long plaits and pinned them together on top of her head with a slide. Irene Dunne had worn her hair like that in a picture she'd seen recently. Flo had been meaning to try it ever since. It looked dead elegant.

She made a face at herself and was about to burst into song, when she remembered the superstition, 'Sing before breakfast, cry before tea.' Anyroad, everyone upstairs was still asleep. She'd make a pot of tea and take them a cup when she heard them stir. Martha and Sally enjoyed sitting up in bed, pillows tucked behind them, gossiping, on days they didn't have to get up for work. Unlike Flo, they both had horrible jobs: Martha was a bottle topper in Goodlad's Brewery, and Sally worked behind the counter of the butcher's on the corner of Smithdown Road and Tunstall Street.

Oh, but it was difficult not to sing on such a glorious day. The sun must be splitting the flags outside, and the whitewashed walls in the backyard dazzled so brightly it hurt her eyes to look. Flo filled the kettle, put it on the hob over the fire in the living room, releasing the flue so the embers from the night before began to sizzle and glow, and decided to dance instead. She took a deep breath and was twirling across the room like a ballerina, when she came to a sudden halt in the arms of their lodger.

'Mr Colquitt! I thought you'd gone.' Flo felt as if she'd blushed right down to her toes. He was wearing his regulation navy blue uniform with red piping, and grinning from ear to ear.

'I'm glad I hadn't, else I'd have missed the sight of a fairy dancing towards me to wish me good morning.'

'Good morning, Mr Colquitt,' Flo stammered, conscious of his arms still around her waist.

'And the same to you, Flo. How many times have I told you to call me Albert?'

'I can't remember.' To her relief, he removed his hands, came into the room and sat in the easy chair that used to be Dad's. Flo didn't mind, because she liked Mr Colquitt – Albert – though couldn't for the life of her understand why Martha was so keen on capturing for a

43

husband a widower more than twice her age. Since her best friend, Elsa, had married Eugene Cameron, Martha was terrified of being left on the shelf. Like Flo, she took after Mam's side of the family, with her slim figure, pale blonde hair and unusual green eyes, but had unfortunately inherited Dad's poor eyesight: she had worn glasses since she was nine and had never come to terms with it. She thought herself the unluckiest girl in the world, whose chances of finding a decent husband were doomed.

Martha had been setting her cap at Albert ever since he arrived on the scene. He was a tall, ungainly man with a round pot belly like a football. Although he was not handsome, his face was pleasant and his grey eyes shone with good humour. His wispy hair grew in sideboards to way below his ears, which Flo thought looked a bit daft. The main thing wrong with Albert, though, was that he didn't get his uniform cleaned often enough, so it ponged something dreadful, particularly in summer. It was ponging now, and she would have opened the window if it hadn't meant climbing on his knee.

'Would you like a bite to eat?' she enquired. Breakfast and an evening meal were supposed to be included in his rent, but he usually left too early for anyone to make breakfast, so compensated by eating a thundering great tea when he came home.

'I wouldn't say no to a couple of slices of toast, and is that water boiling for tea?'

'It is so.' Flo cut two slices of bread and managed to get both on the toasting fork. She knelt in front of the fire and toasted her arm at the same time.

'You've done your hair different,' Albert said suddenly. 'It's very nice. You look like a snow princess.'

'Ta.' Flo had never mentioned it to a living soul, but she sometimes wondered if he liked her better than he did Martha, though not in a romantic way, of course. She also thought that maybe he wasn't too keen to allow pretty, bespectacled Martha Clancy to get her claws into him. He might be twice her age and smell awful, but he didn't want to get married again. Flo hoped Martha wouldn't try too hard so that he'd feel obliged to leave. His thirty bob a week made all the difference to the housekeeping nowadays. It meant they could buy scented soap and decent cuts of meat, luxuries that they could never afford otherwise. Although there were three wages coming in, women earned much less than men.

He ate his toast, drank his tea, made several more flattering remarks about her appearance, then left for work. Flo returned to the living room, poured a cup of tea, and curled up in Dad's chair. She wanted to think about Tommy O'Mara before anyone got up. If Martha was in the room, it was impossible – her sister's mere presence made Flo feel guilty. For a second, a shadow fell over her face. Tommy was married to Nancy, but he'd explained the strange circumstances to Flo's satisfaction. Next year, sooner if possible, he and Flo would be married. Her face cleared. Until the magic day occurred, it was perfectly all right to meet Tommy O'Mara twice a week outside the Mystery.

Upstairs, Mam coughed and Flo held her breath until the house was quiet again. She'd met Tommy on the Tuesday after Easter when he'd come into the laundry by the side door. Customers were supposed to use the front, which led to the office where Mr Fritz was usually behind the counter. It was a dull day, slightly chilly, but the side door was left open, except in the iciest of weather, because when all the boilers, presses and irons were working at full pelt, the laundry got hotter than a Turkish bath.

Flo was pressing sheets in the giant new electric contraption Mr Fritz had only recently bought. She was nearest to the door, wreathed in steam, only vaguely aware of someone approaching through the mist until a voice with a strong Irish accent said, 'Do you do dry-cleaning, luv?'

'Sorry, no, just laundry.' As the steam cleared, she saw

a young man with a brown suit over his arm. He wore a grey, collarless shirt and, despite the cold, the sleeves were rolled up to his armpits, showing off his strong, brown arms – there was a tattoo of a tiger on the right. A tweed cap was set jauntily on the back of his untidy brown curls. His waist was as slim as a girl's, something he must have been proud of as his baggy corduroy trousers were held up with a leather belt pulled as tight as it would go. A red hanky was tied carelessly around his neck, emphasising the devil-may-care expression on his handsome, sunburnt face.

'The nearest dry-cleaner's is Thompson's, that's along Gainsborough Road on the first corner,' she said. There was a peculiar feeling in the pit of her tummy as she watched him over the pressing machine. He was staring at her boldly, making no attempt to conceal the admiration in his dark eyes. She wanted to tear off her white turban and let him see she looked even prettier with her blonde hair loose.

'What's your name?' he asked.

Flo felt as flustered as if he'd asked to borrow a pound note. 'Flo Clancy,' she stammered.

'I'm Tommy O'Mara.'

'Are you now!' You'd think she was the only one there the way he kept his eyes locked on hers, and seemed unaware that the other five women had stopped work for a good look – Josie Driver was leering at him provocatively over the shirts she was supposed to be ironing.

'I suppose I'd better make me way round to Thompson's,' he said.

'I suppose you had.'

He winked. 'Tara, Flo.' With a swagger, he was gone.

'Tara,' Flo whispered. Her legs felt weak and her heart was thumping madly.

'Who was that?' Josie called eagerly. 'Jaysus, he could have me for sixpence!'

Before Flo could reply, Olive Knott shouted, 'His name's Tommy O'Mara. He lives in the next street to us, and before you young 'uns get too excited, you might like to know he's well and truly married.'

Flo's thumping heart sank to her boots. Married!

Mr Fritz came out of the office to ask what all the fuss was about.

'We've just had Franchot Tone, Clark Gable and Ronald Colman all rolled into one asking if we did dry-cleaning,' Olive said cuttingly.

'Why, Flo, you've gone all pink.' Mr Fritz beamed at her through his wire-rimmed spectacles. He was a plump, comfortable little man with a round face and lots of frizzy brown hair. He was wearing a brown coat overall, which meant he was about to go out in the van to deliver clean laundry and collect dirty items in return. Olive, who'd been there the longest and was vaguely considered next in command, would take over the office and answer the telephone.

'I didn't mean to,' Flo said stupidly.

'It must be nice to be young and impressionable.' He sighed gloomily, as if he already had one foot in the grave though he wasn't quite forty. For some reason, Mr Fritz was forever trying to make out he was dead miserable, when everyone knew he was the happiest man alive – and the nicest, kindest employer in the whole wide world. His surname was Austrian, a bit of a mouthful and difficult to spell, so everyone called him by his first name, Fritz, and referred to his equally plump little Irish wife, Stella, as Mrs Fritz, and their eight children – three girls and five boys – as the little Fritzes.

He departed, and the women returned to their work, happy in the knowledge that on Tuesdays he called at Sinclair's, the confectioner's, to collect the overalls and would bring them back a cream cake each.

Try as she might, Flo was unable to get Tommy O'Mara out of her mind. Twice before, she'd thought she was in love, the first time with Frank McGee, then Kevin Kelly – she'd actually let Kevin kiss her on the way home from the Rialto where they'd been to a St Patrick's Day dance – but the feelings she had for them paled to nothing when she thought about the man who'd looked at her so boldly. Was it possible she was properly in love with someone she'd exchanged scarcely more than half a dozen words with?

When they were having their tea that night Martha asked sharply, 'What's the matter with you?'

Flo emerged from the daydream in which an unmarried Tommy O'Mara had just proposed. 'Nowt!' she answered, just as sharply.

'I've asked three times if you want pudding. It's apple pie.'

'For goodness sake, Martha, leave the girl alone.' Mam was having one of her good days, which meant she resented Martha acting as if she owned the place. At other times she was too worn out and listless to open her mouth. More and more often, Flo found her in bed when she arrived home from work. Mam patted her youngest daughter's arm. 'She was in a lovely little world of her own, weren't you, luv? I could tell. Your eyes were sparkling as if you were thinking of something dead nice.'

'I was so.' Flo stuck out her tongue at Martha as she disappeared into the back kitchen.

'Can I borrow your pink frock tonight, Flo?' Sally enquired. 'I'm going to the Grand with Brian Maloney.'

'Isn't he a Protestant?' Martha shouted from the kitchen.

'I've no idea,' Sally yelled back.

Martha appeared, grim-faced, in the doorway. 'I'd sooner you didn't go out with Protestants, Sal.'

'It's none of your bloody business,' Flo said indignantly.

Mam shook her head. 'Don't swear, luv.'

Sally wriggled uncomfortably in the chair. 'We're only going to the pictures.'

'You can never tell how things develop with a feller. It's best not to get involved with a Protestant from the start.'

'I'll tell him I won't see him again after tonight.'

'In that case, you won't need our Flo's best frock. Go in something old. He might get ideas if you arrive all dolled up.'

Flo felt cross with both her sisters, one for being so bossy and the other for allowing herself to be bossed.

'What are you doing with yourself tonight, luv?' Mam asked.

'I thought I'd stay in and read a book – but I'll play cards with you if you like.' When Dad was alive, the two of them used to play cards for hours.

'No, ta, luv. I feel a bit tired. I might go to bed after I've had a cup of tea. I'll not bother with the apple pie, Martha.'

'I wish you'd go to the doctor's, Mam,' Flo said worriedly. Kate Clancy had never been a strong woman, and since the sudden, violent death of her beloved husband, she seemed to have lost the will to live, becoming thinner and more frail by the day.

'So do I.' Martha stroked Mam's hair, which had changed from ash-blonde to genuine silver almost overnight.

'Me, too,' echoed Sally.

But Mam screwed her thin face into the stubborn expression they'd seen many times before. 'Now, don't you girls start on that again,' she said tightly. 'I've told you, I'm not seeing a doctor. He might find something wrong with me, and there's no way I'm letting them cut me open. I'm just run down, that's all. I'll feel better when the warm weather comes.'

'Are you taking the bile beans I bought?' Martha demanded.

'They're beside me bed and I take them every morning.'

The girls glanced at each other with concern. If Mam died so soon after Dad, they didn't think they could bear it.

Mam went to bed and Sally got ready to meet Brian

Maloney. Martha made her remove her earrings before she left, as if sixpenny pearl earrings from Woolworths would drive a man so wild with desire that he'd propose on the spot and Sally would feel obliged to accept!

It was Flo's turn to wash and dry the dishes. She cleared the table, shook the white cloth in the yard, straightened the green chenille cloth underneath and folded one leaf of the table down, before putting the white cloth on again for when their lodger came home. A meal fit for a giant was in the oven keeping warm. Flo set his place: knife, fork and spoon, condiments to the right, mustard to the left. As soon as she'd finished, she sank into the armchair with the novel she was halfway through, *Shattered Love, Shattered Dreams*.

Martha came in and adjusted everything on the table as if it had been crooked. 'You've always got your head buried in a book, Flo Clancy,' she remarked.

'You moan when I go out and you moan when I stay in.' Flo made a face at her sister. 'What do you expect me to do all night? Sit and twiddle me thumbs?'

'I wasn't moaning, I was merely stating a fact.' Martha gave the table a critical glance. 'Will you look after Albert when he comes?'

'Of course.' There was nothing to be done except move the plate from the oven to the table, which Albert could no doubt manage alone if no help was available.

'I'd stay meself, but I promised to go and see Elsa Cameron. That baby's getting her down something awful. I'm sure she smacks him, yet the little lad's not even twelve months old.'

'Norman? He's a lovely baby. I wouldn't mind having him meself.'

'Nor I.' Martha shoved a hatpin into a little veiled cocked hat, then sighed as she adjusted her glasses in the mirror. She was smartly dressed, although she was only going around the corner, in a long grey skirt with a cardigan to match. The whole outfit had cost ten bob in Paddy's Market. 'Trouble is, Flo, I'm beginning to think

Elsa's not quite right in the head. She's been acting dead peculiar since Norman arrived. The other day when I turned up she was undoing her knitting, but when I asked why, she'd no idea. She mightn't be so bad if Eugene was there, but him being in the Merchant Navy, like, it means he's hardly ever home.'

'It's a terrible shame,' Flo said sincerely. Norman Cameron was Martha's godson and the most delightful baby she'd ever known. It was terrible to think he was getting his mam down. 'Can't Eugene get a different job?'

'Not with a million men already out of work,' Martha said. 'Mind you, that'll soon change if there's a war.'

'There won't be a war,' Flo said quickly. She looked at her sister, scared. 'Will there?'

'Oh, I don't know, luv. According to the papers, that Hitler's getting far too big for his boots.'

Like Mam dying, war was something best not thought about. After Martha left, Flo tried to bury herself in her book, but the man over whom the heroine was pining was a pale, insipid creature compared to Tommy O'Mara, and instead of words, she kept seeing *him* on the page: his dark, shameless eyes, his reckless face, the cheeky way he wore his cap. She reckoned it was a good job she wouldn't be seeing him again. If he'd been as knocked sideways by her as she'd been by him, he might ask her out, and although a good Catholic girl should never, never go out with a married man, Flo wasn't convinced she'd be capable of resisting Tommy O'Mara.

She *did* see him again, only two days later. He came into the laundry, this time bearing two white shirts that already looked perfectly clean. She looked up from the press and found him smiling at her intently as if she was the only woman in the world, never mind the laundry.

'I'd like these laundered, please.'

Flo had to swallow several times before she could answer. 'You need to take them round the front and Mr

Fritz will give you a ticket,' she said, in a voice that sounded as if it belonged to someone else.

He frowned. 'Does that mean I won't see you when I collect them?'

'I'm afraid not,' she said, still in someone else's voice.

He flung the shirts over his shoulder, stuck his thumbs in his belt and rocked back on his heels. 'In that case, I'll not beat about the bush. Would you like to come for a walk with me one night, Flo? We can have a bevy on the way – you're old enough to go in boozers, aren't you?'

'I'll be nineteen in May,' Flo said faintly. 'Though I've never been in a booz – a pub before.'

'Well, there's a first time for everything.' He winked. 'See you tomorrer night then, eight o'clock outside the Mystery gates, the Smithdown Road end.'

'Rightio.' She watched him leave, knowing that she'd done something terribly wrong. She felt very adult and worldly wise, as if she was much older than Sally and Martha. Tomorrow night she was going out with a married man and the thing was *she didn't care!*

'What did he want?' Olive Knott brought her down to earth with a sharp nudge in the ribs.

'He brought his shirts to the wrong place. I sent him round the front.'

Olive's brow creased worriedly. 'He didn't ask you out, did he?'

For the first time in her life Flo lied. 'No.'

'He's got his eye on you, that's plain to see. Oh, he has a way with him, there's no denying it, but it's best for nice girls like you to stay clear of men like Tommy O'Mara, Flo.'

But Flo was lost. She would have gone out with Tommy O'Mara if Olive had declared him to be the divil himself.

Friday was another dull day and there was drizzle on and off until early evening when a late sun appeared. It looked as soft as a jelly in the dusky blue sky, and its gentle rays filled the air with gold dust.

Flo felt very odd as she made her way to the Mystery. Every step that took her nearer seemed of momentous significance, as if she was walking towards her destiny, and that after tonight nothing would ever be the same again. She thought of the lie she'd told at home – that she was calling on Josie Driver who'd been off sick and Mr Fritz wanted to know how she was, which had been all she could think of when Martha demanded to know where she was going.

When she arrived Tommy was already there. He was standing outside the gates, whistling, wearing a dark blue suit that looked a bit too big, a white and blue striped shirt with a high stiff collar, and a grey tie. A slightly more respectable tweed cap was set at the same jaunty angle on the back of his curly head. The mere sight of the swaggering, audacious figure made Flo feel quite faint.

'There you are!' He smiled. 'You're late. I was worried you might have changed your mind.'

The thought had never entered her head. She smiled nervously and said, 'Hello.'

'You look nice,' he said appreciatively. 'Green suits you. It sets off your eyes. That was the first thing I noticed when I came into the laundry, those green eyes. I bet you have stacks of fellers chasing after you.'

'Not exactly,' Flo mumbled.

'In that case, the fellers round here must be mad!' When he linked her arm Flo could smell a mixture of strong tobacco and carbolic soap. She got the peculiar feeling in her tummy again as they began to stroll through the park, though the Mystery was more like a playing-field: a vast expanse of grass surrounded by trees. The Liverpool-to-London railway line ran along one side. The trees were bursting into life, ready for summer, and pale sunlight filtered through the branches, making dappled patterns on the green grass underneath.

Without any prompting, Tommy briefly told her the story of his life. He'd been born in Ireland, in the county of Limerick, and had come to Liverpool ten years ago when he was twenty. 'I've got fourteen brothers and sisters, half of 'em still at home. I send me mam a few bob when I've got it to spare.'

Flo said she thought that very generous. She asked where he worked.

'I'm a fitter at Cammell Laird's in Birkenhead,' he said boastfully. 'You should see this ship we're building at the moment. It's a T-class submarine, the *Thetis*. Guess how much it's costing?'

She confessed she had absolutely no idea.

'Three hundred thousand smackeroos!'

'Three hundred thousand!' Flo gasped. 'Is it made of gold or something?'

He laughed and squeezed her arm. 'No, but it's the very latest design. You should see the instruments in the conning tower! *And* it's got ten torpedo tubes. I don't envy any German ships that come near the *Thetis* if there's a war.'

'There won't be a war,' Flo said stubbornly.

'That's what women always say.' He chuckled.

She realised he'd omitted to tell her about one important aspect of his life – his wife. There was silence for a while, except for his whistling, as they strolled across the grass and the April sun began to disappear behind the trees.

Perhaps Tommy had read her thoughts, because he said suddenly, 'I should have told you this before, Flo. I'm married.'

'I know,' Flo said.

He raised his finely drawn eyebrows in surprise. 'Who told you?'

'A woman at work, Olive Knott. She lives in the next street to you.'

'Does she now.' He made a face. 'I'm surprised you came, knowing, like.'

54

Flo wasn't in the least surprised: she'd have come even if she'd been told he had ten wives.

They'd arrived at the other side of the Mystery and emerged into Gainsborough Road. Tommy steered her inside the first pub they came to. 'What would you like to drink?' he asked.

'I've no idea.' The only alcohol that ever crossed Flo's lips was a small glass of sherry at Christmas.

'I'll get you a port and lemon. That's what women usually like.'

The pub was crowded. Flo glanced round when Tommy went to be served, worried someone might recognise her, but there were no familiar faces. She noticed that quite a few women were eyeing Tommy up and down as he waited at the bar, legs crossed nonchalantly at the ankles. Without doubt he was the best-looking man there – and he was with *her*! Flo gasped at the sheer magic of it all, just as Tommy turned round and winked.

Her eyes flickered as she tried to wink back, but couldn't quite manage it. Tommy laughed at her efforts as he came over with the drinks. 'You know,' he whispered, 'you're the most beautiful girl here, Flo Clancy, perhaps the most beautiful in the whole of Liverpool. There's something special between us, isn't there? I recognised it the minute I set eyes on you. It's something that doesn't happen often between a man and a woman, but it's happened between you and me.'

Flo felt as if she wanted to cry. She also wanted to say something meaningful, but all she could think of was, 'I suppose it has.'

Tommy swallowed half his beer in one go, then returned the pint glass to the table with a thump. He took a tin of tobacco from his pocket and deftly rolled a ciggie out of the thick dark shreds that smelt of tar. He shoved the tin in Flo's direction, but she shook her head. 'It's time I explained about Nancy,' he said grandly.

'Nancy?'

'Me wife. It's not a genuine marriage, Flo, not in any respects.' He looked at her knowingly. 'I met Nancy in Spain when I was fighting in the Civil War. She's a gypsy. I won't deny I fell for her hook, line and sinker. I would have married her proper, given the opportunity, but 'stead, I did it Nancy's way.' The way he told it it sounded like the most romantic novel ever written. He and Nancy had 'plighted their troth', as he put it, at a gypsy ceremony in a wood near Barcelona. 'It means nowt in the eyes of British law or the Roman Catholic Church,' he said contemptuously. He'd been meaning to leave for a long time, and as soon as Nancy got better he'd be off like a shot. 'Then I'll be free to marry an English girl, proper, like, this time.' He clasped Flo's hand and gazed deep into her eyes. 'And you know who that'll be, don't you?'

Flo felt the blood run hot through her body. She gulped. 'What's wrong with Nancy?'

Tommy sighed. 'It's a bit embarrassing to explain, luv. It's what's called a woman's complaint. She's been to Smithdown Road ozzie and the doctors said it'll all be cleared up in about six months. I don't like to leave till she gets better,' he added virtuously.

The guilt that had been lurking in a little corner of Flo's mind about going out with a married man disappeared, along with the suspicion that he'd only told her about Nancy in case someone else did. Why, he was almost single! It seemed wise, though, not to mention him and his peculiar circumstances to her family. Martha, in particular, would never understand. She'd say nothing until they got engaged.

'I trust you'll keep what I've just said under your hat for now, luv,' Tommy said conspiratorially. 'I don't want people knowing me private business, like, till the time comes to tell them.'

'I won't breathe a word,' Flo assured him. 'I'd already decided to keep you a secret.'

'A secret! I like the idea of being the secret man in Flo

Clancy's life.' His brown eyes sparkled. 'How about another drink before we go?'

'No, ta.' The port and lemon had already gone to her head.

'I'll just have another quick pint, then we'll be off.'

It was dark when they went outside. The sky glowed hazy orange where the sun had set, but was otherwise dark blue, almost black. They wandered hand in hand through the Mystery, the noise of the traffic behind growing fainter, until nothing could be heard except their feet on the grass, the slight rustle of the trees, and Tommy's musical whistle.

'What's that tune?' Flo enquired. 'I can't quite place it.'

' "Dancing in the Dark." Have you never heard it before?'

'I couldn't remember what it was called.'

He began to sing. ' "Dancing in the dark . . ." C'mon, Flo.' He grabbed her by the waist and twirled her around. Flo threw back her head and laughed. ' "Dancing in the dark," ' they sang together.

They stopped when two men walked past and Flo shivered. 'I forgot to bring a cardy.'

Tommy put his arm around her shoulders. 'You don't feel cold.' He placed his hand on the back of her neck. 'You feel hot. Your neck's sweating.'

She wasn't sure if she was hot or cold. Her body felt as if it was on fire, yet she shivered again. Tommy's hand pressed harder on her neck as he began to lead her towards a tree not far away. He pushed her against the broad trunk and took her in his arms. 'I've been thinking of nothing else but this for days.'

A train roared past on the furthest side of the park, the engine puffing eerie clouds of smoke. Flo thought about Dad, who'd been knocked down on that very same railway line, but not for long: Tommy's lips were pressed against hers and she felt as if she was being sucked into a whirlpool. Her head spun and she seemed

.to be slipping down and down and down. She came to briefly and found herself lying on the damp grass with Tommy bent over her. He'd undone the front of her dress and his lips were seeking her breasts, his tongue tenderly touching her nipples. Flo arched her back and almost screamed because the sensation was so wonderful. She knew what was to come, she knew it was a bad thing, but she could no more have stopped him than she could have stopped the sun from rising the next morning.

Tommy was pushing up her skirt, pulling away her underthings. There was the sound of her stockings tearing and she felt his callused hand between her legs. He was groaning, murmuring over and over, 'I love you, Flo,' and she could hear other little breathless cries that she realised came from her own throat. All the while, she was running her fingers through his thick dark curls, kissing his ears, his neck . . .

He felt so *big* when he entered her, and it hurt, but the hurt soon faded and turned into something else, something that no words had been invented to describe.

It all ended in a wild, feverish explosion that left them shaken and exhausted, and with Flo convinced that the only reason she'd been born was to make love with Tommy O'Mara.

'Jaysus, Flo!' he said hoarsely. 'That was the best I've ever known.' After a while, he began to pull her clothes back on. 'Get dressed, luv, else you'll catch cold.'

Flo touched his sensually curved lips with her finger, feeling the love flow from her heart right down her arm. 'I love you, Tommy.'

'I love you, girl.'

There was the faint murmur of voices upstairs: Martha and Sally were awake. Flo leaped out of the chair to take them up a cup of tea. On the way to the back kitchen, she did a pirouette. She'd always been happy, but nowadays she was so happy she could bust – and it had all begun that night in the Mystery when she'd danced in the dark with Tommy.

She and Sally had a wonderful day in New Brighton. They went on every single ride in the fairground, even the children's ones. Sally complained afterwards she felt quite sick, though it was more likely caused by the fish and chips followed by a giant ice-cream cornet with strawberry topping. She recovered swiftly on the ferry back when they clicked with two sailors who invited them to the pictures. 'Why did you turn them down?' she grumbled, on the tram home to Wavertree.

'I didn't fancy that Peter,' Flo replied. In fact, both sailors had been quite nice, but she was meeting Tommy at eight o'clock. Even if she wasn't, she would have felt disloyal going out with another man.

'I quite fancied Jock.' Her sister sighed. Sally was neither plain nor pretty, a bit like Dad with her neat brown hair and hazel eyes. She hadn't had a date since the one with Brian Maloney, almost two months ago.

Flo felt bad about the sailors. If it hadn't been for Tommy she'd have gone like a shot. 'You gave Jock your address, Sal. He might write,' she said hopefully.

'And where are you off to?' Martha demanded that night when Flo came downstairs ready to go out.

'I'm going to see Josie.' Unknown to Josie Driver, she and Flo had become the greatest of friends since Tommy had appeared on the scene. She met Josie twice a week, Mondays and Fridays. Josie would have been surprised to learn she was thinking of becoming a nun and needed someone in whom she could confide her deepest, most intimate thoughts while coming to such a major decision.

Martha's eyes looked suspicious behind her thick glasses. 'Why do you need a red bow in your hair just to see Josie?'

'I bought the ribbon in New Brighton,' Flo replied haughtily.

'It looks very nice,' Albert Colquitt said, from the table where he was having his tea.

'I think so, too,' Mam concurred.

Martha gave up. 'Don't be too late.'

'Have a nice time,' Flo called, as she slammed the door. Albert had just bought a wireless and everyone was staying in to listen to a play, Mam armed with two bottles of Guinness to 'build her up', although she'd been feeling better since the weather had improved. Flo shuddered to think of her sisters sitting in the parlour on Albert's bed-settee. What a way for two young women to spend a bank-holiday evening!

'I like your bow,' said Tommy.

'I like your tie,' Flo sang.

'I like your face, your eyes, your lips. I like every single little thing about you!' He picked her up and spun her around until they both felt dizzy and fell, laughing, on to the grass, whereupon he began to kiss her passionately.

'It's still broad daylight,' Flo murmured.

'So it is.' He kissed her again and caressed her breasts.

'We might get arrested and it'd be in the *Echo*.'

'Would that matter?'

'Not to me it wouldn't,' Flo giggled, 'but me mam wouldn't be pleased and our Martha'd have a fit. Nancy wouldn't like it either.'

'Nancy would just have to lump it.' Nevertheless, he sat up and smoothed his unruly curls.

Flo had never told him she'd seen Nancy. One day when she knew he was at work she'd set out for Clement Street, off Smithdown Road. It was a respectable street of small two-up, two-down houses. The windows shone, the steps had been scrubbed that morning. Flo paused across the road opposite number eighteen.

So this was where he lived. Nancy must take pride in her house. The curtains were maroon cretonne, upstairs and down, and there were paper flowers in the parlour window. The front door and the window-sills were dark

60

green, freshly painted. Flo's heart missed a beat – had *he* painted them? She'd never ask because she didn't want him to know she'd spied on his house.

She walked up and down the street several times, keeping a close eye on number eighteen in case Nancy came out to clean the windows or brush the step. After about half an hour, when she was about to give up, a woman carrying a shopping basket came towards her from the direction of Smithdown Road. Flo knew it was Nancy because she looked exactly like the gypsy Tommy had said she was. She was outstanding in her way, the sort of woman that would be described as handsome. Her skin was the colour of cinnamon, her eyes as black as night, and she had a big beaked nose and glossy black hair drawn back in a cushiony bun at the nape of her thin neck.

'Mercy me!' Flo muttered. She wasn't sure why, but something about the woman disturbed her. And what peculiar clothes she wore to go shopping! A flowing black skirt, red satin blouse and a brightly embroidered garment that wasn't quite a jacket and wasn't quite a shawl.

The two women passed. Flo had no idea if Nancy glanced in her direction because she kept her own eyes fixed firmly on the ground. After a few seconds, she turned and saw the colourful figure cross the road and go into number eighteen.

In the Mystery, Tommy got to his feet and reached down to pull her up. 'We'll come back later when it's dark. And then . . .' His dark eyes smouldered and Flo's tummy did a cartwheel.

'And then . . .' she whispered. Then they would come as close to heaven as it was possible to get on earth.

She told him about the sailors because she wanted to make him jealous and he duly was. 'You belong to me, Flo Clancy,' he said angrily. 'We belong to each other till the end of time.'

'I know, I know!' she cried. 'I wouldn't dream of going out with another man when I've got you.'

He looked sulky. 'I should hope not!'

In the pub, he informed her that the submarine he'd been working on, the *Thetis*, was taking its first diving exercise on Thursday. 'Some of the shipyard workers are sailing with it, but my name wasn't on the list. You get extra pay, at least ten bob.' He looked wistful. 'I would have gone for nothing.'

'Never mind.' Flo was keeping a close eye on the sky outside. She wasn't bothered about the *Thetis*. All her concentration was centred on how swiftly night would fall so they could go to the Mystery and make love.

2

The Fritz family had been to Anglesey for Whit, a regular haunt, and Mr Fritz didn't return to the laundry till Thursday when the children were due back at school. He'd bought a camera, there was one exposure left on the roll, and he wanted a snapshot taken of him with his girls. Later that morning, Mrs Fritz came bustling along to take it. It was the first of June and a perfect day for taking photographs. The weather had been brilliantly sunny all week.

The six women trooped outside, excited. 'You stand by me, Flo,' Mr Fritz hissed. 'It's an excuse to put my arm around you. I want a record of that smile. It's always been enough to dazzle the strongest eyes, but lately it's not just a smile, it's a miracle.'

Mrs Fritz stationed her plump body in the middle of the street. 'Try and get the sign in over the door, Stella,' her husband shouted, as everyone shuffled into position.

'Say cheese!' Mrs Fritz called.

'*Cheese!*'

There was a click. 'All done!'

'If it turns out all right, I'll order a copy each.' Mr Fritz squeezed Flo's waist and whispered, 'I enjoyed that.'

Flo knew he was only joking, because he adored his

sweet little wife and eight children, but she hoped no one had noticed – Josie was always complaining that Flo was Mr Fritz's favourite.

The rest of the day passed in a dream, as the days did since she'd met Tommy. She lived for Monday, lived for Friday, then lived for Monday again. They would have met more often, but he didn't like to leave Nancy while she felt so poorly.

Six o'clock came and she made her way home, still immersed in her dream, and scarcely noticed the crowd that had gathered on the corner of the street next to hers until she reached it.

'What's up?' she asked.

A woman grabbed her arm. 'There's been a terrible accident, girl. Haven't you heard?'

'What sort of accident?'

'It's some ship, a submarine called the *Thetis* – it's trapped underwater in Liverpool Bay and they can't find its position. There's over a hundred men on board.'

'Holy Mary, Mother of God!' Flo crossed herself. At first she felt relieved that Tommy hadn't been on board, but concern followed quickly for the men who were. She could think of nothing more horrific than to be trapped beneath the sea in a vessel she imagined being shaped like a big black fish. 'They'll be rescued, won't they?' she said anxiously.

An elderly man butted in. 'Of course they will, luv. I'm an ould salt meself, so I know Liverpool Bay's no more than twenty-five fathoms deep. They'll have them men up in no time.'

When she got home Mam and her sisters had already heard the bad news. Martha was wondering if they dared invade Albert's room and turn on the wireless.

'It's not been declared official yet,' Mam said. 'So far it's just rumour.'

'You mean it might not have happened?' Sally looked hopeful.

'Oh, it's happened all right.' Mam shook her head

sadly. 'Mrs Cox's nephew works in Cammell Laird where everyone knows full well there's been an accident. Women have already started to collect outside to wait for news of their men. It's just that nothing's been confirmed, so the news won't have reached the wireless.'

It wasn't until ten o'clock that the plight of the *Thetis* was conveyed to the nation by the BBC. One hundred and three men were on board, fifty of them civilians. The Admiralty assured everyone concerned that rescue ships were on their way and there was every hope the men would be saved.

'I should think so!' Flo said indignantly. 'It's only twenty-five fathoms deep.'

'How much is that in feet?' Martha asked Albert, as if men automatically knew everything. Albert confessed he had no idea.

There was a search for Dad's dictionary, which had conversion tables at the back. Twenty-five fathoms was 150 feet.

In bed that night, Flo was unable to get the trapped men out of her mind. She tossed and turned restlessly.

'Are you awake, Flo?' Sally whispered.

'Yes. I can't stop thinking of those men in the *Thetis*.'

'Me neither.'

Martha's voice surprised them because she usually slept like a log, despite the metal curlers. 'Let's say a silent prayer. Remember that one we learned at school for shipwrecked mariners?'

Eventually the sisters fell asleep, the words of the prayer on their lips.

When they woke next morning the *Thetis* came straight to mind. The weather was lovely, gloriously sunny, and it seemed incongruous and unfair that those safe on land should be blessed with such a perfect day in view of the disaster unfolding beneath the sea.

Albert had given them permission to listen to his wireless, from which they learned there'd been no developments overnight. Ships and aircraft were still trying to pinpoint the position of the stricken submarine.

On her way to work, Flo passed several groups of people gravely discussing the tragedy, which had touched the hearts of everyone in Liverpool. Twice she was asked, 'Have you heard any fresh news, luv?' All she could do was shake her head.

She bought a *Daily Herald*. Everyone in the laundry had bought a paper and the *Thetis* was the main headline on them all, as well as the sole topic of conversation all morning. Betty Bryant knew a woman who knew a woman whose cousin's husband was on board.

'I know someone on board even better than that,' Olive Knott said smugly. 'In fact, we all do. Remember that feller who brought his suit in for dry-cleaning a couple of months ago, Tommy O'Mara? He's a fitter with Cammell Laird. His poor ould wife wasn't half making a scene last night! Running up and down the street she was, screaming her head off. It took half a dozen neighbours to calm her. Mind you, Nancy O'Mara's always had a couple of screws loose.'

'But he wasn't supposed to go!' Flo's horrified words were lost in the chorus of dismay.

'Such a dead handsome feller, what a shame!'

'He was a cheeky-looking bugger, but I liked him.' Josie Driver looked close to tears.

Olive made a sour face. 'I don't wish him any harm, but Nancy'll be better off without the bugger. He drove the poor woman doo-lally with his philandering. No woman, married or single, was safe near Tommy O'Mara.'

That's not true! Flo wanted to scream that Olive was talking nonsense. Tommy may have been a bit of a blade in the past – in fact, he'd hinted so more than once – but it was only because Nancy hadn't been a proper wife in a long time. Since he'd met Flo, he wouldn't have given another woman a second glance. Oh, if only she could tell them! But why on earth was she thinking like this when it didn't matter a jot what Olive thought? What mattered was that Tommy might die! If he did, Flo wanted to die, too.

In her agitation she nearly scorched a shirt. Then Betty made things worse by reading out something from the newspaper. There was only enough oxygen on board to last thirty-six hours. Once the supply dried up, the men would die from carbon-dioxide poisoning. 'It means there's not much time left.' Betty clasped her hands together as if she were praying. 'Holy Mary, Mother of God, please save those poor men!'

Then Mr Fritz came hurrying in, panting for breath. 'The *Thetis* has been spotted with its stern sticking out of the water fourteen miles from Great Ormes Head. It was on the wireless just before I left.'

'Thank the Lord!' Josie shouted. 'They're bound to save them now.'

Relief swept through Flo's body so forcefully that, for a moment, she felt sick. She swayed, and Mr Fritz snatched the gas iron from her hand. 'Are you all right, Flo?'

'I hardly slept last night. I feel a bit ragged, that's all.'

'You go home, girl, if you don't feel better soon,' he said concernedly. 'I don't want you on your feet all day if you've got problems.'

'Problems' meant he thought she had a period. Standing for ten hours in the equivalent of a steambath was hard on women who had trouble with their monthlies, and Mr Fritz was always sympathetic if someone needed a day off. Flo, however, had always sailed through hers without so much as a twinge. Apart from a week's holiday each year, she hadn't had a single day off since she'd started five years ago straight from school.

'I'll see how I feel,' she told him gratefully.

The feeling of sickness soon left her, but for the first time the noise in the laundry began to get on her nerves: the churning of the washing in the boilers, the clatter of the belt-driven wringers, the hiss of the irons. Flo knew

66

she couldn't work all day with the sounds pressing against her brain while she remained ignorant of the fate of the *Thetis*.

At midday, she went into the office and told Mr Fritz she felt no better. 'I wouldn't mind going home, after all.' She felt slightly ashamed of how good she'd become at lying over the last two months.

He fussed around, patted her cheek, and said she didn't look anything like her usual glowing self. He even offered to take her to Burnett Street in the van.

'No, ta,' she said. 'I might walk around a bit to clear me head. I'll go to bed this avvy.'

'Good idea, Flo, I hope you feel better tomorrow.'

Several hundred men and women had congregated in front of the gates of Cammell Laird. Some of the women held babies in their arms with slightly older children clutching their skirts. Some faces were hopeful, others blank with despair. A woman she couldn't see was shouting for her man. Flo's heart sank. It would seem there hadn't been more good news.

A girl with a glorious head of red hair, about the same age as herself, was standing at the back. 'What's happening?' Flo asked.

'Four men got out through the escape hatches, otherwise nowt.' The girl's face was extraordinarily colourful: pink lips, rosy cheeks, black-lashed eyes the colour of violets, all framed in the cloud of red waves.

'But someone at work said the stern was sticking out the water,' Flo groaned. 'I'd have thought they'd have hauled it up by now.'

The girl shrugged. 'I'd have thought so, too, but they haven't.' She looked at Flo sympathetically. 'Have you got someone on board?'

Flo bit her lip. 'Me feller.'

'Aye, so's mine. Well, he's only a sort of feller.' She didn't look the least bit upset. 'I only came out of curiosity. I'm always looking for an excuse to get off

67

work. I suppose it's about time I went – I called in and said I had to see the doctor.'

'I told a lie to get away meself,' Flo confessed.

The girl made a face as if implying they were partners in a crime. 'Are you from Liverpool or Birkenhead?' She spoke in a loud, musical voice that rose and fell as if she was singing.

'Liverpool. I came on the ferry.'

'Me, too. I'll catch the next one back. Are you coming?'

'I only just got here. I'd sooner stay and see if anything happens.' Flo wished the girl didn't have to go. She rather liked her friendly, down-to-earth manner.

'I might go to the pics tonight. It'll be all about the *Thetis* on the Pathé News. Tara, then.' She clattered away on her high heels.

'Tara.' Flo sighed. If the submarine hadn't been brought up by tonight, it would be cutting things fine for those on board.

She turned her attention to the crowd. 'What I'd like to know,' a man muttered aggressively, 'is why they don't bore a hole through the hull and get everyone out that way, or at least pass in a hose of oxygen.'

Somewhere a woman was still shouting: 'What have you done with my man?' Flo edged her way through the throng.

'There's no need for that carry-on,' an elderly woman remarked acidly. 'Most of us are feared for our lads, but we're not reduced to weeping and wailing like a bloody banshee. Just look at the way she's throwing herself about an' all!'

Flo didn't answer. She had almost reached the front when she froze. Nancy O'Mara was kneeling on the ground, her hands clasped imploringly towards the closed gates of the ship-builder's. Her crow-black eyes burned unnaturally bright, as if with fever. Long strands of hair had escaped from the big bun coiled on her neck, and writhed like little snakes as she rocked to and fro. She looked almost insane with grief. Every now and then she turned her tragic face towards the men and women standing silently each side of her. 'Why?' she pleaded. 'Why, oh, why?'

Nobody answered, the faces remained impassive. They had no idea why. At that moment, there wasn't a person on earth who knew why ninety-nine human beings still remained on the stricken vessel when it was surrounded by rescue ships and the stern was visible for all to see.

Flo stood stock-still as she watched Tommy's wife throw herself back and forth on the pavement. Nancy paused to seek succour from those around her yet again. 'Why?' Then she caught sight of Flo, who stood transfixed as the burning eyes bored into hers, so full of hate that she felt her blood turn to ice.

Nancy knew!

With a cry that almost choked her, Flo turned and pushed her way through the crowd. She ran, faster than she'd ever run before, past the docks, the half-built ships, the vessels waiting to be loaded or unloaded. She ran until she reached the ferry, where a seaman was just about to raise the gangplank, and launched herself on to the deck. 'Just made it, luv.' He grinned.

Flo hardly heard. She climbed the stairs until she reached the top deck where she leaned on the hand-rail and stared into the calm greeny-brown waters of the Mersey. A warm breeze fanned her face, and her mind was blank, devoid of emotion or thought.

'Hello, there,' said a familiar voice. 'I thought you were going to stay and see what happened?'

'I decided not to.' Flo turned. The red-haired girl was the only person she didn't mind seeing at the moment. 'I felt too upset.'

'You shouldn't get upset over a feller.' The girl leaned on the rail beside her. She wore a smart emerald-green frock that accentuated her vividly coloured face. At any other time Flo would have felt ashamed of the shabby blouse and skirt she wore for work. 'There's plenty more where he came from. Someone with your looks will soon get fixed up again.'

'I don't want to get fixed up again,' Flo whispered. 'I'll never go out with anyone else. Never!'

'Don't tell me you're in love?' The girl sounded faintly disgusted.

Flo nodded numbly. For the first time since she'd heard the news about Tommy, she began to cry. The tears flowed freely down her cheeks and fell silently on to the smooth waters below.

'Come on, girl.' Flo felt her shoulders being painfully squeezed. 'What's your name?'

'Flo Clancy.'

'I'm Isobel MacIntyre, but everyone calls me Bel.' She gave Flo a little shake. 'Look, the ferry's about to dock. Shall we find somewhere and have a cup of tea?'

'I'd love to, but what about your job?'

'Sod me job! I'll tell them the doctor said I was run down and I needed a day off to put me feet up. Anyroad, it says almost half past two on the Liver building clock, so it's not worth going in.'

Flo couldn't help but smile through her tears. 'You're the healthiest-looking person I've ever seen.'

There was a café a short way along Water Street, almost empty after the dinner-time rush. They were about to enter, when Flo remembered she had only enough money for her tram fare home.

'Don't worry,' Bel said, when she told her. 'I'm flush so it can be my treat.'

As they drank their tea and Flo nibbled at a sticky bun, Bel informed her that she worked as a waitress at La Porte Rouge, a restaurant in Bold Street. 'That's French for the Red Door. It's dead posh and I get good tips, particularly off the fellers. Last week, I got fifteen bob altogether.'

'Just in tips! Gosh, I don't get much more than that in wages.'

Bel asked where she worked and where she lived and all about her family. Flo could tell she was trying to keep

70

her mind off the events taking place above and below the sea not too many miles away. She gladly told her all about Fritz's Laundry, about Mam and her sisters, and how they'd had to take in a lodger when Dad died. 'He's dead nice, Albert. The thing is, our Martha's determined to marry him. I can't think why, 'cos though he's nice, he's no oil painting, and he's forty-five. She wears glasses, though, and she thinks she'll never catch a feller. You should hear the way she bosses me and our Sal around, just 'cos she's the oldest,' Flo said indignantly.

'She couldn't be any worse than me auntie Mabel,' Bel said flatly. 'She's an ould cow if there ever was one.' She explained that her mam had died when she was only four and she'd been dumped on Auntie Mabel who lived in Everton Valley. 'Me dad's away at sea most of the time. I can't wait to get away meself. I'm eighteen, and the very second the war starts, I'm going to join the Army.'

'But the Army only take men!'

'Of course they don't, soft girl! They take women an' all. They're called the ATS, which stands for Auxiliary Territorial Service.'

Just then, two men came in, talking volubly, and sat at the next table. After they had given the waitress their order, they continued their conversation.

'It's bloody disgraceful!' one said angrily. 'If I had a son on board, I'd kick up a stink all the way to Parliament. Why was she allowed to dive with twice the normal complement on board? Why was the Navy so long finding her position? And I'll never understand why cutting gear hasn't been brought by now and a hole made in her stern. The men would be free if the powers-that-be had any sense of urgency.'

'If someone doesn't get their finger out pretty soon, it'll be too late,' the other man said.

'If it isn't already! That business about there being enough oxygen for thirty-six hours, I'd like to know if that takes account of the extra men as well as the crew.'

'Do you ever go dancing, Flo?' Bel asked brightly.

But Flo's mind had been distracted long enough. 'I wonder if anything's happened,' she whispered.

'Don't sound like it. But try not to lose heart, Flo. There's still hope.'

Flo gave a deep, shuddering sigh. It was strange, but she couldn't help thinking about Nancy.

'Your chap's married, isn't he?' Bel said knowingly.

'How did you guess?' Flo gasped.

'If he was a proper boyfriend, this Mr Fritz would have let you off like a shot. Instead, you had to tell a lie to get away.'

'So did you,' Flo pointed out. 'Your chap must be married, too.'

Bel made a face. 'It so happens he's not. Tuesday was only the second time I'd seen him. That's when he told me he was sailing with the *Thetis* because some other feller had been taken poorly. When I saw the headlines in this morning's papers, it seemed a good excuse for a ride on the ferry – I often go on me own. In fact, that's where I met my chap, on the Birkenhead ferry.' She pursed her red lips primly. 'I'm not the sort of girl who goes out with married men, thanks all the same. Mind you, Flo, you don't look the sort, either, particularly with you being a Catholic an' all, not like me.'

Flo felt it was important to explain the nature of her relationship with Tommy. 'My chap wasn't married proper. We were going to get married next year.' She paused, frowning. 'His wife – I mean, his sort-of-wife – was outside Cammell Laird's. You never heard such a carry-on.'

'Was she the one who was shouting?'

'That's right, Nancy. The thing is, I'm sure she recognised me.'

'Maybe she's been following you and your bloke around?'

Flo shuddered. 'Oh, don't! Tommy would have a fit at the very idea.'

'Who?'

72

'Tommy. Tommy O'Mara. What's your chap's name?'

Bel was scowling at the teapot as she poured more water in. Her cheeks were flaming. 'Er, Jack Smith,' she said shortly. Despite having refilled the pot, she leaped to her feet and paid the bill. Outside, she began to walk quickly, for no reason that a rather confused Flo could see, back towards the river.

They arrived at the Pier Head just as a ferry returning from New Brighton was docking. Children came running off the boat on to the landing-stage carrying buckets and spades, their hair full of sand, faces brown from the sun. Flo remembered going to New Brighton with Mam and Dad and her sisters. It seemed a hundred lifetimes ago. The area was unusually crowded for a weekday. People were staring out to sea, as if hoping to see signs of the attempts being made to rescue the ill-fated submarine. The girls wandered across to join them.

They stood for a long while in silence, until Flo said dully, 'I don't know what I'm going to do if Tommy's dead. I'll never love another man the way I loved him. If they don't fetch the *Thetis* up, me life's over.'

'I've never heard such nonsense!' Bel's expressive face conveyed a mixture of sympathy and impatience. 'No one's life's over when they're only nineteen. What about all the proper wives? Are their lives over, too? You're dead stupid you are, Flo Clancy, letting yourself get all worked up over a chap who's not worth twopence.'

The criticism was rather blunt and scathing coming from someone she'd only just met, but Flo was too upset to take offence. She began to cry again. 'How would you know what he's worth?' she sobbed. 'Tommy O'Mara's worth a million pounds to me.'

'I've never met a chap worth twopence meself,' Bel said brusquely. 'When I meet a threepenny one, I'll marry him like a shot. The trouble with you is you're dead soft. I'm as hard as nails, me. You'll never see me cry over a man, not even a threepenny one.' She seemed unable to grasp the extent of Flo's despair. 'C'mon, let's

73

walk into town. It might take your mind off things, though we'd best steer clear of Bold Street case someone from work sees me.'

It wasn't until half past five that Flo and Bel parted. They exchanged addresses and promised to keep in touch. Flo wanted to arrive home as she usually did from work. She wouldn't tell anyone where she'd been that afternoon.

'Good heavens, Flo!' Mam remarked, when she went in. 'You're as white as a ghost and you're shivering. I hope you're not coming down with a cold. Summer colds are the worst to shake off.'

'Has anything happened?' Flo demanded abruptly.

Mam knew exactly what she meant. 'No, luv,' she said sadly. 'According to Mrs Cox, they managed to get a hawser to the hull, but it snapped and the ship sank underwater. I went to church today to say prayers with the Legion of Mary, but they don't seem to have done much good.'

Flo refused anything to eat. At Mam's insistence, she went to bed after a cup of tea. She felt uncomfortable when Martha came up later with a hot-water bottle and tucked her in. Martha wouldn't be so sympathetic if she knew the reason why her sister felt so out of sorts.

That night, she slept fitfully. Each time she woke, she was left with the memory of the same dream: she'd been wandering alone through the Mystery when an orchestra wearing full evening dress appeared before her, the sort she'd seen in films. But these were hollow, insubstantial figures – she could see right through them. They were playing 'Dancing in the Dark', and equally shadowy couples began to waltz in a circle around her. Instead of staring at each other, they gazed at Flo, unpleasant, gloating expressions on their faces. They were sneering because she was the only person without a partner. Her sense of isolation was so acute that she felt as if she was encased in a block of ice. Then the couples disappeared, the music stopped, and all that could be heard was the rustle of the trees. Flo was alone with only the moon for company.

Next morning, Mam came up with a cup of tea. 'To save you asking, I just listened to the BBC and there's no news, I'm afraid.'

Flo sat up. To her amazement there was no sign of Martha and Sally, and their bed was neatly made.

'They've gone to work,' Mam explained. 'We decided not to wake you. It wouldn't hurt to have the day off, it being Saturday, like, and you'd only be there till one. I'm sure Mr Fritz won't mind – you've never been off before.'

Flo was only too willing to comply. After Mam had gone, she pulled the bedclothes over her head and sobbed her heart out. She wasn't sure what time it was when she heard a knock on the front door, followed by Mr Fritz's voice asking how she was. 'We're all worried about her. It's not like Flo to be sick.' She hoped he wouldn't say she'd been off yesterday. It seemed he didn't, because Mam came up shortly afterwards and didn't mention it.

'He's a lovely man,' she said warmly. 'I'm very fond of him. You're ever so lucky, Flo, working in such a nice place.'

By late afternoon everyone was home, including Albert. Flo got up, and after tea they all trooped into the parlour to listen to the six o'clock news. In a chilling voice the announcer read a statement: 'The Admiralty regrets that hope of saving lives in the *Thetis* must be abandoned.'

Liverpool, the entire country, was stunned. A cablegram arrived from King George VI in Canada. His mother, Queen Mary conveyed her sympathies to the grieving relatives, and Adolf Hitler sent condolences from the citizens of Germany. When this was announced in the cinema, the audience set up a chorus of boos. A fund was set up for relatives of the dead; within days it had reached thousands of pounds. The Clancy family clubbed together and managed to raise a pound between them. Albert Colquitt added another pound and promised to take it to the collection point in the town hall.

The following Tuesday was a day of mourning. Birkenhead Cenotaph was said to be a mass of wreaths. Fifteen thousand attended the service and five thousand workers marched in honour of the memory of those who had died.

While the country mourned and salvage work began on the *Thetis*, the press were asking questions. It was impossible to grasp that so many lives had been lost when only a few feet had separated the men from their rescuers. Why hadn't experienced divers been rushed to the scene? Where was the oxyacetyline gear? A tribunal was appointed to investigate.

It wasn't until November that the *Thetis* was salvaged and able to deliver her dead for proper burial. The ship was pronounced sound enough to return by sea to its place of birth in Birkenhead. At any other time, this would have been headline news, but by now the country was already in the grip of a tragedy that would result in far greater loss of life than on a single submarine. The unthinkable had happened: Great Britain was at war with Germany and immersed in the struggle to survive.

Flo Clancy drifted through the months after Tommy O'Mara died. Everyone wanted to know what had happened to her lovely smile. Mr Fritz gave her the lightest jobs, much to the chagrin of Josie Driver who turned quite nasty. Mam bought an iron tonic, which Flo took dutifully three times a day, though she knew it wouldn't do any good. Only Bel MacIntyre, whom she saw regularly, knew why Flo no longer smiled. But Bel knew only the half of it. Flo had more things than the loss of Tommy to worry about.

On the first Sunday in September, a day blessed with shimmering sunshine and an atmosphere as heady as wine, Flo sat in the parlour listening to Albert's wireless. She heard Neville Chamberlain, the Prime Minister, announce that the country was at war and wished it mattered as much to her as it did to the rest of her family. Sally had burst into tears. 'What's going to happen to Jock?' she wept.

Jock Wilson had been writing to Sally ever since Whit Monday when they'd met on the New Brighton ferry. He'd been back to Liverpool to see her whenever he could manage a few days' leave.

Albert turned off the wireless. He looked grim. Martha reached across and self-consciously took his hand. Poor Mam's face seemed to collapse before their eyes. 'Oh, I don't half wish your dad was here!' she cried.

But Flo was too concerned with her own luckless state to care. She'd scarcely noticed missing the first period, and it wasn't until July that she had become alarmed. By the time July had given way to August and there was still no sign, she realised, with increasing horror, that she was pregnant with Tommy O'Mara's child.

Millie

I

Sharp fingers of light strobed the dark ceiling of the nightclub, interlocking briefly; blue, red, green, then yellow, followed by blue again. The disc jockey's overwrought, grating voice announced a change of record, though his words could scarcely be heard above the music booming from the huge speakers on either side of him.

In the centre of the large room, which was mainly painted black, the dancers gyrated, faces blank. Only their bodies reacted to the pounding rhythm of Joey Negro's 'Can't Take it With You', the sound bouncing off the ceiling and the walls.

I could feel the noise vibrating through the plastic seat and the soles of my shoes. It throbbed through the table and up my arms. Although I hadn't danced so far, the heat felt tremendous and my neck was damp with perspiration.

Beside me, James didn't look bored exactly, but definitely fed up. He'd been like that since we met earlier, which wasn't a bit like him. I felt put out. After a stressful week, I'd been looking forward to Saturday and his relaxing company. The friends we'd come with, Julie and Gavin, had got up to dance about half an hour ago, though I could see no sign of them on the floor.

I put my mouth against James's ear and shouted, 'Enjoying yourself?'

'Oh, I'm having a wonderful time.' He spoke with a sarcasm I'd never heard before. 'Want another drink?'

I shook my head just as Julie and Gavin returned.

78

Gavin was an old schoolfriend of James, a massively built yet graceful man who played amateur rugby. He surreptitiously removed a piece of folded paper from the breast pocket of his silk jacket and emptied the contents on to the table. Three pink tablets rolled out.

'Eleven quid each,' he shouted. He pushed one towards James. 'Have this on me.'

'Not tonight, thanks,' James said stiffly.

'Come on, James,' Julie coaxed. She was a pretty girl with a cascade of blonde curly hair. 'You look way down in the dumps. An E will put a different perspective on things.'

'I said no, thanks.'

Gavin shrugged. 'How about you, Millie? Does Miss Morality fancy changing the habit of a lifetime and popping a pill for once?'

I was tired of explaining that refusing Ecstasy had nothing to do with morality, but that the thought of not having full control of my faculties frightened me. Before I could refuse, James said angrily, 'No, she doesn't.' He looked at me, irritated at his own impatience, because he knew I would resent his answering on my behalf. 'Aw, shit!' He groaned. 'I can't stand it here. I'm going out for some fresh air.'

'He's not himself,' I said in excuse. I collected my coat and bag and James's jacket. 'We might see you later, but don't wait.'

I pushed my way through the crowded tables and found James outside in the car park. He was already shivering without his coat. October had brought an end to the beautiful Indian summer and the temperature must have dropped twenty degrees. I handed him the jacket. 'Put this on or you'll catch cold.'

'Yes, ma'am.' He forced a smile. 'Sorry about that, but I'm getting too old for clubbing.'

I linked his arm as we strolled through the car park towards the rear of the club. I had no idea where the place was situated; over the water, somewhere between

Birkenhead and Rock Ferry. 'You'd think you were ready to collect your pension.'

'Seriously, Millie, once you reach a certain age, life has to have more to it than the non-stop pursuit of a so-called "good time". Life's got to mean something.' There was a tinge of desperation in his voice. 'Oh, hell! I'm no good at explaining. It's just that, at twenty-nine, I feel I should be doing something rather more worthwhile than prancing round a nightclub, taking happy pills.'

'Such as?' To my surprise, I found we'd reached a stretch of lumpy sand and the Mersey glinted blackly in the distance, reflecting a wobbly quarter-moon. We climbed the chain-link fence and walked towards the water.

'You'll be annoyed if I tell you.'

'I promise, on my heart, not to be.'

'I'd like us to get married and have kids,' James said flatly. 'And I'd prefer to do a job that made some sort of contribution towards society.'

Astonished, I came to a standstill on the sand. 'You'd give up the garage? What would your father have to say?' The business was to be his one day.

'Sod Pa, and sod the garage,' James said, even more astonishingly. 'I'm sick to death of selling poncy, over-powered cars to idiots like myself. The job's as worthless as my life. It's useless, *I*'m useless.' He kicked moodily at a stone. 'I took today off and went to Liverpool. There was a march, hundreds of dockers who've been turfed out by Mersey Docks and Harbour Board because they refused to sign contracts that meant worse conditions and less pay. They've been out of work a year. There were fathers and sons among them. Men like that are the salt of the earth. I feel so . . . so *inadequate* compared to them.'

We reached the water. James released my arm and stuffed his hands in his pockets. He stared into the black waves. 'I've led a charmed life, Millie. I've never had to struggle for anything. Everything I've wanted has just dropped into my lap without my needing to ask. We're very lucky, the pair of us.'

I wanted to laugh out loud and say, 'You speak for yourself! Nothing has ever dropped into *my* lap. I've worked very hard for what I've got.' But what did he know about it? I'd told him virtually nothing about myself. Instead, I muttered, almost inaudibly, 'Marriage may not be the answer, James. It sounds to me like you're going through some sort of crisis.'

'Oh, God, Millie!' He pulled me into his arms, so tightly I could hardly breathe. 'Then help me through, darling. I've been going out of my mind over the last week.'

Only a week, I thought wryly. It was only during the past two or three years that I'd vaguely begun to feel an acceptable member of the human race. I put my arms around his neck and laid my head on his shoulder, not sure what to say. A dredger, barely lit, was moving silently down the river. The music from the nightclub was a muted throb. A memory returned, as it so often did, of one of the worst beatings. Mam had been out, working evenings to make ends meet. I didn't hear him come in. I heard nothing until the slithering footsteps sounded on the stairs and my body froze with fear. *I was reading in bed with a torch!* I was six and had only just learned to read. The teacher was amazed at how quickly I'd taken to it, but books offered undreamed-of pleasures, as well as escape from grim reality. I read in the lavatory, at break-times, and in the canteen. I had no idea why my father should detest the idea of my reading. It was as if he couldn't stand his children, or his wife, getting enjoyment from something, being happy.

So I'd been ordered not to read in bed. At the sound of the footsteps, I fumbled frantically with the torch, but it wouldn't go off. My hands were clammy with terror and I dropped it on the floor. The book followed. Two little thuds that sounded like thunderclaps in the quiet house.

'I thought I told yer not ter read in bed.' His voice was low and quiet, full of menace. The words travelled the years, as if they'd been spoken only a few minutes ago.

'I'm sorry, Dad.' I quaked with fright. I could feel my insides tearing apart, the way the ground erupts in an earthquake.

'I'll give yer summat to be sorry for. Gerrout!'

But I was still frozen, terrified, under the covers. I couldn't move. He pulled them back, roughly dragged me on to the floor, and began to undo the buckle of his wide leather belt. 'Kneel down,' he ordered. 'Kneel down against the bed and pull yer nightie up.'

'I didn't mean it, Dad. I won't read again, I promise,' I wailed. This was before I vowed never to let him see me cry. In her bed on the other side of the room, our Trudy stirred. 'Whassa matter?'

'Get back ter sleep,' our father snarled.

With my face buried in the bedclothes, I began to whimper. 'I won't do it again, Dad, honest.'

'Yer can bet yer life on that, yer little bitch! Bend over further.'

My arms tightened around James's neck as I remembered and felt the blows rain down on my bare bottom for the millionth time. The hard leather cut into my soft, childish flesh and I felt blood trickle down my legs. I heard my screams of pain, my pleas for mercy. 'I won't read again, Dad, I promise.'

I never did, not for a long time. The teacher was mystified as to why words no longer meant anything to her best pupil. 'It must have been a flash in the pan,' she said.

Perhaps it was Trudy, sobbing hysterically, that made him stop or perhaps he was exhausted. I was never sure. My face was still pressed against the bed, when I heard him going downstairs, the most welcome sound on earth. 'Thank you, God!' I breathed.

I broke free of James's arms and began to walk along the sands. My heart was beating rapidly and my legs were shaking. The tide rippled in over my shoes, but I didn't notice.

James caught up and grabbed my arm. 'Darling, what's wrong? What did you just say? Thank you, God, for what?'

'Nothing.' I hadn't realised I'd spoken aloud.

'You're trembling. How can it be nothing?' He regarded me sadly. 'Why are you keeping things from me?'

'Because there are things I don't want you to know.'

'If we're to be married, we should know everything about each other.'

I put my hands over my ears to shut him – everything – out, I shouted, 'Who said we're to be married? *I* didn't. When you brought the subject up last Sunday I said I'd sooner talk about it some other time. I didn't mean a few days later.'

'Darling, your feet are getting soaked.' Before I knew what was happening, he'd picked me up in his arms and carried me back to where the sand was dry. He crouched down beside me and started to take off my wet shoes. 'We're a mixed-up pair, Millie,' he said.

'You were perfectly well adjusted when we met. If you're mixed up now, it must be my fault.'

He stroked my hair. 'That's probably true. You're driving me nuts, Millie Cameron.'

I relaxed against him. Perhaps marrying James wouldn't be such a bad thing, though I'd have to think long and hard before having children. He was so comfortable to be with, so nice. But, then, no one could have been nicer than Gary, who'd bored me silly, and presumably Dad had been as nice as pie when he was courting Mum.

He was hurt when I insisted that he leave immediately after lunch next day. 'I thought we'd be spending Sunday together,' he said forlornly.

But I was firm. 'I'm clearing out my auntie's flat. I told you about it, remember? This is my only free day.'

83

'Why can't I go with you?' he pleaded. 'I could help. I could carry stuff out to the car. Anyway, it isn't safe for a woman on her own round there. Isn't William Square a red-light area?'

'Don't be silly,' I said dismissively. I couldn't wait to get to Flo's flat and had no intention of taking anyone with me. Mum had telephoned on Friday night and offered to lend a hand after she'd finished in the news-agent's shop where she worked till noon. 'You could meet me off the bus in town and let me have the key – I'll leave it with the woman upstairs. As long as I'm home before your dad, he'd never know I'd been.'

'It's quite all right, Mum,' I assured her. 'I can manage on my own.' I felt as if the flat was mine.

'Are you sure, luv? Last Sunday I got the impression you didn't want to be bothered.'

'I don't know where you got that idea from,' I said innocently. 'I don't mind a bit.'

After James had gone, I dressed in jeans and sweatshirt, and was brushing my hair when the phone rang. I ignored it, and heard the answering-machine click on. It was Mum. I sat on the off-white settee with a sigh and listened to the whining voice.

'Millicent, it's Mam. Your dad and Declan are out. Are you there, luv? It's just that I got this letter yesterday from the charity that runs our Alison's home. They can only keep her till she's eighteen. Next April she'll be transferred to this adult place in Oxford. Is that far, luv? I daren't show the letter to your dad – you know how he feels about Alison – and I can't find the atlas anywhere . . .'

My mother rambled on, as if the answering-machine itself was enough to talk to. I felt tears prickle my eyes as I listened. Mum loved her youngest child to distraction. She spent any spare money saved from the housekeeping on little presents for Alison, and had never stopped pining for her lost daughter. I couldn't bear to think how she would feel if Alison was placed out of reach of her weekly visits.

Oh, if only I could get shot of my family as easily as I'd got shot of Gary! If only I could divorce them and never see them again! By now, tears were pouring down my cheeks and I couldn't stand my mother's pain another second. I stumbled across the room and picked up the receiver.

'Mam!' But she had hung up. I had neither the strength nor the courage to ring back.

I breathed a sigh of relief as I closed the door of Flo's flat behind me. It felt like coming home. There were letters on the mat. As I lit the fire I scanned through them quickly, then turned on the lamp and went into the kitchen to put the kettle on. Nothing important; circulars, a market-research survey, a reminder that the TV licence was due. I put them aside and made a cup of tea. This time, I'd brought teabags, fresh milk and sandwiches. Still dunking a teabag, I returned to the living room and sank into the middle of the settee.

After a few minutes, I got up and put on Flo's record. Listening to Bing Crosby's soothing voice, I relaxed even more. The newspaper cuttings about the lost submarine, the *Thetis*, were still on the coffee table. I'd meant to ask someone about it, but the only elderly person I knew was Gran.

For almost an hour, I breathed in the peaceful atmosphere of the room, and the tension flowed from my body. I would have been quite happy to stay there for ever, but after a while I got up and began to wander round, poking in cupboards and drawers. Flo had been only superficially tidy. One sideboard drawer was full of gloves, another full of scarves, all in a mess. Another contained balls of string, a tangle of old shoelaces, an assortment of electric plugs, and a wad of money-off coupons held together with a rusty paperclip, which were years out of date.

For some reason, I found it necessary to untangle the laces, and was concentrating hard on undoing knots and trying to find pairs when there was a knock at the door. It would be Charmian I thought, and went to answer it. An elderly woman, very thin, with a huge cloud of unnatural mahogany-coloured hair and a still lovely though deeply wrinkled face, was standing outside. She wore a fake leopardskin jacket over a purple mohair jumper and black leggings, and appeared to be in the middle of a conversation with someone.

'Can't you wear a jacket or something?' she demanded angrily. There was a mumbled reply I couldn't catch, then the woman said, 'You'll do even less business if you catch the flu.' She turned and smiled at me ruefully, revealing a set of over-large false teeth. 'That bloody Fiona! She's wearing a dress with no sleeves that barely covers her arse. She'll perish in this weather. Hello, luv.'

No one waited for an invitation into Flo's, it seemed: the woman bounced into the room with the vitality of a teenager, although she must have been well into her seventies, followed by a waft of expensive perfume. 'I'm Bel Eddison, Flo's friend,' she said loudly. 'I know who you are – Millicent Cameron. I asked Charmian to give me a ring next time you came. She was right. You're the spitting image of Flo, and it's even more obvious to me 'cos I knew her when she was a girl. It gave me quite a turn when you opened the door.'

I'd already recognised the woman from the snapshot taken in Blackpool. It felt strange shaking hands with Flo's best friend, as if I was stepping back into the past, yet Bel was very much part of the present. 'How do you do?' I murmured. 'Please call me Millie.' I don't think I had ever seen such lovely eyes before, genuine violet. They were heavily made up, though, far too much for someone so old. The purple shadow had seeped into the crêpy lids, giving the effect of cracked eggshells.

'I'm tip-top, luv. How are you?' Bel didn't wait for an answer. Instead, she put her hands on her hips and regarded the room with exaggerated surprise. 'You haven't touched a thing,' she remarked. 'I was expecting to see the place stripped bare by now.'

'I was working out a plan of action,' I said guiltily, pushing the laces back into the drawer and closing it. 'Would you like a cup of tea?' I asked, when the newcomer removed her coat and threw herself on to the settee as if she'd come to stay. The springs squeaked in protest.

'No, ta, but I wouldn't mind a glass of Flo's sherry,' she said. Not only did she speak loudly, but also very quickly, in a strong, melodic voice that gave no hint of her age. 'Me and Flo sat here getting pissed on sherry more times than you've had hot dinners.'

Flo pissed didn't quite fit the image I'd built up in my mind, and I said as much to Bel when I gave her a glass. I poured one for myself too.

'It was her only vice,' Bel said. 'That's if you could call sherry a vice. Otherwise she led the life of a saint. For a long while, she went on retreat once a month to some convent in Wales. What's these?' She picked up the newspaper cuttings. 'Oh, you found them.' She grimaced.

'They were by the bed. Why did she keep them?' I asked.

'Draw your own conclusions, luv. It should be obvious.'

'She was in love with someone and he died on the *Thetis*?' I did a quick calculation: Flo would have been nineteen at the time.

'I said, draw your own conclusions.' Bel pursed her lips. I got the impression she enjoyed being mysterious. 'I'm not confirming or denying anything. I'd be betraying Flo's memory if I told things she kept to herself all her life.' She regarded me with her bright violet eyes. 'So, you're Kate Colquitt's eldest girl?'

'You know my mother?' I said, surprised.

'I did once. She used to come and see Flo a long time ago, but not since she married your dad. She was a lovely girl, Kate Colquitt. How is she these days?'

'She's okay,' I said abruptly.

Bel wriggled contentedly on the settee. Her expressive face displayed even the most fleeting emotion. 'This is nice! I never thought I'd sup sherry in Flo's again – pass us the bottle, there's a good girl. Ta!' she said comfortably. 'I'll top your glass up, shall I? We used to do this regular every Sunday. Sometimes Charmian joined us. It's uncanny, what with Flo dead, but you looking so much like her. Actually,' she continued with a frown, 'I'm racking me brains trying to bring to mind your husband's name. Was it Harry? You'd only been married a couple of years when Sally died – can you remember me at the funeral? Sally was the only contact Flo had with your family. When she died, Flo had no way of knowing how you were all getting on.'

'I'm sorry I don't remember you. I looked out for Flo, wondering what she was like. She disappeared before anyone could speak to her.'

'And how's Harry getting on?' Bel probed.

'Actually, it was Gary. We're divorced.'

'Really!' Bel sipped her sherry, clearly interested. 'What's your position now?' She looked all set for a long jangle. I felt less annoyed than I'd expected that the afternoon I'd anticipated having to myself had been interrupted. In fact, I *wasn't* annoyed. I liked Bel: she was so cheerfully vivid and alive. I wondered if we could trade information. If I told her a few things about myself, would she provide some details about Flo?

'I've got a boyfriend,' I explained. 'His name's James Atherton and we've been going out for a year. He's twenty-nine, and his father owns three garages on Merseyside. James manages the Southport one.'

'Is it serious?' Bel enquired gravely.

'On his side, not mine.' I thought about what James had said last night on the sands outside the nightclub. 'He's been going through some sort of crisis for an entire week.'

'Poor bugger,' Bel said laconically. 'Fellers wouldn't

88

recognise a crisis if it crept up behind and threw them to the ground.'

'It's all my fault.' I wrinkled my nose.

'It shouldn't do him any harm. Men generally have it too easy in relationships with women.'

'Where did you meet Flo?' It was time she answered a few questions.

'Birkenhead, luv, a few months before the war began. She was a year older than me. She lived in Wavertree in those days.'

'Did Flo join the forces like you?'

'How did you know . . . ?' Bel began, then nodded at the photographs on the table. 'Of course, the photo of yours truly getting hitched to dear ould Bob. That was me in the ATS. No, Flo stayed working in the laundry during the war. I was posted to Egypt and it was years before I saw her again.' She glanced sadly around the room. For the first time she looked her age as her face grew sober and her eyes darkened with sadness. She appeared to be slightly drunk. 'She was such a lovely girl. You should have seen her smile – it was like a ray of sunshine, yet she buried herself in this place for most of her life. It's a dead rotten shame.'

'Would you like more sherry?' I asked. I much preferred the cheerful Bel, even if it meant her getting even drunker.

'I wouldn't say no.' She perked up. 'The bottle's nearly gone, but there'll be more in the sideboard. Flo always had half a dozen in. She said it helped with her headaches. Is there anything to eat, luv? Me stomach's rumbling something awful. I would have had summat before I left, but I never thought I'd be out so long.'

In the kitchen, I found several tins of soup in a cupboard. I opened a tin of pea and ham, poured it into two mugs and put them in the microwave to heat, then unwrapped the ham sandwiches I'd brought with me. I didn't realise I was singing until Bel shouted, 'Someone sounds happy! You've been listening to Flo's record.'

It was totally different from how I'd spent Sunday afternoons before and I wasn't doing anything that could remotely be considered exciting, yet I felt contented as I watched the red figures count down on the microwave. I wondered if Flo had bought the microwave and other things like the record player and the television on hire purchase. During my rather pathetic forays into drawers and cupboards, I hadn't come across any papers. Flo must have a pension book somewhere, possibly an insurance policy, and there were bound to be other matters that had to be dealt with; electricity and gas bills, council tax, water rates. I was being negligent in dealing with her affairs. This was the second time I'd come and the flat was no different now than it was when Flo died, except that there was less sherry and less food. As soon as Bel went, I'd get down to work, clear a few drawers or something.

I searched for a tray and discovered one in the cupboard under the sink. There was salt and pepper in pretty porcelain containers – 'A Gift from Margate'. I put everything on the tray and took it into the living room where Bel was half asleep.

'Who paid for the funeral?' I asked.

Bel came awake with a furious blinking of her thickly mascaraed lashes and immediately attacked a sandwich. 'Both me and Flo took out special funeral policies. She showed me where hers was kept and I showed her where to find mine. We used to wonder which of us would go first. Flo swore it would be her. I never said anything but I thought the same.' She made one of her outrageous faces. 'I'll have to show someone else where me policy is, won't I?'

'Haven't you got any children?'

'No, luv.' For a moment, Bel looked desolate. 'I was in the club three times but never able to bring a baby to term. Nowadays, they can do something about it, but not then.'

'I'm sorry,' I said softly. In fact, I was so sorry that a lump came to my throat.

Unexpectedly Bel smiled. 'That's all right, luv. I used to joke with Flo sometimes that we were a barren pair of bitches but, as she'd say, kids don't automatically bring happiness. Some you'd be better off without.' She went on tactlessly, 'How's that sister of yours, the sick one? I can't remember her name.'

'Alison. She's not sick, she's autistic.' I shrugged. 'She's the same as ever.'

'And what about your other sister? And you've got a brother, haven't you?'

I was being cross-questioned again, I told her about Trudy. 'As for Declan, he just drifts from job to job. He's getting nowhere.'

Bel screwed up her face in an expression of disgust. 'There's not much hope for young people nowadays.' She sipped her soup for a while, then said casually, 'How's your gran?'

I had the definite feeling that Bel had been leading up to this question from the start. 'She's fine. She was eighty in June.'

'Is she still in the same place in Kirkby?'

'Yes.'

Bel stared at her ultra-fashionable boots: lace-ups with thick soles and heels, not quite Dr Marten's, but almost. 'I don't suppose,' she said wistfully, 'you know what that row was all about?'

'What row?'

'The one all them years ago between your gran and Flo.'

'I don't know anything about it,' I said. 'We were always led to believe Flo had done something terrible, and Gran never spoke to her again.'

Bel pulled one of her peculiar faces. 'I heard it the other way round, that it was Martha who'd done wrong and Flo who'd taken umbrage. More than once she said to me, 'Bel, under no circumstances must our Martha be told if I go to meet me Maker before she does – at least not till the funeral's over,' but she'd never tell me why, although she wasn't one to keep secrets from her best friend. We knew everything about each other except for that.'

At six o'clock, Bel announced that she was going home, but changed her mind when Charmian arrived with a plate of chicken legs and a wedge of home-made fruitcake. By then I was a bit drunk and gladly opened another bottle of sherry. At half past seven we watched *Coronation Street*. It was hours later that my visitors left, and I was sorry to see them go. Charmian was natural and outgoing, with a sharp wit, and I felt completely at ease, as if I'd known them both all my life. It was as though I had inherited two good friends from Flo.

'I've had a great time today,' Bel said, with a satisfied chuckle when she was leaving. 'It's almost as if Flo's still with us. We must do this again next Sunday. I don't live far away in Maynard Street.'

I was already looking forward to it, forgetting that I was there to sort out Flo's possessions, not enjoy myself.

Charmian said, 'Our Jay's twenty-one this week, Millie, and we're having a party on Saturday. You're invited if you're free – bring a boyfriend if you've got one.'

'Of course she's got a boyfriend, a lovely girl like her!' Bel exclaimed. 'A party might be just the thing to help your James through his crisis.'

Charmian rolled her eyes. 'It's a party, not a counselling session.'

'I'll ask him, but I'm sure he's already got something arranged.' I was convinced that James would hate the idea.

The flat felt unusually still and quiet without Bel and her loud voice, though it still smelt strongly of her perfume. A police car came screeching round the corner, the flashing blue light sweeping across the room through the thin curtains. It made me realise that I'd had more glasses of sherry than I could count. If I was stopped and breathalysed, I would lose my licence, and I couldn't afford that: a car was essential to my job. I'll have to stay here tonight, I thought.

The idea of sleeping in the soft, springy bed was appealing. I made coffee, put it in the microwave and went into the bedroom to take stock. There were night-dresses in the bottom drawer of the chest. I picked out a pretty blue cotton one with short puffed sleeves and white lace trimming on the hem. A dramatic quilted black dressing-gown, patterned with swirling pink roses, was hanging behind the door, and I remembered the pink furry slippers under the bed. I undressed quickly and put on the nightie. It felt crisp and cold, but the dressing-gown was lined with something fleecy and in no time I was warm. I shoved my cold feet into Flo's slippers. Everything smelt slightly of that lovely scent from the Body Shop, Dewberry! It seemed odd, because I kept thinking of Flo as belonging to another age, not someone who frequented the Body Shop.

It didn't seem the least bit odd or unpleasant to be wearing a dead woman's clothes. In fact, it seemed as if Flo had left everything in place especially for me.

There wouldn't be time in the morning to go home and change, and George disapproved of jeans in the office. A quick glance in the wardrobe showed it to be so tightly packed with clothes that I could barely get my fingers between them. There was bound to be something I could wear.

I collected the coffee, took it into the bedroom and climbed into bed. I switched on the bedside lamp and picked up the book Flo had been reading before she died, turning to the first page. I was deeply involved when my eyes started to close, although it wasn't yet ten o'clock, hours before I usually went to bed. I turned off the lamp, slid under the bedclothes and lay in the cool darkness, vaguely aware of the saints staring down at me from the walls, and the crucifix above my head.

There were shouts in the distance, followed by a crashing sound, as if someone had broken a window. A car's brakes shrieked, there were more shouts, but I scarcely noticed. I thought about James. Perhaps I was too hard on him. I resolved to be nicer in future. My thoughts drifted briefly to Bel, but she had scarcely occupied my mind for more than a few seconds before I fell into a deep, restful and dreamless sleep.

2

'That's a charming dress,' said George. 'You look exceptionally sweet and demure this morning.'

'So do you,' I replied tartly. I always resent men considering it their prerogative to make comments on a woman's appearance. 'The dress belonged to my aunt. I stayed the night in her flat.'

George looked at me askance. 'That's a bit risky, isn't it? I hope you weren't alone.'

'I was, but seem to have survived the experience.'

The extension rang on my desk and George disappeared into his office. It was James. 'Where on earth were you last night?' he demanded crossly. 'I rang and rang and left increasingly desperate messages on your answering-machine. Then I called early this morning and you still weren't there.'

I frowned in annoyance. What right had he to know my whereabouts for twenty-four hours a day? 'I had visitors at my aunt's flat and we drank a bottle of sherry between us. It didn't seem safe to drive.'

'If I'd known what number your aunt had lived at, I'd have come to William Square in search of you.'

'If you had, I'd have been very cross,' I said coldly.

James groaned. 'Darling, I've been out of my head with worry. I thought you might have come to some harm.'

I remembered that I'd vowed to be nicer to him, so bit back another sharp reply. 'I'm perfectly all right,' I said pleasantly. 'In fact, I had the best night's sleep in years.'

Even Diana had remarked on how well I looked. 'Spark-ling' was how she had put it. 'You never usually have much colour, but your cheeks today are a lovely pink.'

'Shall we meet tonight, catch a movie, have dinner? *Leaving Las Vegas* is on at the Odeon.'

"Not tonight, James. I really need to get on with some work at home. I haven't touched my report in ages.' George had muttered something earlier about having found an ideal site in Woolton for the new office. 'Perhaps Wednesday or Thursday.'

'Okay, darling.' He sighed. 'I'll call you tomorrow.'

I hadn't time to worry if I'd hurt him because the phone rang again immediately I put the receiver down. The Naughtons wished to view a house in Ormskirk; they'd received the details that morning. This time they'd make their own way there, and I arranged to meet them outside the property at two o'clock.

The phone scarcely stopped ringing for the rest of the morning. I ate lunch at my desk, and remembered my appointment with the Naughtons just in time to avoid being late. Snatching the keys off the wall, I told George I'd probably be gone for hours. 'They take for ever, wandering around discussing curtains and stuff.'

'Humour them, Millie, even if it takes all day,' George said affably. He grinned. 'I must say you look a picture in that dress.'

I stuck out my tongue at him because I knew he was teasing. Flo's dress was a pale blue and pink check with a white Peter Pan collar, long sleeves and a wide, stiff belt. The material was a mixture of wool and cotton. It fitted perfectly and didn't look in the least old-fashioned. Neither did the short pink swagger coat that had been tucked at the back of the wardrobe, though I'd had an awful job pressing out the creases with a damp tea-towel. Even Flo's narrow, size seven shoes could have been bought with me in mind: the clumpy-heeled cream slingbacks went perfectly with everything.

Until I reached the countryside, I hadn't noticed how

miserable the weather was. Mist hung over the fields, drifting in and out of the dank wet hedges. The sky was a dreary grey with blotches of black.

When I drew up outside the house the Naughtons were waiting in their car. It was a compact detached property on a small but very smart estate that had been built only five years ago.

I got out and shook hands with the rather homely middle-aged couple. Their children had left home and they were looking for something smaller and easier to clean. The trouble was, they were unwilling to give up a single item of furniture and seemed unable to visualise life without their present curtains. 'Let's hope this is it!' I smiled. They were registered with several other agents and had been viewing properties for months. 'The vendors are both at work, so we'll have the place to ourselves.'

The house was owned by schoolteachers who were moving south. It had been very untidy when I had called to take details a few days before, but I'd assumed they would tidy up when they knew prospective purchasers were coming – I'd never known a seller yet who hadn't. However, when we went in, the place was a tip. Heaps of clothes lay on the stairs to be taken up, the remains of breakfast was still on the kitchen table and there were years of ground-in dirt on the tiled floor.

'This is disgusting,' Mrs Naughton expostulated indignantly. Her husband nudged her, embarrassed, but she refused to be silenced. 'It smells!' she claimed.

After a brief glance in the lounge, which looked as if a hurricane had swept through it, Mrs Naughton refused to go upstairs. 'I dread to think what the bathroom must be like. I couldn't possibly live here.' She made for the door.

Seconds later, I found myself shaking hands again and apologising for the state of the house. They drove away, Mrs Naughton in high dudgeon, and I returned to my car. I had expected the view to take at least an hour but it had been over within a few minutes.

I drove out of the estate and was about to turn right towards Liverpool when I remembered that the St Osyth Trust, where Alison lived, was only about five miles away. On impulse, I turned left in the direction of Skelmersdale. I'd tell George the Naughtons had taken their usual lengthy time. 'I'm normally very conscientious,' I told myself virtuously. 'I rarely take time off. I'm never ill.'

It was months since I'd seen my sister. I preferred to go without Mum, who frequently made a big emotional scene, patting and kissing a mystified Alison who had no idea what all the fuss was about.

The sky was growing darker and it began to drizzle. I hated driving with the windscreen wipers on, and it was with relief that I turned off the narrow, isolated road into the circular drive of the gloomy red-brick mansion.

The big oak trees bordering the grounds at the front had shed their leaves and a gardener was leisurely raking them into little heaps on the lawn. Round the side of the house, a bonfire smouldered reluctantly. I parked in the area reserved for visitors. Perhaps because it was Monday, I appeared to be the only one there.

The heels of Flo's shoes clicked loudly on the polished wooden floor as I went over to Reception where a woman was typing. She looked up questioningly. 'Can I help you?'

'I've come to see Alison Cameron. I'm her sister.' I felt uncomfortable. The woman, Evelyn Porter, had worked there for as long as I could remember, yet she didn't recognise me because I came so rarely.

'Of course. I should have known. Alison's in the lounge. She's already got a visitor. You know the way, don't you?'

I nodded and turned to go, when Evelyn Porter said, 'I should warn you that Alison's a little upset today. We had to have the upstairs redecorated – it was in a terrible state, and the painters are in her room. Alison can't stand her precious things being disturbed and you'll find her rather agitated.'

The lounge was built on to the rear of the house, a sturdy conservatory that went its entire width, filled with brightly cushioned cane furniture. I paused before going in, praying it would be Trudy who was visiting, not Mum. Trudy's car hadn't been outside, though, and Mum couldn't fit in the bus journey to Skelmersdale between finishing work and being home in time to make my father's tea. During the week he monopolised the car – it would have been fixed quick enough when he needed it himself, assuming there'd been anything wrong in the first place.

To my pleased surprise, when I opened the door I found Declan, who was supposed to be at work, alone in the lounge with Alison. 'What on earth are you doing here?'

He stood up and hugged me. 'Hi, Sis. You're the last person I expected to see.'

We stayed in each other's arms for several seconds. It was only when I saw him that I remembered just how much I loved my little brother, though he was several inches taller than me now. 'Declan, love, you're thinner than ever,' I said. I could feel the bones protruding from his neck and shoulders, and I remembered the violence meted out to his puny body by our father. I gave him an affectionate push and turned to my sister. 'Hallo, Alison. It's Millie. I've come to see you.'

Over the last few years, Alison Cameron had grown into a beautiful young woman. She'd always been the prettiest of us three sisters, but now she was breathtaking. Her eyes were large and very green, like a luminous sea in sunlight, the lashes long and thick, several shades darker than her abundant ash-blonde hair, emphasising the creamy whiteness of her flawless skin. Her condition was only evident in the movements of her lovely body: stiff, clumsy, lacking grace.

'Hallo, hallo, hallo.' Alison flicked her long fingers in front of her eyes. 'You want to go upstairs.'

She meant, 'I'. 'I want to go upstairs.'

'Sorry, luv. You can't,' Declan said gently. 'Your room's being painted a nice new colour.'

I kissed the smooth, porcelain cheek, but Alison didn't seem aware of the gesture. 'It will look very pretty when it's done, darling. Then you can spread all your lovely things out again.' She kept her talcum powder, hairslides, toys and other odds and ends in neat rows on the bedside table and window-sill, and was always deeply distressed if anything was put in the wrong place.

'You want to go upstairs.'

'Later, darling, later.'

Alison looked at the floor, avoiding eye-contact. 'Come in thing with wheels?'

'I came in my car, yes.'

'You go in thing with wheels.'

'You've been in a car? Whose car, darling?'

'I think Trudy and Colin took her for a drive yesterday,' Declan whispered, when Alison shook herself irritably and began to flick her fingers again.

I had never been able to comprehend what went on in my sister's mind, although one of the doctors had once tried to explain it to Mum. It was something to do with mind blindness, the inability to perceive another person's emotions, which was why she sometimes laughed when our mother cried. Poor Mum was unable to accept that Alison wasn't laughing at *her*. My sister just wasn't aware of tears.

'Would you like to do a jigsaw puzzle, luv?' Declan suggested. 'The woman brought some in before,' he said. 'Thought they might calm her down, like.'

But Alison was looking out of the window, where a narrow line of smoke was drifting upwards from the bonfire. She had an uncanny, inexplicable ability to do the most complicated jigsaws in a fraction of the time it would have taken most people.

Declan and I looked at each other. As far as Alison was concerned, we might as well not be there.

'You know,' Declan said softly, 'I used to think me dad was responsible for the way Alison is. I thought he shook and slapped her so hard it damaged her brain. I envied her something rotten. I always hoped he'd do the same to me so I'd be sent here, too.'

'He did more than shake and slap you, Dec. He leathered the three of us regularly.'

'You had it the worst, Mill. You were the oldest, and he seemed to have it in for you more than the rest of us.'

I made a face. I seemed to have caught the habit from Bel. 'Maybe there was something about me that drove him over the edge,' I suggested lightly.

'Still, it didn't damage our brains. We all stayed quite normal.' Declan grinned. 'Least, relatively normal. Mind you,' the grin disappeared, 'there's still time for one of us to snap. I'll end up behind bars if I stay in that house much longer. I swear one day I'll kill the bastard because of the way he treats Mam. He hasn't given her any money in weeks. It used to be the horses, now it's that bloody lottery. Yet you should hear him moan if the food isn't up to scratch. He nearly hit the roof when we got a reminder for the electricity bill, as if she could pay everything out of the fifty quid a week she earns and what I hand over for me keep. He called her a lazy bitch and said it was about time she got a full-time job. If she did, there'd be hell to pay if his meals weren't ready on time.'

Declan's soft, rather feminine voice was rising, and I noticed that his hands, long and white like Alison's were gripping the arms of the chair, the knuckles taut. His gentle face was drawn and tired. I leaned back in the chair and sighed. My brother's unhappiness was painful to watch and it was to avoid that pain that I kept as far away from my family as I could. I almost wished I hadn't come or that Declan hadn't been there. 'Why don't you leave, Dec?' I pleaded. Then there'd only be Mum for me to worry about.

'As if I could leave Mam on her own with that bastard.'

'You can't stay for ever, love.'

'I'll stay as long as I have to.'

I got up and walked down the long room to the coffee machine provided for visitors. The light was on, which meant the machine was working. 'Fancy a coffee, Dec?' I called. Alison remained fascinated by the smoke.

'Please.'

'What are you doing here, anyway?' I asked, when I returned with the drinks. 'You're supposed to be at work.'

Declan recovered his good humour swiftly. His knack of making a joke of things that would have driven another person to despair was impressive. Dad's belt had broken once in the middle of a thrashing. 'Never mind, Dad,' he had said chirpily. 'I'll get you another for Christmas.'

'I lost me job.' He smiled. 'I got the sack three weeks ago.'

'Mum never said!'

He shrugged his delicate shoulders. 'That's because she doesn't know. She gets dead upset every time I get the shove. No one knows except our Trudy. I've looked for other work, Millie, honest, but I can't get anything. I've got no references because I've never held a job down long enough. The thing is, all I know is labouring and I'm not up to it.'

'Oh, Dec! What do you do with yourself all day?' I felt hurt that he had confided in Trudy and not in me. I was his sister, too. I wanted, reluctantly, to help.

'I wander the streets, go to the Job Centre, call on Trudy, then go home for six o'clock so Mam thinks I've been to work. This is the third time I've come to see Alison, but it means hitching lifts and last time I had to walk all the way back.'

'You should have told me.' I would have given him the key to my flat, where he could watch TV and help himself to food.

'I didn't think you'd be interested,' Declan said, which hurt more.

'I'll have to go soon,' I said. 'They'll be expecting me at the office. We don't seem to be doing much good here.' I made a quick decision. 'Look, I'll take you into town and you can go to the cinema – *Leaving Las Vegas* is on at the Odeon. When I finish work, we'll go back to my place for a meal. I've got pizza in the freezer.'

Declan's big green eyes sparkled. 'Great idea, Sis. I'll ring Mam and tell her I'm working late or she'll want to know how I met you. The pictures are out 'cos I'm skint. I give Mam all I get off the social, but it'll be nice to look round the shops. I haven't been to town in ages.'

It was even worse than I'd thought. 'What have you been doing for money all this time?' I asked, dismayed.

'Trudy gives me the odd few quid, but she doesn't want Colin to know what's happened. She reckons he's had enough of the Camerons.'

Despite Declan's protests that he didn't want to scrounge, I insisted he take all the money I had with me, twenty pounds.

A woman in a white overall came in to ask how Alison was. 'She doesn't want to know us today, do you, Sis?' Declan chucked his beautiful sister under the chin, but she remained as unaware of the gesture as she'd been of my kiss. 'Slippers,' she muttered. 'Slippers, slippers, slippers.'

'The builders are just packing up for the day so we can put her things back in place. They've only got the ceiling to do tomorrow. Would you mind if I took her upstairs? I think she'll feel happier once she knows everything's back to normal. Next time you come she'll be fine.'

Well, as fine as she'll ever be, I thought sadly. I watched Alison being led away, oblivious to the presence of her brother and sister.

When it came down to it, I was no good at telling blatant lies. I couldn't bring myself to tell George that the Naughtons had taken ages viewing the house when it wasn't true. 'I hope you don't mind, but I went to see my sister. She only lives a few miles away. It was a spur-of-the-moment thing.'

'The one in the home?'

'That's right.' Sometimes I forgot George knew things about me that no one outside my family did.

'No problem,' George said easily.

'I should have let you know on the mobile.'

George laughed. 'I said, no problem. You could get away with murder in that dress, Ms Millicent Cameron. What prompted your folks to call you that, by the way?'

'It's after a singer my mother liked, Millicent Martin.'

'Oh, Lord!' he groaned. 'I liked her, too. Does that show my age?'

'Very much so, George,' I said gravely, getting my own back for his comments on Flo's frock.

We grinned at each other amiably, and George said, 'I was wondering where you were. Mrs Naughton telephoned to complain to a higher authority about the state of that house. I'll give the vendors a ring tonight, suggest they tidy up, but be prepared to warn people in future, just in case.'

I hung up the keys and went over to my desk, aware of how close I'd come to blotting my copybook with George.

It was my job to prepare a list of properties to advertise in the local press and I was gathering together details to feed into the computer when I became aware that Diana, whose desk was next to mine, was crying quietly. Tweedledum and Tweedledee were out, and Oliver Brett was in George's office. June, the receptionist, was on the phone, her back to us.

'What's the matter?' I asked. The woman's eyes were red with weeping.

'It's my father. I don't know if I told you he was ill. It's cancer of the stomach. A neighbour's just called to say she found him unconscious on the kitchen floor. He's been taken to hospital.'

'Then go and see him straight away. George won't mind.'

'Why should I?' Diana looked at me mutinously. 'I've got work to do – I'm just finishing off those notes on Woolton. It could affect my prospects of promotion.'

I said nothing, but wondered where my priorities would lie in the same situation.

'Parents are a pain,' Diana said, in a hard voice. 'When they grow old, it's worse than having children.' She blew her nose, wiped her eyes, and began to cry again. 'I don't know what I'll do if Daddy dies!'

'I think you should go to the hospital.'

Diana didn't reply. She typed furiously for a while, then said, 'No. I'm too busy. I wish that bloody neighbour hadn't phoned. There comes a time when you've got to put yourself first.'

'If you say so.' I tried to ignore her as I finished off the adverts then faxed them through to the press, by which time it had gone six o'clock. I was meeting Declan in a pub in Water Street close to where I'd parked the car. When I left Diana was still typing, her brow creased in concentration, her eyes still red. I stood for a moment, looking at her and wondering what to say. Eventually, all I could think of was, 'Goodnight, Diana.'

'Night,' Diana replied, in a clipped voice.

Declan had thoroughly enjoyed the film. 'Dad would be in his element in Las Vegas,' he said, chuckling, on the way to Blundellsands.

'Only if he had a few thousand pounds to play with,' I said drily, 'and he'd probably lose that within a day.' I patted his knee. 'Try to forget about him and enjoy yourself for a change. We can watch a video later, if you like.'

'That'd be the gear, Sis.' Declan sighed blissfully as I drove into the parking area at the side of my flat. 'I feel dead honoured. I've only been here once before.' His voice rose an octave and became a squeak. 'Jaysus, look at that car! It's only a Maserati!'

A low-slung black sports car was parked against the boundary wall. It wasn't possible to see through the dark-tinted windows who was inside it, but a terrible suspicion entered my mind.

'I'd sell me soul for a car like that!' Declan murmured reverently. He leaped out of the Polo as soon as it stopped and went over to the black car with the deference of a pilgrim approaching the Pope. My suspicions were confirmed when the car door opened and James climbed out. He frequently turned up in strange cars belonging to the garage.

'Millie?' His voice contained a great deal of anger and hurt. It even sounded slightly querulous. 'Millie?' he said again.

I realised he thought that Declan was a boyfriend. He'd asked me out that night and I'd refused, saying I had work to do. Instead I was seeing someone else. I felt irritated. Why shouldn't I go out with another man if I wanted? I was cross that James had turned up uninvited. Now I would have to introduce him to Declan, and I wanted the Camerons and the Athertons kept apart for as long as possible. For ever would be even better.

'This is my brother, Declan,' I said stiffly. 'Declan, this is James.'

James's broad shoulders sagged with relief. 'Declan!' he said jovially, as he shook hands. 'I've heard a lot about you.' He was being polite: he knew nothing about my brother other than that he existed.

'Is this your car?' Declan's jaw dropped in disbelief: he had a sister who had a boyfriend who drove a Maserati.

'No, I just borrowed it for tonight. My own car is an Aston Martin.'

'Jaysus! Can I look under the bonnet? Would you mind if I sat behind the wheel, only for a minute, like?'

James was happy to oblige. He got back into the car and pulled the lever to raise the bonnet. Seconds later the pair were bent over the engine and James was explaining how things worked. I trudged upstairs, dreading the evening ahead.

I put the kettle and the oven on, and began to prepare a salad. James would probably expect to stay to dinner and fortunately the pizza was a large one. I opened a bottle of wine and drank a glass to steady my nerves. By the time James and Declan arrived, almost half an hour later, I'd drunk half the bottle and had to open another to have with the meal. I blamed Flo. It wouldn't have crossed my mind to drink alone if I hadn't come face to face with all that sherry.

The two men were getting on famously. The conversation had turned to football. 'There's a match on TV later, Liverpool versus Newcastle.' James rubbed his hands. 'You don't mind if we watch it, do you, Millie?'

'Not at all.' By now, I was terrified Declan would say something, give the game away, and the whole respectable edifice I'd built around myself would come tumbling down.

It wasn't until they had finished their meal that he revealed the smallest of my secrets. 'That was great, Sis. I haven't had such decent grub in ages.' He turned to James. 'Our mam does her best, but everything comes with mashed spuds and cabbage.' He patted his stomach. 'I'm not half glad I went to see Alison in Skem, else I wouldn't have met our Millie.'

'I thought Alison lived in Kirkby with you,' James said, puzzled.

'Oh, no. Alison's autistic. She's in a home. Hasn't Millie told you?'

'Who'd like coffee?' I said brightly. I went into the kitchen, bringing that line of conversation to an abrupt end. When I returned with the coffee, Declan had just rung home. 'I forgot to tell Mam I'm supposed to be working late. I lost me job the other week,' he explained to James, 'and I still haven't got round to telling our mam and dad.'

James looked sympathetic. 'What sort of work do you do?'

I gritted my teeth as Declan replied, 'Only labouring. I was working on this demolition site, but it seemed to be me who got demolished more often than the building.'

'You're wasted as a labourer. Why don't you take a college course like Millie did?'

To my surprise, Declan's face turned bright red. He blinked his long lashes rapidly and said, 'It's never entered me head.'

Fortunately, it was time for the match to start. I switched on the television, then the computer. I wanted to finish my report, but my brain was incapable of competing with the sound of the television and James and Declan's bellows of support alternated with groans of despair whenever Newcastle went near the Liverpool goal. I tried to read a book, gave up, and went into the kitchen where I caught up with the ironing and prayed the match wouldn't go into extra time. The minute it was over, I'd take Declan home. It was imperative that my brother and my boyfriend were separated before any more of the Camerons' dirty linen was aired.

To my dismay, James had already offered Declan a lift. I thought of the burnt-out car abandoned opposite my parents' house – hopefully James wouldn't notice in the dark – of the lads who'd still be playing outside and might not feel too charitably towards the driver of a Maserati.

'Tara, Sis.' Declan punched me lightly on the shoulder. 'It's been a smashing evening.'

'We must do it again soon. Perhaps next time there's a match, eh?' James kissed me on the lips. 'I'll call later.'

'Oh, no, you won't,' I cried as soon as I'd closed the door. I took the phone off the hook, ran a bath, and finished off the wine while I soaked in the warm, scented water. The events of the day swirled through my mind: the Naughtons and that filthy house, Alison, Declan, Diana and her father, James.

James! What was Declan saying to him? It wasn't that I

cared about him loving me less, I only cared about him – anybody – *knowing*. And when it came down to it, it was nothing to do with the house in Kirkby, or being poor, or Mum letting herself go, or Alison. It was the terror of my childhood that I wanted to keep to myself: the beatings, the fear, the sheer indignity of it all. I'd felt as if my body didn't belong to me, that it could be used by someone else whenever the whim took them. What I wanted more than anything was to put the past behind me so that the dreams would stop. I wanted to forget everything and become a person not a victim. But this would never happen while my family remained a haunting reminder, always there to ensure that the past was part of the present and, possibly, the future. The only solution would be to go far away, start a new life elsewhere – but although my mother set my teeth on edge, I loved her so much that it hurt. I could never desert her.

The water in the bath had gone cold. I climbed out, reached for a towel, and was almost dry when the door-bell rang.

'Blast!' I struggled into a bathrobe.

'I tried to call you on the car phone,' James said, as he came breezing in, 'but you seemed to be incommunicado.' He noticed the receiver was off the hook. 'Is this deliberate or accidental?'

'Deliberate,' I said irritably. 'I want some peace. I want to be left alone.' He tried to take me in his arms, but I pushed him away. 'Please, James.'

He threw himself on to the settee with a sigh. 'Why didn't you tell me all that stuff before?'

My heart missed a beat. 'What stuff?'

'You know what I mean. About Alison, and about Declan being gay.'

'Declan's not gay!' I gasped.

'Of course he is, Millie. It's obvious.'

'You're talking utter rubbish,' I said half-heartedly, remembering how Declan had blushed when James paid him a compliment. Then I remembered all sorts of other things about my brother. He was girlish, no doubt about it, but gay?

'Darling, I guessed straight away.'

I shook my reeling head. It was too much, coming after such an eventful day. 'What did you and Declan talk about on the way to Kirkby?'

'Cars, mainly, football a bit. Why?'

'I just wondered.'

'After I dropped him off, I gave some kids a ride around the block. They were very impressed with the Maserati.'

'That was nice of you.'

I made him a coffee, then insisted he went home. Before going to bed, I took three aspirins. Even so, unlike last night at Flo's, it was several hours before I eventually fell asleep, a restless, jerky sleep, full of unwelcome, unpleasant dreams.

Diana's father was kept in hospital overnight. The fall had nothing to do with his illness; he had had a dizzy spell. Next morning she said that a neighbour had offered to bring him home. 'I suppose you think I'm awful, not going myself,' she went on.

'Why should I?'

'Well, I think I'm awful. Daddy's being incredibly brave. At times, I wish he'd have a good old moan and I'd really have something to complain about. I'd feel less of a louse.' She wrinkled her nose. 'I'm all mixed up.'

'Who isn't?' I snorted.

3

James had been told bluntly that I needed time to myself, time to think. If he turned up uninvited again, I would be very cross. He agreed meekly that we wouldn't meet again until Saturday. 'Will you be very cross if I call you?' he asked, in a little-boy voice.

'Of course not, but if I'm not around I don't want anguished messages left on my answering-machine.'

'No, ma'am. Thank you very much, ma'am.'

I kissed his nose, because he was so patient and understanding. I couldn't imagine allowing a man to mess me about as much as I did him. Nor could I understand why he put up with it from someone like me.

Throughout the week, I did my utmost to get to the flat in William Square, but the estate-agency business, while not exactly booming, was picking up. On Wednesday and Thursday I was still hard at work in the office until well past seven o'clock.

On Friday night, I finished off the report and stapled together the eight pages. I decided to read through it again and give it to George on Monday: he'd begun negotiations for the empty shop, which he hoped to have open by Christmas. Even if Diana got her 'notes' in first, it would show that I was equally keen.

Afterwards, I phoned home, which I'd been meaning to do all week, and was relieved when Declan answered.

'Where's Mum?' I asked.

'Out. Dad went to the pub, so I gave her five quid of that twenty I got off you on condition she went to bingo.' He chuckled. 'She was dead chuffed.'

'Declan?'

'Yes, luv?'

'That suggestion James made, about you going to college, why don't you do it? You could learn car mechanics or something, get a job in a garage.' Unlike me, he had left school with two reasonable O levels.

'Oh, I dunno, Millie. Me dad would blow his top.'

'You're twenty, Declan. It's nothing to do with him what you do with your life.'

'That's easy for you to say. It's not you who'd face the consequences when he finds out I've given up work for college.' He sounded peevish, as if he thought I'd forgotten the way my father's powerful presence still dominated the house in Kirkby.

'You've already given up work, Declan — or, rather, work's given up on you.' He was too soft, too unselfish, not like me and Trudy, who couldn't wait to get away. He was also weak. In a strange way, the horror had made my sister and me stronger, but our father had beaten all of the stuffing out of his only son. Declan's sole ambition seemed to be to exist from day to day with as little effort as possible.

'I suppose it wouldn't hurt to make a few enquiries,' he said grudgingly. 'What I've always fancied is learning about fashion — y'know, designing dresses or material, that sort of thing.'

'In that case, go for it, Dec,' I urged, and tried to imagine what our father would say when told his son was training to be a dress designer. Even worse, how would he react if James was right and he, too, realised that Declan was gay? I would have liked to discuss it with Declan there and then, but it was up to him to out himself. Until he did, I would never breathe a word to a soul.

I had expected James to claim he'd missed me dreadfully, but when he picked me up on Saturday night he said 'I've had a great week. I've joined the SWP.'

'The what?' I felt a trifle put out, particularly when he didn't even notice my new outfit, a short black satin shift, nor that I'd parted my hair in the middle and smoothed it back behind my ears for a change.

'The Socialist Workers' Party.'

'Good heavens, James!' I gasped. 'Isn't that a bit over the top? What's wrong with the Labour Party?'

'Everything!' he said crisply. 'This chap, Ed, said that they're all a shower of wankers. This morning I helped collect money for those dockers I told you about. I nearly brought my placard into Stock Masterton to show you.'

'I'm glad you didn't!' I hid a smile. 'Does this mean you're over your crisis?'

'I'm not sure, but for the first time in my life, I feel as if

I have some connection with the real world, real people. I've learned an awful lot this week. You wouldn't believe the tiny amount single mothers have to live on, and I never knew the National Health Service was in such a state.'

All the way into town, he reeled off statistics that most people, me included, already knew. Only a tiny percentage of the population owned a huge percentage of the country's wealth; revenue from North Sea oil had disappeared into thin air; privatisation had created hundreds of millionaires.

In the restaurant, a favourite one in the basement of a renovated warehouse, with bare brick walls and a Continental atmosphere, he didn't show his usual interest in the food. 'I went to Ed's place on Wednesday to watch a video. Did you know that in the Spanish Civil War the Communists fought on the side of the legally elected government? I'd always thought it was the other way round, that the Communists were the revolutionaries.'

I stared at him, aghast: he'd been to public school, followed by three years at university during which he'd studied history, for God's sake, and he hadn't known that! 'What does your father have to say about your miraculous conversion?' I asked. 'A couple of weeks ago, you were in the Young Conservatives.'

He frowned and looked annoyed. 'My folks think it jolly amusing. Pop said he's glad I've started to use my brain at last. My sister got involved with a group of anarchists at university, and he thinks I'll grow out of it, like Anna did.'

Anna was married with two children and lived in London. So far, we'd not met. I sipped my coffee thoughtfully. I wasn't sure if I wanted him to grow out of it. The trouble was, like his folks, I found the whole thing rather amusing. Although, no doubt, he felt sincerely about his newly found beliefs, he didn't sound sincere, more like a little boy who'd discovered a rare stamp for his collection.

'Where shall we go?' He looked at his watch. 'It's only half past ten.'

All I could think of was a club, but James reminded me he'd gone off them. 'I've just remembered,' I said, 'We're invited to a party in William Square.' It was Charmian's son's twenty-first.

'Great,' James said eagerly. 'Let's go.'

'But you'd hate it,' I laughed. 'They're not at all your sort of people.'

He looked hurt. 'What do you mean, not my sort of people? You'd think I came from a different planet. I quite fancy partying with a new crowd. Wherever we go it's always the same old faces.'

The same old middle-class professionals; bankers and farmers, stockbrokers and chaps who were something in insurance. Some of the women had careers, and those who'd given up their jobs to have children complained bitterly about the horrendous cost of employing cleaners and au pairs. I always felt out of place, just as I probably would at Charmian's. I wondered if there was anywhere I'd feel right.

'We'll go to the party if you like,' I said, but only to please James. After all, now he'd joined the SWP he'd have to get used to mixing with the hoi polloi.

Charmian looked exotic in a cerise robe with a turban wound round her majestic head. 'Lovely to see you, girl,' she murmured, and kissed me.

Rather to my own surprise, I kissed her back as I handed over the wine James had bought in the restaurant for a ludicrous price because he couldn't be bothered to search for an off-licence. I introduced him to Charmian, who seemed taken aback when he shook her hand and said, in his beautifully cultured voice, 'How lovely to meet you.'

The Smiths big living room was packed, though several couples in the middle were managing somehow to dance to the almost deafening sound of Take That's

'Relight My Fire'. I met Herbie, Charmian's husband, a mild, good-humoured man with greying hair who was circulating with a bottle of wine in each hand. 'Our Jay's around somewhere.' Charmian peered over the crowd. 'You must meet the birthday boy.' With that, she plunged into the fray.

I found a bedroom and left my coat. When I returned, there was no sign of James so I helped myself to a glass of wine and leaned against the wall, hoping Bel had been invited so that I would have someone to talk to.

A young man with a wild head of shaggy black curls and a fluffy beard came and stood beside me, his dark eyes smiling through heavy horn-rimmed glasses. 'You look like the proverbial wallflower.'

'I'm waiting for my boyfriend,' I explained.

'Fancy a dance in the meantime?'

'I wouldn't mind.' I felt rather conspicuous on my own.

He took my hand and led the way through to the dancers. There wasn't room to do anything other than shuffle round on the spot.

'Do you live round here?' I asked politely. I'd never been much good at small talk.

'Next door, basement flat. Do you still live in Kirkby?'

'You know me!' I never liked coming across people from the past.

'We were in the same class together at school. You're Millie Cameron, aren't you?'

I nodded. 'I'm at a disadvantage compared to you,' I said. 'I don't recall anyone in class with a beard.'

'I'm Peter Maxwell, in those days known as Weedy. You can't have forgotten me. I usually had a black eye, sometimes two, and an inordinate amount of cuts and bruises. The other lads used to wallop me because I was no good at games. Me mam wasn't slow at walloping me either but she didn't need a reason.'

'I remember.' He'd been a frail, pathetic little boy, the smallest in the class, smaller even than the girls. There never seemed to be a time when he wasn't crying. Rumour had it that his father had been killed during a fight outside a pub in Huyton. I envied his ability to talk about things so openly: there'd been no need for him to tell me who he was. Maybe he knew my own history. It had been no secret that Millie and Trudy Cameron's father hit his girls.

'How come you grew so big?' I asked. He was only as tall as I was, about five feet eight, but his shoulders were broad and I could sense the strength in his arms.

'Turned sixteen, left home, found work, spent all my spare time in a gym, where I grew massively, but mainly sideways.' He grinned engagingly. 'Having developed the brawn, it was time to develop the brain, so I went to university and got a degree in economics. I teach at a comprehensive a mile from here.'

'That's a tough job!' I admired him enormously, particularly his lack of hang-ups.

'It helps to have muscles like Arnold Schwarzenegger,' he conceded, 'particularly when dealing with bullies, but most kids want to learn, not cause trouble. Now, that's enough about me, Millie. What are you up to these days? If I remember rightly, you married Gary Bennett.'

'I did, yes, but we're divorced. I'm a property negotiator with Stock —'

Before I could say another word, a young woman in a red velvet trouser suit pushed through the dancers and seized his arm. 'There you are! I've been looking everywhere for you.' She dragged him away, and he turned to me, mouthing, 'Sorry.'

I was just as sorry to see him go — it had been interesting to talk to someone with a background similar to my own. I spotted James, deep in conversation with a middle-aged couple. He seemed to have forgotten about me. I felt a bit lost and made my way to the kitchen where I offered to help wash dishes. Herbie shooed me away with an indignant, 'You're here to enjoy yourself, girl.'

By now, the party had spilled out into the hall. I went

out in the hope of finding Bel, but there was no sign of her so I sat on the stairs and was immediately drawn into an argument over the acting ability, or lack of it, of John Travolta.

'He was great in *Pulp Fiction*,' a woman maintained hotly.

'He stank in *Saturday Night Fever*,' someone else said.

'That was years ago.' The woman waved her arms in disgust. 'Anyroad, no one expected him to act in *Saturday Night Fever*. It was a musical and his dancing was superb.'

The front door opened and a man came in, a tall, slim man in his twenties with a pale, hard face and brown hair drawn back in a ponytail. He wore small gold gypsy earrings and was simply dressed in jeans, white T-shirt, and black leather jacket. There was something sensual about the way he moved, smoothly and effortlessly, like a panther, that made me shiver. At the same time, his lean body was taut, on edge. Despite his hard expression, his features were gentle: a thin nose, flaring wide at the nostrils, full lips, high, moulded cheekbones. I shivered again.

The man closed the door and leaned against it. His eyes flickered over the guests congregated in the hall. I held my breath when our eyes met and his widened slightly, as if he recognised me. Then he turned away, almost contemptuously, and went into the living room.

'What do you think? What did you say your name was?' The woman who had been defending John Travolta was speaking to me.

'Millie. What do I think about what?'

'Didn't you think he was fantastic in *Get Shorty*?'

'Amazing,' I agreed, still preoccupied with the man who'd just come in.

For the next hour I barely listened as the discussion moved on to other Hollywood stars. Someone brought me another glass of wine, then James appeared, gave a thumbs-up, and vanished again. I contemplated looking for the man with the ponytail to find out who he was –

but I had left it too late: the front door opened and through the crowd I glimpsed him leaving.

At one o'clock, the party was still going strong. There were sounds of a fight from the living room, and Herbie emerged holding two young men by the scruff of the neck and flung them out of the door.

By now, I was tired of Hollywood and longed to go home. I searched for James and found him sitting on the floor with half a dozen people who were all bellowing at each other about politics. He'd removed his jacket and was drinking beer from a can. I didn't like to disturb him when he appeared to be enjoying himself so much. Nevertheless, I fancied some peace and quiet and knew exactly where I could find it.

William Square, bathed in the light of a brilliant full moon, was quiet when I went outside, though the silence was deceptive. Women, barely clothed, leaned idly against the railings, smoking and waiting for their next customer. A car crawled past, then stopped, and the driver rolled down the window. A girl in white shorts went over and spoke to him. She got in, the driver revved the engine and drove away. Two dogs roamed the pavements, casually sniffing each other. In the distance, the wail of a siren could be heard, and in the even further distance, someone screamed. A cat rubbed itself against my legs, but ran away when I bent to stroke it.

Suddenly, a police helicopter roared into the sky, like a monstrous, brilliantly lit bird. The noise was almost deafening. It really was a war zone, as George had said. I ran down the steps to Flo's flat. To my consternation, I saw that the curtains were drawn and the light was on, yet I could distinctly remember switching off the light and pulling back the curtains the last time I was there. Perhaps someone, Charmian or Bel, had decided it would be wise to make the place look lived in. But there was only one key, the one I held in my hand right now.

Cautiously I unlocked the door. It was unlikely I'd come to any harm with fifty or sixty people upstairs. I opened the inner door and gasped in surprise. The man with the ponytail was lounging on Flo's settee, his feet on the coffee table, watching the swirling lamp and listening to her record.

'Who are you? What are you doing here?' I snapped.

He turned and regarded me lazily, and I saw that his eyes were green, like mine. His face seemed softer than when I'd seen him upstairs, as if he, too, was under the spell of the blurred shadows flitting around the room and the enchanting music.

'I never thought I'd do this again,' he said. 'I came to leave me key on the mantelpiece and found Flo's place no different than it's always been.'

'Where did you get the key?'

'Off Flo, of course. Who else?' His voice was coarse, his Liverpool accent thick and nasal. He was the sort of man from whom I'd normally run a mile, and yet, and yet . . . I did my level best to hide another shiver.

'You still haven't told me who you are.'

'No, but I've told you why I'm here.' He swung his feet off the table with obvious reluctance, as if he wasn't used to being polite, and stood up. 'I was a friend of Flo's. Me name is Tom O'Mara.'

Flo

I

'Tommy O'Mara!' Martha's voice was raw with a mixture of hysteria and horror. 'You're having a baby by Tommy O'Mara! Didn't he go down on the *Thetis*?'

Flo didn't answer. Sally, sitting at the table, pale and shocked, muttered, 'That's right.'

'You mean you've been with a married man?' Martha screeched. Her face had gone puffy and her eyes were two beads of shock behind her round glasses. 'Have you no shame, girl? I'll never be able to hold up me head in Burnett Street again. We'll have to start using a different church. And they're bound to find out at work. Everybody will be laughing at me behind me back.'

'It's Flo who's having the baby, Martha, not you,' Sally said gently.

Flo was grateful that Sally appeared to be on her side or, at least, sympathetic to her plight. A few minutes ago when she had announced that she was pregnant, Martha had exploded but Mam had said quietly, 'I can't stand this,' and had gone straight upstairs, leaving Flo to Martha's rage and disgust. The statement had been made after tea deliberately, just before Albert Colquitt was due when Martha would feel bound to shut up. After Albert had been seen to, she might have calmed down a bit, but Flo knew that she would be at the receiving end of many more lashings from her sister's sharp tongue.

'It might be Flo having the baby, but it's the whole family that'll bear the shame,' Martha said cuttingly. She turned to her youngest sister, 'How could you, Flo?'

'I was in love with him,' Flo said simply. 'We were going to get wed when Nancy got better.'

'Nancy! Of course, he married that Nancy Evans, didn't he? Everyone used to call her the Welsh witch.' Martha scowled. 'What do you mean, you were going to get wed when she got better? She's never been sick, as far as I know. Anyroad, what's that got to do with it?'

As Martha was unlikely to know the intimate details of Nancy O'Mara's medical history, Flo ignored the comment, but she was disconcerted to learn that Nancy was Welsh when she was supposed to have been Spanish. In a faltering voice she said, 'He wasn't married proper to Nancy.' She didn't mention the gypsy ceremony in a wood near Barcelona because it sounded ridiculous. In her heart of hearts, she'd never truly believed it. It was too far-fetched. She wondered bleakly if Tommy had ever been to Spain, and realised that everything of which Martha accused her was true: she was a fallen woman, lacking in morals, who'd brought disgrace upon her family.

It wasn't surprising to hear Martha say that there was no question of Tommy O'Mara not being married proper to Nancy Evans, because she had been in church when the banns were called. 'He used to lodge with the family of this girl I met at Sunday school,' she said, and added spitefully, 'She said her mam couldn't wait to get shot of him because she had a terrible job getting the money off him for his bed and board.'

Sally gasped. 'Shush, Martha. There's no need for that.'

'I'm sorry,' Flo said brokenly. 'I'm so sorry.'

'There, there, Sis.' Sally slipped off the chair and put her arms around her sister, but Martha wasn't to be swayed easily by expressions of regret.

'And so you should be sorry,' she blasted. 'You realise everyone will call the kid a bastard? No one will speak to it at school. It'll be spat upon and kicked wherever it goes.'

'Martha!' Mam said sharply, from the doorway. 'That's enough.'

Flo burst into tears and ran upstairs, just as the front door opened and Albert Colquitt arrived.

A few minutes later, Sally came in and sat on the bed where Flo was lying face down, sobbing.

'You should have taken precautions, luv,' she whispered. 'I know what it's like when you're in love. It's hard to stop if things get out of hand.'

'You mean, you and Jock . . .' Flo raised her head and looked tearfully at her sister. Jock Wilson continued to descend on Liverpool whenever he could wangle a few days' leave.

Sally nodded. 'Don't tell Martha, whatever you do.'

The idea was so preposterous, that Flo actually laughed. 'As if I would!'

'She doesn't mean everything she says, you know. I don't know why she's so bitter and twisted. You'd think she was jealous that you'd been with a man.' Sally sighed. 'Poor Martha. Lord knows what she'll say when she finds out me and Jock are getting married at Christmas, if he can get away. She'd have expected to go first, being the eldest, like.'

'Sally, Oh, Sal, I'm so pleased for you.' Flo forgot her own troubles and hugged her sister. Sally made her promise to keep the news to herself: she didn't want anyone to know until it was definite.

After a while, Sally went downstairs because it was her turn to do the dishes and she didn't want Martha getting in a further twist.

Flo sat up, leaned against the headboard, and rested her hands on her swelling tummy. She'd put off breaking the dreadful news for as long as possible, but it was October, she was four and a half months' pregnant, and it was beginning to show. One or two women in the laundry had been eyeing her suspiciously, and the other day when she'd been hanging out sheets in the drying room she'd turned to find Mrs Fritz at the door, watching keenly.

Then Mrs Fritz had spent quite a long time in the office with Mr Fritz.

At first Flo had considered not telling a soul, running away and having the baby somewhere else. But she didn't want to stay away for ever and there'd be a baby to explain when she came back. Anyroad, where would she run to and how would she support herself? She had no money and wouldn't be able to get a job. She realised, sadly, that she would have to leave the laundry and it would be dreadful saying goodbye to Mr Fritz.

The door opened and Mam came in. 'I'm sorry I walked out, girl, but I couldn't stand our Martha's screaming. Perhaps it would have been best if you'd told your mam first and left me to deal with Martha.' She looked at her daughter reproachfully. 'How could you, Flo?'

'Please, Mam, don't go on at me.' Flo began to cry again at the sight of her mother's drawn face. Mam had seemed much better since the war began, as if she'd pulled herself together and was determined to see her family through the conflict to its bitter end. 'I'll leave home if you want. I never wanted to bring shame on me family.' Getting pregnant had been far from her mind when she'd lain under the trees in the Mystery with Tommy O'Mara.

'The man, this Tommy O'Mara, he should have known better. Martha says he was at least thirty. He was wrong to take advantage of a naïve young girl.' Mam pursed her lips disapprovingly.

'Oh, no, Mam,' Flo cried. 'He didn't take advantage. He loved me, and I loved him.' The lies he'd told meant nothing and neither did the promises. It was only because he was worried she might not go out with him that he'd said the things he had. 'If Tommy hadn't died, he'd have left Nancy by now and we'd be together.'

This was altogether too much for her mother. 'Don't be ridiculous, girl,' she said heatedly. 'You're talking like a scarlet woman.'

Perhaps she *was* a scarlet woman, because Flo had meant every word she said. Perhaps other couples didn't love each other as much as she and Tommy had. To appease her mother, she said meekly, 'I'm sorry.'

'Anyroad, that part's over and done with,' Mam sighed. 'What we have to deal with now are the consequences. I've had a word with Martha and Sal, and we think the best thing is for you to stay indoors until you've had the baby, then have it adopted. No one in the street will have known a thing. I'll go round and see Mr Fritz tomorrer and tell him you've been taken ill and won't be coming back. I hate to deceive him, he's such a nice feller, but what else can I do?'

'Nothing, Mam,' Flo said calmly. She was quite agreeable to the first part of the suggestion, that she stay indoors until the baby was born, but there was no way she intended giving up Tommy O'Mara's child, which was the next best thing to having Tommy himself. She wouldn't tell Mam that, otherwise there would be non-stop rows for months. Once it was born, she would move to another part of Liverpool, a place where no one knew her, but not too far for her family to come and visit. She'd say she was a widow who had lost her husband in the war, which meant there was no reason for anyone to call her child a bastard. She would support them both by taking in laundry and possibly a bit of mending – Mr Fritz often declared that no one else could darn a sheet as neatly as Flo.

War had made little impact so far on the country and people had begun to refer to it as 'phoney'. Lots of lads had been called up and ships were sunk frequently, with enormous loss of life, but it all seemed very far away. There was no sign of the dreaded air-raids and food was still plentiful.

Flo passed the days knitting clothes for the baby: lacy matinée coats and bonnets, unbelievably tiny booties and mittens, and dreaming about how things would be when her child was born. Occasionally, she could hear Mam and her sisters having whispered conversations in the kitchen, and the word adoption would be mentioned. It seemed that Martha already had the matter in hand. Flo didn't bother to disillusion them – anything for a quiet life. When she wasn't knitting, she read the books that Sally got her from the library. Once a month, she wrote to Bel McIntyre, who'd joined the ATS and was stationed up in the wilds of Scotland where she was having a wonderful time. 'There's a girl for every fifteen men,' she wrote. 'But there's one chap in particular I really like. Remember I said once I'd never met a chap worth twopence? Well, I've come across one worth at least a hundred quid. His name is Bob Knox and he comes from Edinburgh like me dad.' Flo didn't mention the baby in her letters. Bel had thought her daft to become involved with a married man, and she didn't want her to know just how involved and completely daft she'd been.

Often, she wished she could go for a walk, particularly when it was sunny, and as the time crawled by, she ached to go out even in the pouring rain. The worst time was when visitors came or their lodger was at home and she had to spend hours shut in the bedroom. According to Martha, of all the people in the world, Albert Colquitt was the one who must remain most ignorant of Flo's dark secret. If he knew what sort of family he was living with he might leave, and that would be disastrous, 'seeing as you're no longer bringing in a wage.' She sniffed. Sally thought Martha was mainly worried that he wouldn't want to marry her, a goal she was still working towards with all her might.

'How do you explain that I'm never there?' asked Flo.

'He's been told you're run down, anaemic, and have to stay in bed and rest.'

'I've never felt so healthy in me life.'

She was blooming, her cheeks the colour and texture of peaches, her eyes bright, and her hair unusually thick and glossy. She wondered why she should look so well when she felt so miserable without Tommy, but perhaps it was because she couldn't wait to have the baby. Also, Mam had ordered extra milk especially for her, and Martha, for all her carping comments and sniffs of disapproval, often brought home a pound of apples and made sure there was cod-liver oil in the house, which was what Elsa Cameron had taken when she was pregnant. 'And look what a lovely baby Norman turned out to be.' Flo knew she was lucky: another family might have thrown her out on to the street.

It was on a black dreary morning in December that the Clancys' lodger discovered the secret he was never supposed to know. Mam had gone Christmas shopping and Flo was in the living room, knitting, when the key turned in the front door. It wasn't often anyone used the front door apart from Albert. She assumed Mam's shopping bags were too heavy to carry round the back, and hurried out to help. To her horror, she came face to face with Albert.

'I forgot me wallet,' he beamed, 'least I hope I did, and it's not lost. It's not just the ten-bob note I had, but there's me identity card, and some photos I'd hate to lose, as well as . . .' His voice faded and his eyes widened in surprise as he took in Flo's condition. 'I didn't know, luv,' he whispered. 'Jaysus, I didn't know.'

Flo was stumbling up the stairs. Halfway, she turned, 'Don't tell our Martha you've seen me,' she implored. 'Please!'

'Of course not, luv.' He looked stunned. 'Flo!' he called, but by then Flo was in the bedroom and had slammed the door.

She heard him go into the parlour, and a few minutes later Mam returned from the shops. 'Are you all right, girl?' she called.

'I'm just having a little lie-down, Mam.'

'I'll bring a cup of tea up in a minute, then I'm going round to St Theresa's to do the flowers for Sunday.'

Mam was obviously unaware that Albert was in the

parlour and remained unaware for the whole time she was at home. After she'd gone, Albert didn't stir or make even the smallest of sounds. Flo wondered if he was still searching for his wallet. Perhaps he was contemplating handing in a week's notice and finding somewhere more respectable to live.

Another half-hour passed, and still no sound. Then the parlour door opened and heavy footsteps could be heard coming upstairs. There was a tap on the door and a voice said hesitantly, 'Flo?'

'Yes?'

'Would you come downstairs a minute, luv? I'd like to talk to you.'

'What about?' Flo said warily.

'Come down and see.'

A few minutes later she and Albert were sitting stiffly in the living room. She felt over-conscious of her enormous stomach and hoped Albert wasn't intent on giving her a lecture, because she'd tell him it was none of his business. She felt deeply ashamed when, instead of a lecture, Albert mumbled, 'I've missed you, Flo. The house doesn't seem as bright and cheery without you.'

'I've been . . . upstairs,' she said lamely.

He shifted uncomfortably in the chair, then, without looking at her directly, said, 'I hope you don't mind me seeming personal, luv, but what's happened to the feller who . . . ?' Words failed him.

'He's dead,' said Flo.

'I thought he might be in the forces, like, and one day he'd turn up and you'd get married.'

'There's no chance of that, not when he's dead.'

'Of course not.' His face was cherry red, and she could see beads of perspiration glistening on his forehead. That he was sweating so profusely made his uniform pong even more strongly than it normally did. She wondered why on earth he was so embarrassed, when if anyone should be it was her. 'It'll be hard, bringing up a kiddie without a husband,' he said awkwardly.

'I'll manage. I'll have to, won't I?'

'It'll still be hard, and the thing is, I'd like to make it easier if you'll let me.' He paused and his face grew even redder before he plunged on. 'I'd like to marry you, Flo, and provide you and the little 'un with a home. I earn decent money as an inspector on the trams, and it's a good, secure job with prospects of promotion to depot superintendent. We could get a nice little house between us, and I've enough put away to buy the furniture we'd need. What do you say, luv?'

Flo hoped the distaste she felt didn't show on her face: the last thing in the world she wanted was to hurt him, but the idea of sharing a bed with a middle-aged man with a pot belly and a dreadful smell made her feel sick.

'It's kind of you, Albert —' she began, but he interrupted, as if he wanted to get everything off his chest.

'Of course, I wouldn't expect to be a proper husband, luv. We'd have separate rooms, and if you ever wanted to leave, it'd be up to you. There'd be no strings. To make it easier, we could get wed in one of those register-office places. I'd just be getting you out of a temporary hole, as it were. You'd have marriage lines, and if we did it quick enough, the baby'd have a dad, at least on paper.'

He was incredibly unselfish, and Flo was angry with herself for finding his proposal so disagreeable. But she'd once dreamed of sharing her life with Tommy O'Mara, beside whom Albert Colquitt was — well, there wasn't any comparison. On the other hand, she thought, as she leaned back in the chair and stared into the fire, would it really be so disagreeable? It would be getting her out of a hole, as he put it. No one would call the baby names if it had a father, and Flo wouldn't have to take in laundry but would have a nice, newly furnished house in which to live. She wouldn't be taking advantage of him, not in a mean way, because it was his idea. Of course, everyone would kick up hell at the idea of a Clancy getting married in a register office but, under the circumstances, Flo didn't care. And Martha would be livid, claiming Flo had stolen Albert from right under her nose.

She was still wondering how to respond when Albert said wistfully, 'Me wife died in childbirth, you know, along with the baby. It was a girl. We were going to call her Patricia, Patsy, if we had a girl. I've always wanted a kiddie of me own.'

If he hadn't said that she might have agreed to marry him, if only on a temporary basis – he'd made it clear that she could leave whenever she wanted. But she knew she could never be so cruel as to walk out once he'd grown to love the baby he'd always wanted. She would feel trapped. It would be like a second bereavement and he would lose another wife and child. No, best turn him down now.

So Flo told him, very nicely and very gently, that she couldn't possibly marry him but that she would never forget his kind gesture. She never dreamed that this decision would haunt her for the rest of her days.

Much to Martha's disappointment, Albert took himself off to stay with a cousin in Macclesfield over Christmas, though Flo was glad because it meant she could remain downstairs except when the occasional visitor came. She wondered if he'd gone for that very reason, and said a little prayer that he would enjoy himself in Macclesfield and that the scarf she'd knitted him would keep him warm – the weather throughout the country was freezing cold with snow several feet deep. Before Albert went, he gave the girls a present each: a gold-plated chain bracelet with a tiny charm. Martha's charm was a monkey, Sally's a key and Flo's a heart.

'I bet he meant to give me the heart,' Martha said.

'We'll swop if you like,' Flo offered.

'It doesn't matter now.'

On Christmas Eve, a package arrived from Bel containing a card and a pretty tapestry purse. When Flo opened the card, a photograph fell out. 'Bel's married!'

she cried. 'She's married someone called Bob Knox, he's a Scot.'

'I only met her the once, but she seemed a nice young lady,' Mam said, pleased. 'You must pass on our congratulations, Flo, next time you write. Why not send her one of those Irish cotton doilies as a little present?'

'I wanted those doilies for me bottom drawer, Mam,' Martha pouted.

Flo shook her head. 'Thanks all the same, Mam, but she won't want a doily in the Army. She'd prefer a bottle of scent or a nice pair of stockings.'

'And have you got the wherewithal to buy scent and nice stockings?' Martha asked nastily.

'I'll get a present when I'm earning money of me own,' Flo snapped.

Their mother clapped her hands impatiently. 'Now, girls, stop bickering. It's Christmas, the season of goodwill.'

'Sorry, Flo.' Martha smiled for once. 'I love you, really.'

'I love you too, Sis.'

Later, Martha said to Flo, 'How old is Bel?'

'Eighteen.'

'Only eighteen!' Martha removed her glasses and polished them agitatedly. 'I'll be twenty-four next year.'

Flo wished with all her heart that she could buy a husband for her unhappy sister and hang him on the tree. It didn't help when, on Boxing Day, a telegram arrived for Sally. GOT LICENCE STOP GOT LEAVE STOP BOOK CHURCH MONDAY STOP JOCK.

'I'm getting married on Monday,' Sally sang, starry-eyed.

Flo whooped with joy, and Mam began to cry. 'Sally, luv! This is awful sudden.'

'It's wartime, Mam. It's the way things happen nowadays.'

'Does it mean you'll be leaving home, luv?' Mam sobbed.

'Jock doesn't have a regular port. I'll stay with me family till the war's over, then we'll get a house of our own.'

At this, Mam's tears stopped and she became practical. She'd call on Father Haughey that very day and book the church. Monday afternoon would be best, just in case Jock was late. Even trains had a job getting through the snow. At this, Sally blanched: she had forgotten that the entire country was snowbound. 'He's coming from Solway Firth. Is that far?' No one had the faintest idea so Dad's atlas was brought out and Solway Firth was discovered to be two counties away.

'I'll die if he doesn't get here!' Sally looked as if she might die there and then.

'Surely he'll be coming by ship.' Martha hadn't spoken until then. Her face was as white as the snow outside and her eyes were bleak. She was the eldest, she was being left behind, and she couldn't stand it.

'Of course!' Sally breathed a sigh of relief.

Mam continued to be practical. Did Sally want a white wedding? No? Well, in that case, tomorrow she'd meet her outside the butcher's at dinner-time, and they'd tour the dress shops in Smithdown Road for a nice costume, her wedding present to her daughter. 'It's no use getting pots and pans yet. And we'll have to have a taxi on the day. It's impossible to set foot outside the house in ordinary shoes in this weather, and you can't very well get married in Wellies. As for the reception, I wonder if it's too late to book a room?'

'I don't want a reception, Mam. I'd prefer tea in a café afterwards. Jock's mate will be best man. All I want is me family, you, Martha and Flo.'

'Our Flo can't go,' Martha pointed out. 'Not in her condition.'

Everyone turned to look at Flo, who dropped her eyes, shame-faced. 'I hate the idea of missing your wedding, Sal,' she mumbled.

'I'll be thinking of you, Flo,' Sally said affectionately. 'You'll be there in spirit, if not in the flesh.'

Flo summoned up every charitable instinct in her body. 'Albert will be back from Macclesfield by then,' she said. 'Perhaps he could go instead of me. He'd be a partner for our Martha.'

Albert declared himself supremely honoured to be invited to the wedding. 'He likes to feel part of the family,' Sally said. 'I suspect he's lonely.'

On the day of her sister's wedding, Flo sat alone in the quiet house, thinking how much things had changed over the last twelve months. A year ago Mam was ill, and the sisters' lives had been jogging along uneventfully. Now, Mam had bucked up out of all recognition, Flo had found, and lost, Tommy O'Mara, and was carrying his child, and at this very minute Sally, wearing an ugly pinstriped costume and a white felt hat that made her look like an American gangster, was in the process of becoming Mrs Jock Wilson. Martha was the only one for whom everything was still the same.

She laid her hands contentedly on her stomach. It was odd, but nowadays she scarcely thought about Tommy O'Mara, as if all her love had been transferred to the baby, who chose that moment to give her a vicious kick. She felt a spark of fear. It wasn't due for another six weeks, on St Valentine's Day, exactly nine months and one week since the date of her last period – Mam had worked it out – but what if it arrived early while she was in the house by herself? Martha had booked a midwife under a 'vow of confidentiality', as she put it, who would deliver the baby when the time came. Flo couldn't wait for everything to be over, when her life would change even more.

Snow continued to fall throughout January, and February brought no respite from the Arctic weather. By now Flo was huge, although she remained nimble on her feet. As the days crept by, though, she lost her appetite and felt increasingly sick. Martha left instructions that she was to be fetched immediately if the baby started to arrive when she was at work.

'Surely it would be best to fetch the midwife first?' cried Mam. 'If you'll tell me where she lives, I'll get her.'

'I'd sooner get her meself,' Martha said testily. 'There'll be no need to panic. First babies take ages to arrive. Elsa Cameron was twenty-four hours in labour.'

'Jaysus!' Flo screamed. 'Twenty-four whole hours! Did it hurt much?'

Martha looked away. 'Only a bit.'

The phosphorous fingers on the alarm clock showed twenty past two as Flo twisted restlessly in bed – it was such a palaver turning over. St Valentine's Day had been and gone and still the baby showed no sign of arriving. She lifted the curtain and looked outside. More snow, falling silently and relentlessly in lumps as big as golf balls. The roads would be impassable again tomorrow.

Suddenly, without warning, pain tore through her belly, so forcefully, that she gasped aloud. The sound must have disturbed her sisters, because Martha stopped snoring and Sally stirred.

Flo waited, her heart in her mouth, glad that the time had come but praying that she wouldn't have a pain like that again. She screamed when another pain, far worse, gripped her from head to toe.

'What's the matter?' Sally leaped out of bed, followed by Martha. 'Has it started, luv?'

'Oh, Lord, yes!' Flo groaned. 'Fetch the midwife, Martha, quick.'

'Where does she live?' demanded Sally. 'I'll go.'

'There isn't time for a midwife,' Martha said shortly, 'not if the pains are this strong. Wake Mam up, if she's not awake already, and put water on to boil – two big pans and the kettle. Once you've done that, fetch those old sheets off the top shelf of the airing cupboard.'

'I still think I should get the midwife, Martha. You and Mam can see to Flo while I'm gone.'

'I said there isn't time!' Martha slapped her hand over Flo's mouth when another pain began. 'Don't scream, Flo, we don't want the neighbours hearing. It would happen the night Albert's not out fire-watching,' she added irritably.

'I can't help screaming,' Flo gasped, pushing Martha's hand away. 'I've got to scream.'

Mam came into the room in her nightdress. 'Help me pull the bed round a bit so's I can get on the other side,' she commanded. When it had been moved, she knelt beside her daughter. 'I know it hurts, luv,' she whispered, 'but try and keep a bit quiet, like.'

'I'll try, Mam. Oh, God!' Flo flung her arms into the air and grasped the wooden headboard.

'Keep her arms like that,' Martha instructed. 'I read a book about it in the library.'

Sally brought the sheets, and Flo felt herself being lifted, her nightie pulled up, and the old bedding was slipped beneath her.

'You didn't book a midwife, did you, our Martha?' Sally said in a low, accusing voice. 'It was all a lie. God, you make me sick, you do. You're too bloody respectable by a mile. You'd let our poor Flo suffer just to protect your own miserable reputation. I don't give a sod if me sister has a baby out of wedlock. You're not human, you.'

'Is it true about the midwife, Martha?' Mam said, in a shocked voice.

'Yes!' Martha spat. 'There's not a single one I'd trust to keep her lip buttoned. It's all right for Sal, she's married. I bet Jock wouldn't have been so keen if he'd known what her sister had been up to.'

'It so happens, Jock's known about Flo for months, but it was me he wanted to marry, not me family.'

'Stoppit!' Flo screamed. 'Stoppit!'

'Girls! Girls! This isn't the time to have a fight.' Mam stroked Flo's brow distractedly. 'Do try to keep quiet, there's a good girl.'

'I'm trying, Mam, honest, but it don't half hurt.'

'I know, luv, I know, but we've kept it to ourselves all these months, there's only a short while to go.'

'Can I go for a walk once it's over?'

'Yes, luv. As soon as you're fit, we'll go for a walk together.'

In her agony, Flo forgot that by the time she was fit again she would be gone from the house in Burnett Street. She would be living somewhere else with her baby.

Afterwards, she never thought to ask how long the torment lasted: one hour, two hours, three. All she could remember were the agonising spasms that seized her body regularly and which wouldn't have felt quite so bad if only she could have screamed. But every time she opened her mouth, Martha's hand would slam down on her face and Mam would shake her arm and whisper, 'Try not to make a noise, there's a good girl.'

She was only vaguely aware of the argument raging furiously over her head. 'This is cruel,' Sally hissed. 'You're both being dead cruel. It's only what I'd expect from our Martha, but I'm surprised at you, Mam.'

Then Mam replied, in a strange, cold voice, 'I'm sorry about the midwife, naturally, but one of these days, you'll leave this house, girl, all three of you will. I don't want to be known for the rest of me life as the woman who's daughter had an illegitimate baby, because that's how they'll think of me in the street and in the Legion of Mary, and I'd never be able to hold me head up in front of Father Haughey again.'

Later, Sally demanded, 'What happens if she tears? She'll need stitches. For Christ's sake, at least get the doctor to sew her up.'

'Women didn't have stitches in the past,' Martha said tersely. 'Flo's a healthy girl. She'll mend by herself.'

'I want to go to the lavatory,' Flo wailed. 'Fetch the chamber, quick, or I'll do it in the bed.'

'It's coming!' Mam said urgently.

'Push, Flo,' Martha hissed. 'Push hard.'

'I need the chamber!'

'No, you don't, Flo. It's the baby. *Push!*'

Flo felt sure her body was going to burst and the hurt was so tremendous that the room turned black and little stars appeared, dancing on the ceiling. ' "Dancing in the dark," she bellowed. "Dancing in the dark. Dancing . . ." '

'Oh, Lord!' Sally was almost sobbing. 'She's lost her mind. Now see what you've done!'

Which was the last thing Flo heard until she woke up with a peculiar taste in her mouth. She opened her eyes very, very slowly, because the lids felt too heavy to lift. It was broad daylight outside. Every ounce of strength had drained from her body, and she could barely raise her arms. Unbelievably, for several seconds she forgot about the baby. It wasn't until she noticed her almost flat tummy that she remembered. Despite her all-out weariness, she was gripped by shivers of excitement. She forced herself on to her elbows and looked around the room, but the only strange thing there was a bottle of brandy on the dressing-table which accounted for the funny taste in her mouth, though she couldn't remember drinking it. There was no sign of a baby.

'Mam,' she called weakly. 'Martha, Sal.'

Mam came into the room looking exhausted, but relieved. 'How do you feel, luv?'

'Tired, that's all. Where's the baby?'

'Why, luv, he's gone. Martha took him round to the woman who arranged the adoption. Apparently a very nice couple have been waiting anxiously for him to arrive, not that they cared whether it was a boy or a girl, like. They'll have him by now. He'll be one of the best-loved babies in the whole world.'

It was a boy *and he'd been given away!* Flo's heart leaped to her throat and pounded as loudly as a drum. 'I want my baby,' she croaked. 'I want him this very minute.' She struggled out of bed, but her legs gave way and she fell to the floor. 'Tell me where Martha took him, and I'll fetch him back.'

'Flo, luv.' Mam came over and tried to help her to her feet, but Flo pushed her away and crawled towards the door. If necessary, she'd crawl in her nightdress through the snow to find her son, Tommy's lad, their baby.

'Oh, Flo, my dear, sweet girl,' Mam cried, 'can't you see this is the best possible way? It's what we decided ages ago. You're only nineteen, you've got your whole life ahead of you. You don't want to be burdened with a child at your age!'

'He's not a burden. I want him.' Flo collapsed, weeping on to the floor. 'I want my baby.'

Martha came in. 'It's all over, Flo,' she said gently. 'Now's the time to put the whole thing behind you.'

Between them, they picked her up and helped her back to bed. 'C'mon, luv,' Martha said, 'Have another few spoons of brandy, it'll help you sleep and you need to get your strength back. You'll be pleased to know none of the neighbours have been round wanting to know what all the racket was last night, which means we got away with it, didn't we?'

Why, oh, why hadn't she just taken a chance, run away and hoped everything would turn out all right? Why hadn't she made it plain that she wanted to keep the baby? Why hadn't she married Albert Colquitt?

In the fevered, nightmarish days that followed, Flo remained in bed and tortured herself with the same questions over and over again. She cursed her lack of courage: she'd been too frightened to run away, preferring to remain in the comfort of her home with her family around her, letting them think she was agreeable to the adoption to avoid the inevitable rows. She cursed her ignorance in assuming that she'd have the baby, leap out of bed, and carry him off into the unknown. Finally, she cursed her soft heart for turning down Albert's

136

proposal because she didn't want him hurt at some time in the far-distant future.

All the time, her arms ached to hold her little son. The unwanted milk dried up, her breasts turned to concrete, and her insides felt as if they were shrivelling to nothing. She didn't cry, she was beyond tears.

'What did he look like?' she asked Sally one day.

'He was a dear little thing. I'm sure Mam wished we could have kept him. She cried when Martha made her give him up.'

'At least Mam held him, which is more than I did,' Flo said bitterly. 'I never even saw him.'

'That's what happens when women give their babies up for adoption. They're not allowed to see them, let alone hold them, least so Martha says. It's what's called being cruel to be kind.' Sally's eyes were full of sympathy, but even she thought that what had happened was for the best.

'Our Martha seems to know everything.' Flo had refused to speak to Martha until she revealed the whereabouts of her son.

'That's something I'll just have to get used to,' Martha said blithely, 'I couldn't tell you even if I wanted to because the names of adoptive parents are kept confidential. All I've been told is the baby's got a mam and dad who love him. That should make you happy, not sad. They'll be able to give him all the things that you never could.'

Flo gripped her painful breasts and glared contemptuously at her sister. 'They can't give him his mother's milk, can they? There'll be no bond between him and some strange woman who didn't carry him in *her* belly for nine whole months.'

'Don't be silly, Flo.' For once, Martha was unable to meet her sister's eyes. She turned away, her face strangely flushed.

March came, and a few days later the weather changed dramatically. The snow that had lain on the ground for months melted swiftly as the temperature soared.

Spring had arrived!

Flo couldn't resist the bright yellow sunshine that poured into the bedroom, caressing her face with its gentle warmth. She threw back the bedclothes, and got up for the first time in a fortnight. Her legs were still weak, her stomach hurt, her head felt as if it had been stuffed with old rags, but she had to go for a walk.

She walked further every day. Gradually, her young body recovered its strength and vigour. When she met people she knew, they remarked on how fit and well she looked. 'You're a picture of health, Flo. No one would guess you'd been so ill.'

But Flo knew that, no matter how well she looked, she would never be the same person again. She would never stop mourning her lost baby, a month old by now. There was an ache in her chest, as if a little piece of her heart had been removed when her son was taken away.

2

Sally had left the butcher's to take up war work at Rootes Securities, an aircraft factory in Speke, for three times the wages. She was coping well in the machine shop in what used to be a man's job. Even Mam was talking about looking for part-time work. 'After all, there's a war on. We've all got to do our bit.' Albert was out most nights fire-watching, though so far there hadn't been a fire for him to watch.

Flo realised it was time she got back to work. Sally suggested she apply to Rootes Securities. 'If we got on the same shift we could go together on the bus. You'll find it peculiar, working nights, but it's the gear there, Sis. All we do the whole time is laugh.'

Laugh! Flo couldn't imagine smiling again, let alone laughing. Sally fetched an application form for her to fill in and took it back next morning. Later, as Flo roamed the streets of Liverpool, she thought wistfully of Fritz's

Laundry. She'd sooner work there than in a factory, even if the pay was a pittance compared to what Sal earned.

Since emerging from her long confinement, she'd passed the laundry numerous times. The side door was always open, but she hadn't had the nerve to peek inside. She felt sure the women, including Mrs Fritz, had guessed the real reason why she'd left.

On her way home the same day, she passed the laundry again. Smoke was pouring from the chimneys, and a cloud of steam floated out the door.

'I'll pop in and say hello,' she decided. 'If they're rude, then I'll never go again. But I'd like to thank Mr Fritz for the lovely necklace he sent at Christmas.'

She crossed the street, wondering what sort of reception she would get. To her astonishment, when she presented herself at the door, the only person there was Mr Fritz, his shirtsleeves rolled up, working away furiously on the big pressing machine that Flo had come to regard as her own.

'Mr Fritz!'

'Flo!' He stopped work and came over to kiss her warmly on the cheek. 'Why, it's good to see you. It's as if the sun has come out twice today. What are you doing here?'

'I just came to say hello, like, and thank you for the necklace. Where is everyone?'

He spread his arms dramatically. 'Gone! Olive was the first, then Josie, then the others. Once they discovered they could earn twice as much in a factory they upped and went. Not that I blame them. I can't compete with those sort of wages, and why should they make sacrifices on behalf of Mr and Mrs Fritz and their eight children when they have families of their own?'

Mrs Fritz came hurrying out of the drying room with a pile of bedding. Her face hardened when she saw Flo. 'Hello,' she said shortly. She scooped clean washing out of a boiler and disappeared again.

Her husband wrinkled his stubby little nose in

embarrassment. 'Don't take any notice of Stella. She's worn out. Her mother is over from Ireland to look after the children, as we work all the hours God sends, including weekends. You see, Flo,' he went on earnestly, 'lots of hotels and restaurants have lost staff to the war and they send us the washing they used to do themselves. Business has soared, and I hate to turn it away, so Stella and I are trying to cope on our own. I've hired a lad, Jimmy Cromer, to collect and deliver on a bike with a sidecart. He's a right scally, but very reliable for a fourteen-year-old.' He managed to chuckle and look gloomy at the same time. 'One of these days, Stella and I will find ourselves buried under a mountain of sheets and pillow-cases, and no one will find us again.'

'Would you like a hand?' Flo blurted. 'Permanent, like.'

'Would I!' He beamed, then bit his lip and glanced uneasily towards the drying room. 'Just a minute, Flo.'

He was gone a long time. Flo couldn't hear what was said, but sensed from the sound of the muffled voices that he and Stella were arguing. She supposed she might as well get on with a bit of pressing rather than stand around doing nothing, so folded several tablecloths and was wreathed in a cloud of hissing steam when he returned.

'We'd love to have you, Flo,' he said, rubbing his hands together happily, though she guessed he was putting it on a bit. Mrs Fritz had probably agreed because they were desperate. As if to prove this, he went on, 'You'll have to make allowances for Stella. As I said, she's worn out. The children daren't look at her in case she snaps their heads off. As for me, I'm very much in her bad books. She regards me as personally responsible for the war and our present difficulties.'

As the profit from the laundry had provided the Fritz family with a high standard of living and a big house in William Square, one of the best addresses in Liverpool, Flo thought it unfair of Stella to complain. She said nothing, but offered to go home, change into old clothes and start work that afternoon.

140

Mr Fritz accepted her suggestion gratefully. 'But are you sure you're up to it, Flo? Your mother said you were very ill each time I called.' He looked into her eyes and she could tell he knew why she'd been 'ill' but, unlike his wife, he didn't care. 'There'll be three of us doing the work of six.'

'Does that mean the wages will be more?' She was glad to be coming back, but it seemed only fair that if she was doing the work of two women, she should get an increase in wages. He might not be able to compete with a factory, but if business was soaring he should be able to manage a few extra bob.

He blinked, as if the thought hadn't entered his head. Just in case it hadn't, Flo said, 'I've applied for a job in Rootes Securities where our Sally works. She's paid time and a half if she works Saturdays.'

Mr Fritz's shoulders shook with laughter. 'Don't worry, my dear. I promise your pocket won't suffer if you work for me. I'll pay you by the hour from now on, including time and a half on Saturdays.'

Flo blushed. 'I didn't mean to sound greedy, like.'

He pecked both her cheeks and chucked her under the chin. 'I haven't seen you smile yet. Come on, Flo, brighten up my day even further and give me one of your lovely smiles.'

And to Flo's never-ending astonishment, she managed to smile.

Stella Fritz had seemed such a sweet, uncomplaining person in the days when Flo hardly knew her, but after they'd worked side by side for a short while, she turned out to be a sour little woman who complained all the time. Perhaps she was worn out and missed being with her children, but there was no need to be quite so nasty to Mr Fritz, who was blamed for every single thing, from exceptionally dirty sheets that needed boiling twice to food rationing, which had just been introduced.

'Bloody hell! She was only a farm girl back in Ireland,'

Martha said indignantly, when Flo brought up the subject at home – Flo's vow never to speak to her eldest sister had been forgotten. 'She's dead lucky to have hooked someone like Mr Fritz. Have you seen their house in William Square?'

'I hope she's not nasty to you,' Mam remarked. 'If she is I'll go round there and give her a piece of me mind.'

'Oh, she just ignores me, thank goodness.' It was a relief to be beneath the woman's contempt. It meant she could get on with things without expecting the wrath of Cain to fall on her because the chain in the lavatory had stopped working or the soap powder hadn't arrived.

Mr Fritz said privately that he'd never felt so pleased about anything in his life as he was to have Flo back. She told him he was exaggerating, but he maintained stoutly that he meant every word. 'I love my wife, Flo, but she was beginning to get me down. The atmosphere has improved enormously since you reappeared on the scene. Things don't seem so bad if you can make a joke of them. Until you came, it all seemed rather tragic.' Every time Stella went into the drying room, or outside for some fresh air, he would make a peculiar face and sing, 'The dragon lady's gone, oh, the dragon lady's gone. What shall we do now the dragon lady's gone?'

When the dragon lady returned, he would cry, 'Ah, there you are, my love!' Stella would throw him a murderous look and Flo would do her best to stifle a giggle. She thought Mr Fritz was incredibly patient. A less kind-hearted person might have dumped Stella in one of the boilers.

She scarcely noticed spring turn into summer because she was working so hard, sometimes till eight or nine o'clock at night, arriving home bone weary, with feet swollen to twice their normal size, ready to fall into bed where she went to sleep immediately. Sally was equally tired and Martha's brewery was short-staffed, which meant she often had to work late. In order to hang on to their remaining staff, the brewery increased the wages, or the pubs might run out of beer, a situation too horrendous even to contemplate. Mam got a part-time job in a greengrocer's in Park Road. The Clancy family had never been so wealthy, but there was nothing to spend the money on. Rationing meant food was strictly limited, and the girls hadn't time to wander round the shops looking at clothes. They all started post-office accounts, and began to save for the day when the war would be over, though that day seemed a long way off.

By now, the war could no longer be described as 'phoney'. Adolf Hitler had conquered most of Europe; in June, he took France, and although thousands of British and French soldiers were rescued in the great evacuation of Dunkirk, thousands more lost their lives or were taken prisoner. The British Isles was separated from the massed German troops by only a narrow strip of water. People shivered in their beds, because invasion seemed inevitable, although the government did all it could to make an invasion as hazardous as possible. Road signs and the names of stations were removed, barricades were erected, aliens were sent to detention camps all over the country, including nice Mr and Mrs Gabrielli who owned the fish-and-chip shop in Earl Road.

One Monday, Flo arrived at work to find Mrs Fritz all on her own, ironing a white shirt with unnecessary force. Her eyes were red, as if she had been weeping. The two women rarely spoke, but Flo felt bound to ask, 'What's the matter? Is Mr Fritz all right?'

'No, he isn't,' Stella said, in a thin voice. 'He's been rounded up like a common criminal and sent to a detention camp on the Isle of Man. Oh, I said he should have taken British nationality years ago but he was proud of being Austrian, the fool. Not only that, we've lost two of our biggest customers. It seems hotels would sooner have dirty sheets than have them washed in a laundry with a foreign name.' Her Irish accent, scarcely noticeable before, had returned in full force with the power of her anger.

'Oh, no!' Flo was sorry about the lost orders, naturally, but devastated at the thought of dear Mr Fritz, who wouldn't have hurt a fly and loathed Hitler every bit as much as she did, being confined behind bars or barbed wire, like a thief or a murderer. 'How long are they keeping him?' she asked.

'For the duration of the bloody war.'

'Oh, no,' Flo said again.

'I suppose I'll just have to close this place down,' Mrs Fritz said bleakly. 'I can't manage on me own. Anyroad, those cancellations could be the start of an avalanche. Soon, there mightn't be any customers left. I suppose we're lucky the building hasn't been attacked. The German pork butcher's in Lodge Lane had all its winders broken.'

'But you can't close down!' Flo cried. 'You've got to keep going for when Mr Fritz comes home. The laundry is his life. And his old customers won't desert him, not the ones who know him personally. We can cope, just the two of us, if there's going to be less work.'

Mrs Fritz attacked the shirt again and didn't answer. Flo took a load of washing into the drying room and was hanging it on the line when Stella Fritz appeared at the door.

'All right, we'll keep the laundry going between us,' she said, in a cold voice, 'but I'd like it made plain from the start, Flo Clancy, that I don't like you. I know full well what you've been up to, and just because I've agreed we should work together, it doesn't mean that I approve.'

Flo tried to look indifferent. 'I don't care if you approve or not. I'm only doing it for Mr Fritz.'

'As long as we know where we stand.'

'Rightio. There's just one thing. What about changing the name from Fritz's Laundry to something else?'

'Such as?'

144

'Oh, I dunno.' Flo pondered hard. 'What's your maiden name?'

'McGonegal.'

'McGonegal's Laundry is a bit of a mouthful. What about White? White's Laundry. It's got the same number of letters as Fritz, so it'll be easy to change the sign outside. Of course, it won't fool the old customers but it'll certainly fool the new.' It seemed rather traitorous because no one could have been more patriotic than dear Mr Fritz, but if his foreign name was a hindrance to his business, she felt sure he wouldn't mind it being changed.

After a few hiccups – another two big customers withdrew – by August, White's Laundry was back on its feet. More large hotels sent enormous bundles of washing, including one who'd used the laundry before and seemed content to use it again now the name had been changed.

'That was a good idea you had,' Stella Fritz said grudgingly, the day she heard their old customer had returned.

'Ta,' Flo said.

'Though it means we'll be even more snowed under with work than ever,' she muttered, half to herself.

'Hmm,' Flo muttered back. The two women still rarely spoke. There wasn't the time and they had nothing to say to each other. Occasionally Flo asked if Stella had heard from her husband, and was told he'd written and sounded depressed. It was hard to make out whether Stella was upset or angry that Mr Fritz had gone.

Mam had been discussing with her friends at the Legion of Mary the long hours her youngest daughter worked. One night she said, 'There's these two spinsters in the Legion, twins, Jennifer and Joanna Holbrook. They're in their late seventies, but as spry and fit as women half their age. They want to know if you'd like a hand in the laundry.'

'We're desperate. Stella's tried, but there's better jobs around for women these days. I doubt if two old ladies in their seventies would be much good, though, Mam.'

'I told them to pop in sometime and have a word with Mrs Fritz, anyroad.'

Two days later the Holbrook twins presented themselves to an astonished Stella Fritz. They were nearly six feet tall, stick thin, with narrow, animated faces, and identical to each other in every detail, right down to each item of their clothing. Papa had been in shipping, they explained between them, in their breathless, posh voices, and they'd never done a day's work in their lives, apart from in a voluntary capacity in the other great war.

'Of course, we've been knitting squares for the Red Cross . . .' said one – Flo was never able to recognise one twin from the other.

'. . . and rolling bandages . . .'

'. . . and collecting silver paper . . .'

'. . . but we'd far sooner go *out* to work . . .'

'. . . it would be almost as good as joining up.'

Mrs Fritz looked flummoxed. She glanced at Flo, who rolled her eyes helplessly.

'We wrote to the Army and offered our services . . .'

'. . . but they turned us down . . .'

'. . . even though we explained we could speak French and German fluently.'

'I don't know what to say.' Normally blunt, often rude, Mrs Fritz was stuck for words before the two women towering over her.

'What about a week's trial?' Flo suggested.

One twin clapped her hands and cried, 'That would be marvellous!'

'Absolutely wonderful!' cried the other.

'The money isn't important . . .'

'. . . we'd work for peanuts . . .'

'. . . and regard it as our contribution towards the war.'

Stella Fritz offered them peanuts and agreed that they should start tomorrow.

The twins turned up next day in uniforms that had once been worn by their maids: identical white ankle-length pinafores and gathered caps that covered their eyebrows. They were undoubtedly fit, but not quite as spry as Mam had claimed. Every now and then, they required a 'little sit-down', and would produce silver cigarette cases from the pockets of their pinnies and light each other's cigarette with a silver lighter. Then they would take long, deep puffs, as if they had been deprived for months.

'I needed that, Jen.'

'Same here, Jo.'

When their first week was up, there was no suggestion of them leaving, and once again the atmosphere in the laundry improved. Observing the Holbrook twins at close quarters was like having the front seat in a theatre, because they were as good as a top-class variety act. Even Stella Fritz seemed happier, particularly as they didn't have to work so hard and could leave at a civilised hour. It was nice to have a proper break at dinner-time instead of trying to eat a butty and iron a shirt at the same time. Flo didn't bother going home for dinner, and continued to take butties, which she sometimes ate as she wandered along Smithdown Road peering in shop windows. Once or twice, she ventured into the Mystery, but that part of her life no longer seemed real. It was impossible to believe that eighteen months ago she hadn't even met Tommy O'Mara. She felt like a very old woman trying to recall events that had happened more than half a century before. Flo had once had a lover, then she'd had a baby, but now both were gone, she was back at work in the laundry, and it was as if nothing had ever happened. Nothing at all.

Perhaps Hitler felt too daunted by the English Channel, because the threat of invasion faded, to be replaced by a more immediate terror: air raids. Liverpudlians dreaded the ominous wail of the siren warning them that enemy planes were on their way, while the sweetest sound on earth was the single-pitched tone of the all-clear to announce that the raid was over.

Over tea, Mrs Clancy would reel off the places that had been hit: the Customs House, the Dunlop rubber works, Tunnel Road picture house and Central Station. Edge Hill goods station, where Dad had worked, was seriously damaged. Then Albert Colquitt would come home and reel off a different list.

Sally came home from work one morning to report that Rootes Securities had been narrowly missed, and did Flo know that Josie Driver, who used to work in the laundry, had been killed last week when Ullet Road was bombed? 'I thought she'd gone in a convent.'

Flo was wandering along Smithdown Road in her dinner hour, thinking about last night's raid, when she saw the frock and the war was promptly forgotten.

'Oh, it's dead smart!' She stood in front of the window of Elaine's, Ladies' and Children's Fashions, eyeing the frock longingly. It was mauve, with long sleeves, a black velvet collar and velvet buttons down the front. 'It's dead smart, and only two pounds, nine and eleven. I could wear it for church, or to go dancing in. It's ages since I've been to a dance. And I've enough money saved.' She caught sight of her reflection in the window. She looked a fright. It was about time she smartened herself up, did something with her hair, started to wear powder and lipstick again. She couldn't mope for ever. 'If I bought that frock, perhaps Sally would come dancing with me. I bet Jock wouldn't mind.' It was no use asking Martha because she was convinced that no one would ask a girl with glasses to dance, even though Flo assured her there were plenty of men in glasses who didn't hesitate to ask girls up.

'I'll buy it – least, I'll try it on. If it fits, I'll ask them to put it on one side and come back tomorrer with the money.' Excited, she was about to enter the shop when she saw Nancy O'Mara coming towards her pushing a big black pram.

Nancy was dressed less flamboyantly than the last time Flo had seen her, outside the gates of Cammell Laird, in a plain brown coat that looked rather old. Her hair was in the same plump bun on the back of her thin yellow neck. Long earrings with amber-coloured stones dangled from her ears, dragging the lobes so that they looked elongated and deformed. She stopped at the butcher's shop next door, nudged the brake of the pram with her foot, and went inside.

Curious, Flo temporarily put aside her longing for the mauve frock, and walked along to the butcher's. Nancy had joined the small queue inside and her back was to the window. The hood of the pram was half up. Inside, a pretty baby, about seven or eight months old, with fair hair and a dead perfect little face, half sat, half lay against a frilly white pillow, playing sleepily with a rattle. She supposed it was a boy, because he wore blue: blue bonnet and matinée coat, both hand-knitted. Nancy must be minding him for someone. Flo thought of all the baby clothes she'd knitted which had been left behind when her son had been taken away. She'd asked Sally to hide them, because she hadn't wanted ever to see them again. For the first time, she wondered what her little boy had been wearing when Martha took him out into the snow to give to the couple who'd been so anxiously waiting for him to be born.

One of the baby's mittens had come off. 'You've lost a mitt, love,' she said softly.

At the sound of her voice, the baby turned his head. He smiled straight at her, shook the rattle, and uttered a contented little gurgle. As Flo stared into the two huge pools of green that were the baby's eyes, she felt a tingling creep down her spine, and knew that he was hers. *Martha had given her baby to Nancy O'Mara!*

'Aaah!' she breathed. Her arms reached down to pick her son out of the pram, when a scrawny yellow hand appeared from nowhere and gripped her right arm like a vice.

'Stay away from him!' Nancy O'Mara hissed. 'Don't think you'll ever get him back because I'll kill him first. He's mine. D'you hear?' Her voice rose hysterically and became a shriek. *'He's mine!'*

3

Flo's feet scarcely touched the pavement as she flew along the narrow streets, her mind in turmoil. It would always hurt, but she'd more or less got used to the idea that her baby was with someone else, but she would never get used to him being with Nancy O'Mara. She'd get him back, she'd claim him as her own.

Her face was on fire, and there were waves of pain like contractions in her belly. She had no idea where she was going, but when she found herself in Clement Street, where Nancy O'Mara lived, she realised she'd known all along. Without even thinking what she was going to say, she knocked at the house next door. A woman in a flowered overall answered almost immediately. She wore a scarf over a head crammed with metal curlers. A cigarette was poking out of the corner of her mouth.

The words, the lies, seem to come to Flo quite naturally. 'I'm looking for me friend, Nancy O'Mara, but she doesn't seem to be in. I haven't seen her in ages and thought I'd check if she still lived in the same place before I came all the way back.'

'She's out shopping with the baby, luv. I expect she'll be along any minute.'

Flo feigned surprise. 'Baby! I never knew she was expecting.'

The woman seemed amenable to an unexpected gossip on the doorstep. She folded her arms and leaned nonchalantly against the door frame. 'To tell you the truth, luv, it came as a shock to everyone. Did you know her feller died on the *Thetis*?'

'Yes. That was the last time I seen her. We went together on the ferry to Cammell Laird's. She didn't say she was in the club.'

'She wouldn't have known then, would she?' The woman took a puff of her cigarette and narrowed her eyes. 'Let's see, when was Hugh born? – February, Tommy'd been gone a few months before she told me that she'd copped one.'

Hugh! She'd called him Hugh! How can I ask if she actually saw Nancy pregnant? Flo was wondering desperately how she could frame such a question, when the woman gave a rather sardonic smile, 'It's funny,' she said, 'but Nancy O'Mara's always kept herself to herself. Hardly a soul knocks on that door, yet you're the second friend who's turned up out the blue. Actually, she looked a bit like you, 'cept she wore glasses. I don't suppose the two of you are sisters?'

'I haven't got a sister.'

'Mind you, she doesn't come so often since Hugh was born.'

'Doesn't she?' Flo said faintly.

'No. Y'see, Nancy was one of those women who hides out of sight when she's pregnant. I've a sister-in-law in Wallasey like that, me poor brother has to do all the shopping. Nancy not having a feller, like, this friend used to get her ladyship's groceries for her.'

'The friend with the glasses?'

' 'Sright, luv.'

'Did she have the baby at home or in the hospital?'

'No one's sure about that, luv. Typical of Nancy, she just appeared with him in a pram one day. Proud as punch she was, pushing him round in the snow.' She laughed coarsely. 'If she hadn't announced all those months ago that she was in the club, I'd have thought she'd pinched him.'

'You don't say.'

'Know Nancy well, do you, luv?' The woman looked quite prepared to talk all day.

'Not all that well. Me brother worked at Cammell Laird's and Nancy and Tommy came to his wedding,' Flo explained. 'I've only seen her a few times since.' She was wondering how to get away.

'Well, she certainly fell on her feet when Tommy kicked the bucket. A bob a week she used to pay in life insurance – I only know because me friend's husband's the collector and we used to joke she was planning on doing away with him one of these days, randy bugger that he was. Oh, look, here comes Nancy now.'

Nancy O'Mara had just turned the corner. She didn't notice Flo and the neighbour because all her attention was concentrated on the occupant of the pram. She was shaking her head, laughing and clucking. Then she stopped, tipped the pram towards her, and said something to the baby inside. She laughed again. Her face wore an expression Flo had rarely seen on anyone before: a radiance so intense that it was as if every wish she'd ever made had come true.

'She don't half dote on that baby,' the woman in the flowered overall murmured.

To the woman's astonishment, Flo turned on her heel and walked away.

When she returned to work more than half an hour late Stella Fritz threw her a questioning look, but Flo wasn't in the mood to make apologies or excuses. Throughout the afternoon, she worked like a madwoman, well making up for the time she'd been late. She swung wildly between sorrow, rage and loathing for the sister who had so comprehensively betrayed her. But the feeling that towered above all others was jealousy. She kept seeing Nancy's radiantly happy face; happiness caused solely by the fact that she'd been blessed with the gift of Flo's baby. For eight months, Tommy's wife had had him all to herself, nursed him, soothed him, watched him grow; unique, wonderful experiences that had been denied his real mother. There was the oddest feeling deep within Flo, almost akin to making love with Tommy, when she imagined holding her baby to her breast.

'I'll get him back,' she swore, but remembered Nancy's face again and felt uneasy. '*Don't think you'll ever get him back, because I'll kill him first. He's mine!*' the woman had said. The way she'd looked at the baby wasn't quite natural. She loved him too much. Tommy had always claimed she wasn't quite right in the head, and even Martha had called her funny, a Welsh witch, though it hadn't stopped her from handing over her sister's child, Flo thought bitterly. As the afternoon progressed, it became easy to visualise Nancy O'Mara suffocating the tiny boy with that frilly pillow before she'd let Flo have him.

Perhaps she could snatch him from his pram, take him to another town . . . but Flo knew there would never be an opportunity to steal him. She'd like to bet a hundred pounds that the baby would never be left outside a shop again. Now Nancy knew that Flo had recognised him, she would hang on to him like grim death.

When her youngest sister came storming in Martha was setting the table. Flo thought she looked furtive and immediately guessed why: Nancy O'Mara had been waiting outside the brewery to relay what had happened that afternoon.

Now that the moment had come to pour out the rage that had been mounting ever since dinner-time, scream about the terrible injustice that had been done, Flo couldn't be bothered. What was the point?

Mam was humming to herself in the back kitchen. 'Is that you, Flo?' she called.

'Yes, Mam.'

'I was just telling our Martha, I ordered a chicken today for Christmas. I couldn't believe they were taking orders so early but, as the butcher said, it's only eleven weeks off.'

'That'll be nice, won't it, Flo?' Martha said brightly. 'Maybe Albert will stay with us this year. You know, Mam,' she called, 'it might be possible to put Albert's name down for a chicken as well.'

'I suppose it might. I didn't think o' that.'

'I won't be living here by Christmas,' Flo said. The words seemed just to come out without any previous thought.

Martha's jaw dropped and she looked frightened. 'Why not?'

'You know darn well why not. Because I can't bear to live in the same house as you another minute.'

Mam came bustling in with plates of stew. 'Sal!' she yelled. 'Dinner's on the table. It's blind scouse,' she explained. 'There wasn't a scrap of meat to be had in the butcher's.' She wiped her hands on her pinny. 'What was that I heard about someone not living here by Christmas?'

'Ask our Martha,' Flo said abruptly. 'I don't want any tea tonight, Mam. It's been an awful day and I feel like a lie-down.'

Sally burst into the room, full of beans because she'd had a letter from Jock that morning. She kissed her sister's cheek. 'Hello, Flo,' she sang.

Sally's evident happiness only emphasised Flo's all-embracing misery, but she gave her a long, warm hug before going upstairs. To her surprise, she only lay down for a few minutes before she fell asleep.

It was pitch dark when she woke up. Someone must have been in, because the curtains were drawn. She was collecting her thoughts, remembering the events of the day, when she became conscious of a movement in the room. As her eyes became used to the dimness, she saw that her mother was sitting on the edge of the double bed watching her sleep.

Mam must have sensed she was awake. 'I've been thinking about your uncle Seumus,' she said softly.

'I didn't know I had an uncle Seumus,' Flo said dully.

'He died long before you were born, shot by the English on the banks of the Liffey. He was smuggling arms for the IRA.'

'How old was he?' Another time Flo would have been interested to discover she'd had a romantic, if disreputable, uncle. Right now, she didn't care.

'Nineteen. I was only ten when he died, but I remember our Seumus as clearly as if he died yesterday. He was a grand lad, full of ideals, though not many people, particularly the English, would have agreed with them.' Mam sighed softly. 'I still miss him.'

'What made you think of him just now?'

'You remind me of him, that's why – hot-headed, never thinking before you act. Oh, Flo!' Mam's voice rose. 'Did it never enter your head the trouble it could cause by sleeping with a married man? God Almighty, girl, we were such a happy family before. Now everything's ruined.'

Flo didn't answer straight away. She recalled the first time she'd been on her way to meet Tommy O'Mara outside the Mystery, and the strange feeling she'd had, as if nothing would ever be the same again. It had turned out to be true, but not in the way she'd imagined. Mam was right. The Clancy family was about to break up. Flo could no longer live in the same house as Martha. 'I'm sorry, Mam,' she whispered. 'I'll leave home, like I said. Things'll be better if I'm not here.'

'Better!' Mam said hoarsely. 'Better! How will they be better without you, girl?' She reached out and stroked Flo's cheek. 'You're me daughter and I love you, no matter what you've done. I just wish I could feel so charitable about our Martha.'

'Did she tell you – about Nancy O'Mara?'

Mam nodded bleakly. 'That was a terrible thing to do. I wish to God I'd known what she was up to. The thing is, I've relied too much on Martha since your dad died. I thought she was strong, but she's the weakest of us all. The only way she can feel important is by meddling in other people's lives. If anyone's going to leave home, I'd rather it be Martha, but I suppose she needs me more than you and Sal ever will, particularly if she doesn't manage to catch poor Albert.'

'Oh, Mam!' Her mother seemed to accept that she was leaving, and Flo felt the future loom up before her, dark and uncertain.

'Come on, girl.' Mam stood up with a sigh. 'There's scouse left if you feel like it. Albert's fire-watching, Sal's at work, and Martha's gone to see Elsa Cameron – Norman's had another bad fall. The little lad's only two, and every time I see him he's covered in bruises.'

'Mam?'

'Yes, luv?' Her mother paused at the door.

'D'you think I could get him back – my baby?'

'No, luv. According to Martha, the birth certificate has Nancy down as the mother and Tommy O'Mara as the dad. Everyone in the street believed she was pregnant. Legally, he's hers, fair and square.'

'But you know that's a lie, Mam,' Flo cried. 'We could go to court and swear he's mine.'

Mam's entire demeanour changed. 'Court! Don't talk soft, Florence Clancy,' she said sharply. 'I've no intention of setting foot inside a court. For one thing, we haven't got the money, and second, there'd be a terrible scandal. It'd be in all the papers and I'd never be able to hold me head up in Liverpool again.'

The raid that night was short and not too heavy. The Clancys usually stayed in bed until the last minute, then when danger seemed imminent, they would go down and sit under the stairs. That night, the all-clear sounded before anyone had stirred, but Flo remained wide awake long afterwards. Where would she live? Would Mam let her have some sheets and blankets and a few dishes? They hadn't got a suitcase, so how would she carry her few belongings?

'Are you awake, Flo?' Martha whispered.

Flo made no sign she'd heard, but Martha persisted, 'I know you're awake because you're dead restless.'

'So what if I am?' Flo snapped.

'I thought we could talk.'

'I've nothing to say to you, Martha. You're nothing but a bloody liar. All that talk about me little boy going to a nice mam and dad!'

'Just listen to me a minute. What I did was only for the best.'

'You mean giving my baby to a Welsh witch was only for the best?' Flo laughed contemptuously.

'Nancy's always longed for a child, but the good Lord didn't see fit to answer her prayers. No one could love that baby more than she does.'

'*I* could! And the good Lord had nothing to do with it. It was because Tommy hadn't touched her that way in years. He told me.'

'I was only thinking of you, luv,' Martha said piteously. 'I wish you'd change your mind about leaving home. Mam's dead upset, and I feel as if it's my fault.'

'It *is* your fault,' Flo spat. It was all she could do not to leap out of bed and beat her sister to a pulp until every ounce of frustration and anger had been spent. 'And you weren't thinking of me, you were thinking of yourself, about your stupid reputation and what people would say.' Her voice rose shrilly. 'You couldn't even arrange the adoption properly, could you? I bet you enjoyed conspiring with Nancy, doing her shopping, being her best friend.' She imagined her sister bustling round to Clement Street, eyes gleaming behind her round glasses, sounding Nancy out, skirting round the matter of Flo's pregnancy until she had established that the woman would jump at the chance of having Tommy's child. Neither had dreamed Flo would recognise her own baby, because neither had given birth to a child of their own. Flo buried her face in her hands and began to rock to and fro. 'I wish I'd had the nerve to leave once I realised I was expecting, I wish I'd married Albert, I wish –'

Martha sat up. 'What was that about Albert?' she asked tersely.

Flo blinked. She hadn't meant to mention Albert. There was still time to pretend she'd meant something else or used the wrong name, but all of a sudden she saw an opportunity to hurt her sister, not nearly so badly as she'd been hurt herself but enough to wound. Still she hesitated, because she'd never intentionally hurt anyone in her life. A hard voice inside her insisted that Martha needed to be taught a lesson. '*She took your baby and gave him to Nancy O'Mara*,' the voice reminded her.

'I've never mentioned it before,' she said lightly, 'but Albert knew about the baby. He offered to marry me there and then. He told me about his wife dying in childbirth, and his little girl, Patsy, who died at the same time. He was going to use his savings to buy furniture for our house. In view of what's happened, I'm dead sorry I turned him down.'

'I don't believe you!'

'Ask him.' Flo yawned and slid under the bedclothes. She didn't sleep another wink that night as she lay listening to her sister's sobs, unsure whether to feel glad or ashamed.

She had less trouble than she had expected in finding somewhere to live. Next day, after asking the twins if they would keep their eyes open for a room to let, Stella Fritz sidled up. 'Why are you leaving home?'

Flo resisted telling her to mind her own business. The woman was her employer and they'd been getting on much better lately. 'I just want to, that's all,' she said.

'Is it, I mean, are you . . . ?' Stella's face grew red. It was obvious she thought Flo might be in the club again.

'I'm leaving because our Martha's driving me dotty. Now our Sal's married, there's only me left to boss around. I'll be twenty-one next year, and I thought it was time I lived on me own.'

'I see. You can have our cellar, if you want. It's never used.'

'Cellar!' Flo had visions of a little dark space full of coal. 'I'm not living in a cellar, thanks all the same.'

Stella shook her head impatiently. 'I call it the cellar, but it's really a basement. It's where the housekeeper used to live in the days when William Square was full of nobs. There's a few odds and ends of furniture, and I can let you have some stuff from upstairs. The walls will need a coat of distemper. Otherwise, it's very clean.'

William Square was becoming a bit seedy, Flo thought when she went to see the basement. There was nothing you could put a finger on, but the gracious houses weren't being maintained as they used to be.

The living room was very big, only partially furnished and rather dark, but there was a separate bedroom, a kitchen, and, wonder of wonders, a bathroom with a lavatory. There was even electric light. Everywhere smelt strongly of damp, but all in all, the place was much grander than anywhere Flo had hoped to find.

'Fritz had the gas fire installed. He used to turn it on now 'n' again during the winter, case the damp spread through the house.'

Flo gazed in awe at the efficient-looking fire. Imagine not having to fetch in coal every day! Imagine just pressing a switch for the light, and sitting on the lavatory indoors!

'I'm not sure if I can afford the rent for a place like this.'

'I haven't said what the rent will be, have I? You'd make your own meals and pay your own gas and electricity – there's separate meters down here.' Stella pursed her lips. 'Five bob a week'll do.'

'But you could get as much as seven and six!'

'I could ask ten bob in this part of town, but you'd be doing me a favour if you take it.'

'What sort of favour?'

Stella ignored her and went to stand at the rear window, which overlooked a rather grubby little yard. 'Just look at that!' she said tonelessly. 'Walls, bricks, dirt! Back in Ireland all we could see from our winders was green fields, trees and sky, with the lakes of Killarney sparkling in the distance. It's like living in a prison here.' She seemed to have forgotten that Flo was there. 'It was something Fritz could never understand, that there's some things more important than money, like good clean air and a sweet, blowing wind. All that concerned him was his bloody laundry.'

Flo twisted her hands together uncomfortably, not sure what to say. The Fritzes had always seemed such a happy couple.

'Oh, well.' Stella turned away. 'The palliasse for the bed's up in the loft, case it got damp. I'll fetch it down, as well as a mat for in front of the fire and a few other bits and pieces. Those chairs aren't too comfortable, but there's not much I can do about it – Fritz used to come down here sometimes for a bit of peace and quiet. Me mam'll give the place a good clean, though if you want it painting you'll have to do it yourself. There's some tins of distemper in the yard. It should be ready to move in by Monday.'

It was awful leaving Sally, but when it came to saying goodbye to her mother, Flo felt cold. Mam hadn't acted as badly as Martha, but Flo had never dreamed she could be so hard, preferring her daughter to go without her beloved baby rather than risk the faintest whiff of scandal.

When she made her departure directly after tea on Monday Albert Colquitt wasn't home. 'Give him my love, Mam,' she said. 'Tell him he's been the best lodger in the world and I'll never forget him.' She was aware of a white-faced Martha across the room. Her sister still looked stunned from their row the other night. Flo had ignored her ever since.

Mam was close to tears. 'For goodness sake, luv, you'd

think you had no intention of setting foot in Burnett Street again. You can tell Albert that to his face next time you see him.'

'Tara, Mam. Tara, Sal.' Flo slung the pillowcase containing all her worldly possessions over her shoulder like a sailor. She tried to force her lips to say the words, but they refused to obey, so she left the house without speaking to Martha.

The first few months in William Square were thoroughly enjoyable. Perhaps the favour Stella had mentioned was having Flo look after the little Fritzes – not that the two eldest, Ben and Harry, were little any more. Aged thirteen and fourteen, they were almost as tall as Flo. They invaded the basement flat, all eight of them, on her first night there.

'Have you come to live with us?'

'Did you know our dad?'

'Will you read us a book, Flo?'

'Do you know how to play Strip Jack Naked?' Ben demanded.

'The answer to every question is yes,' Flo grinned. 'Yes, yes, yes, yes. Sit on me knee – what's your name? – and I'll read you the book.'

'I'm Aileen.'

'Come on, then, Aileen.'

From that night on, Flo scarcely had time to have her tea before the children would come pouring down the concrete steps. By then Stella's mother, Mrs McGonegal, had seen enough of her lively grandchildren. She was a withdrawn woman, shy, with a tight, unhappy face. According to Stella, she missed Ireland and its wide open spaces even more than her daughter and couldn't wait to get back. 'And she's petrified of the air raids. She won't come with us to the shelter but crawls under the bed and doesn't come out till the all-clear goes.'

On Sunday afternoons, Flo took the children for walks. They formed a crocodile all the way to the Pier

Head and back again. Sometimes, she took the older ones to the pictures, where they saw Will Hay and Tommy Trinder and laughed till they cried. She suspected Harry had a crush on her, so treated him more tenderly than the others, which only made the crush worse.

A week after Flo moved, Sally came to see her and was startled to find the room full of little Fritzes. 'Have you started a school or something?'

'Aren't they lovely?' Flo said blissfully. 'I can't wait for Christmas. I thought I'd be spending it all by meself for the first time in me life, but Stella's invited me upstairs.' She still saw a trace of disapproval in the little Irish-woman's eyes whenever they spoke. 'I'm making dec-orations for the tree and it's lovely wandering round the shops at dinner-time looking for prezzies for the kids. I'm buying one a week.'

But by the time Christmas arrived, Stella Fritz, her mother, and her eight children had all gone.

After what everyone called 'the raid to end all raids' at the end of November, when for seven and a half long hours the city of Liverpool suffered a murderous attack from the air, a night when 180 people were killed in one single tragic incident, December brought blessed relief. 'I think Mr Hitler is going to let us spend the festive season in peace,' one of the twins remarked.

She spoke too soon. At twenty past six that night, all hell broke loose as wave after wave of enemy bombers unloaded their lethal cargo of incendiary and high-explosive bombs. The city was racked by explosions for nine and a half hours. Fires crackled furiously, the flames transforming the dark sky into an umbrella of crimson. Ambulances and fire engines screamed through the shattered streets.

Would the dreadful night ever end, Flo wondered, as she sat in the public shelter with the two smallest Fritzes on her knee. It hardly seemed possible that William Square could still be standing. As she tried to comfort the children, she was overcome with worry for her family and her little son.

At one point, Stella muttered, 'It's all right for Fritz, isn't it? He's safe and sound on the Isle of Man.'

At last the all-clear sounded at four o'clock in the morning; the long piercing whine had never been so welcome. Stella gathered the children together and made for home. William Square was just round the corner, and in the red glow the houses appeared miraculously intact. A small fire sizzled cheerfully in the central garden area where an incendiary bomb had fallen and several trees and bushes were alight.

'I'll help put the kids to bed,' Flo offered.

'It's all right,' Stella said tiredly, 'you see to yourself, Flo. Forget about opening up on time tomorrer. The twins have got a key – that's if they turn up themselves.' She sighed. 'I wonder how me mammy is?'

When Flo woke it was broad daylight. The birds were singing merrily. She jumped out of bed, intent on getting to work as quickly as possible – not because she was conscientious but she wanted to make sure that Clement and Burnett Streets hadn't been hit. After a cat's lick, she threw on the clothes she'd worn the day before.

Before leaving, she went upstairs to ask after Mrs McGonegal. To her astonishment, Stella Fritz opened the door wearing her best grey coat and an astrakhan hat with a matching grey bow. Her eyes were shining, and she looked happier than Flo had ever seen her, even in the days when she and Mr Fritz had seemed such an ideal married couple. 'I was about to come and see you,' she cried. 'Come in, Flo. We're off to Ireland this afternoon, to me uncle Kieran's farm in County Kerry. Me mam's over the moon. Oh, I know there's no gas or electricity, the privy's in the garden and you have to draw water from a well, but it's better than being blown to pieces in a raid.'

'I'll miss you.' Flo was devastated when she saw the

row of suitcases in the hall. It was the little Fritzes she'd really miss. She looked forward to their regular invasion of her room, the walks, the visits to the pictures. Upstairs, she could hear their excited cries as they ran from room to room and supposed they were collecting their favourite possessions to take to Ireland.

'The children are dead upset you're being left behind,' Stella said, looking anything but upset herself, 'but I said to them, "Flo's going to take care of things back here. She'll look after the house." I'll leave you the keys, luv, and if you'd just take a look round once a week, like, make sure everything's all right.'

So, that was the favour. Flo had been installed downstairs so that Mrs Fritz could up and leave whenever she liked, safe in the knowledge that the house would be cared for in her absence. Flo wasn't too bothered that she'd been used. It still meant she'd got a lovely flat dead cheap. But now it appeared she'd have the flat for nothing in return for 'services'. Would she mind running the water in cold weather, save the pipes from icing up, lighting a fire now and then to keep the place aired, opening the windows occasionally so it wouldn't smell musty?

'What's happening to the laundry?' Flo asked, when Stella had finished reeling off instructions.

'You'll be in charge from now on, luv,' Stella said carelessly. 'Take on more women, if you can. I'll write and tell you how to put the money in the bank each week.'

'Right,' said Flo stoutly, as yet more responsibility was heaped on her young shoulders. 'I'll just go upstairs and say tara to the children.'

She was about to leave the room, when Stella came over and gripped her by the arms. Her good humour had evaporated and her face was hard. 'There's something I'd like cleared up before I go.'

'What's that?' Flo asked nervously.

'I know full well why you left the laundry that time.

Tell me truthfully, was it my Fritz who fathered your child?'

The question was so outlandish that Flo laughed aloud. 'Of course not! What on earth gave you that idea?'

'I just wondered, that's all.' She smiled and squeezed Flo's arms. 'You're a grand girl, Flo. I'm sorry I was horrible in the past, but everything got on top of me. And I always had me suspicions about you and Fritz. Now, say tara to the kids, and tell them to come down and we'll be on our way.'

It didn't seem possible but the raid that night was even heavier than the one the night before. For more than ten hours, an endless stream of fire-bombs and explosives fell on Liverpool. Flo didn't bother with the shelter, but stayed in bed trying to read a novel she'd found upstairs. She did the same the following night when the raid was even longer. The house seemed no less safe than a brick shelter, and at least she was warm and comfortable and could make a cup of tea whenever she liked.

Each morning, she left promptly for work, although she hadn't had a wink of sleep, and on the way made sure that Clement Street and Burnett Street were still standing.

On Christmas Day she went early to Mass, then spent the morning tidying up after the Fritzes. In their excitement, the children had left clothes and toys everywhere, and there were dirty dishes in the back kitchen. Flo moved from room to room, feeling like a ghost in the big silent house, picking things up, putting them away, gathering together the dirty clothes to wash. She helped herself to a few items for downstairs; a tablecloth, a saucepan, a teapot, more books, and supposed she'd better use up the fresh food that had been left behind – the bacon looked like best back – and Mrs McGonegal had walked miles in search of dried fruit for that Christmas cake.

She went into the living room and sat in the huge bay

window beside the tree that she'd helped to decorate. William Square was deserted, though there must be celebrations going on behind the blank windows. As if to confirm that this was so, a motor car drew up a few doors away and a couple with two children got out. The man opened the boot and handed the children several boxes wrapped in red paper. Flo remembered the presents she'd bought for the Fritzes, which were still hidden under her bed, away from their prying eyes. She'd take them to one of them rest centres that looked after people who'd lost everything in the blitz, let some other kids have the benefit.

The house was so quiet, you could almost sense the quietness ticking away like a bomb. They'd just be finishing dinner in Burnett Street and starting on the sherry. Sally had said that Albert would be there, and Jock. No one would be coming to see Flo because they thought she was spending Christmas with the Fritzes. Flo sniffed dejectedly. It would be easy to have a good ould cry, but the situation was entirely of her own making. If she'd turned down Tommy O'Mara when he'd asked her to go for a walk, she'd be part of the group sitting round the table in Burnett Street with Martha rationing out the sherry.

Sherry! There were half a dozen bottles on the top shelf of the larder. She went into the kitchen, collected a bottle, and was about to take everything downstairs when she noticed the wireless in an alcove beside the fireplace. Unlike Albert's battery set, this one had an electric plug. It was also far superior to Albert's. The Bakelite casing had a tortoiseshell pattern, the gold mesh shaped like a fan.

She spent the rest of the day drinking sherry, half reading a book, half listening to the wireless, and told herself she was having a good time. It wasn't until a man with a lovely deep voice began to sing 'Dancing in the Dark', that she had a good ould cry.

★

On Boxing Day Flo moved the furniture into the middle of the room and distempered the basement a nice fresh lemon. It needed two coats and she was exhausted by the time she had finished and stood admiring her handiwork. The room had brightened up considerably, but the blackout curtains looked dead miserable. She raided upstairs and found several sets of bronze cretonne curtains, which she hung over the blackout. The place was beginning to look like home.

Home! Flo sat on one of the lumpy chairs and put her finger thoughtfully to her chin. She had a home, yes, but she hadn't got a life. The idea of spending more nights alone listening to the wireless made her spirits wilt, and she didn't fancy going to dances or the pictures on her own. Having two sisters not much older than herself meant she'd never gone out of her way to make friends. Bel was the closest to a friend she'd ever had, but Bel wasn't much use up in Scotland. Of course, she could always change her job so that she worked with women of her own age, but she felt honour-bound to keep the business going for Mr Fritz.

'I'll take up voluntary work!' she said aloud. It would occupy the evenings, and she'd always wanted to do something towards the war effort. 'I'll join the Women's Voluntary Service, or help at a rest centre. And Albert said there's even women fire-fighters. I'll make up me mind what to do in the new year.'

Next day, Sally and Jock whizzed in and out, but Flo didn't mention that the Fritzes had gone because Sally might have felt obliged to stay – and you could tell that she and Jock couldn't wait to be by themselves. The day after, Mam came into the laundry to see how she was and Flo said she was fine. She didn't want Mam thinking she regretted leaving home, because she didn't. She might have experienced the most wretched Christmas imaginable, but she'd willingly go through the whole thing again rather than live in the same house as Martha. More than anything, she couldn't stand the idea of anyone feeling sorry for her, though by the time New Year's Eve arrived, Flo was feeling very sorry for herself.

A party was going on across the square, a pianist was thumping out all the latest tunes: 'We'll Meet Again', 'You Were Never Lovelier', 'When You Wish Upon a Star . . .' In Upper Parliament Street, people could be heard singing at the tops of their voices. There'd been little in the way of raids since Christmas, and no doubt everyone felt it was safe to roam the streets again. She switched on the wireless, but the disembodied voices emphasised rather than eased her sense of isolation. She contemplated going early to bed with a book and a glass of sherry – there were only two bottles left – but ever since she was a little girl she'd always been up and about when the clocks chimed in the New Year. She remembered sitting on Dad's knee, everybody kissing and hugging and wishing each other a happy new year, then singing 'Auld Lang Syne'.

I could gatecrash that party! She smiled at the thought, and a memory surfaced: Josie Driver, God rest her soul, had once mentioned ending up on St George's Plateau on New Year's Eve. 'Everyone was stewed to the eyeballs, but we had a dead good time.'

Flo threw on a coat. She'd go into town. At least there would be other human beings around, even if she didn't know them, and they could be as drunk as lords for all she cared. She hadn't been a hundred per cent sober herself since finding that sherry.

The sky was beautifully clear, lit by a half-moon and a million dazzling stars, so it was easy to see in the blackout. Music could be heard coming from the Rialto ballroom and from most of the pubs she passed. People seemed to be enjoying themselves more than ever this year, as if they had put the war to the back of their minds for this one special night.

When she arrived in the city centre it was far too early, and her heart sank when there wasn't a soul to be seen on

St George's Plateau. What on earth shall I do with meself till midnight? she wondered. She began to walk slowly towards the Pier Head, aware that she was the only woman alone. The pubs were still open – they must have got an extension because it was New Year's Eve. She paused outside one. She could see nothing, because the windows had been painted black, and there was a curtain over the door, but inside a girl with a voice like an angel was singing, 'Yours Till the Stars Lose Their Glory', as it had never been sung before.

Flo stared into the black window, seeing Tommy O'Mara's reckless, impudent face gazing back at her, his cap perched on the back of his brown curly hair. Their eyes met and her insides glowed hot. She wanted him, oh, how she wanted him! 'Nobody understood how much we loved each other,' she whispered.

'D'you fancy a drink, luv?'

She turned, startled. A young soldier was standing beside her, twisting his cap nervously in his hands. Lord, he was no more than eighteen, and there was an expression on his fresh, childish face that reflected exactly how she felt herself: a look of aching, gut-wrenching loneliness. She'd like to bet he'd never tried to pick up a girl before, that this was his first time away from home, the first New Year's Eve he hadn't spent within the bosom of his family, and that he was desperate for company. She also saw fear in his eyes. Perhaps he was going overseas shortly and was afraid of being killed. Or perhaps he was just afraid she'd turn him down.

The girl inside the pub stopped singing, everyone thumped the tables, burst into enthusiastic applause, and Flo was hit with an idea that took her breath away. She knew exactly what she could do as her contribution towards the war.

'What a nice idea, luv!' she cried gaily. 'I'd love a drink. Shall we go in here?'

Millie

I

'Are you the Tom who gave her the lamp?' I'd always imagined Flo's friend being as old as Flo herself.

' 'Sright. I got it her in Austria.'

I sat in the armchair, resentful that Tom O'Mara was occupying my favourite spot on the settee, his feet back on the table. 'What were you doing in Austria?'

'Skiing,' he said abruptly.

He looked more the type to prefer a Spanish resort full of bars and fish-and-chip shops, I thought. I said, 'I've always wanted to ski.'

'I didn't know Flo had these.' He ignored my observation and picked up the newspaper cuttings. His fingers were long and slender and I imagined . . . Oh, God! I did my best to hide another shiver. 'That's how me grandad died,' he said, 'On the *Thetis*.'

'Do you know much about it?' I asked eagerly. 'I keep meaning to get a book from the library.'

'Me gran used to pin me ear back about the *Thetis*. She had a book. It's at home. You can have it, if you like. I'll send it round sometime.'

'Thanks,' I said. A pulse in my neck was beating crazily, and I covered it with my hand, worried he'd notice. What on earth was happening to me? Usually, I wouldn't give a man like Tom O'Mara the time of day. I glanced at him surreptitiously and saw that he was staring at the lamp, oblivious of me. I almost felt a nuisance for having interrupted his quiet sojourn in the flat. There was little sign that a party was going on upstairs, just a muffled thumping as people danced, and music that sounded as if it came from some distance away. 'How come you knew, Flo?' I asked.

'She was a friend of me dad's. I knew her all me life.'

'Would it be possible to meet your father? I'd love to talk to him about Flo.'

'"Would it be possible to meet your father?"' he repeated after me, in such a false, exaggerated impersonation of my accent that I felt my face redden with anger and hurt. 'Christ, girl, you don't half talk posh, like you've got a plum in your gob or something. And you can't talk to me dad about anything. He died fourteen years ago.'

'Is there any need to be so rude?' I spluttered.

Our eyes met briefly. Despite my anger, I searched for a sign that he didn't despise me as much as he pretended, but there was none. He turned away contemptuously. 'People like you make me sick. You were born in Liverpool, yet you talk like the fucking Queen. I think it's called "denying your roots".'

'A day never goes by when I don't remember my roots,' I said shortly. 'And there are people around who could have a great deal of fun with the way you speak.' I stared at him coolly, though cool was the opposite of what I felt. 'I came down for some peace and quiet, not to be insulted. I'd be obliged if you'd go.'

Before he could reply, there was a knock on the window and James called, 'Are you there, Millie?' He must have been looking for me, and someone, Charmian or Herbie, had suggested where I might be.

'Coming!' I stood, aware that Tom O'Mara's eyes had flickered over my body, and felt exultant. My ego demanded that he found me as attractive as I found him, not that it mattered. He was an uncouth lout. Anyway, there was no likelihood of us meeting again. He could keep his book on the *Thetis*, I'd get one for myself. In my iciest voice, I said, 'I've got to go. Kindly put the key on the mantelpiece when you leave. Goodnight.'

★

For James's sake, I decided reluctantly to give Flo's flat a miss the next afternoon. I couldn't bring myself to ask him to leave after refusing to see him all the previous week. Bel and Charmian would be expecting me, I thought wistfully, though I really should get down to clearing things out – and I still hadn't found out about the rent. I was anxious to speak to the landlord and pay another month before the flat was let to someone else, if that hadn't happened already. One of these days I might turn up and find the place stripped bare. The rent book was bound to be among Flo's papers, but I hadn't even discovered where her papers were kept.

'This is nice.' James sighed blissfully as we lay in bed in each other's arms after making love for the third time. 'An unexpected treat. I thought I'd be sent on my way ages ago.' It was almost three o'clock.

'Mmm.' I was too exhausted to reply. I felt guilty and ashamed. James wouldn't feel quite so happy if he knew that every time I closed my eyes he turned into Tom O'Mara.

He nuzzled my breasts. 'This is heaven,' he breathed. 'Oh, darling, if only you knew how much I love you.'

I stroked his head and said dutifully, 'I think I do.'

'But you never tell me you love me back!' he said sulkily. He pulled away and threw himself on to the pillow.

'James, please,' I groaned, 'I'm not in the mood for this.'

'You're never in the mood.'

I leaped out of bed and grabbed my dressing gown. 'I wish to God you'd give me some space,' I snapped. 'Why do you keep nagging me to say things I don't want to say, to feel things I don't feel?'

'Will you ever say them? Will you ever feel them?' He stared at me forlornly.

I stormed out of the room, 'I can't stand any more. I'm going to have a shower and I'm locking the door. I expect you to be gone when I come out.'

When I emerged from the bathroom fifteen minutes later there was no sign of a contrite James begging forgiveness. No doubt he would telephone or come back later, in which case he wouldn't find me in. I got dressed quickly in jeans and an old sweatshirt and raced down to the car. It was already growing dark and I couldn't wait to be in Flo's flat where I knew I would find the tranquillity I craved.

It wasn't to be, but I didn't mind. I was unlocking the front door when Bel Eddison appeared in her leopardskin jacket. 'I thought I heard you. I've been helping Charmian clear up after the party. We were expecting you hours ago.'

'I was delayed. Come and have some sherry. Why weren't you at the party? I looked everywhere for you.'

'I had another engagement.' She smirked. 'I wouldn't say no to a glass of sherry, but me and Charmian have been finishing off the bottles left over from last night. I'm not exactly steady on me legs.' She staggered into the basement and made herself comfortable on the settee. 'Charmian can't come. Jay's going back to university in the morning and she's still sorting out his washing.'

I turned on the lamp and poured us both a drink. I noticed Tom O'Mara's key on the mantelpiece. As the lamp began slowly to revolve, I said, 'I met the man who gave her that last night.'

'Did you now.' Bel hiccuped.

'He told me how his grandad died, and you said Flo was in love with someone who was lost on the *Thetis*. I wondered if they were one and the same person.'

'I said no such thing, luv,' Bel remarked huffily. 'I said, "Draw your own conclusions," if I remember right.'

'Well, I've drawn them, and that's the conclusion I've reached.' I felt that I'd got one up on Bel for a change.

To my consternation, the old woman's face seemed to shrivel, her jaw sagged, and she whispered hoarsely, 'Flo said, "I don't know what I'm going to do if Tommy's dead. Me life's over. I'll never love another man the way I loved him." The thing is, he was a right scally, Tommy O'Mara, not fit to lick Flo's boots. It sticks in me craw to think she wasted her life on a chap like him.'

I hoped Bel wouldn't be angry, but I had to ask, 'Last night, Tom talked about his gran. Does that mean this Tommy was married when . . . ?'

Bel nodded vigorously. 'She was the last girl in the world to go out with a married man, but he spun her a tale. He was such a charmer. He told *me* he was single.'

'You mean, you went out with him, too?' I gasped.

'Yeh.' Bel grimaced. 'I never let on to Flo, it would have killed her, but I'd been out with him twice just before the *Thetis* went down. Some men aren't happy unless they've got a string of women hankering after them. Tom O'Mara's another one like that. He was a nice lad once, but he's grown up without his grandad's charm. A woman would be mad to have anything to do with him.'

'I agree about the lack of charm. I found him very rude.' I would have liked to know more about Tom O'Mara, but Bel might have thought I was interested when I definitely wasn't. Well, I told myself I wasn't. 'Would you like some tea or coffee to sober you up?' I asked instead.

'A cup of coffee would be nice, but only if it's the instant stuff. I can't stand them percolator things. Flo's got one somewhere.'

For the next few hours we chatted amiably. I told her about my job and my problems with James, and she told me about her three husbands, describing the second, Ivor, in hilarious detail. Before she left, I asked where Flo had kept her papers.

'In that pull–down section of the sideboard, the old one. Flo called it her bureau. You'll have your work cut out sorting through that lot. I think she kept every single letter she ever got.'

Bel was right. When I opened the bureau I found

hundreds, possibly thousands, of pieces of paper and letters still in their envelopes, crammed in every pigeon-hole and shelf. I felt tempted to close it again and snuggle on the sofa with sherry and a book, but I'd been irresponsible for far too long. I sighed and pulled out a thick wad of gas bills addressed to Miss Florence Clancy, which, to my astonishment, went back as far as 1941, when the quarterly bill was two and sevenpence.

I wondered what the flat had looked like then – and wasted ages envisaging a young Flo, living alone and pining after Tommy O'Mara. Perhaps that's what the row with Gran had been about, Flo going out with a married man. Gran was incredibly straitlaced, though it didn't seem serious enough to make them lifelong enemies.

The cardboard boxes I'd brought were in the bathroom so I fetched one and threw in the bills. Then I almost took them out again. Flo had kept them for more than half a century and it seemed a shame to chuck them away. I pulled myself together, and more than fifty years of electricity bills quickly joined them. I decided I deserved a break, made coffee and helped myself to a packet of Nice biscuits. On my way to the settee, I jumped when something clattered through the letterbox.

It was a book: *The Admiralty Regrets*. I opened the door, but whoever had delivered it had disappeared.

Fiona was leaning against the railings, smoking. 'Hi,' I said awkwardly.

She glared at me malevolently through the railings. 'Sod off,' she snarled.

Shaken, I closed the door, and put the book aside to read later. I returned to the bureau with my coffee and continued to throw out old papers. One thick wedge of receipts was intriguing. From a hotel in the Isle of Man, they were made out to a Mr and Mrs Hoffmansthal, who had stayed there for the weekend almost every month from 1949 until 1975. I decided to ask Bel about them, then changed my mind. Bel had mentioned that Flo went on retreat to a convent in Wales once a month. Perhaps Flo had kept a few secrets from her old friend and I certainly wasn't about to reveal them after all this time. I threw away the receipts with a sigh. How I'd love to know what lay behind them, and especially the identity of Mr Hoffmansthal.

The contents of the bureau were considerably diminished by the time the unimportant papers had been discarded. All that remained were letters, which I had no intention of throwing away until I'd read every one. Some looked official, big fat brown envelopes, the address typed, but most were handwritten. I tugged out a wad of letters held together with an elastic band. The top one bore a foreign stamp. It had been posted in 1942.

It dawned on me that I hadn't found the rent book that had prompted my search, or a pension book. Flo might have had them in her handbag, which, like Gran, she had kept hidden. After a fruitless search through all the cupboards, I found what I was looking for under the bed, where dust was already beginning to collect.

I took the black leather bag into the living room and emptied the contents on to the coffee table. A tapestry purse fell out, very worn and bulging with coins, followed by a set of keys on a Legs of Man keyring, a wallet, shop receipts, bus tickets, cheque book, metal compact, lipstick, comb . . . I removed a silver hair from the comb and ran it between my fingers. It was the most intimate thing belonging to Flo I'd ever touched, actually part of her. The room was very still, and I almost felt as if she was in the room with me. Yet I wasn't scared. Even when I opened the compact to compare the hair with mine in the mirror, half expecting to see Flo's face instead of my own, I didn't feel frightened, more a comfortable sensation of being watched by someone who cared about me. I knew I was being silly because Flo and I had only set eyes on each other once, and then briefly.

'One day my hair will turn that colour,' I murmured,

and wondered where I would be and who I would be with, should I live to be as old as Flo. For the first time in my life, I thought it would be nice to have children, so that a strange woman I hardly knew wouldn't sort through my possessions when I died.

I came back to earth, told myself to be sensible. The cheque book meant that, like Gran since she'd been robbed, Flo's pension had probably been paid straight into the bank. I flicked through the stubs to see if cheques had been made out for rent, but most appeared to be for cash, which was no help. I would have asked Charmian for the landlord's address, but glancing at my watch, I saw it was past midnight.

Good! It was a perfect excuse to sleep in Flo's comfortable bed again.

One by one, I returned the things to the bag, glancing briefly in the wallet, which held only a bus pass, a cheque guarantee card, four five-pound notes, and a card listing a series of dental appointments two years ago. I was putting the bag away in the bureau when there was a knock on the door.

James! He'd been to my flat, waited, and when I didn't arrive he had guessed where I would be. I wouldn't let him in. If I did, he'd never keep away and this was the only place where no one could reach me. It was one of the reasons why I always seemed to forget to bring my mobile phone. I fumed at the idea of him invading what I'd come to regard as my sanctuary.

'Who is it?' I shouted.

'Tom O'Mara.'

I stood, transfixed, in the middle of the room, my stomach churning. I knew I should tell him what I'd intended to tell James, to go away, but common sense seemed to have deserted me, along with any will-power I might have had. Before I knew what I was doing, I'd opened the door.

Oh, Lord! I'd thought this only happened in books – turning weak at the knees at the sight of a man. The jacket of his black suit was hanging open, and the white collarless shirt, buttoned to the neck, gave him a priest-like air. Neither of us spoke as he followed me inside, with that sensually smooth walk I'd noticed the night before, bringing with him an atmosphere charged with electricity. I patted my hair nervously, aware that my hand was shaking. He was carrying a plastic bag that smelt of food. My mouth watered and I realised I was starving.

He held it out. 'Chinese, from the takeaway round the corner. Joe said there was someone in when he came with the book so I thought I'd see if you were still here on me way home.'

'What's this in aid of?' I gulped.

'Peace-offering,' he said abruptly. 'Flo would have slagged me off for behaving the way I did last night. No one can help the way they speak, you and me included.'

'That's charitable of you, I must say.' I'd worked hard to get rid of my accent, and felt annoyed that Tom O'Mara seemed to regard the lack of one as an affliction.

'Shall we forget about last night and start again?' He bagged my favourite spot on the settee and began to unpack the cartons of food. 'You're Millie, I'm Tom, and we're about to have some nice Chinese nosh – I don't know if you want to use these plastic forks, Flo used to fetch proper ones, and she'd warm plates up in the microwave. She didn't like eating out of boxes.'

I hurried to do as I was told, sensing that he was accustomed to giving orders, when he shouted, 'Fetch a corkscrew and some glasses while you're at it. I've got wine.'

'It's red,' he said, when I obediently brought everything in. 'I'm an ignorant bugger and I don't know if that's what you have with this sort of food.'

'Neither do I.' James always knew what sort of wine to order but I'd never taken much notice.

'I thought you'd be one of those superior sort of people who know about such things.' He shared out the food on to the plates.

'And I thought we'd made a fresh start.'

'You're right. Sorry!' His smile took my breath away. His face softened and he looked charmingly boyish. I could understand what the nineteen-year-old Flo must have seen in his grandfather.

'Did you and Flo do this often?' I asked, when he handed me my plate.

'Once a week. Mondays, usually, when I finish work early.'

'Where do you work?'

'Minerva's. It's a club.'

I'd heard of Minerva's, but had never been there. It had a terrible reputation as a hang-out for gangsters and a source of hard drugs. Scarcely a week passed when there wasn't something in the *Echo* or on local TV about the police raiding it in search of a wanted criminal or because a fight had broken out. As I sipped the rich, musky wine, I wondered what Tom O'Mara did there.

'The wine's nice,' I said.

'So it should be. It's twenty-two quid a bottle at the club.'

'Wow!' I gasped. 'All that much to have with a take-away!'

He dismissed this with a wave of the hand. 'It didn't cost me anything, I just helped meself.'

'You mean you stole it?'

He managed to look both amused and indignant. 'I'm past the stage of nicking things, thanks all the same. Minerva's belongs to me. I can take anything I like.'

I felt a chill run through my body. He was almost certainly a criminal – he might have been in prison for all I knew. If he owned Minerva's, it meant he was involved in the drugs trade and other activities that didn't bear thinking about. But the awful thing, the really appalling thing, was that he became even more desirable in my eyes. I was horrified. I'd never dreamed it was in me to be attracted to someone like Tom O'Mara. Perhaps it was something passed down in the blood: Flo had wasted her life on a scally who, according to Bel, wasn't fit to lick her boots, Mum had fallen for my loathsome father. Now I found myself weak at the knees over possibly the most unsuitable man in the whole of Liverpool. I thought about James, who loved me and was worth ten Tom O'Maras, and for a moment wished it really had been him at the door.

I put my plate on the table and Tom said, 'You haven't eaten much.'

'I've eaten half,' I said defensively. 'I haven't a very big appetite.' He'd already finished, the plate scraped clean.

'I tell you what, let's have some music.' He went over to the record player and lifted the lid.

'Flo's only got the one record.'

'She's got a whole pile in the sideboard. Neil Diamond and Tony Bennett were her favourites. I got her this last year when she started humming it non-stop. She'd play it over and over.' The strains of 'Dancing in the Dark' began to fill the room. 'She said something once, she was half asleep, about dancing in the dark with someone in the Mystery years ago.'

'The Mystery?' I wondered if it had ever crossed his mind that the 'someone' might well have been his grandad.

'Otherwise known as Wavertree playground. There's a sports stadium there now.' He removed his jacket, saying, 'It's hot in here,' and I felt my insides quiver at the sight of his long, lean body, his slim waist.

'You were very fond of Flo?'

'I wasn't just fond of her, I loved her,' he said simply. 'I dunno why 'cos she weren't a relative, but she was more like a gran than me real one. Christ knows what I'd have done without Flo when me dad died.'

Surely he couldn't be so bad if he'd thought so much of Flo. Bing Crosby was singing and I had no idea why I should have a feeling that history was repeating itself when Tom held out his hand and said with a grin, 'Wanna dance, girl?'

I knew I should refuse. I knew I should just laugh and shrug and say, 'No, thanks, I'm not in the mood,' because I also knew what would happen when he took me in his arms. And if it did, if it did, the day might come when I would regret it. The trouble was, I had never before wanted anything so much. My body was crying out for him to touch me.

The lamp continued its steady progress, round and round, casting its dark, blurred shadows on the low ceiling of the room, and I stared at the shifting patterns, looking for the girl in the red coat. Tom O'Mara came across the room, put his hands on my waist and lifted me out of the chair. For a moment I resisted, then threw all caution to the wind. I slid my arms around his neck and kissed him. I could feel him, like a rock, pressing against me. My veins seemed to melt when our exploring tongues met, while his hard, eager hands stroked my back, my waist, my hips, burning, as if his fingers were on fire.

Still kissing, swaying together almost imperceptibly to the music, we moved slowly towards the bedroom. Outside the door, in the little cold lobby, our lips parted, and Tom cupped my face in his hands. He stared deep into my eyes, and I knew that he wanted me every bit as much as I wanted him. Then he opened the door, where the bed with its snowy white cover was waiting, and led me inside. By now, I felt weak with longing, yet once again I hesitated. There was still time to back out, to say no. But Tom O'Mara was kissing me again, touching me with those hot fingers, and I couldn't have said no to save my life. He kicked the door shut behind us.

In the living room, 'Dancing in the Dark' played through to a glorious crescendo. When it finished, I imagined, in a little corner of my mind, the needle raising itself automatically and the arm returning to nestle in the metal groove. There was silence in Flo Clancy's flat, though I knew that the lamp continued to cast its restless shadows over the walls.

★

I was woken by Tom O'Mara stroking my hip. 'You should have eaten the rest of that meal,' he whispered. 'You could do with a bit more flesh on you.'

Turning languorously into his arms, I began to touch him, but he caught my hand. 'I've got to go.'

'Is there nothing I can do to keep you?' I said teasingly. 'Nothing.'

He got out of bed and began to get dressed. I could have kept James in bed if the building was on fire. I lay, admiring his will-power and his slim brown limbs. His skin was as slippery as polished marble, the hollow of his neck as smooth as an egg. There was a tattoo on his chest, a heart with an arrow through it, and a woman's name I couldn't make out. I'd always thought tattoos repulsive, though it was a bit late in the day to remember that. 'What's the hurry?' I enquired.

'It's nearly seven o'clock. Me wife doesn't mind me staying out all night, but she likes me home for breakfast.'

'Mightn't it have been a good idea to mention you had a wife last night?' I said mildly. I wasn't the least bit shocked because I didn't care. We had no future together.

He paused while pulling on his trousers. 'Would it have stopped you?'

'No, but it might have stopped some women.'

'Then those sort of women should ask before leaping into bed with a bloke they hardly know.'

I made one of Bel's faces. 'You sound as if you disapprove of women who sleep with strange men.'

'It so happens that I do.'

'But you don't disapprove of men who do the same?' I laughed, pretending outrage.

'Blokes take what's on offer.' He was buttoning his shirt.

I eased myself to a sitting position. 'Do you know?' I said thoughtfully, 'I truly can't remember offering myself last night.'

'You didn't, but it's different with me and you, isn't it?'

'Is it?'

He sat on the bed. 'You know it is.' He held my face in both hands and kissed me soundly on the lips. I put my arms around his neck and kissed him back, greedy for him, and determined to keep him if I could, even if it meant I'd be late for work.

'I said I've got to go.' His voice was steely. He removed my arms none too gently and went over to the door.

'Oh, well,' I sighed exaggeratedly, 'see you around sometime, Mr O'Mara.' I was still teasing, though my heart was in my mouth, dreading he might take me at my word and say, 'See you too, Millie.'

'What the hell do you mean by that?' I was taken aback by the anger in his green eyes. The muscles were taut in his slender neck. 'Is that all it was to you, a night's shag?'

'You know it wasn't.' I blushed, remembering the night, so different from any I'd ever known. I looked at him directly. 'It was magic.'

I could have sworn he breathed a sigh of relief. 'In that case, I'll be round tonight, about twelve.' He left abruptly. A few seconds later, the front door opened and he shouted, 'It was magic for me, too.'

I got out of bed, removed the crucifix, the statues, and holy pictures off the wall, and put them in the drawer of Flo's bedside cabinet.

'You've been raiding your aunt's wardrobe again,' George said, when I arrived at Stock Masterton. 'I can tell.'

'Is it so obvious?' I stared down at the long, straight black skirt and demure white blouse with a pointed collar.

'Only because you don't usually wear those sort of clothes. You look very appealing. I could eat you for lunch.'

I tried to think of a put-down remark in reply, but couldn't.

George went on, 'That young man of yours must have had the same idea. You've got a love bite on your neck.' He sighed dolefully. 'It's called a hicky in America. I can't remember when I last gave a girl one. I must have been in my teens. Those were the days, eh?' He hooted.

Embarrassed, I went over to my desk and switched on the computer. Diana had just arrived. 'How's your father?' I asked.

'He seemed much better over the weekend,' Diana replied. Her face had lost the tense lines of the previous week. 'In fact, we had a lovely time. He told me all about his experiences during the war. I knew he'd been in Egypt in military intelligence, but I never realised he'd been in so many dangerous scrapes. He was very much a James Bond in his day.' She took an envelope from her bag. 'I managed to finish those notes I mentioned. Did George tell you his offer for the shop in Woolton has been accepted? We could be open by the new year.'

My own report was at home but didn't seem all that important any more. Nevertheless, I had to go back to the flat to collect a few things if I was going to stay at Flo's so I'd pick it up then.

'I'll give this to George.' Diana winked conspiratorially and hurried into his office. She seemed rather pathetic, I thought, yet until recently I'd wanted the job in Woolton just as much, which meant I'd been just as pathetic myself. Now, I didn't care.

The realisation surprised me. I stared at my blurred reflection in the computer screen and wondered what had changed. Me, I decided, though I had no idea why. I felt confused but, then, I'd felt confused throughout my life. Perhaps it was Flo who'd made me see things differently. Perhaps. I wish I'd known her, I thought wistfully, remembering the warm, comfortable sensation I'd had in the flat last night, as if she had been there with me. I had a feeling I could have talked to her about stuff I wouldn't dream of telling anyone else.

And there was Tom O'Mara. I cupped my chin in my

hands and my reflection did the same. I'd been a married woman for four years, and there'd been other men before James, yet it was as if I'd made love for the very first time. My body had never felt so alive, so *used* in the most gratifying way. I held my breath and felt my scalp prickle when I thought about the things that Tom O'Mara and I had done to each other.

'Millie! *Millie!*'

Darren thumped my desk, and I became aware that June was shouting, 'Wake up, sleepyhead. There's a call for you.'

It was the Naughtons again. They'd had details of another house, which sounded ideal, this time in Crosby. I arranged to meet them there at noon, though felt sure it would be another waste of time. Crosby was close to Blundellsands, which meant I could call at home afterwards.

It felt strange going into my flat, as if I'd been away for weeks not merely twenty-four hours. It smelt dusty and unused, long empty. I opened the windows of the balcony to air the place, and had a shower. There was a bruise beneath my breast and another on my thigh and I wondered if Tom O'Mara also bore scars of our night together. I covered the bite on my neck with makeup. The red light was flickering on the answering-machine.

My mother's tearful voice announced that Declan had lost his job. 'He was sacked ages ago. Your dad only found out by accident off some chap in the pub. Of course he's livid, called poor Declan all the names under the sun. And, Millicent, I'd like to talk to you about Alison . . . Oh, I'll have to ring off now, luv. Your dad's on his way in.'

I waited. There was no message from James. I was glad, but thought about calling him at work to make sure he was all right. In the end, I decided not to. It might encourage him to think I cared, which I did but not nearly enough to satisfy him. I reversed the tape, packed a few clothes and toiletries in a bag, along with the folder containing the report. As I'd gone to the trouble of writing it, it wouldn't hurt to let George take a look.

He was working alone in his glass cubicle when I got back, so I took the folder in. 'You'll never guess what that bloody woman's gone and done,' he barked immediately he saw me.

I pretended to back away, frightened. 'What woman?' I couldn't recall seeing George so angry before.

'That Diana bitch. She's only given me a list of reasons why I should open the new office! I couldn't believe my eyes when I read it. Does she seriously imagine I haven't thought the whole thing through myself? Jesus Christ, Millie, I've been in the estate-agency business for over thirty years. I know it back to front, yet an idiot woman with a stupid degree thinks she knows better than I do.'

'She was only being helpful, George.'

'More likely after the boss's job,' he sneered. 'As if I'd give it her, the pushy little cow. The job's Oliver's. He never makes a decision without referring to me first, which is the way I like it.' He grinned. 'I guess I must be a control freak.'

'Did you say anything to Diana?'

'I bawled her out and she left for lunch in tears.'

'Oh, George!' I shook my head. 'You'll feel sorry about that tomorrow.' A few weeks ago I would have been as pleased as punch at Diana's fall from grace, but now, for some strange reason, I felt nothing but pity for the woman.

'I know.' He sighed. 'I'm a disagreeable sod. I'll apologise later, though it was still a stupid, tactless thing for her to do.' He nodded at the folder in my hand. 'Is that for me?'

'No. I just came to tell you about the Naughtons. Apparently, the draining board was on the wrong side.'

Later that afternoon, I fed my report into the shredder. I'd never stood the remotest chance of getting the manager's job, and it made me feel acutely embarrassed to have thought that I had.

Tom O'Mara didn't arrive at midnight as he'd promised. An hour later he still wasn't there. I lay on the settee, half watching an old film, not sure what to think. Had I been stood up? Maybe he'd had second thoughts. Maybe he'd meant tomorrow night. I tried to work out how I'd feel if I never saw him again. Hurt, I decided, hurt, insulted and angry, but definitely not heartbroken, possibly a little bit relieved. However, right now relief wasn't uppermost in my mind. I wasn't in love with Tom and never would be, yet my body ached for him and I could have sworn he felt the same. It was easy to while away the time imagining his lips touching every part of me. My pulse began to race, and I felt hot at the thought. 'Please come, Tom,' I prayed. 'Please!'

At some time during the night I fell asleep, and was woken when it was barely daylight by a kiss and the touch of a hand stroking me beneath my dressing-gown.

'How did you get in?' I whispered.

'Took me key back off the mantelpiece, didn't I?'

'You're late,' I yawned. 'Hours late.' It was delicious just lying there, feeling sleepy, yet conscious of his exploring hands.

'There was trouble at the club, and I couldn't ring. Flo always flatly refused to have a phone. How do I undo this knot?'

'I'll do it.' I unfastened the belt and he pulled the robe away.

'Anyroad, I'm here now,' he said, 'and that's all that matters.'

He was kneeling beside me, his face hard with desire. He would never say soft, tender things as James did, yet this only made me want him more. I held out my arms. 'Yes, Tom, that's all that matters.'

Time seemed to stand still; it had lost its meaning, all because of Tom O'Mara. I returned to my flat on Sunday morning to collect more clothes and take a shower – bathing at Flo's was like bathing in the Arctic – and found an increasingly frantic series of messages from my mother on the answering-machine. It was the last Sunday in October and it had completely slipped my mind.

'Don't forget, luv, we're expecting you for dinner on Sunday.'

'Why don't you ever ring back, Millicent? I hate these damn machines. It's like talking to the wall.'

'Have you gone away, Millicent?' the voice wailed fretfully. 'You might have told me. I'd ring your office if I didn't think it would get you into trouble.'

As usual, I felt a mixture of guilt and annoyance. I phoned home immediately. 'I'm sorry, Mum,' I said penitently. 'You were right, I've been away.' I hated lying to my mother, but how could I possibly tell her the truth? 'I know I should have called, but it was a spur-of-the-moment thing, and I was so busy when I got there, I forgot about everything. I'm sorry,' I said again, assuming this would be enough to satisfy her, but apparently not.

'When you got where?' she demanded.

I said the first place I could think of. 'Birmingham.'

'What on earth were you doing there?'

'George sent me.'

'Really!' Mum sounded so impressed that I hated myself even more. 'He must think highly of you, sending you all the way to Birmingham.'

To please her, I took particular pains with my appearance. I wore a cherry red suit with a black T-shirt underneath. To assuage my guilt, and make amends for lying, I stopped on the way to Kirkby and bought a bunch of chrysanthemums and a box of Terry's All Gold.

'You shouldn't have, luv,' Mum protested, though she looked gratifyingly pleased.

When we sat down to lunch, Flo's flat immediately became the main topic of conversation.

'I thought you'd have it well sorted by now,' Mum remarked, when I claimed there were still loads of things to do.

'I only have Sundays free, don't I?' I said defensively. 'You wouldn't believe the amount of stuff Flo had. It's taking ages.'

'Your gran keeps asking about it. I said you'd call in and see her on your way home.'

I groaned. 'Oh, Mum, you didn't!'

'She is your gran, luv. She's desperate for a little keepsake, something to remind her of Flo. A piece of jewellery would be nice.'

Flo mightn't be too pleased at the idea of anything of hers going to someone she'd specifically not wanted at her funeral. As for jewellery, I hadn't come across any so far. Everything's becoming incredibly complicated, I thought worriedly.

Things became even more complicated when Declan asked, 'How's James?'

'He's fine,' I said automatically, only then realising it was a whole week since I'd seen him, and he hadn't called once. Perhaps he'd decided being chucked out was the last straw. I dismissed him from my mind – there was already enough to think about – and said to Declan, 'Have you done anything about college?'

My father choked on his steak and kidney pudding. 'College? Him? You must be joking.'

'I think it's a very good idea,' Colin said quietly. 'If he took an engineering course, he could come and work for me. I could do with another pair of hands.'

'He'd prefer something different, wouldn't you, Declan?' I was determined to air the matter of Declan's future because I had a feeling he would never have the courage to do it himself. 'Something artistic.' I thought it wise not to mention fashion design or my father might choke to death before our very eyes.

My mother regarded him warily. 'It wouldn't hurt, would it, Norman, for our Declan to go to college? After all, Millicent went to night school and look where it got her.'

While Trudy and Colin did the dishes, I wandered down to the bottom of the garden with Scotty. The little dog jumped up and down like a yo-yo in front of me. I eased myself through the gap in the hedge that separated the main garden from the compost heap, and sat down on an enormous hump of hard soil, cuddling Scotty. This was the only place we had been allowed to play when we were little: our father wouldn't allow us on the lawn. I remembered the day when five-year-old Trudy had broken a window in the greenhouse with a tennis ball. She'd been so petrified she was literally shaking with fright and couldn't stop crying. 'He'll kill me when he gets home,' she sobbed hysterically.

Then I'd had the brilliant idea of pretending someone from the houses behind had done it. We exchanged the ball, which our father would have recognised, for a stone, and claimed ignorance when the broken pane was discovered. It was one of the few crimes we ever got away with.

'Penny for them!' Trudy murmured, as she squeezed through the hedge and sat beside me. Scotty, fast asleep, stirred and licked my knee.

'I won't say what I was thinking about. It would only depress you.'

'It was me smashing that window, I bet. I always remember when I come down here. Even now I break out in a sweat.'

I put an arm around her shoulder. 'How's things, Sis?'

Trudy shrugged. 'Okay. I'm growing a hair on me chin. See?'

'You've always had that,' I said. 'It appeared when you were about fourteen.'

'Did it? I've never noticed before. It must be the glasses.'

'What glasses?'

'I need glasses for close work, reading and painting. I've had them for months. I thought you knew.'

'No,' I said sadly. 'There was a time when we knew every single little thing about each other, but now . . .' In the darkness of our room, when our father was out, we'd whisper our innermost secrets to each other.

'Sorry, Sis.'

'Don't be.' I squeezed Trudy's shoulder. 'I'm not complaining. There's all sorts of stuff you don't know about me.'

'Such as?'

'That would be telling.' I grinned enigmatically.

Trudy pulled a face. 'Actually, there's things I can't even talk about with Colin.'

'Would you like to talk about them now?'

'No, Sis. It would take much too long.'

I watched a bee, well past its prime, buzz weakly on a dandelion. I was conscious of feeling far less fraught than I usually did on these occasions. Today hadn't been nearly as bad as other Sundays. Instead of constant reminders of the way things used to be, I was preoccupied with how things were now.

Mum appeared in the gap in the hedge, looking flustered, though she rarely looked anything else. 'You'll get your lovely clothes all dirty sitting on that soil.' She pushed her bulky frame through the sharp twigs and, ignoring her own advice, plopped down heavily beside us. Immediately Scotty jumped off my knee and on to hers. 'I wanted to talk to you both about Alison.' She began to pull at a weed. 'I found Oxford on the atlas,' she said hesitantly. 'It's almost as far as London. I was scared enough driving to Skem so I'll never make it that far in the car — that's if your dad would let me have it — and I couldn't afford to go every week by train.'

'I'll pay your fare, Mum,' I offered at the same time as Trudy said, 'Colin and me will take you.'

'No.' She shook her head. 'I don't want to be dependent on other people. Alison's me daughter. I don't love her any better than I do you and our Declan, but she needs me more than you lot ever will.'

It seemed to me that Alison didn't need anyone in particular, but perhaps the faithful figure of her mother appearing every Sunday provided a sense of security, a vague feeling that she was special in at least one person's eyes. On the other hand, perhaps the need was the other way round, and it was Mum who'd miss Alison. One day, Declan was bound to leave home and Alison, detached and indifferent, would be the only one of her children left. But, somewhat cruelly, fate had decreed she'd be miles away in Oxford.

'I want her to stay with the St Osyth Trust,' Mum was saying. 'They know and understand her. I'd have her home like a shot, but that's out the question with your dad. He's ashamed of her, for one thing, and he's no patience with her funny little ways. So I've decided to move to Oxford.'

'What!' Trudy and I cried together. It was the last thing we'd expected to hear.

'Shush!' She glanced nervously through the hedge, but the garden was empty. Her husband was inside playing with his beloved grandchildren, and Colin was on guard.

'You mean you'd actually leave him?' I gasped. Why hadn't she thought of this years ago when we were all being beaten regularly for the least little thing, and sometimes for nothing at all?

Mum said huskily, 'I should have left him a long time ago, I know, but it never crossed me mind. I always thought that if I became a better wife he'd stop hitting us, but the harder I tried, the worse he got. In the end, perhaps I was punch-drunk or something, but it all seemed quite normal.' Her voice broke. Scotty opened his eyes and looked at her curiously. 'I could never imagine things being any other way. I'm sorry, but at least I got Alison out the road, didn't I?'

'Don't rake over the past, Mum,' Trudy said softly. 'About Oxford, I don't know what to say.'

'Nor me,' I said, and then, meaning it with all my heart, 'I'll miss you, Mum.'

She dug me in the ribs with her elbow. 'Don't talk daft, Millicent. I only see you once a month as it is, and you're never there when I phone. I talk to that silly machine more than I do you.'

'I'd miss your messages,' I cried. 'Honest, Mum, I really would.' Suddenly I felt that there would be a dreadful hole in my life.

'I could still ring and leave messages.' She chuckled.

'Yes, but it wouldn't be the same if you weren't around.'

Trudy was frowning, as if she, too, was trying to contemplate a future that had so unexpectedly changed. 'Melanie and Jake would be lost without their gran,' she said, close to tears.

'They'll still have their grandad,' Mum said comfortably. Behind her back, Trudy grimaced at the idea that she'd still bring her children to Kirkby if Mum wasn't there.

'I'll get meself a full-time job,' Mum was saying, 'and look for a bedsit close to the home so's I can see Alison every day.'

'It's a big step, Mum,' Trudy said. 'Getting a job won't be easy at your age, and bedsits might cost the earth in Oxford.'

'Then I'll go on social security or whatever it's called these days,' Mum said serenely. 'I've never claimed a penny in me life, yet I've always paid me stamps.' She beamed at us. 'I feel better now I've talked to you two. Not a word about this to your dad, mind.'

Trudy shuddered. 'I wouldn't like to be in your shoes

when you tell him. Would you like me and Colin to be here, give you moral support, like?'

'I don't need moral support, luv. I'll tell him to his face, and if he doesn't like it, he can lump it. Anyroad, it's months off yet.'

'Grandma,' Melanie piped, from the other side of the hedge.

'I'm here, sweetheart.' Mum scrambled to her feet, dislodging an indignant Scotty.

'Grandad said he wants a cup of tea.'

'Tell Grandad to make his own tea,' Trudy said curtly.

'No, no, don't say that, Melanie, whatever you do.' A stubby branch caught her cheek, drawing blood, as she frantically pushed her way back through the hedge.

Trudy glanced at me meaningfully. 'I wonder if she'll do it?'

I remembered the photo of Flo taken in Blackpool, the still pretty face, the lovely smile, when Gran opened the door. Age hadn't been as kind to Martha Colquitt as it had to her sister. I could never remember her smiling much, or looking anything but old. Her face was creased into a permanent scowl, and behind the severe, black-framed spectacles with their thick lenses, her eyes were unfriendly, disapproving. Her best feature was her hair, thick and silvery, which she kept in neat waves under a fine, almost invisible net.

'Oh, it's you,' she said sourly. 'Come in. I might as well not have grandchildren, I never see them.' I followed her into the spotlessly clean, over-furnished room, which stank of a mixture of cigarettes, disinfectant and the vile-smelling ointment she rubbed on her rheumatic shoulder.

'Well, I'm here now,' I said brightly. I would have come more often, or so I told myself, if the welcome was ever warm, but even my kindhearted mother found visiting Gran an ordeal, fetching her weekly shopping out of a sense of duty.

The television beside the fireplace was on without the sound. Gran turned it off. 'Nothing on nowadays but rubbish.'

I sat down in an overstuffed armchair. 'Mum said to remind you there's an old film on later that you might like. It's a musical with Beryl Grable.'

'Betty Grable,' Gran corrected irritably. Her faculties were sharper than those of most people half her age, her memory for names and faces prodigious. 'I might watch it, I'll see. It depends on how long you stay. Do you want a cup of tea?'

'Yes, please,' I said politely.

Gran disappeared into the kitchen and I went over to the window. I'd lived in this flat until I was three, and the view from the fifth floor was one of the few things I could remember clearly. It couldn't be called magnificent: a shopping precinct, the Protestant church, miles and miles of red-brick houses, with a glimpse of flat fields in the far distance, a few trees, but it seemed to change from day to day. The sky was never the same, and I always seemed to glimpse a tree or a building I hadn't noticed before. It was certainly better than no view at all, but Gran felt the need to block it out with thick lace curtains, although no one could see inside except from a passing helicopter.

The curtains had been drawn back a few inches, as if Gran had been looking out, which, apart from going to Mass on Sundays, was all she had to do: she looked out of the window, watched television and smoked – an ashtray on the sill was full of butts. Each day must seem endless.

I adjusted the curtain and returned to my seat. God, it was depressing. The room seemed much darker than Flo's basement.

'I can't remember if you take sugar.' Gran came in with tea in two fine china cups, a cigarette poking from her mouth. Because she'd been to Mass that morning she wore a neat brown woollen blouse and skirt, though Mum reported that she usually spent the day in her dressing-gown. She had no friends, no one called, so what was the point in getting dressed?

'I don't, thanks.'

'Your mam forgot to get me favourite fig biscuits. All I've got is digestives.' Poor Mum could never get the shopping right.

'I don't want a biscuit, thanks all the same.' I sipped the tea, doing my best to avoid the ash floating on the top.

The wall above the sideboard was full of photographs in identical cheap plastic frames: Grandad Colquitt, long dead, a genial-looking man with erratic facial hair, various weddings, including mine and Trudy's, lots of photos of the Cameron kids taken at school – the happy faces, grinning widely, telling a terrible lie.

'There's a photo in Flo's of my father as a baby with his mother – my other grandma,' I said. At home his parents were rarely mentioned. All I knew was that his father had been a sailor, and his mother had died when he was twenty.

'Is that so? Your other gran, Elsa, used to be me best friend.' The thin yellow lips trembled slightly. 'What's it like in Flo's place?'

'Nice.' I smiled. 'I found gas bills the other day going back to nineteen forty-one.' At least this showed I'd been making an effort to get things done.

'It was nineteen forty when she moved in,' Gran said. 'November.' Her voice was surprisingly soft, considering she was talking about her lifelong enemy. 'Just before Christmas. Mam didn't find out till later that Mrs Fritz had gone to Ireland, leaving her in that big house all by herself.'

The name seemed familiar. 'Fritz?'

'Mr Fritz owned the laundry where she worked. He was sent to an internment camp during the war.'

'There's a snap of Flo outside the laundry.' In a fit of generosity, I said, 'Would you like me to take you?' Flo might turn in her grave if she knew, but Gran looked so wretched.

'To the laundry!' The crumpled jaw fell open. 'They knocked it down years ago, girl.'

'I meant Flo's. I'm on my way there now to try to get a few more things done,' I said virtuously. 'I'll bring you home in the car.'

Gran shook her head adamantly. 'Toxteth's the last place on earth I'd go. A man was murdered there only last week, stabbed to death right on the pavement. Even the town centre isn't safe any more. A woman at church had her gold chain snatched from round her neck when she was walking through St John's precinct. She almost had a heart attack.' She looked at me with frightened eyes. 'It's a terrible world nowadays, Millicent.'

'Flo lived in Toxteth most of her life without coming to any harm.' I vaguely remembered my father saying the same thing a few weeks ago. 'And Bel lives not far away. She comes and goes all the time.'

'Bel?'

'Flo's friend.'

'I know who Bel is,' Gran said bitterly. 'I met her once when she was young. So, even she didn't bother to tell me when our Flo died!'

'Maybe she didn't know your address.'

'There aren't many Mrs M. Colquitts in the Liverpool phone book. And someone knew where to contact me, didn't they? But only when it was too late.'

'I'm sorry, Gran,' I said awkwardly. I put the cup and saucer down; the dregs were grey with ash. 'I'd better be going. Don't forget to watch that film.'

'I wish you hadn't come,' Gran said tonelessly. She fumbled in the packet for another cigarette. 'You've raked up things I'd considered long forgotten.'

'I'm sorry,' I said again. I'd only come because I'd been told she wanted to see me.

'I expect you can see yourself out.'

'Of course. 'Bye, Gran.'

There was no answer. I closed the door and flew down the stone staircase where the walls were scrawled with graffiti. As I drove towards Toxteth, it was difficult to rid myself of the memory of the stiff, unhappy woman smoking her endless cigarettes.

I parked in William Square, and as I walked back towards Flo's, Bel and Charmian must have seen me arrive for they were standing by the basement stairs. Charmian waved a bottle of wine, and my heart lifted.

'Hi!' I called, beginning to hurry. Gran was forgotten and I had the strangest feeling, as if I *was* Flo, coming home to my friends.

It would seem that the banging wasn't part of a dream. Beside me Tom O'Mara was dead to the world. I almost fell out of bed, pulled on Flo's dressing-gown and hurried towards the door before whoever was there demolished it. The noise was even louder in the living room. Any minute now Charmian or Herbie might appear, wanting to know what was going on.

'Who's there?' I shouted crossly. It must be a drunk who'd come to the wrong house. I looked blearily at my watch — ten past two — and wondered if I should have woken Tom.

The banging stopped. 'It's James. Let me in.'

James! I was wide awake in an instant, and leaned against the door. 'Go away, James, please.'

'I've no intention of going away.' He began to hammer on the door again. 'Let me in!'

'I don't want to see you,' I yelled, but he almost certainly couldn't hear me above the noise he was making. A police siren sounded in the distance, and just in case it had been alerted by a neighbour to investigate the disturbance in William Square, I opened the door.

'You're not . . .' I began, as a wild-eyed James, smelling strongly of alcohol, brushed past me into the room, '. . . coming in.' Too late. I switched on the main light. Flo's room looked so different with every corner brightly illuminated.

James stood in the middle of the room. I'd never

thought him capable of such anger. I shrank before it, terrified, my heart racing. His face, his neck, his fists were swollen, as if at any minute he would explode. 'What the hell do you think you're playing at?' he demanded furiously.

'I don't know what you mean.' I kept my voice mild, stifling my own anger, not wanting to provoke him further.

He glared at me, as if I was the stupidest woman on earth. 'I've been outside your flat since five o'clock waiting for you,' he raged. 'When it got to midnight, I decided to come here, but I couldn't remember where the fucking place was. I drove round and round for ages before I found it.'

I didn't know what to say, so remained silent. Once again I thought about rousing Tom, but it seemed weak. I was determined to handle the situation on my own: with Tom there, things might turn ugly. James began to pace the floor, waving his arms, his face scarlet. 'Last week, after you threw me out, I thought, I'll give her till Sunday, then that's it. If she doesn't phone, it's over.' He thrust his red face into mine. 'You didn't phone, did you? You didn't give a fuck how I was.' He mimicked my voice, which seemed to be becoming a habit with all the men I knew. '"I'm taking a shower and I expect you to be gone when I come out." And I went, like the good little boy I am. Then I waited for you to get in touch, but apparently you were willing to let me just walk out of your life as if I'd never existed.'

'James.' I put my hands on his arms to try to calm him. The police car screamed along the main road, William Square obviously not its destination. 'You're not making sense. You said it would be over if I didn't phone. Perhaps that would be the best thing.'

'But I love you! Can't you get into your stupid head how much I love you?' His eyes narrowed. 'You know, all my life I've had girls throw themselves at me. I've never gone short, as they say. But you, an uppity little bitch from Kirkby, you're the one I fell in love with, wanted to marry. How *dare* you turn me down?'

This wasn't happening! I closed my eyes for a second, then said quietly, 'I don't love you, James.'

At this, his hands and arms began to twitch, his blue eyes glazed. He raised his huge fist, ready to strike.

I felt myself grow dizzy. I was a little girl again, wishing I were invisible, waiting, head bowed, for a blow to fall. It was no use trying to escape, because wherever I went, wherever I hid, my father would find me and then the punishment would be even worse. I wanted to weep because this was the story of my life.

The blow I was expecting never came. The dizziness faded, reality returned. That part of my life was over. I took a step back. James was still standing, arm raised. 'Christ! What's the matter with me?' he gasped, in a horrified voice.

'What the hell's going on in here?' Tom O'Mara came out of the bedroom fastening his trousers and bare to the waist.

James's face turned ashen, his shoulders slumped. 'How could you, Millie?' he whispered.

Tom wasn't quite as tall as James, or so broad, but before I knew what was happening, he had James's right arm bent behind him with one hand, the other on his collar, and was propelling him roughly towards the door. Despite the way James had just behaved, I was shocked at the sheer brutality of it. 'There's no need for that,' I cried.

The door slammed. After a while, I could hear James stumbling up the concrete steps. I switched on the lamp, turned off the central light, and sat in the middle of Flo's settee, trembling and hugging myself tightly with both arms.

'What was that all about?' asked Tom from behind.

'Can't you guess?'

'Hadn't you told him about me?'

'It was nothing to do with you until you appeared,' I sighed.

A few seconds later, Tom sat on the settee beside me and put a glass of sherry on the coffee table. 'Drink that!' he commanded. 'It'll do you good. Flo took sherry for her nerves.'

I was actually able to smile. 'I get the impression Flo took sherry for an awful lot of things.'

He put his arm around me companionably. It was the first time he'd touched me when I didn't automatically melt. 'So, what's the story with the bloke I just chucked out? Is he the one you were with at the party?'

'Yes, and there isn't a story. He loves me and I don't love him, that's all. He'll feel worse now he's seen you.' I swallowed half the sherry in one go. Thank goodness Tom had been there. Even if James had calmed down he would have been difficult to get rid of. I thought about him driving home, drunk as a lord. The whole thing was my fault. I should have made it plain the minute he said he loved me that I didn't love him. But I did! The trouble with James is that he's spoilt, too used to having girls throw themselves at him to grasp that this one wasn't blinded by his fatal attraction. I sipped more sherry, conscious of Tom's arm, heavy on my shoulders. I would have let him hit me! I just stood there. I'd never have dreamed James had such an ugly side. He was always so gentle. I watched the lamp, waiting for the girl in the red coat, hating James for bringing ugliness into the place I loved, where I'd always felt supremely safe. I'll never see him again, I vowed.

'Better?' Tom enquired. 'You've stopped trembling.'

'Much better.' I snuggled my head against his shoulder. 'Were you happy as a child?'

'That's a funny thing to ask.' He thought for a while. 'I suppose I was. Knowing Flo helped a lot.'

'What was your dad like?'

'Me dad? Oh, he was a soft ould thing. Everyone pissed him about something rotten – Gran, me mam and me, I suppose, as well as the firm he worked for.' His voice became hard. 'That's why I swore I'd be me own boss when I grew up.'

'Where's your mother?'

He shrugged carelessly. 'No idea. She did a runner when I was five. Went off with another bloke.'

I patted his knee. 'I'm sorry.'

'Don't be,' he said carelessly. 'It were good riddance as far as I was concerned.' He kissed my ear. 'What about you?'

'What about me?'

'Were you happy – how did you put it? – as a child?'

'Sometimes I wish I could be reborn and start all over.'

'Well, you can't. You're here and that's it, you can't change anything.'

'Are these your wife's initials?' I traced the heart on his chest with my finger.

'No. Clare's always trying to persuade me to get rid of it. You can get it done with a laser.'

'Have you any children?'

'Two girls, Emma and Susanna.' He raised his eyebrows, and I sensed he was annoyed. 'What's this? The third degree?'

'I wanted to know a few things about you, that's all.'

'What's the point?' he said coldly.

Just as coldly, I replied, 'I thought it would be nice to know a little about the man I've been sleeping with for the past week.' I looked at him. 'Is there nothing you'd like to know about me?'

'You're a great fuck, that's all I care.'

I stiffened and pulled away. 'Do you have to be so coarse?'

He dragged me back against him. 'The less we know about each other the better, don't you understand that?' he whispered urgently. 'I may be coarse, but I'm not thick. I've always taken me wedding vows seriously. I love me kids, and I don't want to spoil things between me and Clare.' He twisted me around, so that I was lying on his knee, and undid the belt on my dressing-gown. 'Let's keep things the way they are. Getting to know each other could be dangerous.'

His hands were setting my body on fire. I told myself that I had no intention of falling in love with someone like him. But he aroused feelings in me that no other man had. His lips came down on mine, and we rolled on to the floor. The pleasure we gave each other was sublime, and in the midst of everything, when I was almost out of my head with delight too exquisite to describe, I could have sworn I shouted, 'I love you.'

Or perhaps it was Tom.

At some time in the early hours of the morning, he carried me into the bedroom. I pretended to be asleep when he tucked the bedclothes around me, and remained like that while he got dressed. It wasn't until the front door clicked behind him that I sat up. 'Did you ever get yourself into a mess like this, Flo?' I asked. 'If your bureau is anything to go by, you led a very neat, ordered life.'

It was ages before I had to leave for work but I got up, ran a few inches of water in the bath and splashed myself awake. I made coffee in the microwave and carried it into the living room, where I tried, unsuccessfully, to empty my mind. But as soon as I got rid of Tom O'Mara, James would take his place, followed by Mum, Alison, Declan, Trudy – what were the things my sister couldn't talk about to Colin?

I was back to Tom again when I noticed that the rising sun was shining through the rear window and the walls of the little yard were glowing a rosy pink. I'd never been up this early before, and it looked so pretty.

So far, I hadn't ventured into the yard. I went outside, wondering if Flo had sat here in the summer with her first cup of tea of the day, as I did on my balcony. A black cat regarded me benignly from the wall and graciously allowed me to stroke its back. The wooden bench was full of mould and needed scrubbing, and the pansies in the plant-holders were dead now. I nearly jumped out of my skin when a head covered with untidy black curls appeared over the neighbouring wall.

'Hi,' Peter Maxwell grinned. 'Remember me? We met the other week at Charmian's party.'

'Of course! You said you lived next door. What are you doing up so early?' I could only see him from the shoulders up and he appeared to be wearing a sleeveless T-shirt.

He flexed a bulging muscle in his arm. 'I work out every morning. I'm off for a jog in a minute.' He winked. 'You can come with me, if you like.'

'You must be joking!'

He rested his arms on the wall and said conversationally, 'Are you all right?'

'Don't I look all right?'

'You look great, even without my glasses. It's just that I heard a commotion in your place last night. I contemplated coming round, but the sounds died down.'

'It was a drunk,' I said dismissively. 'I soon got rid of him.'

'By the way, I'd like to apologise for Sharon.'

'Who's Sharon?'

'Me girlfriend – ex-girlfriend. I tore her off a strip for dragging me away when I was dancing with you at the party. She was very rude.'

'I hardly noticed.'

He looked dismayed. 'And I was quite enjoying our little chat. I thought you were, too.'

'Well, yes, I was,' I conceded.

'It means I've got a spare ticket for the school concert in December. I wondered if you'd come.'

I pulled a face. 'I hate schools.'

'So did I, but they're different when you're an adult. No one will test your spelling or demand the date of the battle of Waterloo. Come on,' he coaxed, 'it's Charles Dickens's *A Christmas Carol*. I'd love you to be there.'

'Why?'

'Because you used to know me as Weedy and I want

you to see me as Peter Maxwell, MA, economics teacher, and scriptwriter of genius – I wrote the script for *A Christmas Carol* and set it in the present day. Tell you what,' he said eagerly, 'if you come to the concert, I'll let you show me round a property and we can negotiate. Then we'll have both proved to each other that we've made it.'

I smiled. 'How could I possibly refuse?'

Still smiling, I went indoors. Peter Maxwell had cheered me up. We'd both been through the mill and emerged unscathed. I paused in the act of pulling down the front of Flo's bureau, which hadn't been touched since the night Tom had arrived with a Chinese takeaway.

Unscathed? Was that true? Until that moment, I'd never thought I'd ever get over the tragedy of my childhood. I'd thought that, along with Trudy and Declan, I'd been irreparably damaged. But maybe time was fading the shadow of my father, and perhaps one day it would go away altogether. One day, the three of us would emerge, truly unscathed.

I decided not to think about it any more on such a lovely morning. I fetched a chair up to the bureau and took out the bundle of letters held together with the elastic band. It was rotten, and snapped when I pulled it off.

William Square began to wake up to the new day: cars drove away, others came to take their place; feet hurried past the basement window; children shrieked on their way to school – a football came over the railings and landed with a loud clang on the dustbin. But I was only vaguely aware of these activities. I was too engrossed in Flo's letters. It wasn't until I returned the last letter to its envelope that I remembered where I was. The letter was one of several from the same person, a Gerard Davies from Swansea, in which he implored Flo yet again to marry him. 'I love you, Flo. I always will. There'll never be another girl like you.'

Which was more or less what every other letter had said. They were love letters from a score of different men, all to Flo, and from the tone of quite a few, the relationships hadn't been platonic.

And Bel had claimed that Flo had led the life of a saint!

I remembered the mysterious receipts from the hotel in the Isle of Man. 'Oh, I bet you were a divil in your day, Flo Clancy,' I whispered.

Flo

I

1941

'Oh, Flo, you'll never guess!' Sally threw herself on to the sofa. 'Our Martha's captured Albert Colquitt at long last. They're getting married on St Patrick's Day.'

'Only two weeks off!' Flo sank beside her sister and they collapsed into giggles. 'How on earth did she manage that?'

Sally dropped her voice, though the entire house, all five floors of it, was empty and no one could have overheard. 'I think she seduced him,' she whispered dramatically.

'She what!' screamed Flo, giggling even more. 'You're joking.'

'I'm not, Flo, honest,' Sally assured her, round-eyed. 'One night after we'd gone to bed our Martha got up again. I didn't say anything, and she must have thought I was asleep. I thought she was going to the lavvy, but she sat at the dressing-table and started combing her hair. The moon was shining through the winder, so I could see her as clearly as I can see you now.' Sally frowned thoughtfully. 'I wondered why she hadn't put her curlers in or smothered herself with cold cream. Not only that, she was wearing that pink nightdress – you know, the one Elsa Cameron bought her for her twenty-first. Are you with me so far, Flo?'

'Yes, yes, I'm with you.' Flo wanted to throttle her sister for stretching the tale out so long. 'What happened then?'

'She just disappeared.'

'What d'you mean she just disappeared? You mean she vanished before your very eyes?'

'Of course not, soft girl. She left the room and was gone for ages. I was asleep by the time she got back.'

'Is that all?' Flo said, disappointed. 'I don't know how you worked out she seduced Albert. She might have dozed off on the lavvy. I've nearly done it meself in the middle of the night.'

'Why didn't she put her curlers in, then? Why didn't she use her cream? And she was keeping that nightdress for her bottom drawer. Not only that,' Sally finished triumphantly, 'she wasn't wearing her glasses.'

That seemed to provide final proof of Sally's claim. It was no longer a laughing matter. 'If that's how she caught him, then she's been dead devious,' Flo said soberly. 'Not many men could resist if a girl got into bed with them. She's shamed him into getting married.'

Sally nodded knowingly, with the air of a woman of the world, well aware of men's lack of will-power when it came to sex. 'They're very weak,' she agreed. 'Anyroad, Martha and Albert are going to live at home till the war's over. Mam said she's expecting you at the wedding.'

'In that case, Mam's got another think coming.' Even if she wasn't dead set against her sister, she'd feel peculiar, knowing that Albert had asked her first and that Martha was his second choice – that's if he'd had a choice. She would, though, write him a little note. In the time she had remained in Burnett Street after his kind proposal, she'd always made sure they'd never been alone. He didn't know the truth of what had happened to her baby but it would have been a sore reminder that she shouldn't have turned him down. Last week, her son had had his first birthday. She'd sent a card, writing simply, 'To Hugh, from Flo'. But the card had come back by return of post.

Sally sighed. 'She must have been desperate. Poor Martha.'

'Poor Albert,' Flo said cynically.

The young sailor stood before her, agonisingly shy, his face red with embarrassment. She had noticed him watching her all night. 'Would you like to dance, miss?'

'Of course.' Flo lifted her arms and he clasped her awkwardly. It was the first time he'd ventured on to the floor.

'I'm not very good at this,' he stammered, when he stood on her toe.

'Then you must learn,' she chided him. 'All service-men should learn to dance. This is a waltz, the easiest dance of all. You'll find yourself in all sorts of different towns and cities and it's the best way to meet girls.'

He swallowed, and said daringly, 'I won't meet many girls like you. I hope you don't mind me saying, but you're the prettiest one here.'

'Why on earth should I mind you saying a lovely thing like that? What's your name, luv?'

'Gerard Davies. I come from Swansea.'

'Pleased to meet you, Gerard. I'm Flo Clancy.'

'Pleased to meet you, Flo.'

It always started more or less the same. She only picked the shy ones, who were usually, though not always, very young. Gerard looked eighteen or nineteen, which meant he'd not long left home and would be missing his family.

When the waltz was over, she fanned herself with her hand and said, 'Phew! It's hot in here,' knowing that almost certainly he would offer to buy her a drink. He took the opportunity eagerly, and she chose the cheapest, a lemonade. They sat in a corner of the ballroom, and she asked him about his mum and dad, and what he'd done for a living before he was called up.

His dad ran a smallholding, he told her, and his mum worked in the shop where their vegetables were sold. He had two sisters, both older than him, and everyone had been very proud when he'd passed the scholarship and gone to grammar school. Less than three months ago, he'd gone straight from school into the Navy, and he had no idea what he wanted to do when the war was over. Flo noticed that he had the merest trace of a moustache on his upper lip, and his hands were soft and white. It was easy to believe that until recently he'd been just a school-boy. His brown eyes were wide and guileless. He knew nothing about anything much, yet he was about to fight for his country in the worst war the world had ever known. Flo felt her heart contract at the thought.

The drink finished, they returned to the dance floor. Flo could tell that he was gaining confidence because he had a girl on his arm, and it grew as the night progressed.

At half past eleven, she said she had to be getting home. 'I have to be up for work at the crack of dawn.'

'In the laundry?'

'That's right, luv.' She'd told him quite a lot about herself. She gave a little shudder. 'I don't live far away, but I'm terrified of walking home in the blackout.'

'I'll take you home,' he said, with alacrity, which Flo had known he would. She wasn't a bit scared of the blackout.

Outside, she linked his arm in case they lost each other in the dark. 'Have you got long in Liverpool?'

'No, we're sailing tomorrow, I don't know where to. It's a secret.' She felt his thin, boyish arm tighten on her own, and reckoned he was frightened. Who wouldn't be, knowing about all the ships that had been sunk and the lives that had been lost, mainly of young men like him?

When they got to her flat she made him a cup of tea and something to eat – he appeared to be starving the way he downed the two thick cheese sarnies.

'I'd better be getting back to the ship.' He looked at her shyly. 'It's been a lovely evening, Flo. I've really enjoyed myself.'

'So've I, luv.'

By the door, he flushed scarlet and stammered, 'Can I kiss you, Flo?'

She didn't answer, just closed her eyes and willingly offered her lips. His mouth touched hers, softly, and his arms encircled her waist. She slid her own arms around his neck, and murmured, 'Oh, Gerard!' and he kissed her again, more firmly this time. She didn't demur when his hands fumbled awkwardly and hesitantly with her breasts. She had thought this might happen. It nearly always did.

It was another half-hour before Gerard Davies left Flo in her bed. 'Can I write to you?' he pleaded, as he got back into his uniform. 'It'd be nice to have a girl back home.'

'I'd like that very much, Gerard.'

'And can I see you if I'm in Liverpool again?'

'Of course, luv. But don't turn up unannounced, whatever you do.' She worried that more than one of her young lovers might turn up at the same time. 'Me landlady upstairs wouldn't like it a bit. I'll give you the phone number of the laundry so you can let me know beforehand, like.'

'Thanks, Flo.' Then he said, in an awestruck voice, 'This has been the most wonderful night of my life.'

Gerard Davies was the seventh young man she'd slept with. Flo told herself earnestly that it was her contribution towards the war. Tommy O'Mara had taught her that making love was the most glorious experience on earth, and she wanted to share this experience with a few bashful young men who were about to fight for their country. It made her heart swell to think that they would go into battle, perhaps even die, carrying with them the memory of the wonderful time they'd had with Flo, the pretty young woman from Liverpool, who'd made them feel so special.

It was important that she didn't get pregnant. She'd asked Sally, casual, like, what she and Jock used.

'It's something called a French letter, Flo. They're issued by the Navy. I think you can get them in the chemist's, but I'm not sure.' Sally grinned. 'Why on earth d'you want to know?'

'No reason, I just wondered.'

There was no way Flo would even consider entering a chemist's to ask for French letters, so she inserted a sponge soaked in vinegar which she'd once heard the women in the laundry say was the safest way. But Flo had the strongest feeling she would never have another baby. It was as if the productive part of her had withered away to nothing when her little boy was taken away.

Just after Martha's wedding, Bel wrote to say she was expecting. 'I'll be leaving the ATS, naturally. Bob's being posted to North Africa, so I'll be back in Liverpool soon, looking for somewhere to live. Perhaps I can help out in the laundry if there's a sitting-down job I could do.'

Flo wrote back immediately to say she'd love to have Bel stay until she found a place of her own and that, if necessary, she'd invent a sitting-down job in the laundry. She bought two ounces of white baby wool to knit a matinée jacket, but in April another letter arrived: Bel had had a miscarriage. 'You can't imagine what it's like to lose a baby, Flo. I'm staying in the ATS, though I was looking forward to living in William Square and working in this famous laundry.'

The knitting was put away, unfinished. She seemed to waste a lot of time making baby clothes that would never be worn, Flo thought sadly. She wrote to Bel. 'I wouldn't know, of course, but I can imagine how heartbreaking it must be to lose a baby.'

Flo was proud of the way she'd run the laundry since Stella Fritz had returned to Ireland four months ago. As well as the Holbrook twins, she now employed two young mothers, friends, who worked half a day each. Lottie would turn up at midday with several lusty tod-dlers in a big black pram, and Moira would take them home. There was also Peggy Lewis, a widow, only four and a half feet tall, who worked like a navvy. Peggy had to leave early to prepare a massive meal for her three lads who worked on the docks and arrived home famished and ready to eat the furniture if there was no food ready.

When the delivery-boy, Jimmy Cromer, a cheeky little bugger but reliable, gave in his notice, having been offered a job with a builder at five bob a week more, Flo immediately increased his wages by ten. Jimmy was thrilled. 'If I stay, can I paint "White's Laundry" on me sidecart?'

'Of course, luv. As long as you do it neat and spell it proper.'

Every Friday, Flo sat in the office working out the week's finances, putting the wages to one side, and taking the surplus to the bank. There were usually several cheques in settlement of their big customers' bills. She paid everything into the Fritizes' account, then made out a statement showing exactly what money had come in and what had gone out, to send to Stella Fritz in County Kerry. At the bottom, she usually added a little message: the laundry was doing fine, there were no problems with the house, the window-cleaner still came once a month and she assumed this was all right. She kept all her own personal bills, stamped 'paid' by the gas and electricity companies, just in case there was ever any argument.

Not once did Stella acknowledge the hard work Flo was putting in to keep the business going and looking after the house. I suppose she's too busy breathing in the good clean air and looking out the winder, Flo thought. In the absence of any authority to tell her otherwise, she promoted herself – she'd remembered a white overall in the office cupboard with Manageress embroidered in red on the breast pocket. It had been there for as long as she could remember, together with a few other odds and ends that customers had forgotten to collect.

'You look dead smart, luv,' Mam exclaimed. She often called in on her way to or from work. 'Manageress at twenty! Who'd have thought it, eh?' Flo did her utmost not to preen. 'Which reminds me,' Mam continued, 'we were talking about you the other night. It's only a fortnight off your twenty-first, May the eighth. Martha and Sal both had a party. We can't let yours go without a little celebration, drink your health an' all. What do you say, Flo?'

'Where would the party be?'

'At home, luv, where else?'

Flo shook her head stubbornly. 'I'm not coming home, Mam, not while our Martha's there.'

'Oh, luv!' Mam's face was a mixture of grief and vexation. 'How long are you going to keep up this feud with Martha? After all, the girl's expecting. I can't wait to have me first grandchild,' she added tactlessly, as if Hugh O'Mara had never existed.

'Sal told me about the baby, Mam, and it's not a feud with Martha. I'm not sure what it is.'

'You'll have to speak to her sometime.'

'No, I won't.' Flo thought about Hugh. Then she thought about Nancy O'Mara, and that no one would take Martha's baby away and give it to a Welsh witch. 'I don't have to speak to our Martha again as long as I live,' she said abruptly.

Mam gave up. 'What about your twenty-first then?'

'You and Sal can come to William Square. I'll ask the women from the laundry, get a bottle of sherry and make sarnies. You can drink me health there.'

Sally reported that Albert seemed relatively content now that he was a member of the family he'd grown so fond of. 'He's started calling Mam "Mother" and she's a bit put out – she's two years younger than him! He always asks about you, Flo. He can't understand why you never come to visit.'

'Tell him I can't stand his wife,' Flo suggested. 'How's her ladyship taken to married life, anyroad?'

'All she's ever wanted was a wedding ring and Mrs in

front of her name. She goes round looking like the cat that ate the cream.'

Now that Albert was to become a father, his joy knew no bounds. Flo was pleased for him: he was a nice man who deserved happiness. But when it came to Martha, she felt only bitterness.

Frequently, in the dinner hour or on her way home, she walked down Clement Street, but she never set eyes on Nancy and there was never a pram outside number eighteen. Once, she thought she heard a baby cry as she passed, but that might have been her imagination.

Everyone in the laundry was pleased to be invited to Flo's twenty-first. 'It won't be much,' she warned. 'There won't be any fellers, for one thing.'

'We don't mind,' Jennifer and Joanna Holbrook said together.

'Me husband wouldn't let me go if there were,' remarked Moira.

Lottie's husband was away in the Army. Nevertheless, she would have felt disloyal going to a party where there were fellers.

'I'm not bothered,' Peggy said, from somewhere within a cloud of steam. 'Anyroad, I see enough of fellers at home. You could ask Jimmy Cromer if he'd like to provide some masculine company.'

'I'm not going to a party full of ould married women,' Jimmy said in a scandalised voice.

'I'm not old and I'm not married,' Flo reminded him.

Jimmy leered at her far too maturely for a fifteen-year-old. 'Will you come out with me, then?'

'I'll do no such thing!'

'In that case, I'm not coming to your party.'

The first week of May brought air raids worse than any the city had known before. For a week, it seemed as if the Luftwaffe's intention was to blast Liverpool out of existence. Flo was convinced that her party would never take place. By the eighth no one would be left alive and there wouldn't be a building still standing. At night she stayed indoors, worried that if she went dancing a raid might start and that she really would be too scared to come home alone. In bed, with her head under the covers, she listened to the house grinding on its foundations as the bombs whistled their way down to earth and the ground shook, though it was the parachute mines, drifting silently and menacingly, that caused the greatest carnage. Bells clanged wildly as fire engines raced to put out the hundreds of fires that crackled away, turning the sky blood red.

Next morning, exhausted but still in one piece, Flo would go to work. There was rarely any sign of public transport and she had to make her way carefully along pavements carpeted with splintered glass, passing the sad, broken remains of buildings that had been the landmarks of a lifetime, and the little streets with yawning gaps where houses had been only the day before. The air was full of floating scraps of charred paper, like black confetti at a funeral.

Everyone at the laundry was miraculously still there to exclaim in horror about the events of the previous night: the narrow escapes, the bomb that had dropped in the next street killing a girl they'd gone to school with, or a chap who'd nearly married their sister. Moira lost the godmother of her youngest child. Peggy's brother-in-law, an ARP warden, was killed outright when the building he was in got a direct hit. How long, everyone wondered, would the terror continue?

'It can't go on for ever,' Peggy maintained.

It was that thought that kept them going. It had to stop sometime.

Flo arrived on the Friday of the nightmarish week to find that during the night all the mains had been fractured. There seemed little point in a laundry without electricity, gas or water so she told everyone they might as well go home. 'You'll still get paid,' she promised, not caring if Stella would approve or not. 'It's not your fault you can't work. It's that bloody Hitler's.'

'What are you going to do?' one of the twins enquired.

'I'll stay, just in case things come on again.'

'We'll stay with you.'

'Same here,' echoed Peggy.

'Me, too,' said Moira.

The next few hours always remained one of Flo's most vivid memories, proof that the human spirit obstinately refused to give in, even in the face of the worst adversity. Peggy produced a pack of cards and they played Strip Jack Naked, Rummy and Snap, and shrieked with laughter for no reason at all, though anyone listening would have thought the laughter a mite hysterical and a bit too loud. Every now and then, they'd pause for a sing-song: 'We'll Meet Again', 'Little Sir Echo', 'Run Rabbit Run'. In their quavery soprano voices, the twins entertained them with a variety of old songs, 'If You Were the Only Girl in the World', and 'Only a Bird in a Gilded Cage'.

Mid-morning, when they would normally have stopped for a cup of tea, Moira said wistfully, 'I'd give anything for a cuppa.'

As if in answer to Moira's prayer, Mrs Clancy appeared suddenly at the side door carrying a teapot. 'I expect you're all parched for a drink,' she said cheerfully. 'I always run a bucket of water before I go to bed, just in case, like, and Mrs Plunkett next door's got one of them paraffin stoves.'

There was a mad dash for cups. As usual, the twins had brought milk because they never used all their ration.

'I've got Albert at home,' Mam said to Flo. 'He hurt his leg fire-watching. He's a terrible patient. All he does is complain about people getting away without paying their fares.'

'There's hardly any trams running.'

'That's what I keep telling him. There's lines up everywhere.' She patted Flo's hand. 'I'm off to work now, luv. I'll call in for the teapot on me way home.'

'It's all right, Mam, I'll bring it. I wouldn't mind having a word with Albert. What time will you be back?' She would take the opportunity of Martha's absence to reassure Albert, though not in words, that they would always be friends. She'd prefer him not to be alone, just in case there was a message in his eyes it would be wiser not to see.

'I'll be home about half two. Sal's on mornings, so she'll be back not long afterwards.'

Later that morning the gas supply was reconnected, and just after one o'clock water came gushing out of the tap in the lavatory, which had been left turned on. There was still no electricity, so the steam-presser remained out of use, but the boilers could be loaded with washing and the ironing done. Flo gave a sigh of relief as the laundry began to function almost normally, the women setting to work with a will. Normality seemed precious in an uncertain, dangerous world, though it didn't last for long.

Just as Flo was thinking that it was almost time to nip round to Burnett Street with the teapot, the air-raid siren began its sinister wail. She particularly hated daylight raids. They were rarely heavy and usually brief but, unlike the night raids, were impossible to ignore – or, at least, pretend to. The women groaned, but when Flo suggested they abandon work for the shelter on the corner, they flatly refused.

'The shelter's just as likely to get a direct hit as the laundry,' said Lottie, who'd recently changed shifts with Moira. 'I'd sooner stay.'

There seemed no argument to this, although the laundry was flimsy in comparison. Soon afterwards a solitary plane could be heard buzzing idly overhead. Everyone went outside to take a look. They could see the German crosses on the wings.

'Is that a Messerschmidt, Jo?'

'No, Jen. It's a Heinkel.'

Suddenly the plane went into a dive. It appeared to be coming straight for them. Peggy screamed and they ran inside and slammed the door. Almost immediately, there was a loud explosion, followed by another, then several more. The plane must have dropped a stick of bombs. From somewhere within the building, there was a thud and the crash of breaking glass.

'Jaysus! That was close!' someone gasped.

They stood still, scarcely breathing, as the plane's engine grew fainter. Then the sound disappeared and the all-clear went. The raid was over.

The laundry had suffered superficial damage. At least, Flo assumed that a shattered office window and the door blown off its hinges could be described as superficial. 'The thing is,' she said shakily, 'I'd forgotten today's the day I do the accounts, otherwise I'd have been in here sorting out the wages, or writing the statement for Mrs Fritz.' There was a small crater in the street outside, and the houses opposite had also lost their doors and windows, but thankfully, no one had been hurt.

The twins began calmly to sweep up the broken glass and restore the room to relative order. Flo decided to take the money home and leave the bank till Monday, but it was important that the women were paid. Using the presser as a desk, she counted out the money and wrote each name on a little brown envelope. She felt angry with herself because her hands were trembling and her writing was all over the place. She'd had a close shave, that was all. Some people suffered far worse without going to pieces. Her stomach was squirming. She felt uneasy, full of dread. 'Pull yourself together, Flo Clancy,' she urged.

'Flo, luv,' a voice said softly.

Flo looked up. Sally was standing at the side door and the feeling of dread grew until it almost choked her. She knew why Sally had come. 'Is it Mam?' she breathed.

Her sister nodded slowly. 'And Albert.'

Sally said, 'Promise you'll make things up with Martha.'

'Why should I?' demanded Flo.

It was almost midnight. The sisters were as yet too exhausted to grieve. They paid no heed to the raid going on outside, which was as bad as any experienced so far, decimating the beleaguered city even further. They were in William Square, the only place Sally had to go now that she'd lost her home in Burnett Street. The joint funeral would take place on Monday, the day after Flo's twenty-first birthday. There was room for Albert in his mother-in-law's grave, where she would join her beloved husband. The wreaths had been ordered, a Requiem Mass arranged, and a friend of Mam's had offered to provide refreshments after the service. Father Haughey was trying to track down Albert's cousin in Macclesfield. The address would have been in the parlour, but there was no longer a parlour, no longer a house, nothing left of the place to which Mr and Mrs Clancy had moved when they married, where they'd brought up their three girls. The bomb had gone through the roof and exploded in the living room, demolishing the houses on both sides. Martha had been safe at the brewery but Mam and Albert, sheltering under the stairs, had been killed instantly. Their shattered bodies lay in the mortuary, waiting for the funeral director to collect.

'Oh, Flo,' Sally moaned, 'how can you be so unChristian and unforgiving? Martha's pregnant and she's lost both her mam and her husband.'

Martha had been whisked from the brewery to Elsa Cameron's house. When Sally went to see her, she was fast asleep, the doctor had given her a sedative.

'I can't begin to imagine how I'd feel if I'd lost Jock and Mam at the same time,' Sally shuddered.

'But you're in love with Jock,' Flo pointed out. 'Martha was no more in love with Albert than I was – and all three of us loved Mam.'

'You're awful hard, Sis.'

'I'm only pointing out the obvious. What's hard about that?'

'Oh, I dunno. It's just that you always seemed such a

soft ould thing. I never dreamed you could be so un-sympathetic.'

'I feel sorry for our Martha,' Flo conceded. 'I just don't want anything more to do with her, that's all.' She felt irritated that Sally didn't seem to appreciate the enormity of what Martha had done. Maybe, because Flo's baby was a bastard, she wasn't supposed to love him the way a married mother would.

'Despite our Martha being an ould bossy-boots, she depended on Mam far more than we did.' Sally sighed. 'She'll miss her something awful. We loved Mam, but we didn't need her.' She turned to her sister and said, 'Don't think I've forgotten about Tommy O'Mara and the baby, Flo. But you're a strong person, a survivor. You've got yourself a nice little home, an important job. It's time to forgive and forget.'

'I'll never forgive Martha, and I'll never forget.' Flo's voice was like ice. 'I'll speak to her politely on Monday, but that's as far as I'm willing to go.'

But Martha was too ill to attend the funeral. And Sally had been right: Elsa Cameron reported that it was her mother Martha kept calling for. There was no mention of Albert.

2

The momentous year had flown by. Suddenly, it was Christmas again and Liverpool, though battered and badly bruised after the week-long May blitz, had survived to fight another day. The raids continued fitfully, but it was rare that the siren went nowadays. Life went on, and mid-December, Martha Colquitt gave birth to a daughter, Kate, named after the grandmother she would never know.

'She's the prettiest thing you've ever seen,' Sally told Flo. 'Ever so placid and good-humoured.'

'That's nice.' Flo did her utmost to sound generous.

'But I wish Martha'd find somewhere else to live.' Sally's brow puckered worriedly. 'I wouldn't want that Elsa Cameron anywhere near a baby of mine. She treats Norman like a punch-bag, poor bugger. He's only four, and such a lovely little chap.'

'What's happened to her husband?'

'Eugene used to come home from sea every few months, but last time he told her she was crackers and he's never been back since. I reckon he's done a bunk, permanent, like.'

'Martha said once Elsa had a sort of illness,' Flo remarked. 'She said some women go that way when they have a baby. Afterwards they're never quite right in the head.'

Sally nodded. 'There's summat wrong with the woman. By rights, Norman should be taken off her. She's not fit to be a mother.'

It seemed grotesquely unfair that Elsa Cameron, unfit to have a child, and Nancy O'Mara, unable to have one, should both have become mothers, yet Flo was childless. She changed the subject before she said something she might later regret.

'What d'you think of me decorations?' she asked. The room was festooned with paper chains and tinsel. Clusters of imitation holly hung in both windows.

'It looks like a grotto. I tried everywhere for decorations, but there's none to be had in the shops.' After living for a few months with Flo, Sally had found herself a small flat not far from Rootes Securities in Speke, which meant that she and Jock could be alone together during the precious times he was on leave.

'I got them from upstairs,' Flo said smugly. 'There's plenty more, if you'd like some. It's like having a big shop up there all to meself.'

'I wouldn't mind a few. I'm expecting Jock any minute, and it'd be nice to have the place looking Christmassy. Don't forget you're invited to Christmas dinner, will you?'

'No. And don't you forget me party the Saturday before. I feel as if I owe the girls in the laundry a party. I never had the one that was planned for me twenty-first.'

Sally twisted her lips ruefully. 'Mam was really looking forward to that. She was trying to get the ingredients for a birthday cake.'

'Was she? You've never mentioned that before.'

'I'd forgotten all about it.'

The sisters were silent for a while, thinking about Mam and Albert and how much their little world had changed over the past few years.

'Oh, well.' Sally sighed. 'I'm on early shift tomorrer. I'd better be getting home.'

It was a sad Christmas, full of bitter-sweet memories of Christmases that had gone before, made even sadder when a letter arrived from Bel to say that Bob had been killed in North Africa. 'I only wish you two had met, Flo,' she wrote. 'He was the dearest husband a woman could have. We were only married two years, almost to the day, and weren't together for a lot of that time, but I'll never stop missing him. Never.'

On New Year's Eve, Flo slipped into the Utility frock that she'd bought especially for the Rialto dance, which would go on till past midnight. It was turquoise linen, made with the minimum amount of material, short sleeves and a narrow collar. She adjusted the mirror on the mantelpiece, took a sip of sherry, and began to curl her hair into a roll.

Would she meet anyone tonight? She was glad Christmas was over and it would soon be 1942. She and Sally had both agreed that they would put the past firmly behind them and start afresh. With a wry smile, Flo glanced at the fluffy blue bunny, still in its Cellophane wrapping on the sideboard. She'd bought it for Hugh, but hadn't had the nerve to take it round to Clement Street, knowing that it would be refused. Anyroad, Hugh would be two in February and had probably grown out of fluffy bunnies. She still looked for him, walking up and down Clement Street two or three times a week. Nancy must have deliberately done her shopping when she knew Flo would be at work because there was never any sign of her out with Hugh. For a while, Flo was worried that she'd moved, but Sally said that Martha had taken Kate to see her.

She sipped more sherry, already slightly drunk and the evening hadn't even started. *She didn't even know what her son looked like!* How could she ever put the past behind her when he would still be on her mind if she lived to be a hundred? She hummed 'Auld Lang Syne', and told herself she was strong, a survivor. She wondered why she wanted to weep when she was getting ready for a dance where she was bound to have a good time. 'Because it's not really what I want,' she told herself bleakly.

When someone knocked on the door she turned, startled. Sal was spending New Year's Eve at Elsa Cameron's with Martha. 'If she's come to persuade me to go with her, she's wasting her time.'

A middle-aged man, sunburned, with hollow eyes and hollow cheeks, was standing outside the door holding a suitcase. He wore an ill-fitting tweed suit, and the collar of his frayed shirt was far too big.

'Yes?' Flo said courteously. She didn't recognise him from Adam.

'Oh, Flo! Have I changed so much?' he said tragically.

'Mr Fritz! Oh, Mr Fritz!' She grabbed his arm and pulled him inside. 'Am I pleased to see you!'

'I'm glad someone is.' He looked ready to shed the tears she'd so recently wanted to shed herself. He came into the flat and she pushed him into a chair, then stared at him as if he were a long-lost, dearly loved relative. He was much thinner than she remembered, but despite his gaunt features and the lines of strain around his jaw, he looked fit and well, as if he'd spent a lot of time working outdoors. His once chubby hands were lean and callused, but without his wire-rimmed glasses he seemed much younger. The more she stared, the less he looked like the Mr Fritz she used to know.

'Are you home for good?' she demanded. She wanted to pat him all over, make sure he was real, and had to remind herself he was only her employer.

He said drily, 'After all this time the powers-that-be decided I wasn't a danger to my adopted country. Just before Christmas they let me go.' His brown eyes grew moist. 'I've been to Ireland, Flo. Stella wasn't pleased to see me, and made it obvious she didn't want me to stay. The younger children didn't know who I was. The others were polite, but they're having such a good time on the farm I think they were scared I'd insist they come home.' He sighed. 'They're known locally as the McGonegals. Stella is ashamed of her married name.'

Flo had no idea what to say. She frowned at her hands and mumbled, 'I always thought you and Mrs Fritz were very happy together.'

'So did I!' Mr Fritz looked puzzled. 'I'm not sure what happened, but as soon as the war started Stella became a different person, bad-tempered, blaming me for things I had no control over. I couldn't produce coal or sugar out of thin air as if I were a magician. I wasn't personally responsible for the air raids. When the women left the laundry for higher wages, that was the last straw as far as Stella was concerned. It was a shock, after so many years, to discover she could be so unpleasant.'

'Perhaps,' Flo said hesitantly, 'once the war's over . . .'

'No.' He shook his head wearily. 'No, it's too late, Flo. I spent eighteen months in the camp. The other married men had letters from their families. Some wives travelled hundreds of miles to see their husbands for just a few hours. I had a single letter from Stella the whole time I was there, and that was to tell me she was back in Ireland and she'd left you in charge of the laundry and William Square.' There was a lost expression on his face.

Something had happened with which he would never come to terms. 'You can't be sure of anything in this life, I hadn't realised that,' he murmured. 'I never thought it possible to feel so very alone, as if I'd never had a family. I still feel like that – alone. Do I actually have a wife and eight children? It seems absurd. It's even worse since I went to Ireland. We were like strangers to each other.'

'Oh, Lord!' Flo was horrified. He was such a dear, sweet man, who wouldn't hurt a fly. She said in her kindest voice, which seemed rather thick and emotional all of a sudden, 'You don't seem like a stranger to me.'

For the first time he smiled. 'That means a lot, Flo. It really does.' He glanced around the room and she hoped he wouldn't recognise the decorations and all the other things she'd pinched from upstairs. 'You've made this place very cosy. It's a relief to have somewhere, someone, to come back to.' He smiled again. 'But you're obviously getting ready for a night out on the town. I expect you have a date with a young man. Don't let me keep you.'

'As if I'd let you spend New Year's Eve all on your own,' Flo cried. 'I was only going to the Rialto by meself.'

Despite his protestations, she refused to leave. 'I'll pretend I got all decked up because I was expecting you,' she said, in the hope that it would make him feel less alone, more welcome.

Apparently it did. By the time she'd made a cup of tea and something to eat, he looked almost cheerful. She poured them both a glass of sherry and told him all about the laundry. 'I hope you don't mind but we changed the name to White's after we lost a lot of business.'

He already knew. Stella had given him the statements Flo had sent. 'It's all I have left now, my laundry.' He sighed, but more like the gloomy Mr Fritz of old than the joyless person who'd just landed on her doorstep.

She described the staff. 'You'll love the twins. They can only manage one person's work between them, but they only get one person's wage, so it doesn't matter.' She told him about Peggy, who had to leave early for her lads' tea, and Lottie and Moira who worked half a day each. 'And, of course, you know Jimmy Cromer, he's a treasure.'

'Jimmy will have to go now I'm back,' Mr Fritz said.

'You can't sack him!' Flo gasped. 'He's a good worker, dead reliable.'

'But there'll be nothing for him to do.' He spread his hands, palms upwards, a gesture she remembered well. 'I'll be able to collect and deliver, won't I?'

'Even so, you can't sack Jimmy for no reason,' Flo said stubbornly.

'He'll be superfluous to requirements, Flo. What better reason is there?'

'It seems very cruel.'

'It's necessary to be cruel sometimes if you run a successful business. It's what capitalism is all about. You can't employ superfluous staff and make a profit.'

'And here's me thinking you wouldn't hurt a fly,' Flo said sarcastically. 'I suppose you'll be reducing the wages next, so you make an even bigger profit. Well, you needn't think I'm working me guts out if everyone leaves.'

His eyes twinkled. 'You've changed, Flo. You would never have spoken to me like that before.'

Flo tossed her head. 'I'm not sorry.'

'Why should you be sorry for expressing an opinion? I like you better this way. But let's have more sherry and save the arguments for tomorrow. It's New Year's Eve. We'll talk about only pleasant things. Tell me, how are your family?'

'I'm afraid there's nothing pleasant to tell.' She explained about Mam and Albert being killed in the same raid that had damaged the laundry.

'So many tragedies.' Mr Fritz looked dejected. 'Hitler has a great deal to answer for. I suppose I should consider myself lucky to be alive.'

As midnight approached, he noticed the wireless and suggested they listen to Big Ben chime in the New Year. 'Is that the set from upstairs?'

'I hope you don't mind. I borrowed it,' Flo said uncomfortably, 'You can have it back tomorrer.'

'Keep it, Flo,' he said warmly. 'It will give me a good excuse to come down and listen to the news.'

'You mean I can stay?' She felt relieved. 'I thought you might prefer to have the house all to yourself, like.'

'My dear Flo,' he laughed, 'would I be silly enough to put my one and only friend out on to the street? Of course you can stay. What's more, this furniture's seen better days. There's a nice little settee and chair in Stella's sitting room that you must have. She's not likely to use it again.'

'Shush!' Flo put her finger to her lips. 'It's about to be nineteen forty-two.'

As the great clock in London chimed in the New Year, they shook hands and Mr Fritz kissed her decorously on the cheek. 'I'd expected it would be dreadful, coming back to the house without Stella and the children, Flo, but it's not been nearly as bad as I'd thought.' He squeezed her hand. 'It really is good to be home.'

He was still the same Mr Fritz, after all, who couldn't hurt a fly. Once face to face with Jimmy Cromer, he couldn't bring himself to dismiss the lad. 'I'm a hopeless capitalist,' he confessed. Instead, he gave him a job in the laundry, which Jimmy said disgustedly was women's work and got bored within a week. As a fit, able sixteen-year-old, he had no problem finding employment in war time, and he left quickly of his own accord.

While she'd been in charge Flo had got used to doing things her way. She had quite a task convincing Mr Fritz that her way was best. He got tetchy when proved wrong, she sulked when he was right, but they were always the best of friends again before the day was over.

He maintained that they provided a substitute family for each other.

'Mam would be pleased,' said Flo. 'She always liked you.'

Life assumed a pleasant pattern. On Sundays, he would come to dinner, armed with a bottle of wine. On Saturday afternoons, Flo had tea upstairs, eating the thick, clumsily made sandwiches with every appearance of enjoyment.

During the week, she continued to go dancing, occasionally bringing home a young serviceman. Upstairs would be in darkness, so Mr Fritz remained ignorant of that part of her life. Not that it was any of his business, she told herself, but it was something she'd sooner keep to herself.

In July, Bel came home on five days' leave prior to being posted to Egypt, and preferred to spend the time with her best friend, Flo, rather than with her horrible aunt Mabel.

Like virtually everyone else, Bel had changed. There was an added maturity to her lovely face, and her violet eyes were no longer quite so dazzling. Even so, she swept into the flat like a breath of fresh air, filling it with noise and laughter. She enthused over the brown plush settee and chair that had once belonged to Stella, the tall sideboard, which had so many useful drawers and cupboards, and was particularly taken with the brass bed from Mr Fritz's spare room. 'It's like a little palace, Flo, but I hate the idea of you living in a hole in the ground.'

'Don't be silly,' Flo said mildly. 'I love it.'

The two girls attracted a chorus of wolf-whistles, and many an admiring glance, as they strolled through the sunlit city streets of an evening in their summer frocks: Bel, the young widow, with her striking red hair and rosy cheeks, and green-eyed Flo, as pale and slender as a lily.

Bel and Mr Fritz took to each other straight away and pretended to flirt extravagantly. On the last night of Bel's leave, he took both girls out to dinner. 'I wonder what

Stella would say if she could see me now.' He chuckled. 'Every man in this restaurant is eyeing me enviously, wondering how such an insignificant little chap managed to get the two most beautiful women in Liverpool to dine with him.'

'Insignificant!' Bel screamed. 'You're dead attractive, you. If I was on the look-out for a feller, I'd grab you like a shot.'

Flo smiled. In the past, no one would have dreamed of describing Mr Fritz as attractive, but since returning from the camp he had acquired a gaunt, melancholy charm. The twins claimed he made their old hearts flutter dangerously, and Peggy declared herself bowled over.

That night, Flo and Bel sat up in bed together drinking their final mug of cocoa. 'I won't half miss you.' Flo sighed. 'The place will seem dead quiet after you've gone.'

'I'm ever so glad I came. It's the first time I've enjoyed meself since Bob was killed.'

'Remember the day we met?' said Flo. 'You were dead impatient because I was upset over Tommy O'Mara. Now you know how I felt.'

'There's a big difference.' Bel's voice was unexpectedly tart. 'Bob was worth crying over, not like Tommy O'Mara!'

'Oh, Bel! How can you say that when you never met him?'

Bel didn't answer straight away. 'Sorry, Flo,' she said eventually. 'It was just the impression I got. But you're well over him now, aren't you?'

'I'm not sure if I ever will be. I've never met a man who comes anywhere near him.' Perhaps if Hugh hadn't always been on her mind to remind her of Tommy's existence, she might have put the memory away.

'It's about time you got yourself a proper feller, girl,' Bel snorted, 'and stopped moping over a man who died three years ago. You're twenty-two. You should be married by now, or at least courting.'

'You sound just like our Martha.' Flo laughed.

'Which reminds me,' Bel went on. 'Why haven't I been to see your Martha's little girl?'

'I thought you didn't like babies.'

'I didn't until I lost the one I was expecting.' Bel's lovely face became unbearably sad. 'You've no idea what it feels like, Flo, having this little person growing inside you. When I had the miscarriage, it was like losing part of meself. Still,' she brightened, 'that's all in the past, and as Bob said to me in his lovely Scots accent just before he was posted to North Africa and we knew he might be killed, "I know you won't forget me, girl, but don't let the memory weigh you down, like unwanted baggage. Go light into the future."' Bel sniffed briefly. 'He was ever so clever, my Bob.'

Flo envied her friend's resilience and ability to look ahead. She spent too much time looking back.

'Anyroad,' Bel persisted, 'what's your Martha's baby like?'

'I've no idea. I haven't seen her.'

Bel's reaction was entirely predictable. 'Why ever not?' she screeched.

'Because me and our Martha had a falling out.'

'What over?'

'Mind your own business,' Flo said irritably, and although Bel pressed for ages to know why, she refused to say another word.

Next morning, the two girls left for Lime Street station, Bel trim and smart in her khaki uniform. Mr Fritz had insisted Flo see her on to the train, even though it meant she'd be hours late for work. He bade Bel a mournful farewell. 'Take care of yourself in Egypt, there's a good girl.' He put his hand over his heart. 'I think I can already feel it breaking.'

Bel flung her arms around his neck. '*You*'re the heart-breaker, Fritz, you ould rascal. Us poor girls aren't safe with chaps like you around. I'm surprised those poor women in the laundry get any work done at all.'

The station was packed with servicemen and women returning from leave or *en route* elsewhere in the British Isles. Bel found herself a seat on the London train and leaned out of the window. 'He's a lovely chap, that Fritz,' she said.

'I know.' Flo nodded.

'I think he fancies you.'

Flo was aghast. 'Don't talk daft, Bel Knox! We're friends, that's all. I'm very fond of him, but he's got a wife and eight children in Ireland.'

Bel winked. 'I think he'd sooner be more than friends. Anyroad, it's over between him and Stella. He told me.'

'Yes, but it still makes him a married man. And they'll never get divorced, they're Catholics.'

'For goodness' sake, Flo. There's a war on. Forget he's married and let yourself go for once.'

The guard blew his whistle, the carriage doors were slammed, and the train began slowly to puff out of the station, Bel still hanging out of the window. Flo walked quickly along beside her. 'One of the first things you said to me was that you didn't approve of going out with married men.'

'Under the circumstances I'd make an exception in the case of you and Mr Fritz,' Bel said. By now, the train was going too fast for Flo to keep up. Bel shouted, 'Think about it, Flo!'

'The thing is,' Flo said under her breath, waving to the red-headed figure until the face was just a blur, 'I'm not sure if I fancy *him*, not in the way Bel's on about. I'm not sure if I'll ever fancy anyone again.'

3

1945

She recognised him immediately, a thin child, delicately boned like Flo herself, hair the colour of wheat. His round, innocent eyes were a beautiful dark green flecked with gold. The other children, boys first, had come charging through the school gates whooping like savages. He came alone, separate from the rest. She could guess one reason why he wasn't part of the gang: the other lads wore shabby jerseys and baggy pants but this five-year old was neatly dressed in grey shorts with a firmly pressed crease, pullover, flannel shirt. Hugh O'Mara was the only child wearing a blazer and tie. Nancy was a good mother, but not very sensitive. Flo would never have allowed her son to stand out in such a ridiculous get-up.

Flo watched as he approached, a sensation in her gut akin to the one she'd had the first time she was on her way to meet his father. She thought of all the times when she'd glimpsed a dark-haired woman with a pushchair on the far side of the Mystery, or crossing the street leading a small boy by the hand. Either it had been someone else, or the woman and child had disappeared when she had hurried to catch up.

Now he was here, and in a few seconds he would be close enough to touch. Not that she would dare. Not just yet.

'Hello,' she said.

He looked at her, and she searched in his eyes for recognition, as if it was inevitable he would sense she wasn't a stranger but his mam, his real flesh-and-blood mam. But there was nothing, just a shy glance.

'What's that you've got there?' she asked. Like all the other children, he was carrying a large brown envelope.

'A photo. It's of all the school taken together.'

'Can I see?'

He opened the envelope and took out the photo. 'The infants are at the front. That's me there.' He pointed to the end of the row, where he was sitting, knees crossed, looking serious. 'Mr Carey said I spoilt it 'cos I'm the only one not smiling.'

'Perhaps there wasn't much to smile about that day.' Flo turned the picture over. The photographer's name was stamped on the back, which meant she could buy a copy for herself.

'I didn't like having me photo taken much,' he said as they began to walk in the direction of Smithdown Road. 'Are you a friend of me mam's?'

'No, but I know some people she knows. I knew your dad quite well.'

His eyes lit up. 'Did ya? He died on a big ship under the sea, but the other boys won't believe me when I tell them.'

'*I* believe you,' Flo declared. 'I've got newspapers at home that tell all about it.'

'Can I come and see them?' he said eagerly. 'I can read a bit.'

There was nothing Flo would have liked more, but she said, 'I live too far away. Tell you what, though, I'll come next Friday and bring the papers with me. We can sit on the grass in the Mystery and I'll read them to you.'

'Can't you come before?' The crestfallen look on his thin face was almost too much to bear. Flo wanted to snatch him up and carry him away. He was much too serious for a five-year-old. She'd like to teach him to laugh and sing, be happy. But it would be cruel to take him from the woman he thought was his mother, the woman he loved more than he would ever love Flo.

She said, 'No, luv. I only get away from work on Fridays when I go to the bank. I should have been back ages ago. Me boss'll be wondering where I am.'

'Me mam works in a sweetshop.'

'I know. Someone told me.' Martha and Nancy O'Mara still saw each other occasionally. Through Sally, Flo had learned that Nancy served in the shop till five o'clock, leaving ninety minutes during which Flo could see her son, although she could only be with him for a fraction of that time because of her own job. St Theresa's junior and infants' school was a few minutes away from the laundry.

'She brings me pear drops home sometimes, and dolly

mixtures.' Unexpectedly, he reached up and put his small hand in hers. Flo could barely breathe as she touched her child for the first time. She stroked the back of his fingers with her thumb, wanting to cry as all sorts of emotions tumbled through her head. She said, knowing it sounded stupid, 'I'd like to be your friend.'

He looked at her gravely. 'Me mam doesn't like me having friends.'

'Why not?' she asked in surprise.

'She said they're a bad inf–' He stumbled over the word and rolled his eyes. 'A bad inflex, or something.'

'A bad influence?'

' 'S right,' he said.

'Perhaps I could be your secret friend.'

'Yes, please. I'd like that.'

They arrived at the laundry, where Mr Fritz was standing by the door looking concerned. He hurried towards them. 'We were worried there'd been a hold-up at the bank. Peggy thought you might have been shot.'

'Peggy's seen too many films.'

'And who's this?' He looked at Hugh benignly.

'This is my friend, Hugh O'Mara.' Flo pushed her son forward. 'Hugh, say hello to me boss, Mr Fritz.'

'Hello,' Hugh said politely.

'Pleased to meet you, Hugh, old chap,' Mr Fritz said jovially.

Flo knelt in front of the little boy and said, in a whisper, 'If ever you're in trouble, this is where you can find me. I'm here every day from eight till half past five, and till one on Sat'days.' She stroked his cheek. 'Remember that, won't you, luv?'

He nodded. 'But I don't know your name!'

'It's Flo Clancy.'

'All right, Flo.'

'Tara, now. I'll see you next Friday.'

He trotted off in his smart clothes, clutching the brown envelope. Flo watched till he turned the corner, and still watched even after he'd gone, imagining him passing the shops in Smithdown Road on his way to Clement Street, where he would remain in the house, alone and friendless, until Nancy came.

'What's the matter, Flo?' Mr Fritz said gently.

'Nothing.' Flo returned to work, and it wasn't until she was inside that she became aware of the tears that were streaming down her cheeks.

For years Gerard Davies had been imploring Flo to marry him. After they'd first met in the Rialto, he'd come to Liverpool whenever he could and he wrote to her regularly. As far as he was concerned, Flo was his girl, his sweetheart. 'We'll see once the war's over,' Flo would say, whenever the subject of marriage was raised.

The war had been over for three months, the lights were on again and the celebrations, the parties, the dancing in the streets were just memories. Gerard Davies had been demobbed and was back in Swansea. He wrote to demand that Flo keep her promise.

He wasn't the only one of her young men to propose – she could have had half a dozen husbands by now – but he was the most persistent. Flo turned down the proposals as tactfully as she could. She didn't want to hurt anyone's feelings. They would never know that things hadn't been quite so wonderful for her as they had been for them. She put the lovely letters away to keep for always.

To Gerard Davies she wrote that she'd only said, 'We'll see,' when the war was over. She hadn't promised anything. She said that she liked him very, very much, and felt honoured that he wanted her for his wife, but he deserved to marry a woman who loved him far more than she did.

Perhaps it was unfortunate that she found Gerard's letter waiting on the doormat when she arrived home the day she'd met Hugh outside school for the first time, otherwise she might have given more serious consideration to his proposal. It would be nice to have a husband, children, a proper house. Sally, who was expecting her first baby in January, had got a nice council house in Huyton with gardens front and back. Jock would complete his naval service in two years' time and they would settle down and raise their family. And Bel had got married again in Egypt to a chap called Ivor, who claimed to be descended from the Hungarian royal family. She enclosed a photo of herself dressed in a lavish lace outfit standing next to a haughty young man with an undeniably regal manner. 'Ivor lives in the land of make-believe,' Bel wrote. 'He's no more royal than my big toe, but he makes me laugh. I'll never love another man the way I loved Bob, but me and Ivor are good company for each other. I'll be back in Liverpool very soon and you can see him for yourself.' The letter was signed, 'Bel (Szerb!)' and there was a PS. 'By the way, I think I'm pregnant!'

Why can't *I* make do with second best? Flo asked herself. Why am I haunted by memories of making love with Tommy O'Mara in the Mystery all those years ago? And why am I obsessed with the son I can never have? She knew that if she married Gerard, she would be only half a wife to him and half a mother to their children. It wouldn't be fair on him or them. She stuck the stamp on the envelope containing the letter to him, thumping it angrily with her fist.

When Bel returned, it was with news of another miscarriage. 'The doctor said I'll never carry a baby to full term. I've got a weak cervix,' she said. Flo nodded sympathetically, as if she knew what it meant.

Bel was upset, but determined not to take the doctor's verdict as final. 'Me and Ivor intend to try again. At least the trying's fun.' She winked. 'It's about time you got married and tried it, Flo.'

'Perhaps, one day.'

'I take it nothing came of you and Mr Fritz?'

'You were imagining things. We're just friends.'

Flo couldn't take to Ivor, whose manner was as haughty as his appearance. He expected his wife to wait on him hand and foot. Bel had a third miscarriage, and went to work behind the handbag counter in Owen Owen's department store, while Ivor lolled around in their flat in Upper Parliament Street, refusing so much as to wash a dish.

'He won't get a job,' Bel raged. She came round to Flo's often to complain and calm her nerves with sherry. 'Whenever I point out a suitable vacancy in the *Echo*, he claims it's beneath him.'

'But it's not beneath him to live off his wife?'

'Apparently not.' Bel snorted so loudly that Flo half expected flames to shoot out of her nostrils. 'I think I'll kick him out, get a divorce.'

'You should never have married him,' Flo said, with the benefit of hindsight.

'I know.' Bel uttered an enormous sigh. 'I don't half envy your Sally. Her little girl's a proper bobby-dazzler, and that Jock seems a dead nice feller.'

'Sal's already in the club again. She's making up for lost time now that Jock'll soon be home for good.'

'Have you been seeing Hugh O'Mara, luv?' Sally asked, one stormy December Sunday when Flo went to see her in Huyton.

'How did you find out?' Flo stammered.

'Someone told Nancy and she told our Martha.' Sally's face was misty with happiness as she nursed nine-month-old Grace on her lap.

'I've been meeting him outside school every Friday for more than a year – I suppose you think I'm daft.'

'Oh, no, luv. I might have done once, but not now.' Sally glanced at her daughter. 'I can't imagine how I'd have felt if someone had taken her away before I'd even seen her, or the little one I've got in here.' She patted her bulging stomach. 'Everyone was dead cruel, Flo, me

238

included. I thought keeping the baby would ruin your life.'

Instead, it was the other way round, Flo thought wryly. 'Is Nancy mad at me?'

'Martha couldn't make out if she was or not. She seemed more resigned than anything. I suppose she thinks it can't do much harm now.'

'I don't suppose it can,' said Flo. 'How is our Martha?' She only asked because it would please Sally, who was forever trying to reunite the sisters.

Sally grimaced and said, predictably, 'I wish you'd go and see her, Flo. She's dead miserable. Kate's starting school in January, and she'll be stuck in the house with Elsa Cameron who's completely off her rocker now. The last time I went she was singing hymns the whole time. By rights, Martha should find a place of her own, but although you'll say she only wants to interfere, Flo, she's not prepared to leave Elsa in sole charge of Norman or the woman's quite likely to kill the poor bugger. Any-road, Norman would be lost without little Kate. They've been brought up together, and he worships the ground she walks on.'

Hugh O'Mara emerged from school wearing a woollen balaclava, a long fringed scarf, and the horrible navy-blue belted mackintosh that Flo thought made him look like a miniature gas man.

It was another terrible winter, bleaker and icier even than the notorious winter of 1940, and the fuel shortages and power cuts made it seem even worse. Food remained rationed, and in such an austere atmosphere it was hard to believe that Great Britain had won the war.

There was a little girl with Hugh, a pretty child, like a fairy, with long fair hair. She wore three-quarter-length socks and patent-leather shoes, and her winter coat was much too big. There was something familiar about her face, though Flo couldn't remember having seen her before.

'I've got another friend,' Hugh beamed happily at Flo. 'She only started last week, but I knew her before school. Me mam goes to their house sometimes. She's nearly two years younger than me, but that doesn't mean we can't be friends.'

'Of course it doesn't, luv.' He would be seven in a month's time and was shooting upwards like a vigorous sapling. Flo had already bought his present, a toy car. If you twisted the steering wheel, the four wheels turned. She was taking the risk that Nancy wouldn't object.

'Can she come with us to the Mystery?' Hugh said eagerly. 'Have you brought the ball?'

Flo was about to say the little girl should ask her mam first, when another boy came up, a dark, handsome lad of about ten, with an ugly purple and yellow bruise on his forehead. She'd noticed him before. He was a bully and most of the children kept well out of his way. He put a possessive hand on the little girl's shoulder. 'I've got to take her home,' he said, scowling. 'We live in the same house together.' He turned to Hugh and spat, 'You leave her alone, Hugh O'Mara.'

'Don't you dare speak to him like that,' Flo said angrily.

The boy ignored her and pulled the child away. 'C'mon, Kate.'

'Is that Kate Colquitt?' Flo enquired, when the children had gone.

'Yes. Do you know her?'

'I'm her auntie.'

'You never are!' Hugh's brow creased in disbelief. 'I don't understand.'

'Her mam and me are sisters,' Flo explained carefully. Then she said, 'The boy with Kate, is that Norman Cameron?'

'Yes.' Hugh wrinkled his thin shoulders. 'He's not very nice. I don't like him. No one does, not even his mam.'

'Perhaps he can't help not being very nice.' She recalled sadly what a beautiful baby Norman had been, so happy – there was a photo somewhere in the flat, taken on his first birthday, that Martha had given her at the time. She hadn't realised the three children would be at the same school – Hugh and Kate were cousins, not that they'd ever know.

Flo took a rubber ball out of her bag and began to bounce it. 'C'mon, I'll race you to the Mystery. Who-ever's last has to climb to the top of the tallest tree and shout "Hallelujah" ten times.' She always won, but Hugh's legs were getting longer. As soon as he was likely to get there first, she'd have to think of a less demanding penalty.

1949

Mr Fritz was stepping out with Mrs Winters, a widow who had tightly permed black hair and wore smart, tailored suits with very short skirts, though her legs were much too thick for ankle-strap shoes – or so Bel claimed when she saw them together. 'I don't like the look of her, Flo. Once she's installed upstairs you'll be out on your arse.'

'Oh, don't!' said Flo. She felt hurt and a touch dis-mayed, as if Mr Fritz was letting her down. Somehow, unreasonably, she'd considered herself the only woman he wanted in his life, though their relationship had always been strictly platonic.

'It's a pity he and Stella can't get divorced,' Bel remarked. It had taken her several years to get rid of Ivor. 'Still, I suppose the poor chap's got to dip his wick somewhere. I'm glad I'm a woman and not panting for it all the time.'

Mrs Winters lasted only two months. 'I couldn't stand the way she stuck her little finger out like a flagpole when she drank her tea,' Mr Fritz confessed to Flo. 'I felt I wanted to hang something on it.' He stared at her gloomily. 'What happened to your chap from the income-tax office?'

'I gave him up. We didn't have much in common.' All Ray Meadows had wanted to talk about was figures. Bel had tried to insist that Flo encourage him. 'He's dead keen, I can tell, and a good prospect. You're not getting any younger – you'll be thirty next year.' But Flo had decided, once and for all, that she would sooner remain single than marry a man she didn't love wholeheartedly. Books and the cinema provided all the romance and excitement she needed, especially as things usually ended happily. She enjoyed the quiet of her flat, buried half under the ground, drinking sherry, and feeling pleasantly cut off from the real world. Her only regret was that she no longer had a family. She missed the love that Mam and Dad had bestowed on her, and since Sally's son, Ian, had developed muscular dystrophy at the age of two, poor little lad, Flo saw her sister rarely now. Whenever she went to Huyton, Sal and Jock seemed so wrapped up in anxiety for their son that Flo felt in the way. Of course, there was always Martha, but if it hadn't been for her, Flo would have had a son of her own for the past nine years.

'I've been invited to the Isle of Man for the weekend in July,' Mr Fritz said, with the air of a man who'd been asked to attend his own funeral. 'Some of the chaps from the camp are having a reunion. Trouble is, they're taking their wives. I've no one to take.'

By now, half of the little Fritzes were in their twenties. The previous year Mr Fritz had been invited to Ben's wedding but had refused to go. 'I'd feel most peculiar,' he said, 'like a stranger at the feast.' A few weeks ago, he'd received a card to say Ben's wife had given birth to a son. He was a grandfather, which made him feel even more peculiar, and also very old, though he was only fifty.

'I'm sure not every chap will be bringing a wife,' Flo said briskly. 'You'll probably have quite a nice time.'

Over the next few weeks, he continued to raise the subject of the reunion, saying miserably, 'I hate the idea of going by myself.' Or, 'It wouldn't have to be a wife. It would be enough to take a friend.'

'If that's the case, why not ask Mrs Winters?' Flo suggested. 'It's only a few days, and you could put up with her little finger for that long, surely.'

'No, no,' he said, distractedly. 'There's someone else I'd far sooner go with.'

Two days before he was due to leave, he came down to the basement, where he sat, sighing continuously and staring moodily into the gas fire, which wasn't even lit. After half an hour of this, Flo said, 'Bel will be round in a minute. We're going to see *The Keys of the Kingdom* at the Odeon. She's mad about Gregory Peck.'

'Gregory Peck's got everything,' he said despondently. 'I bet he wouldn't be stuck for someone to take with him to the Isle of Man.'

Flo burst out laughing. 'If you carry on like this much longer, I'll offer to go with you meself.'

To her astonishment, he jumped to his feet and caught both her hands in his. 'Oh, *would* you, Flo? I've been wanting to ask for weeks.' His brown eyes were shining in a face that had suddenly come alive. 'We'll have separate rooms, of course we will. My intentions are strictly honourable. And we'll have a lovely time. Joe Loss and his orchestra are playing at the Villa Marina. I haven't been dancing in years.'

'But . . .' Flo began.

'But what, my dear girl?' he cried.

Everyone she knew, apart from Bel, would disapprove, despite the separate bedrooms and Bel would ask loads of embarrassing questions. Even so, perhaps it was the same lack of caution that had led her to accept Tommy O'Mara's invitation a decade ago, because all Flo said was, 'Oh, all right. But I don't want Bel and the women in the laundry to know. They'll only get the wrong idea.'

He put a finger to his lips. 'You can count on me not to breathe a word to a soul.'

★

Flo sat on the edge of the double bed and stared out of the hotel window at the choppy, green-brown waves of the Irish Sea. A large black and white ship with a red funnel was approaching Douglas, spewing white foam in its wake. It was the ship on which they would return to Liverpool.

The sky was overcast, the clouds leaden, as if about to unleash another downpour, and the pavements were still wet from the rain that had fallen all night long and the whole of the previous day. Holidaymakers wandered past forlornly in their plastic raincoats, some of the children carrying buckets and spades.

In the *en suite* bathroom, Mr Fritz could be heard humming as he shaved. At the initial gathering of the ex-internees, a man had shouted, 'Fritz Hofmannsthal, you old rascal! How are you?' and she'd been amazed when Mr Fritz went over and shook his hand.

'I didn't realise that was your name,' she whispered.

'I told you it was a mouthful,' he whispered back.

After proudly introducing her all round as 'My dear friend, Miss Florence Clancy,' Mr Fritz seemed to forget he was supposed to be at a reunion. That night, when they should have been at a special dinner, but were tangoing to 'Jealousy' in the Villa Marina, he said, 'Who wants to celebrate a miserable experience like that? It's the sort of thing I'd sooner forget.'

The first night she'd spent alone in the single bedroom he'd booked for her on the floor above. Yesterday, Sunday, they breakfasted together at a table by the window in the dining room with its cream and maroon striped Regency wallpaper. It was raining cats and dogs, and the sky was so dark that the red-shaded wall lamps had been switched on, making the large room cosy and intimate.

'This is nice,' said Mr Fritz. He touched her hand. 'This is lovely.'

They caught a taxi to Mass and back again, then read the newspapers and drank coffee in the hotel lounge until it was time for lunch. Afterwards, they battled their way through the wind and rain to an amusement arcade, then, in the afternoon, they went to the pictures to see *Notorious* with Cary Grant and Ingrid Bergman. 'I must confess,' Mr Fritz said at dinner, 'that I've always nursed a soft spot for Ingrid Bergman.'

They took their time over the meal and it was ten o'clock by the time the wine was finished. They transferred to the bar for a cocktail, and continued to talk about things of mutual interest: the laundry, the little Fritzes, Flo's family, the house in William Square.

It was an unremarkable few days, yet Flo had rarely enjoyed herself more. It was nice to be with someone she knew so much about. There were no awkward silences, no mad scrambling through her mind for what to say next. She'd known Mr Fritz for more than half her life and they were entirely comfortable with each other.

The clock was striking midnight when he offered to escort her upstairs to her room on the third floor. When they reached the second floor, he paused and looked grave. 'Flo, would you, could you . . .' He gestured along the corridor and stuttered, 'Would you consider doing me the honour of – of –'

After their lovely time together, Flo had anticipated that this might happen and was quite prepared. What harm would it do? None, she had decided. Furthermore, she had no intention of making herself out to be a shy virgin and pretending to be coy. If Stella had known she'd had a baby, then so must he. As he looked incapable of saying the words he wanted, she said them for him. 'Of sleeping with you tonight?'

He was an ardent, yet gentle lover. Flo experienced none of the passion there had been with Tommy O'Mara, but as she hadn't expected to she wasn't disappointed. When it was over, she felt cherished and satisfied. Afterwards they sat up in bed like an old married couple. 'We must do this again, Flo,' he said warmly. 'Perhaps next month, August.'

'I'd like that.' She laid her head affectionately on his shoulder.

'In that case, I'll book a double room in a different hotel, and we'll be Mr and Mrs Hofmannsthal.'

'But we'll still be Miss Clancy and Mr Fritz back in Liverpool?'

He looked at her quizzically. 'I think that would be wise, don't you? Friends at home, lovers in the Isle of Man. That way, you're less likely to tire of me. It can be our little monthly treat, our little adventure. You know,' he breathed happily, 'I've always been a tiny bit in love with you ever since the day you came to the laundry for an interview all those years ago.'

So Bel had been right, after all. Flo squeezed his arm. 'I've always been very fond of you.'

'Let's hope Stella didn't notice, eh?'

She couldn't be bothered telling him that Stella had, because it was too late to do anything about it.

'I suppose we should get some sleep,' he suggested. She slid under the covers and he bent and kissed her forehead. 'We have to be up early to catch the boat home.'

He had fallen asleep immediately, but Flo had lain wondering what she'd tell Bel when she went away again in four weeks' time. She wasn't sure why, but she preferred keeping her relationship with Mr Fritz a secret, even from her best friend. Right now, Bel thought she'd gone on retreat to a convent in Wales. I'll say I'm going on another one. It fits in with the image she's got of me. Let her go on thinking I'm as dull at ditchwater . . .

'The boat's just about to dock, Mr Fritz,' she called.

He came out of the bathroom smiling, a towel tucked under his chin, patting his cheeks. His kindly, good-natured face looked young this morning, almost boyish. 'I think we can dispense with the Mr, don't you, Flo?'

As she smiled back, she felt a surge of emotion, not real love but almost. 'I'd sooner not, if you don't mind. I'll always think of you as Mr Fritz.'

Millie

I

I'd been so engrossed in Flo's love letters that I'd for-gotten about the time. I'd be late for work if I didn't hurry. I dragged on the red suit and T-shirt I'd worn the day before, and combed my hair in the car when I stopped at traffic lights. The car behind hooted angrily as I was putting on my lipstick.

Halfway through the morning I answered the phone for the umpteenth time, doing my utmost not to sound as harassed as I felt.

'It's me,' James said humbly.

If I followed my instincts and slammed down the receiver, he would only ring back. 'What do you want?' I snapped.

'To see you, to apologise.'

'I'll take the apology for granted. There's no need for us to see each other.'

'Millie, darling, I don't know what came over me. Let's have dinner tonight. Let me explain.' He sounded desperate, but I hadn't forgotten that he'd raised his fist to strike me. I wasn't interested in explanations or apolo-gies. I could never forgive him.

'I'd sooner not.'

'Please, Millie.' He was almost sobbing. 'Please, dar-ling, I have to see you.'

'Look, James, I'm very busy. I don't like to be rude, but I'm going to ring off. Goodbye.'

An hour later, a van drew up outside the office and a girl came in with a bouquet of red roses for Miss Milli-cent Cameron; two dozen, surrounded by fern, wrapped in gold paper and tied with copious amounts of scarlet ribbon. There was no card, but only one person could have sent them. I thought them ostentatious, but Diana was impressed. I dumped the flowers on her desk. 'In that case, they're yours. Your father might like them.'

'But they must cost the earth!' Diana protested.

'I don't care. I don't want them.' I changed the subject. 'How's your father?'

Diana's face brightened. 'Much improved. We think he might be in remission. It happens sometimes with cancer. Yesterday I took him to Otterspool, and we had a picnic in the car. I can't think why we've never done things like that before.'

'My mother was talking about moving away from Liverpool, and I suddenly realised how much I'd miss her.' I'd never mentioned anything about my family to Diana before, and felt that I'd made the first gesture towards friendship.

We came to the conclusion that most children took their parents too much for granted, and agreed to lunch together if we could get away at the same time. Diana hissed, 'Is George still cross with me over those notes? I suppose I've blown my chances with that job I was after.'

'The job's Oliver's. It always was. As for the notes, I bet George has forgotten all about them.'

'God, I hope so.' Diana pursed her lips. 'I made a terrible cock-up there. I envy you, Millie. You never do anything to rock the boat. You're always so meek and pliable. Men prefer women they think they can control. George doesn't like me because I'm too independent.' It might have been unintentional, but there was a strong note of spite in her voice. She touched a rose. 'No one's ever sent me flowers like this.'

Whether she meant it or not, I still felt affronted. Meek and pliable? Me? I bent my head over my work, and decided to be too busy when Diana suggested it was time for lunch.

★

After work, I drove to Blundellsands to do some washing and take a shower. There was a message from James on the answering-machine, which I refused to listen to. I switched off the machine and rang my mother. 'Is everything okay, Mum?'

'Everything's fine, luv. Why?'

'It's just that my answering-machine's broken, I'll be out most nights this week and I didn't want you to worry.' Nor did I want a repeat of the Birmingham episode. During the week ahead, a minor crisis of one sort or another was bound to occur in the Cameron household and Mum would need someone to talk to. 'Call me at the office if something important crops up,' I told her.

'As long as it won't get you into trouble, luv.'

It wouldn't, I assured her. 'What will you be up to the nights you're out?' she asked.

I imagined telling the truth: that I would be sleeping with the grandson of the man who'd broken Flo Clancy's heart almost sixty years ago. I said, 'I thought it was time I put in a few more hours at Auntie Flo's. I'm getting nowhere at this rate.'

'I'm sorry you were landed with it, Millicent. I never thought it'd turn out to be such a mammoth task.'

'I'm quite enjoying it.'

'Gran said you'd met Bel Szerb.'

'Bel who?'

'Szerb. At least, that's how I knew her. I think she got married again. She was a dead scream, Bel was.'

'She still is.' After impressing on her that she must nag Declan to apply for a college course, I rang off. The washing had finished its cycle so I hung it over the bath, packed a bag and made my way to William Square and Tom O'Mara.

When I got out of the car, Peter Maxwell was going down the steps to his flat with several files under his arm. He wore jeans, a thick check shirt and a donkey jacket. He grinned at me through the railings. 'Hi! Fancy a coffee and a chocolate biccy?'

'I wouldn't mind.' His laid-back, easy-going manner was welcome after James's histrionics.

His flat was completely different from next door: red-tiled floor, red curtains and white walls hung with abstract paintings. It was a man's room. Apart from the paintings and a single white-shaded lamp, there were no other ornaments and the furniture was minimal, mainly of natural wood. Two armchairs were upholstered in black and white check. The effect was cool and airy, tranquil, giving the impression that the occupant was at peace with himself, which I envied.

'This isn't a bit like Flo's,' I remarked. Another difference was that everywhere was warm due to the two large radiators, one at each end of the room.

'I know. I'll just put the kettle on.' He took off his coat, hung it behind the door and disappeared into the kitchen. When he came back, he said, 'I used to see your auntie at least once a week. It was my job to get rid of the bottles.'

'What bottles?'

He grinned. 'The sherry bottles. She didn't want Charmian, the binmen and that aged but gorgeous red-head to know how much she was drinking. Flo was knocking back more than a bottle a day over the last year. She was a nice old girl, though. I liked her.'

'I only saw her once, at another great-aunt's funeral.'

'I wish I'd known you two were related. Flo would have been tickled pink to know we'd been in the same class at school.' He disappeared into the kitchen again, returning with two mugs of coffee and a packet of Jaffa cakes. 'I'm a lousy house-husband. I'm afraid my cupboards are bare. I hope you've eaten.'

'I keep forgetting to eat.'

He ran his fingers through his beard, which already looked like an untidy bird's nest, and said thoughtfully, 'I'm sure there's a tin of corned beef and a packet of instant spuds out there. I'll knock you up a plate of corned-beef hash if you like?'

'No thanks.' I shuddered. 'That's one of my mother's

favourite dishes. It would remind me too much of home.'

'I used to feel like that about *Coronation Street*,' he said. 'Me mam never missed a single episode, and the house had to be dead quiet. You daren't sneeze else you'd get a belt around the ear. For years afterwards if I passed a house and heard the music I got goosebumps.'

We stared at each other and laughed. 'Memories, eh!' he said wryly.

At the end of the room, I noticed there were french windows leading to the tiny yard.

'I had them put in last year.' He looked quite house-proud. 'It's nice to have them open in summer, brightens up the place no end. That's how I met Flo. We used to gab to each other over the garden wall.'

'Does that mean you actually own this flat? It's not rented?' I said, surprised.

'I own about a quarter, the building society has the rest.'

'I can't imagine anyone choosing to live round here if they didn't have to,' I said incredulously.

'How dare you criticise my place of abode, Miss Cameron?' he said mildly. 'I love Toxteth. I've been broken into twice, but that can happen anywhere. The people round here are the salt of the earth, including the girls who hang around the square. Okay, so it's violent, but otherwise it's a good place to live, steeped in atmosphere and history. This is the closest to how Liverpool was when it was the greatest port in the world. And did you know that, centuries ago, Toxteth was a royal park where King John used to hunt deer and wild boar?'

'I'm afraid that piece of information has been denied me until now.'

'If you like, I'll take you on a tour one day, show you precisely where his hunting lodges were situated.'

'I *would* like – it sounds fascinating.'

He looked chuffed. 'Then it's a date.'

I stayed for another cup of coffee before going next

door. A scantily clad Fiona was shivering against the railings. To my surprise, she deigned to speak. 'There's been someone looking for you. She said she'd come back another time. It wasn't Bel or Charmian. It was someone else.'

'Thanks for telling me.'

Fiona yawned. 'Any time.'

As usual the air in Flo's flat smelt damp, and it was freezing cold. I turned the fire on full blast and knelt before the hissing jets, shivering and rubbing my hands, thinking enviously of Peter Maxwell's central heating. When the heat became too much, I retreated to my favourite spot on the settee and promptly fell asleep. It was nearly midnight when I woke up and my legs were covered with red blotches from the fire. Everywhere was still and quiet outside and the flat felt as if it was in a time warp, engulfed in flickering shadows and divorced from anything real.

My life's becoming more and more surreal, I thought. I scarcely ate, slept at the most peculiar times, spent hardly any time at home, and had lost interest in my job, though I still worked hard and hoped George hadn't noticed. Worst of all, I was having an affair with a man who was the epitome of everything I normally loathed about men. Things that had once seemed important, no longer mattered.

I went into the bedroom and changed into a nightdress, Flo's quilted dressing-gown, and her pink slippers, then sprayed myself with perfume ready for Tom, who might arrive at any minute. Until he came, I'd sort out a few more of Flo's papers.

With a sense of anticipation usually reserved for the start of a film or a television programme I was looking forward to, I settled in front of the bureau. The first thing I picked up was a bundle of letters from Bel sent during the war. It didn't seem proper to read them so I put them to one side in case Bel would like them back.

Next, a large, very old brown envelope with 'Wythen-shaw's Photographic Studios – Portraits a Speciality' printed on the top left-hand corner. Predictably, it contained a photograph and, as I pulled it out, I wondered why Flo hadn't put it on the table with the others. It was a school photo: five rows of children, the smallest ones sitting cross-legged at the front. A boy at the end of the front row, the only child not smiling, had been circled with pencil.

What on earth was Flo doing with a photo of our Declan? I looked at the back, but there was only a stamped date, September 1945, a third of a century before Declan was born. There was something else inside the envelope, a piece of yellowing paper folded into four. It was a crude, crayon drawing of a woman with sticks for limbs, yellow hair and gooseberry green eyes. Her mouth was a huge upwards red curve, and she wore a blue dress shaped like a triangle with three buttons as big as Smarties down the front. Underneath was printed, in a careful, childish hand, 'MY FREND FLO'. There was a name at the bottom written in pencil: Hugh O'Mara.

Tom's father must have done the drawing I held in my hand. Despite the stick limbs and the mouth that stretched from ear to ear, there was something undeniably real and alive about the woman, as though the youthful artist had done his utmost to convey the inward radiance of his friend Flo. That both items had been together in the envelope meant that the child in the photograph was almost certainly Hugh O'Mara. I would have loved to have shown it to Tom, but Flo must have had a reason for keeping the photo hidden, and it seemed only right to respect it.

Tom had arrived – I could hear his light footsteps, and forgot about photographs, forgot about everything, as I waited for the sound of his key in the door. He came prowling in, a graceful, charismatic figure, despite the tasteless electric blue suit and white frilly shirt. No words were spoken as we stared at each other across the room. Then I got up and walked into his arms and we began to kiss each other hungrily. It was less than twenty-four hours since we'd parted, yet we kissed as if the gap had been much, much longer.

Another bouquet arrived at the office next morning, this time pink and white carnations. I found a vase and put them in the reception area. 'Diana's late.' June remarked. 'I thought she would have called by now.'

When she still hadn't arrived by midday, George approached me. 'Should I ring to see if she's all right? I'm still annoyed with her, but I suppose she's had it rough lately, and it wouldn't hurt to let her know we're concerned.'

'Would you like me to do it?'

'I was hoping you'd take the hint.' He looked relieved.

When I dialled Diana's home there was no reply. 'Perhaps her father's been taken to hospital again,' I suggested.

George had already lost interest. 'Can I buy you lunch?' He jingled the coins in his pocket. 'I'm desperately in need of a shoulder to cry on. I had a letter from Bill this morning. He and Annabel will stay with me over Christmas but, reading between the lines, I could tell they'd sooner not. They're only coming because their mother's off somewhere exotic with her new husband – his name's Crispin, would you believe?'

'I'm sorry, George, but I'm lunching with my sister, and I've an appointment at the Old Roan with the Naughtons at half past two. Perhaps tonight, after work?'

'You're on,' George said glumly, as he mooched into his office. 'I think I'm about to have a panic attack.'

Trudy had phoned earlier. 'Mum said you'd gone to William Square last night, but you weren't there when I called. That girl draped around the railings, is she what I suspect she is?'

I confirmed that she definitely was.

'Will you be there tonight if I come at the same time? I need to talk to someone and there's only you.'

'I'm not sure when I'll get away,' I said quickly. It was selfish, but I didn't want my sister in Flo's flat, which I regarded as my own property until the place was ready for another tenant – which seemed further away than ever. 'Are you free for lunch?' I enquired. 'My treat.'

'I thought you always worked through lunch?'

'I won't today,' I promised.

We met in Central Precinct under the high domed glass roof, where a woman was playing old familiar tunes on a white grand piano, her fingers rippling languorously up and down the keys. Trudy was already seated at a wrought-iron table, looking very smart in a dark green jacket, long black skirt and lace-up boots. We made a pretty pair, the Cameron sisters, I thought wryly: elegant, with our nice clothes, discreetly made-up faces, and lovely ash blonde hair. No one glancing at us would have guessed at our wretched childhood, though Trudy's face was rather pinched and tight, I thought.

'I've never been here before,' she said, when I sat down. 'I love the pianist.'

'Have you noticed what she's playing?' The strains of 'Moon River' came from the piano. 'Mum's favourite.'

Trudy's laugh was rather strained as she rubbed the scar above her left eyebrow. 'There's no escape, is there?'

When I returned from the counter with prawn salads and two giant cream cakes, she said, 'I've just been thinking about the way Mum used to sing it when us kids had been knocked black and blue, and Dad had probably had a go at her.'

'It was her way of coping, I suppose.' I ate several prawns with my fingers – it was my first proper meal since Sunday. 'What did you want to talk about, Sis?' I was reluctant to rush her, but I had to meet the Naughtons in an hour's time.

Trudy was shoving her food around the plate with her fork. 'I don't know where to begin,' she muttered.

255

'The beginning?'

'That's too far.'

I raised my eyebrows. 'I don't understand.'

My sister threw her fork on to the plate with a sigh. 'It's Colin,' she said.

A knot of fear formed in my stomach. 'What's he done?'

'Nothing,' Trudy said simply. 'He's a good, decent man. I love him, and he loves me, and he adores Melanie and Jake. He works all the hours God sends for us.'

'Then what's the problem, Trude?'

'I don't trust him.' Trudy put her elbows on the table and regarded me with abject misery.

'You mean you think he's having an affair?'

'Of course not. He wouldn't dream of it.' Trudy shook her head impatiently. 'It's nothing to do with affairs. It's to do with the children. Oh, Lord!' She dabbed her eyes with the paper napkin. 'I'm going to cry. Have I smudged my mascara?'

'A bit.' I reached out and rubbed under her eyes. A woman at the next table was watching with interest, but turned away when she saw I'd noticed.

'It's my painting, you see.' Trudy sighed. 'There must be two hundred bottles, jars, decanters and demijohns in the shed, all finished. I've painted light-bulbs, plates, tumblers, brandy glasses – we get them from car-boot sales. The children think it's great, looking for glassware for Mum to paint. And I love doing it, Millie. I get quite carried away, thinking up new ideas, new patterns, and I can't wait to see how they'll turn out. But what am I supposed to do with the damn things?' she said plain-tively.

'Sell them,' I said promptly. I still hadn't grasped what the problem was. 'Didn't Colin suggest you have a stall and he'll look after the kids?'

'Yes. But I don't trust him, Mill. I feel terrible about it, but I don't trust him with me children for an entire day. I'm scared he'll hit them, and if he did I'd have to leave.'

I was beginning to make sense of things. 'Has he ever done anything to make you think he would so much as lay a finger on them?' I asked.

'*No!*'

'In that case, don't you think you're being a bit paranoid?' I said. 'More than a bit, in fact. Over-the-top paranoid, if you ask me.'

'I know I am. But I still can't bring meself to leave them. Colin's nagging me soft to start a stall. There's a church hall in Walton where they have a craft fair every Sunday. He can't understand why I keep putting it off.'

'Neither can I. Our father wrecked our childhood, and now you're letting him wreck your marriage. You've got to trust Colin, Trude. You've *got* to.' Even as I spoke, I recalled James, his fist raised . . . 'I think all of us are capable of violence when the chips are down, but only a very perverted person would hit children the way our father hit us.'

Trudy gnawed her bottom lip. 'I must admit I've smacked Jake's bottom once or twice. He can be a little bugger when he's in the mood.'

'Was Colin there?'

'Yes. He was ever so cross and said I must never do it again.'

'But he didn't leave!' I cried. 'And knowing your history – that children who've been abused often abuse their own children – it's *him* who should be worried about leaving Melanie and Jake with *you*! Think how upset you'd be if you thought he suspected you'd hurt them! He's always trusted you, and he deserves your trust. Start the stall now in case he guesses why you're putting it off. He might never forgive you if he does.'

Trudy began to attack her salad. 'I'm glad I talked to you, Sis. I never looked at it like that before.' She paused, a forkful of prawns halfway to her mouth. 'I wonder if Dad was hit when he was little?'

'That's something we'll never know.'

★

I thought about it later on the way to the Old Roan. The only feelings I'd ever had for my father were fear as a child, and loathing as I grew older. But could there have been a reason for his behaviour? For the first time in my life, I wondered if a badly damaged human being could be lurking inside the monster I'd always known.

The Naughtons found the garden of the property in Old Roan much too big, and I drove back to work irritated by the waste of time.

When I went in, George announced 'Diana's father's dead. She called earlier. He passed away peacefully in his sleep during the night.'

'How did she sound?'

'As hard as nails,' George said indignantly. 'You'd think she was calling to say her car wouldn't start.'

'She's putting it on. I reckon she's devastated.'

'You're an exceedingly charitable person, Ms Millicent Cameron. Anyway, the funeral's Friday afternoon.' He drooped. 'I suppose I'd better put in an appearance, represent the firm, as it were.'

'Do you mind if I come with you?'

'Mind? Of course not. I've rarely had a more welcome offer.'

Later, I called my mother with the news – she was always ghoulishly interested in hearing about a death. 'How old was he?'

'A good eighty,' I replied. 'Diana's parents were middle-aged when she was born.' I decided to change the subject. 'I met our Trudy for lunch.'

'That's nice, luv,' Mum said. 'I like it when you two get together.'

'Perhaps the three of us could have lunch one day, you and me and Trude. You'd love the restaurant, Mum.'

'Oh, I dunno, luv,' she said, flustered. 'I'd never get back in time to do your dad's tea.'

I assured her she'd have bags of time and my father needn't know anything.

'I'll think about it,' she promised.

'You'll have to do more than think, Mum,' I said. 'I'm going to badger you rotten till you say yes.'

There was a pause. 'You sound happy, Millicent. Has something nice happened? Has James proposed?'

'James is history, Mum. Perhaps I'm happy because I've just had lunch with my sister.'

'Whatever it is, luv, I'm glad. You were getting very hard. Not long ago, you wouldn't have dreamed of asking your mam out to lunch. Now, what's all this about James being history?'

Apart from George and me, there were only five other mourners at the funeral: Diana, stiff and unemotional, two women neighbours, and two old men who'd been friends of Diana's father.

It was a bone-chilling November day and a wind flecked with ice blew through the cemetery, whisking in and out of the gravestones, stripping the last few leaves off the trees.

'I didn't think people got buried any more,' George muttered, through chattering teeth. 'I thought they popped 'em in an oven. At least it'd be warmer for the mourners.'

I watched the coffin being lowered into the grave, then the vicar said a few respectful words, and Diana came over and thanked us for coming. I took her hand as we walked towards the cars, George trailing behind.

'I'm sorry about your father. At least he didn't suffer much pain.'

'No, and as everyone keeps saying, he had a good innings.' Diana removed her hand. 'You get over these things. From now on, I'll be able to live my life as I please.'

'If you need someone to talk to,' I said gently, 'then don't hesitate to ring. If I'm not there, I'll be at number one William Square. There's no phone, so you'll just have to turn up.'

'Thank you, Millie, but I'm fine. I can't understand people who go to pieces when somebody dies.'

2

Church bells pealed, nearby and far away, high-pitched and rippling, deep-toned and sonorous. I opened my eyes: a cold sun shimmered through the white curtains, and Tom O'Mara was leaning over me. His brown hair was loose, framing his long face. If it hadn't been for the earrings and the tattoo, he would have resembled one of the saints in the pictures I'd taken down.

'I was just wondering,' he said, 'what is it between us two?'

'I don't know what you're talking about.'

'I mean, the truth is, you're an uppity bitch, full of airs and graces, and your accent gets on me wick.'

My lips quivered as I traced the outline of the heart on his chest. 'I've always steered clear of your sort, and the way you speak sets my teeth on edge.'

He pulled the bedclothes down to my waist and buried his head in my breasts. 'So, what is it between us two?' he asked again. His lips fastened on my left breast, and I squealed in delight when his tongue touched the nipple.

'I haven't a clue,' I gasped truthfully. The deep-down feeling of intimacy was frightening, because I couldn't visualise there ever being an end. The bells were still ringing as we made love, and it wasn't until it was over that I said, 'Why are you still here?' He'd usually gone before sunrise and Flo's alarm clock showed almost half past nine.

'Me wife's taken the girls to see her mam. I thought we'd spend the day together, or at least part of it. I've got to be at the club by five.'

I was thrilled at the notion of spending the day in bed with Tom O'Mara, but he had other ideas. 'C'mon, let's have summat to eat and we'll be off.'

'Off where?' I sat up and blew the hair out of my eyes. Tom was getting dressed.

'Southport.'

'Why Southport?'

'I'll tell you later, after we've had some grub.' He pulled on a blue polo-neck sweater, and went over to the mirror, where he combed his hair and scooped it back into a ponytail with an elastic band. I watched, entranced. It was such a feminine gesture coming from such an overwhelmingly masculine man. 'Me stomach thinks me throat's been cut,' he said. 'I'm starving.'

'There isn't any "grub", as you call it, except for a few old packets of biscuits.'

He groaned. 'In that case, I'll just have a cup of tea and we'll get something to eat on the way. The pubs'll be open by then.'

The sun was as bright as a lemon, and little white clouds were chasing each other across the pale blue sky. The wind was dry and crisp and very cold. I stuffed my hands in the pockets of my tan overcoat, glad that I was wearing boots – after the funeral yesterday I'd gone home for some warm clothes.

Tom's car, a silver-blue Mercedes, was parked round the corner, a suede coat on the back seat. I remarked that he was taking a risk, leaving an expensive coat in full view. 'Someone might steal it.'

'It would be more than their life was worth.' His lips curled. 'Everyone knows whose car this is. They wouldn't dare touch it.'

'You sound like a Mafia godfather!' The words were meant as an insult, but Tom's face was impassive as he replied, 'No one's going to rip me off and get away with it, and the same goes for me friends and family. That's why Flo was always safe in her place. People round here know what's good for them, and that means not mucking around with anything belonging to Tom O'Mara.'

'I see.' The ominous message that lay beyond his words was repellent, yet I didn't hesitate to get into the car with him. I felt very aware of his closeness, the way he held the steering wheel, his long brown hand touching the gear lever.

'What are you looking at?' he asked.

'You. I haven't seen you in daylight before.'

He slid a disc into the CD player and a man with a hard, angry voice began to sing 'The Wild Rover'. 'I love Irish music,' he said. Then he looked at me in a way that made me catch my breath. 'You look great in daylight.' He started up the engine and steered aggressively into the traffic. 'But you're doing me head in, girl. I wish I'd never met you.'

We stopped at a pub in Formby, the first customers of the day. Tom demolished a mixed grill, while I forced myself to eat a slice of toast. As soon as he'd finished, I poured us a second cup of coffee, and said, 'Now will you tell me why we're going to Southport?'

'I thought you'd like to meet me gran.'

I looked at him, startled. 'Your paternal grand-mother?'

'What the hell does that mean?' he almost snarled.

'Is it your father's mother?'

He banged the cup down on the saucer. 'Christ! You talk like a fuckin' encyclopaedia. It's me dad's mam, Nancy O'Mara, eighty-six years old, as fit as a fiddle, but completely gaga.'

The nursing-home was a large, detached house in a quiet road full of equally large houses, all set in spacious, well-tended grounds. The décor inside was subdued and expensive, the floors thickly carpeted in beige. The fees must have been horrendous, and I assumed it was Tom who paid.

The smiling woman in Reception toned perfectly with her surroundings: beige suit, beige shoes, beige hair. When she saw Tom, the smile became a simper. The barmaid in the pub had looked at him in the same way.

'How's me gran been?' he enquired abruptly.

262

'Just the same,' the woman gushed. 'Sometimes she seems very aware of what people say to her, but in the main she lives in a world of her own. We persuade her to do her exercises every day and she's in remarkably good shape for a woman of her age. She's in the garden, which is no place for an old lady on a day like today but there's no arguing with Nancy. We just wrap her up and let her go.'

Tom led the way through to the rear of the house where a door opened on to a vast lawn. On the far side, a woman was sitting ramrod stiff on a wooden bench. She looked tiny beneath the fir trees that towered over the garden on three sides, so thick that not even the faintest glimmer of sunlight could get through.

She watched our approach with interest, ebony eyes flashing brilliantly in her hawk-like, liver-spotted face. Snow-white hair, with streaks of black, was piled in a bun as big as a loaf at the nape of her stringy neck. She wore a crimson coat and fur-trimmed black boots. A black lace stole was draped around her shoulders.

'Have you come to read the meter?' she enquired, in a hoarse, deep voice, when Tom sat down beside her. He motioned to me to sit the other side.

'No, Gran. It's Tom, and I've brought a friend to see you. It's no good introducing you,' he whispered. 'She wouldn't take it in.'

'There's no need to introduce her,' Nancy said unexpectedly. 'I know who she is.' She fixed the glittering eyes in their dry brown sockets on me. 'Oh, yes! I know who she is.'

'Who am I, then?' I felt uncomfortable, slightly afraid, under the woman's piercing gaze.

Nancy cackled. 'That would be telling!' Her long face became fretful. 'The chap hasn't been to read the meter in ages. One of these days, they'll cut the 'leccy off.'

'Stop worrying about the meter, Gran. Everything's all right. It's all been seen to.' Tom's attitude to his grandmother was tolerantly offhand. He hadn't kissed her, and seemed to be there out of a sense of duty, rather than affection.

A woman in a grey cotton frock and a white apron was coming towards us with a tray of tea-things. Nancy grabbed it eagerly, apparently capable of pouring the tea, heaping sugar in all three cups. We were drinking it in silence when I noticed that one of her dangling jet earrings had caught in the stole. I leaned over to unhook it, but was shrugged away with a sharp, 'Don't touch me!'

I made a face at Tom. 'I don't think she likes me.' I was hoping we wouldn't stay long. The garden was a melancholy place, cheerless and dark, the only sound was the dew plopping from the trees on to the thick, wet grass. It was doubtful that the old woman appreciated visitors. I'd hoped to get from her a feeling of the past, of the woman who'd been married to Tommy O'Mara when he'd lost his life on the *Thetis* in 1939, but it was impossible to imagine Nancy being young.

Tom said, 'Gran's never liked anyone much. The only person she ever cared about was me dad.' He glanced at his watch. 'We'll go soon. I don't mind paying the bills, but visiting bores me rigid. I only come once a month to keep the nursing staff on their toes. I don't want them thinking they don't have to look after her proper.'

For the next quarter of an hour, I did my awkward best to engage Nancy in conversation. I admired her coat, asked who did her hair, remarked on the weather, enquired about the food. It was hard to make out whether the old woman was merely being cussed when she didn't answer, or genuinely didn't understand.

'You're wasting your time,' Tom said eventually. 'Sometimes she catches on if you talk about the things she used to know, like the war, or the shops in Smithdown Road.'

'I can't talk about either.' Of course there was the *Thetis*, but under the circumstances that mightn't be a good idea.

264

'C'mon let's go.' Tom squeezed Nancy's shoulder. 'Tara, Gran. See you next month.'

We were half-way across the lawn, when a hoarse voice called, 'Hey, you.' We turned to see her beckoning.

Tom gave me a little push. 'It's you she wants.'

'Are you sure? Why should she want me?' I went back reluctantly, and got a fright when a hand came out and grabbed me painfully by the arm, pulling me downwards until our faces were almost touching. I could smell the fetid breath. 'I know what you're up to, Flo Clancy,' she said, in a voice that sent shivers of ice down my spine. 'But it won't work. Your Martha gave him to me fair and square. He's mine. You'll not get him back, not ever. I've told you before, I'll kill him first.'

'She's making a hole for her own back,' said Bel.

'A rod,' corrected Charmian. 'She's making a rod for her own back, or she's digging herself into a hole. You've got your sayings mixed up.'

'Tch, tch!' Bel snorted loudly. 'She knows what I mean.'

'Would you mind not talking about me in the third person?' I said mildly. 'Furthermore, it's none of your business who I go out with. I can make a hole for my own back if I like.'

'Rod,' said Charmian

'Rod, hole, whatever.' I waved a dismissive hand. I supposed it was inevitable that Tom O'Mara's regular visits to the basement flat wouldn't go unnoticed. When he had dropped me off after we got back from Southport Bel had been watching from Charmian's window to witness my folly.

'Fiona said he'd been in and out, but I didn't believe her.' Bel made no secret of her disapproval. 'Young 'uns nowadays,' she said disgustedly, 'they hop in and out of bed with each other like rabbits. I've only slept with three men in me life, and I married 'em all first.'

'Yes, but times have changed, Bel,' Charmian reminded her. She gave me a wink as she refilled the glasses, though even Charmian looked worried. 'I hope you don't mind me saying this, Millie, but Tom O'Mara's got a terrible reputation. It's not just women but all sorts of other things – drugs, for one. I wouldn't go near that club of his. It worried me to death when our Jay invited him to his twenty-first. I don't think Flo could have known the things he was up to.'

As the evening wore on, my irritation with the pair diminished in proportion to how much I drank. By the time we'd finished a bottle of sherry and started on another, the last, I didn't give a damn what anybody thought. I lay on the rug in front of the fire staring up at the faces of my friends, feeling extraordinarily happy and without a care in the world. 'He's a scoundrel,' I agreed, 'a villain, a good-for-nothing rogue. But he's also drop-down-dead gorgeous.'

'What's happening with poor James?' Bel demanded.

I thought hard, but couldn't remember. Before I could say anything there was a knock at the door and I said, 'Perhaps that's him now.' I walked unsteadily to the door and for several seconds couldn't recognise either of the small, clearly distressed women standing outside.

'You said it was all right to come,' a familiar voice said.

'Of course.' I blinked, and the two women merged into one: Diana, a different Diana from the one I'd always known, with uncombed hair and no makeup, her face white and shrivelled, like melting wax. I asked her in, trying not to sound too drunkenly effusive, and introduced her to Bel and Charmian, adding, because it was obvious that she was in a terrible state. 'Diana's father died last week. He was only buried the day before yesterday.'

Bel, who was over-effusive even when she was sober, jumped to her feet and took the new arrival in her arms. 'You poor girl! Sit down, luv – here, have my place on the settee. Oh, I bet you're feeling dead awful. Charmian, fetch the girl summat to drink. Millie, plump that cushion up and stick it behind her.'

Diana burst into tears. 'I've felt so alone since he died. The house is like a morgue,' she cried. 'I wanted someone to talk to.'

She was eaten up with guilt and anxious to share it. The words came pouring out in a plaintive, childish voice, nothing like her usual terse, clipped tones.

She'd always blamed her father for the fact that she'd never married, she sobbed. 'He said he was sorry. He took the blame but it wasn't his fault at all. No one's ever asked me to marry them. I was using poor Daddy as an excuse for being single, for having to stay in night after night, when I only stayed in because I had nowhere else to go. I'm a total failure as a human being, and it's nobody's fault but my own.'

'Don't be silly, luv,' Bel soothed. 'You stayed with your dad, didn't you? That was very kind and unselfish.'

But Diana wailed, 'I think he wanted to be rid of me so he could have his friends round for bridge. When I came home from university, he offered to buy me a flat. I refused. I told myself it was my duty to stay but I was terrified of being on my own. Then I complained so much about his friends that he stopped asking them. It was me who ruined his life, not the other way round.'

'You're exaggerating,' I said, in what I hoped was a sober, sensible voice. 'I'm sure it wasn't as bad as that.'

'It was,' Diana insisted tearfully.

'In time, you'll see things more reasonably,' Charmian said gently. 'I felt dead guilty when me own mam died. I wished I'd been to see her more often, that I'd been a better daughter.'

Having exhausted the subject of her relationship with her father, Diana turned to her job. She was worried about losing it. George didn't like her, no one did. She'd never fitted in. 'Daddy's gone, and if my job goes, too, I think I'll kill myself.'

'George sometimes gives the impression of being an

ogre, but he wouldn't dream of firing you,' I assured her, adding, though I wasn't convinced that it was true, 'He regards you as an asset to the firm.'

At ten o'clock, Herbie came down to demand the return of his wife, and Charmian went reluctantly upstairs. Bel muttered that it was time she was making tracks.

'I suppose I'd better go, too,' Diana sighed, 'though I dread the thought of spending another night on my own.'

'Come home with me,' Bel said instantly. 'I've got a spare bedroom. I can make the bed up in a jiffy.'

'Can I? Oh, Bel! You're the nicest person I've ever known.' Diana threw her arms around Bel's neck and looked as if she might easily cry again.

Nancy had said, 'I know who she is. Oh, yes, I know who she is.' She had taken me for Flo. They must have known each other, all those years ago. Was Nancy aware that Flo had been in love with her husband? And what did she mean when she said, 'Your Martha gave him to me fair and square. You're not getting him back. I'll kill him first.'

It didn't make sense, but perhaps that wasn't surprising coming from an elderly woman who'd lost her mind. Even so, Nancy must have had a reason for saying it.

I took the newspaper cuttings describing the last days of the *Thetis* over to the bureau and placed them alongside the school photo with the child who looked so much like Declan. Beside the photo, I put Hugh O'Mara's drawing of 'MY FREND FLO'. I looked thoughtfully from the cuttings to the photo to the drawing, then back again. The *Thetis* had gone down in June 1939, the photo had been taken six years later and the little boy was in the bottom class, which meant he must have been five and born in 1940. 'Your Martha gave him to me fair and square.' Flo had left instructions that Gran wasn't to be invited to her funeral. What had she done to make Flo hate her so much?

'*Your Martha gave him to me fair and square.*'

I felt my heart begin to race as I peered closely at the face of the little boy. He was a Clancy, no doubt about it, the same pale hair, slim build, Declan's sensitive features.

Suddenly, everything fell into place. Tommy O'Mara had been the child's father, but his real mother had been Flo. Somehow, Gran had given the baby to Nancy, against Flo's wishes, or she wouldn't have wanted him back. 'I've told you before, I'll kill him first,' Nancy had said.

It meant that Tom O'Mara and I were distant cousins. Tom had the Clancys' green eyes.

Poor Flo! I glanced around the basement room, at its fussy ordinariness, the flowers, lace cloths, abundant ornaments. When I'd first come, it had seemed typical of a place where a pleasant, but rather dull, unmarried woman had lived out most of her life. But as I'd discovered more about Flo, the atmosphere in the room had changed. There was the Flo who'd received those passionate love letters during the war; the woman who'd stayed in the Isle of Man with a man with a foreign name. The flat no longer seemed ordinary, but touched with an aura of romance and a whiff of mystery. This was where a twenty-year-old Flo had come when she was already a mother, but a mother without a child. Now, tragedy was mingled with the romance.

Yet, despite everything, Flo might have been happy. I would never know.

There was a box of drawing-pins in the bureau. I shook some out and pinned the drawing to the wall over the mantelpiece. Flo might have wanted to put it there herself fifty years ago.

The following Tuesday was unusually quiet at Stock Masterton. George went out at midday and hadn't returned by six. Darren and Elliot took the opportunity to leave early, and shortly afterwards June went home. Only Oliver and I were left.

He stretched his arms and yawned. 'I suppose one of us had better stay till George comes back.'

'Where did he go?' I asked.

'He didn't say. He got a phone call and went rushing off.'

'I'll wait,' I offered. Oliver had a long journey home through the Mersey tunnel to a remote village on the Wirral.

'Thanks, Millie.' He gave me a warm, grateful smile. 'You're a chum.'

Oliver had only been gone a few minutes when the light on the switchboard flashed to indicate there was a call. I was astonished to discover an angry Bel at the other end of the line. 'Is that woman there?' she barked.

I assumed she meant Diana, who'd been staying with her since Sunday. 'No, she hasn't been in since her father died. I thought she was with you?'

'She was until this morning,' Bel said. 'She seemed much better when she got up. I went to get us a nice chicken for tea but when I got back she'd upped and gone. Not a word of thanks, no tara, nothing!' she finished, with a high-pitched flourish.

'Perhaps she's coming back,' I suggested. 'She's gone home to collect something.'

'In that case she should have left a note – and it doesn't take five hours to get to and from Hunts Cross.' A loud indignant snort echoed round the empty office. 'Honest, Millie, me ears are numb from listening to her go on and on about bloody Daddy. I'm an ould softheart, me, and I didn't mind a bit, but I'm dead annoyed to think she's just scarpered. She ate me out of house and home. Me freezer compartment's nearly empty!'

'I'm sorry, Bel. I don't know what to say.' If Diana had been there, I could have easily strangled her for treating Bel so rudely. 'Why not come round to Flo's tonight for dinner?' I offered in an attempt to soothe her feelings.

'It'll be a takeaway, mind, from that Chinese place round the corner.'

'Me favourite's sweet and sour pork, and I really go for those little pancakes with roots in.'

'By the way, I found a bundle of letters in the bureau from you to Flo. I thought you might like them to read.'

'No, ta, luv,' Bel said firmly. 'Flo offered them to me once, but I said no to her too. I'm happy now, but I was happier when I wrote them. I'd sooner not be reminded of the ould days. Just chuck 'em out. See you later, luv.'

It was nearly seven by the time George strode into the office. 'I'd like a word with you, Millie,' he snapped, as he passed my desk and went into his cubicle.

Somewhat bemused by his tone, I followed, and was even more bemused when he nodded towards a chair, 'Sit down.' It seemed very formal. People usually sat down without waiting for an invitation.

George placed his arms on the desk and clasped his hands together, his expression grave and accusing. 'I don't think much of the way you treated Diana when she came to you for help,' he said coldly.

I heard the creak of my dropping jaw. 'I haven't the faintest idea what you're talking about.'

'Apparently she called at William Square, as you had invited her to do, desperate for someone to talk to, urgently in need of a shoulder to cry on . . .'

'That's right.' My voice shook. I was at a loss to understand what was wrong.

'But instead of help,' George went on, 'all she found was you and two other women all pissed out of your minds. Not only that, you quickly got her in the same drunken state as yourselves. Even worse, the poor girl was virtually kidnapped by a ghastly old woman who wouldn't let her go. She's been stuck in this woman's dismal little house for days. She rang just before lunch and I was forced to go and rescue her. I found her shaking, crying, and in a terrible state.'

I burst out laughing. 'Rescue her! Don't be so bloody

stupid, George. Bel's anything but ghastly. In fact, Diana said she was the nicest person she'd ever met. Also, she's about seventy-five – a bit old to kidnap someone less than half her age, wouldn't you say?' It wasn't worth adding that although I'd never been in Bel's house I imagined it would be anything but dismal.

But George's face grew colder, if that was possible, and he said, 'I've never pulled rank, Millie. I've always treated my employees as equals, friends. I do, however, own this firm, and take exception to being called stupid by someone whose wages I pay.'

But he *was* being stupid! Diana had fooled him completely, putting on an act so outrageous that I marvelled at her nerve. I said nothing, just sat there, stunned, contemplating her treachery. She'd used us – me, Bel, Charmian – to rid herself of the guilt she'd felt over her father's death. Then she'd probably felt ashamed of having told so much and turned against us, possibly worried I'd tell George or the others in the office the things she'd said when she bared her soul.

'Oh, and another thing, Millie, I'd prefer it if you didn't refer to me in public as an ogre.'

'But I didn't . . .' I began, then remembered that I had. 'I didn't mean it in an offensive way.' I wanted to explain why I'd used the word, but it would probably be a waste of time at the moment. Just now George's mind was made up. It would be sensible to wait until he was able to see sense again, then put him right. 'Where is Diana now?' I asked.

'My place,' he said briefly. 'The poor girl's still very tearful. She's been through a lot lately. Her father dying was bad enough, but you and your friends only made it worse.'

'That's not fair, George,' I felt bound to say. 'If you think about it hard enough, you'll know it's not fair. Diana's having you on.'

For the first time, he looked straight at me and there was a trace of comprehension in his eyes. Then he blinked furiously and said, 'I'd better be getting back. I've promised to take her out to dinner.'

He strode out of the office, a knight on a white charger returning to his damsel in distress. I understood what had happened. His wife and children no longer needed him, his mother was dead, he was a man with no call on his emotions. Diana had got through to the part of him that longed for someone to cherish and protect.

When I sat down at my desk my legs were shaking, my mind a whirl. It was all so unreasonable, so unjust. I picked up the telephone, badly in need of someone sympathetic to talk to. Colin answered when I called Trudy and said she was out. 'She's taken Melanie and Jake to see *101 Dalmatians*. By the way, her bottle stall will be up and running on Sunday. She was going to call you.'

'I'll be there,' I promised.

Then I rang Mum. I couldn't explain what had happened, it would only upset her, but at least she would be a friendly voice. To my dismay, when the receiver at the other end was picked up my father reeled off the number. He always sounded mild, rather genial, on the telephone and it was hard to connect the pleasant voice with the man I knew. I didn't waste time with small talk. 'Is Mum there?'

'She's in bed with a touch of flu.'

'Oh!' I was temporarily flummoxed. 'Oh, well, give her my love and say I'll come and see her tomorrow after work. I'd come tonight, but I've promised to meet someone at Flo's.'

'All right, luv. How's things with you?'

'Fine,' I said brusquely. ' 'Bye.'

Bel would be only too willing to provide sympathy in buckets, though I wouldn't mention anything about kidnapping, or she was quite likely to burst a blood vessel.

273

'It's only me, Mum,' I called, as I ran upstairs. I found her propped up against a heap of pillows looking sleepy, but pleased with herself.

'Hello, Millicent.' She smiled when I went in and planted a kiss on her plump, pasty cheek. 'I'm all on me own. Your dad's gone to the pub and Declan's round at a mate's house.'

'How do you feel? I've been worried about you all day.' Halfway through the morning, I had wondered suddenly if flu was the real reason for her being in bed. Maybe my father had been up to his old tricks again.

'There's no need to worry, luv.' The contented smile was still there, enough to convince me that my suspicions were unwarranted. 'I'm really enjoying lying here and being waited on. Our Declan's been looking after me, and Trudy came this afternoon with some grapes. Now you've brought a lovely bunch of carnations, me favourite.' She buried her nose in them. 'They smell dead gorgeous. It's nice to know me children care about their mam. I even got a get-well card from Alison, though I don't suppose it was her idea to send it. I had to ring up on Sunday and say I couldn't go. The bug had already caught up with me by then, and I didn't feel up to the drive.'

'You should have rung, Mum. I would have come before.'

'I didn't want to bother you, Millicent. I know you're always busy.'

'Oh, Mum!' I stroked her brow, which felt rather hot. 'You've got a temperature,' I said, with a frown

'The doctor's given me some tablets. Look what the women in the shop sent.' She pointed to a little wicker basket of dried flowers on the bedside table next to Alison's card. She seemed far less bothered about being ill than that everybody had been so kind. 'Mrs Bradley from next door keeps bringing bowls of home-made soup. The potato's nice and tasty, but Declan ate the onion.' She giggled girlishly. 'I might be sick more often if this is the sort of treatment I can expect. Your dad's even brought a cup of tea up twice. I think he's a reformed character.'

'Don't bank on it, Mum.'

'I won't, luv. Look!' She patted her stomach. 'I've lost weight. This nightie would hardly go round me before but now it's dead loose. I used to be slim as a girl, just like you.'

'I know. Your wedding photo's downstairs.'

'That's right. I'd like to be slim again by the time I move to Oxford.' She giggled again. 'Start a new life with a new figure.'

I stared at her anxiously. Her expression was as innocent as a baby's. She'd lived under the iron hand of her husband for thirty years and had no idea how to cope with the world outside – how to deal with landlords other than the council, for instance, and the social-security people could easily convince her she wasn't entitled to a penny. 'Are you still set on that idea, Mum?'

'Oh, yes, luv.' She smiled radiantly. 'I'm looking forward to it, not just seeing our Alison more often but living on me own. I thought I might go back to nursing. They say the National Health Service is understaffed.'

'Nursing!' I gasped. 'I never knew you'd been a nurse.'

'I was halfway through training to become state registered when I married your dad.' She sighed. 'I was sorry to give it up.'

'You should have finished your training, then got married,' I said indignantly.

'Life doesn't always go the way you want it, Millicent.'

'I suppose not.'

There was a noise downstairs. 'Jaysus!' she gasped, terrified. 'I hope that's not your dad back! I hope he hasn't heard.'

But it was only Scotty, bored with being left alone and

looking for company. He came bouncing up the stairs and leaped on to the bed, settling himself comfortably between Mum's legs. He pushed his nose between her knees and looked at her adoringly.

'How's Flo's place coming along?'

'I'm nearly there,' I lied.

Mum laughed. 'Oh, come off it, luv. I don't know what you're up to but I've been to Flo's, remember? You can't kid me it takes six or seven weeks to sort out a one-bedroom flat.'

'Oh, Mum!' I slipped off my shoes and sat in my father's place on the bed. It was time I told her the truth. I took my mother's white hand, threaded with startling blue veins. 'I love it there, and I'm having a great time. I've met all sorts of interesting people. You already know Bel, then there's Charmian and Herbie upstairs, a young man next door who comes from Kirkby and was in my class at school, and . . . well, this other guy who knew Flo.'

'Bel used to be very glamorous.'

'She still is.'

'So you haven't done a thing,' Mum said, smiling.

'We've drunk all Flo's sherry and I've cleared out her bureau – well, almost. Otherwise, the place is no different from the first day I went.'

'Have you been paying the rent?'

'No, Mum.' I'd remembered to ask Charmian when the rent collector called. He came monthly, she said, and had been twice since Flo died but had never mentioned the basement flat. Next time he came Charmian had promised to ask about it. 'Flo must have paid several months in advance,' I told Mum. 'So far, I haven't come across a rent book.'

'I'd love to see the place again,' she said wistfully. 'See if it's changed much.'

'Come next week, Mum.' I couldn't keep the flat to myself for ever. 'Come one evening when I can show you round. The weekend would be even better. There's a takeaway round the corner. I'll buy more sherry and we can have a feast. Bel would love to meet you again, and you'll like Charmian.'

Mum squeezed my hand. 'I'll come as soon as I'm better. Now, I'm in a lovely hazy daze, all them tablets. I hope you won't mind if I go to sleep in front of you.'

'I'll make myself a cup of tea when you do.'

We talked in a desultory way about Declan: he'd had a form from a college, had filled it in and sent it off. Wasn't it smashing Trudy having her own stall? 'I hope I'm well enough to go by Sunday,' Mum said sleepily.

When her head began to droop I released her hand. I stayed where I was for a while, glancing round the dismal room. Years ago, Mum had painted all the furniture cream to make it look like a matching set, but she hadn't rubbed the varnish off underneath and the paint had started to peel. Perhaps she'd like that lovely stuff in Flo's bedroom, which I coveted – except that she was moving to Oxford. Where on earth did she get the courage from even to think of changing the course of her life at fifty-five? I sighed, got off the bed, adjusted the pillows and drew the bedclothes up to her shoulders. There was no heating upstairs and the air smelt cold. Scotty, also asleep by now and snoring gently, gave a little grunt when the eiderdown beneath him was disturbed.

Downstairs, I put the kettle on and stood watching until it boiled. It felt strange being in this house, danger free, able to do anything I wanted. Yet I still felt on edge, scared I might break something or put something down in the wrong place. I poured the water into the pot, stirred it to make the tea strong, then took a cup into the lounge. The fire was dying, the hearth full of ash. I threw on a few more coals and watched them slowly catch alight. On the right-hand side of the fireplace an owl made out of string was hanging from a nail that protruded crookedly from the wall. Dad's best belt had hung there once, the one he wore on Sundays: black leather, two inches wide, the heavy brass buckle with a deadly sharp prong. I touched the owl gingerly: such an innocuous thing to put in its place.

The back door opened and my father came in. I was still fingering the owl. 'This is where you used to keep your belt,' I reminded him.

His face flushed a deep, ugly scarlet, but he didn't speak. How did he feel, I wondered, now that his children had grown up and we could see him for what he was? Was he ashamed? Uncomfortable? Embarrassed? Or perhaps he didn't give a damn.

I looked at him, properly for once, and tried to relate the handsome, shambling, probably drunken figure to the photo of the bright-eyed baby at Flo's, but it was inconceivable to think that they were the same person. My gaze returned to the owl. 'You nearly blinded our Trudy with that belt.'

He'd been lashing out at Trudy, the skirt of her gymslip scrunched in a ball in his hand. When she tried to get away, he dragged her back so violently by the collar of her school blouse, that she'd choked and lost consciousness. He probably hadn't meant the buckle to hit her forehead, narrowly missing her eye, but Trudy had been left with a permanent reminder of the incident every time she glanced in the mirror.

My father looked at me, bleary-eyed and bewildered. He still didn't speak.

'Mum's asleep,' I said. 'Tell her goodbye from me.'

He spoke at last. 'Did she seem all right to you? I've been worried. She's had a terrible temperature.' His voice was gruff and querulous.

'I think she'll live.' Could it be that he actually *loved* my mother? That he loved us all? I took my cup into the back kitchen and washed it, then left by the back door without saying another word.

Mrs Bradley was leaning on next door's gate talking to another woman. 'How's your mam, luv?' she asked. She was smartly dressed in a sequinned frock and the gigantic fur coat that she wore when she went ballroom dancing with Mr Bradley.

'She seems much better.'

'That's good,' Mrs Bradley said comfortably. 'I was just saying to Norma here how much better everywhere looks without that wreck of a car littering the place.'

Not only had the burnt out car gone, but the boarded up house was occupied. There were lace curtains in the windows and a television was on in the lounge.

'We got a petition up and sent it to the Council, didn't we, Norma?' Norma nodded agreement. 'What right have some folks got, spoiling the street for the rest of us? It's a respectable place, Kirkby. I remember us moving from Scotland Road in nineteen fifty-eight. It was like a palace after our little two-up, two-down. Will was tickled pink to have a garden.'

I went over to my car, unlocked the door and paused for a moment. Mrs Bradley and Norma were still talking. Mr Bradley came out, a thick car coat over his old-fashioned evening suit. He waved and I waved back.

Still I waited by the car, the door half-open. For the first time, I noticed the pretty gardens. Some of the original front doors had been replaced with more ornate designs, heavily panelled with lots of brassware. There were coachlamps outside several houses. It dawned on me that there was nothing wrong with Kirkby! It was all in my head, all to do with my childhood, my father, school. I'd centred my loathing on the place when it was my life that was wrong!

'What's up with George?' June demanded, for the umpteenth time. 'He's been like a bear with a sore head this week.'

Elliot swung his well-shod feet on to the desk. 'Perhaps he's going through the male menopause.'

'I reckon he's missing Diana.' Darren grinned.

Everyone except me hooted with derision, and Oliver

said miserably, 'She'll be back on Monday, spreading her usual discord and as moody as hell.'

'Actually,' June hissed, 'I didn't say anything before in case I was hearing things, but Diana rang George this morning and when I put her through I could have sworn he called her darling.'

There was a gasp of disbelief.

'Never!'

'I don't believe it!'

'You must have been hearing things, June.'

It figures, I thought. She's managed to wrap him round her little finger. I was glad no one seemed to have noticed that it was me, more than anyone, on whom George vented his bad temper. One day, I'd tried to explain that I'd done nothing wrong, but he was only interested in Diana's version of the story.

What on earth would it be like when she returned? Awful, I decided. She'd be lording it over everyone, particularly me. I wondered if I should look for another job, but my only qualification was a single A level, along with the time spent working at Stock Masterton. Would another estate agent take me on with such a paltry record? I tried to tell myself that it didn't matter, but in my heart of hearts I knew it did. The time I spent at Flo's, the nights with Tom O'Mara, were bound to end sometime, and I'd have to live in the real world again, where my job mattered very much. I had a mortgage, I had to eat. And if I left this job, I'd have to return the car.

Taking advantage of George's absence, Darren and Elliot went home early, followed shortly by June. I suggested that Oliver make himself scarce and I would stay until six in case there were any phone calls: the office closed an hour earlier on Saturday. Oliver accepted the offer thankfully. 'We're in the middle of decorating. I'd like to get it done by Christmas.'

The door had hardly closed when it opened again. I looked up, thinking Oliver had forgotten something.

'I've been waiting across the road for everyone to go,' said James. 'I was praying you'd be the last.'

Over the past few weeks I had almost forgotten James's existence, and was surprised at how glad I was to see the tall, familiar figure; so glad that, for the moment, I put to the back of my mind what had happened the last time we met. He wore a new suit, grey flannel, and a pale blue shirt, and was leaning against the door regarding me shyly.

'Hi,' I said.

'Phew!' He put his hand on his chest in a gesture of relief. 'I was expecting to have something thrown at me – a computer, a telephone, a notebook, at least.' He came down the room and perched on the edge of Diana's desk. 'How's life?'

'Ninety per cent fine, ten per cent lousy.'

'Tell me about the lousy ten per cent.'

I'd always been able to talk to him about humdrum, day-to-day matters. We spent ages discussing the meaning of a film we'd just seen, what frock I should wear to a party, his job, mine. It would have been a waste of time trying to talk to Tom O'Mara about office politics or Mum being ill, Trudy having a bottle stall or Declan going to college. Perhaps that was why I was so pleased to see James – not as a lover but as a friend.

I told him all about the week's events, and about Diana's treachery. 'Now George is really cross with me and I think I've blown my job.'

'But that's totally unfair!' James expostulated angrily.

It was comforting to hear Diana being called a conniving bitch and that George was a fool to let himself be taken in. I felt better after listening to James's loudly expressed indignation and didn't demur when he offered to buy me dinner.

'Shall we go to the wine bar where we first met?'

'I'd prefer to try that new place by the Cavern.' I didn't want to go somewhere that evoked old memories in case he got the idea that everything was back to normal, which it wasn't. 'I'll just ring home, make sure my mother's all right.'

Declan answered and assured me that mum was fine.

'Say hello to Declan for me.' James mouthed.

'James says hello, Declan.'

'I thought mam said James was history?'

I laughed. 'Bye, love.' I took a mirror out of my handbag, powdered my nose, combed my hair, re-touched my lipstick. When I looked up James was watching me with an expression on his rugged face that I remembered well. Our eyes met, he shook his head slightly, as if remonstrating with himself, then turned away. 'I'm sorry,' he said. 'I'm doing my best not to put a foot wrong. I promise not to say a word out of place until the time feels right.'

I began to regret accepting the dinner invitation be-cause I knew I would never feel the same about James after what had happened, but I hadn't the heart to change my mind when he was being so nice.

The restaurant was filled with memorabilia of the Beatles' era. We ordered salad, baked potatoes and a bottle of wine. While we waited, I asked, 'How's the Socialist Workers' Party?'

He looked faintly embarrassed. 'I never went back – it's not really my scene. They were a decent crowd, but I only joined to please you.'

'To please me! I can't remember ever expressing left-wing opinions,' I exclaimed. 'I'm totally uninterested in politics.'

'So am I, though those dockers got a raw deal and I'm on their side. No, I joined because I got the impression you thought I was shallow. I was trying to prove I had some depth.' He glanced at me curiously. 'Did I suc-ceed?'

'I don't know.' I shrugged. 'I never thought about it much.'

'I doubt if you ever thought about me much,' he said drily.

'You promised not to say things like that,' I admonished.

'I'm not criticising,' he assured me. 'I'm trying to be coolly matter-of-fact. I pressurised you too much. I fell in love with you, deeply, passionately, wholeheartedly, and expected you to love me back in exactly the same way at exactly the same time. I wasn't prepared to wait. I wouldn't let you breathe.' He made a face. 'I'm used to getting everything I want, you see.'

'Including girls throwing themselves at you since you were fifteen!' I reminded him.

'Aw, shit, Millie.' He cringed. 'I'd had too much to drink, and I'd been waiting all week for you to call. I couldn't believe it was over between us.'

I played with my food. 'You nearly hit me, James. You would have, if Tom hadn't appeared.'

His face flickered with pain. 'So that's his name.' He leaned across the table, put his hand on mine, then hastily removed it. 'I would never, never have hit you, darling.'

There, in such civilised surroundings, it was easy to believe that he was a decent, honourable man who'd been driven over the edge. If I could feel about him as he did about me, everything would be perfect. He began to eat, but only because the food was there. 'This Tom,' he said, in a strained voice, 'are you in love with him?'

'No.'

'Is he with you?'

'No.'

'Who is he? How did you meet?'

'He was a friend of Flo's.' I smiled. 'She had an affair with his grandfather.'

'So, history is repeating itself.'

'Something like that.' I sipped the wine, which seemed preferable to the food. 'Look, can we change the subject?' I felt uncomfortable discussing my current lover with my old one.

'Perhaps that wouldn't be a bad idea.' James sighed.

'I'm trying valiantly to be grown-up but I think I'm about to explode with jealousy.'

We left the restaurant, the meal hardly touched but the wine finished, and strolled down Water Street towards the Pier Head. After a while, I linked James's arm. 'I'd like us always to be friends,' I said.

'Only a woman would ask a man who was crazy about her to be her friend,' he said with a dry chuckle.

'What would a man do in the same situation?' I asked.

'Run a mile, change his phone number, move house if necessary. If some woman had been chasing me as vigilantly as I was chasing you, I would have done all three in order to get away. You were very patient, Millie.'

The nearer we got to the river, the colder and more sharply the November wind blew. With my free hand, I tried to turn up the collar of my coat. James stopped, released my arm, and did it for me. 'I was with you when you bought this coat. You couldn't make up your mind whether to buy this colour or black. I said I preferred black, so you bought the other.' Still holding the collar by its corners, he said softly, 'Is that really all that's left for us, Millie, to be friends?'

'James . . .'

He released my collar and tucked my arm back in his. 'Okay, friends it is. Am I allowed to ask if I can see you again within the relatively near future?'

'Perhaps one night next week?'

We dodged through the traffic towards the Pier Head, where we propped our arms on the rail and stared at the lights of Birkenhead, reflected, dazzling, misshapen blobs, in the choppy waters of the Mersey.

'You know,' James said softly, 'we see movies about great love affairs that make us conventional folk seem very run-of-the-mill. We never imagine ourselves having the same passionate feelings as the characters on the screen, yet over the last few weeks, no one could have felt more gutted than I have. I was convinced I'd rather die if I couldn't have you.'

I said nothing, but shuddered as the wind gusted up my skirt.

James stared intently at the lights, as if the words he wanted to say were written there, prompting him. 'I wished I were a philosopher, who could cope with things more . . .' he grinned, '. . . more philosophically. Or a spiritual person, who would look at it with an intellectual sort of fatalism. But I don't go to church, I'm not even sure if I believe in God.'

'Did you come to a conclusion?' I asked gently.

'Yes – that I didn't want to die after all. That life goes on, whatever horrendous things might happen.' He grinned again. 'And that I still love you as much as I ever did, but less frenetically. Even so,' he finished, on a mock-cheerful note, 'I could easily throttle this Tom character.'

It had started to rain, so we walked back quickly to where my car was parked. On the way, he asked what was wrong with my mother.

'Flu. She's almost better.'

'I was always kept well hidden from your family. I only met Declan by accident. Were you ashamed of me or something?'

'Of course not, silly. It's them I was –' I stopped. All of a sudden I didn't care if he knew every single thing there was to know about me. 'Actually, James, my sister's having a stall at a craft market tomorrow. Perhaps you'd like to come if you're free.'

I was back at Flo's, going through the remainder of her papers. For the first time, I felt the urge to hurry things along, to finish with the bureau, get started on the rest of the flat. I emptied out the contents of a large brown envelope. Guarantees, all of which had run out, for a variety of electrical goods. I stuffed them back into the envelope and threw it on the floor. The next item was a plastic folder containing bank statements. I leafed through them, hoping they would give a clue to how the rent was paid. If Flo had set up a standing order, it would explain why the collector hadn't called, and also why there'd been little in the post – no electricity or gas bills, no demand for council tax. I admonished myself for being so negligent. I should have done this long ago, got in touch with the bank, sorted out Flo's financial affairs.

To my surprise, the account was a business one, begun in 1976 according to the first statement. The current balance was – my eyes widened – *twenty-three thousand, seven hundred and fifty pounds, and elevenpence*.

'Flo Clancy!' I gasped. 'What the hell have you been up to?'

I grabbed the next envelope in the rapidly diminishing pile. It was long and narrow and bore the name of a solicitor in Castle Street, a few doors along from Stock Masterton. My hands were shaking as I pulled out the thick sheets of cream paper folded inside, the pages tied together with bright pink tape. It was a Deed of Property, dated March 1965, written in complicated legal jargon that was hard to understand. I had to read the first paragraph three times before it made sense.

Fritz Erik Hofmannsthal hereinafter referred to as the party of the first part of Number One William Square Liverpool hereby transfers the leasehold of the section of Number One William Square hitherto known as the basement to Miss Florence Clancy hereinafter referred to as the party of the second part currently resident in the section of the property which is to be transferred for a period of one hundred years . . .

No wonder no one had called to collect the rent! Flo owned the leasehold of the flat in which she'd spent most of her life. My brain worked overtime. Fritz Erik Hofmannsthal! It was Fritz's laundry where Flo had worked; Mr and Mrs Hofmannsthal had spent a weekend on the Isle of Man every month for over twenty years.

'Oh, Flo!' I whispered. I went over and picked up the snapshot taken outside the laundry nearly sixty years before; Flo, with her wondrous smile, Mr Fritz's arm around her slim waist.

I had no idea why I should want to cry, but I was finding it hard to hold back the tears. I felt as if I knew everything there was to know about Flo Clancy: the lover lost on the *Thetis*, the baby who had gone to another woman, the servicemen she'd made love to in this very flat. Now Mr Fritz . . .

Yet the more I knew, the more mysterious Flo became. I wanted to get under her skin, know how she felt about all the tragedies and romances in her life, but it was too late, far too late. Not even Bel knew the things that I did about her lifelong friend. I'm glad it was me who went through her papers, I thought. I'll never tell another soul about all this.

Of course, I'd have to tell someone about the money and the property. It dawned on me that, under the circumstances, Flo would almost certainly have made a will.

Curious, I was about to go back to the bureau, when the front door opened and Tom O'Mara came in, his face, as usual, sombre and unsmiling, and looking like a dark, sinister angel in a long black mac.

I caught my breath, and half lifted my arms towards him as he stood staring at me from just inside the door. 'I'm neglecting the club because of you,' he said accusingly, 'neglecting me family. You're on me mind every minute of every day.' He removed his coat and threw it on the settee. 'You're driving me fucking crazy.'

'I'll be finished here soon, then I'll be back in Blundellsands. You won't want to come all that way to see me.'

'I'd come the length of the country to be with you.'

I wanted him to stop talking, to take me in his arms so that we could make love. I forgot about James, about Flo, Stock Masterton. All I wanted, more than anything on earth, was for Tom O'Mara to bury himself inside me.

Tom shook himself, gracefully, like a cat. 'I think I'm in love with you, but I don't want to be.' He wiped his wet brow with his hand. 'I feel as if I'm under a spell. I want to keep away from you, but I can't.'

'I know,' I murmured. I didn't like him, I couldn't talk to him, he was hard, unsympathetic, a crook. But I felt drawn to him as I'd been drawn to no man before.

We made love in a frenzy, without tenderness, but with a passion that left us both speechless and exhausted. When I woke up next morning, Tom was still asleep, his arm around my waist. I wanted to slip away, escape, because I was frightened. Instead, I turned over and stroked his face. His green eyes opened and stared into mine and he began to touch me. We were locked into each other. There was no escape.

Flo

I

1962

Sally and Jock's son, Ian, died as he had lived; quietly and bravely and without a fuss. He was sixteen. The funeral took place on a suffocatingly hot day in July and the crematorium chapel was packed. The mourners stood and knelt when they were told, their movements slow and lethargic, a sheen of perspiration on their faces, their clothes damp. There were flowers everywhere, their scent sweet and sickly, overpowering.

Flo was at the back, fanning herself with a hymn book. She hated funerals, but who in their right mind didn't? The last one she'd been to was for Joanna and Jennifer Holbrook. Joanna had passed away peacefully in her sleep, and the following night her sister had joined her. But at least the twins had managed more than four score years on this earth, whereas Ian . . . She averted her eyes from the coffin with its crucifix of red and white roses. The coffin was tiny, because he'd grown no bigger than a ten-year-old and every time she looked at it she wanted to burst into tears.

She wished she'd asked Mr Fritz or Bel to come with her. She knew hardly anyone except Sally and Jock. Grace, their daughter, was a cold, aloof girl, who'd always resented the care and attention bestowed upon her invalid brother. She was in the front pew next to her dad, looking bored and not the least upset. She wasn't even wearing dark clothes, but a pink summer frock with a drawstring neck.

The woman on Grace's other side, who was kneeling,

her head buried in her hands, must be melting in that black, long-sleeved woollen frock, she thought. Then the woman lifted her head and whispered something to the girl.

Martha.

Oh, Lord! She looked like an ould woman, her face all wizened and sour. She might well have achieved the coveted title of Mrs before her name and a lovely daughter but, if her expression was anything to go by, it had done nothing to make her happy. Or the nice new flat in Kirkby that she'd moved into a few years ago when Elsa Cameron had stuck her head in the gas oven and ended her tragic life. Perhaps happiness was in the soul, part of you, and it didn't matter what events took place outside. Some people, Martha was one, were born to be miserable.

'I'm happy,' Flo told herself. 'At least on the surface. I make the best of things. I'm happy with Mr Fritz, and me and Bel still have a dead good time, even though we're both gone forty – but I don't half wish we were twenty years younger. I'd love to go to the Cavern, I really would, and see them Beatles lads in the flesh.'

She was vaguely aware of someone genuflecting at the end of the pew. Then the person knelt beside her and whispered, 'Hello, Flo.'

'Hugh!' She flushed with pleasure and patted his arm. He was twenty-three and, as far as Flo was concerned, the finest-looking young man on the planet: tall, slender, with a gentle face, gentle eyes and the sweetest smile she'd ever seen. His hair had grown darker and was now a dusky brown, only a shade lighter than his father's, though it wasn't curly like Tommy's. He was mad about music and haunted the Cavern; she always listened to the charts on the wireless so she could talk to him on equal terms.

'I thought you couldn't get off work?' she said softly. He'd served an apprenticeship as an electrician and worked for a small firm in Anfield.

'I told them it was a funeral. They couldn't very well

refuse. Ian was me friend, he taught me to play chess. Anyroad, I promised Kate I'd come.' He nodded towards the front of the church, and a girl in the row behind Sally and Jock turned round as if she'd sensed someone was talking about her. She had the Clancys' green eyes and silvery hair, and Flo had the strangest feeling she was looking at her younger self in a mirror.

So, this was Kate Colquitt. She'd been at St Theresa's Junior and Infants' school when Flo last saw her, that hulking great lad, Norman Cameron, never far from her side. Sally was right to say she'd grown into a beautiful young woman. Kate twitched her lips at Hugh, almost, but not quite, in a smile, because this was, after all, a funeral. The man kneeling next to her must have noticed the movement. He twisted round and gave Hugh a look that made Flo's blood curdle, a look of hate, full of threats, as if he resented his companion even acknowledging another man's existence.

Norman Cameron, still watching over Kate like an evil guardian of the night.

Everyone stood to sing a hymn: 'Oh, Mary, we crown thee with blossoms today, Queen of the Angels and Queen of the May.' It wasn't May and wasn't appropriate, but it had been Ian's favourite.

Flo saw Norman Cameron find the page for Kate, as if she was incapable of finding it for herself. She felt concerned for the girl, although she hardly knew her. Sally said Norman wanted them to get married and Martha, anxious as ever to meddle in other people's lives, was all for it. Kate had managed so far to hold out. She was working at Walton hospital as an auxiliary and wanted to become a state registered nurse.

'Norman's had a terrible life,' Sally had said, only a few weeks ago. 'No one could have had a worse mam than Elsa, yet the poor lad was inconsolable when she topped herself. I feel dead sorry for him. But he makes me flesh creep, and he's so much in love with Kate it's unhealthy. You'd think he owned her or something.'

'She should find herself another boyfriend,' Flo said spiritedly. 'Try and break away.'

'I reckon Norman would kill any man who dared lay a finger on her.'

'Lord Almighty!' Flo gasped.

The hymn finished, the priest entered the pulpit and began to speak about Ian. He must have known him well because his words were full of feeling: a bright, happy lad who'd borne his illness with the patience of a saint and had almost made it to adulthood due to the selfless commitment of his parents. The world would be a sadder and emptier place without Ian Wilson. Heaven, though, would be enriched by the presence of such a pure, unsullied soul . . .

Flo switched off. Any minute now, he'd start telling Sally and Jock that they should feel privileged their child was dead and had gone to a better place, where he was, even now, safely in the arms of God.

The priest finished. Flo buried her head in her hands when it was time for them to pray. The soft whisper of the organ came from the grille in the wall, the sound gradually growing louder, but not enough to hide a slight whirring noise. Flo peeped through her fingers and saw the curtains behind the altar open slowly and the coffin slide out of sight. The curtains closed and there was an agonised gasp from Sally as her son disappeared for ever. Jock put an arm around her shoulders, and Flo imagined the little curling red and blue flames licking the coffin, spreading, meeting, then devouring it and its precious contents, until only the ashes remained.

'Don't cry, Flo.' Hugh offered her his hanky.

'I didn't realise I was.' She pushed the hanky away. 'You look as if you might need it yourself.'

The service over, they went outside, where the heat was almost as great as it had been in church. When everyone stood round the display of flowers, which were laid out on the parched grass, the blooms wilting rapidly in the hot sunshine, Flo kept to the back. She could see her own wreath, irises and white roses, and would have liked to look for the flowers that Bel and Mr Fritz had sent, but didn't want to come up against Martha, particularly not today.

Hugh was talking to the bereaved parents. He shook hands with Jock and kissed Sally's cheek, very grown-up, very gentlemanly. Nancy O'Mara had raised him well. If she'd been there, she would have felt as proud as Flo. He came over. 'I have to be getting back to work.'

'I'll be going meself in a minute, after I've had a word with our Sally.'

He looked surprised. 'I thought you'd be going back to the house.'

'You're not the only one who has to be at work.'

'In that case,' he said, trying to sound casual, 'I'll give you a lift part of the way.' He had a car, his pride and joy, a little blue Ford Popular.

'That'd be nice, luv. Ta.'

What was she supposed to say to Sally? 'I'm dead sorry, Sal. I feel terrible for you. He was a lovely lad. I don't know how you'll cope without him.' After a few stumbling phrases, she threw her arms around her sister. 'Oh, Lord, Sal, you know what I mean.'

'I know, girl.' Sally nodded bleakly, then grabbed Flo's arm. 'Sis, I want you to do something for me.'

'I'll do anything, Sal, you know that.'

'Make things up with our Martha.' She shook Flo's arm impatiently. 'There's enough misery in the world without adding to it when there's no need. Martha would be overjoyed if you two were friends again.'

Flo glanced at Martha, who was talking to her daughter, Norman Cameron a dark shadow by her side. They weren't exactly a happy family group, but the mother and daughter relationship was there for all to see. Then she looked at Hugh, waiting, hands in pockets, for his 'friend' Flo, and she felt a sense of loss as vivid and painful as the morning she'd woken up and discovered her son had been taken away. Martha hadn't just stolen her son, she'd stolen her life.

Very gently, she removed her sister's hand. 'Anything but that, Sal,' she said.

'I'll miss Ian,' Hugh said, when they were in the car. He smiled shyly. 'I'll miss Kate, too. She was often there when I went to see him. It was the only place she went without Norman Cameron in tow.'

'D'you fancy her, luv?' They would make a perfect couple, Flo thought excitedly. The Catholic Church forbade relationships between cousins, though marriage might be possible with a dispensation. But as neither Hugh nor Kate were aware that they were related, there would be no need for the Church to become involved.

His pale cheeks went pink. 'She's okay.' He'd had several girlfriends, all of whom Nancy had disliked on sight. 'You'd think I was royalty or something,' he'd grumbled to Flo. 'She doesn't think any girl I bring home is good enough for me.'

Flo was inclined to agree, though where Nancy was concerned she always kept her opinions to herself.

Hugh dropped her off in Lime Street. 'See you soon, Flo, perhaps tomorrer.'

It was too nice a day to sit on a bus and Flo decided to walk home. She was in no hurry. Although she'd told Hugh she should be at work, her shift didn't start until two. A few years ago, when launderettes had sprung up all over the place and White's Laundry saw their work trickle away to almost nothing, Mr Fritz had closed the place down. Then he had opened a chain of launderettes, six in all, and put Flo in charge of the biggest, an ex-chandler's shop in Smithdown Road, less than a mile from William Square.

'Hello, gorgeous!' A man, quite good-looking, was standing in front, blocking her way.

'Hello . . .' She stared at him, frowning, before realising that he was a stranger trying to pick her up. 'I thought I knew you,' she said, exasperated.

'You could, very easily. I'd certainly like to know you.'

'Get lost,' she said, but smiled as she dodged past. It was flattering to think that at forty-two she could still attract men. She caught a glimpse of her reflection in the windows as she walked up Mount Pleasant. She never wore black, apart from skirts, and Bel had loaned her a frock for the funeral; very fine cotton with short sleeves and a sunray-pleated skirt. The wide belt made her already slim waist look tiny. She hadn't put on an ounce of weight with age. When they went on their regular visits to the Isle of Man, Mr Fritz complained that she looked no more than thirty. People would think he was spending a dirty weekend with his secretary.

'We're not married, so it is a dirty weekend.' Flo giggled.

He looked horrified. 'Flo! Our weekends together have been the most beautiful times of my life. Nevertheless,' he grumbled, 'all the other guests probably think they're dirty.'

Flo offered to dye her hair grey and draw wrinkles on her face, but he said that wouldn't do either. 'I rather enjoy getting envious glances from other men.' There was no pleasing him, she said.

She passed the women's hospital where Nancy O'Mara had recently had a hysterectomy. Hugh, the dutiful son, had gone to see her after work every night. On the way home, he sometimes called in at the launderette. He usually popped in at least once a week.

'How's Mrs O'Mara?' she asked. It sounded silly, but she could never bring herself to refer to Nancy as his mam.

'Progressing normally, according to the doctor.'

During the time he'd been at secondary modern school, she'd thought she'd lost him. Until then, he'd got into the habit of sticking his head round the door of the laundry on his way home from St Theresa's, just to say hello. When he changed schools, she had the good sense not to wait for him outside when she went to the bank on Fridays, reckoning an eleven-going-on-twelve-year-old in long trousers wouldn't be seen dead playing ball in the Mystery with a woman almost twenty years his senior.

'Where's your little friend?' Mr Fritz asked, after Hugh hadn't shown his face in months.

'He's at a different school and comes home a different way,' Flo explained, doing her best not to appear as cut up as she felt about it.

'That's a shame. I'd grown quite fond of him.' He gave Flo a look full of sympathy and understanding, as if he'd guessed the truth a long time ago.

The months became years. She saw Hugh once when he was fourteen. He was on his way home with a crowd of lads who were kicking a tin can to each other on the other side of the road. She was glad his collar was undone, his tie crooked, that he looked an untidy mess. She was even glad about the tin can. Nancy might not like it, but he'd found his place, he'd made friends, he was one of the lads. She felt a tug at her heart as she melted into a shop doorway out of sight. If only he was coming home to me!

Although Flo had a great time in the launderette – the customers came in with so many funny stories that her sides still hurt with laughter when she went home – she could never get her son out of her mind. She heard through Sally that he'd left school and begun an apprenticeship as an electrician. It wasn't what she would have chosen for him: she would have liked him to become something grander, perhaps even go to university.

It wasn't until almost five years ago, Christmas 1957, that she had seen Hugh again. The launderette was festooned with decorations, drooping in the damp. All afternoon she'd been pressing home-made mince pies and sherry on her 'ladies', as she called them – a few had

even returned with more washing they'd scraped together because they'd had such a good time. The bench
was full of women waiting for the machines to finish, and
Flo was slightly tipsy, having drunk too many people's
health when she wished them merry Christmas. Mr Fritz
usually toured his six establishments daily to ensure that
the automatic machines were working properly and not
in need of his expert attention, but always ended up at
Flo's because it had the nicest atmosphere. His brown
eyes twinkled as he accused her of being in charge of a
launderette while under the influence of alcohol. Just
then the door opened for the hundredth time that day
and he said, 'Why, look who's here!'

Hugh! A shy, smiling Hugh, in an old army jacket
with a small khaki haversack thrown over his shoulder.

My son has grown up! She wanted to weep for all the
years she'd missed. She wanted to hug and kiss him, to ask
why he'd deserted his mam for so long, but merely smiled
back and said, 'Hello, luv.'

'You've grown some,' Mr Fritz said enviously. 'You
must be six foot at least.'

'Six foot one,' Hugh said modestly.

He never explained why he hadn't come before, why
he'd come now, and Flo never asked. She guessed it
was something to do with age, that between eleven and
seventeen, he hadn't felt it proper for her to be his friend,
but as he'd grown older something had drawn him back.
She didn't care what it was. It was enough that he'd
come, and continued to come, to tell her about his job,
his girlfriends, how he was saving up to buy a car. Once, a
few months ago, he had said, 'I wish me mam was a bit
more like you, Flo. She thinks I'm crackers to want a car,
but you wouldn't mind, would you?'

'I should have caught the bus,' she muttered, halfway
home, when the straps of her high-heeled sandals began
to dig into her feet. It would be a relief to reach William
Square, where she'd have a nice cool bath before she
went to work.

Stella Fritz would have a fit if she could see the square now. There was scarcely a house left that hadn't been turned into flats or bedsits and they all looked run down, uncared-for. Even worse, one or two women – Flo refused to believe they were prostitutes – had begun to hang around at night, apparently waiting for men to pick them up. Twice, Flo had been propositioned on her way home in the dark, and Bel had threatened that if anyone else asked how much she charged, she'd thump them. There were frequent fights, which led to the police arriving. Mr Fritz moaned that the place was becoming dead rowdy, and Flo, who loved the square and never wanted to live anywhere else, had to concede that it had deteriorated.

She felt better after the bath and when she had changed into a pale blue cotton frock and canvas shoes. All afternoon, she couldn't get Sally out of her mind. On numerous occasions her ladies wanted to know what was wrong. 'You look as if you've swallowed a quid and shat a sixpence. What's up, Flo?'

If she told them about Ian, she knew what would happen: their great, generous hearts would overflow with sympathy, which would be expressed in flowery, dramatic language a poet would envy. She would only cry, she might possibly howl. She told them she was feeling out of sorts, that the heat was getting her down

Flo loved her ladies. They were coarse, often dirt poor, but they struggled through life with a cheerfulness of spirit that never ceased to amaze her. Through the door they would burst in their shabby clothes, which were usually too big or too small, too long or too short, carrying immense bags of washing. There were black ladies and white ladies, quite often grossly overweight because they existed on a diet of chip butties, but always with a smile on their careworn, prematurely old faces, making a great joke of their bunions and varicose veins, the swollen joints that plagued them, the mysterious lumps that had suddenly appeared on their bodies that they intended to ignore. 'I couldn't go in the ozzie and let them take it away, could I? Not with five kids to look after, and me ould feller propped up in the boozer all day long.'

It could be seven kids, ten kids, twelve. Most of the husbands were unemployed, and more than a few of Flo's ladies went out cleaning early in the morning or late at night. It was their money that paid the rent and put food on the table, but that didn't stop some husbands taking out their frustration with the government and society in general on their wives. Flo often found herself bathing bruises or bandaging cuts, cursing the perpetrators to high heaven.

But the women refused to listen to a word of criticism of their men – 'He couldn't help it, luv. He was stewed rotten. He wouldn't dream of hitting me when he's sober,' which Flo found an unsatisfactory explanation for her ladies' sometimes appalling injuries. She cosseted them, made them tea, laughed at their jokes, admired them. The only thing she refused was to let them do their washing on tick, which Mr Fritz had strictly forbidden. 'Before you can say Jack Robinson, they'll have run up a huge bill and we'll never get paid. No, Flo. They put their own coins in the machine and that's final. And if I find you've been loaning your own money, I'll be very cross indeed. They're a canny lot, and pretty soon you'll be subsidising washing for the whole of Toxteth.'

The thought of Mr Fritz being cross wouldn't have caused a tremor in a rabbit, but Flo was careful to take heed of his advice.

At seven o'clock on the day of Ian's funeral, it was a relief when she could turn the Open sign to Closed. Mr Fritz came and went, promising to have some iced tea ready for when she came home – he was obsessed with his new refrigerator. It would be another hour before all the machines were finished and she could tidy up and leave. The place felt like an oven. Perhaps that was why she had remained so slim: since she was thirteen, she'd spent a high proportion of her waking hours in the equivalent of a Turkish bath.

Bel had been promoted to manageress of ladies' outer-wear in Owen Owens: long coats, short coats, raincoats, furs. She was frequently wined and dined by representa-tives of clothing firms who wanted her to stock their products. Occasionally, when Flo had nothing better to do, she would go to Owen Owens and listen while Bel dealt with a customer.

'Modom, that coat looks simply divine on you. Of course, Modom has a perfect figure, and red is definitely your colour.' The accent, Bel's idea of 'posh', and the voice, haughty yet obsequious, was stomach-churning. When the customer wasn't looking, Bel would make a hideous face at Flo, and mouth, 'Sod off!'

On her way home from the launderette, Flo let herself into her friend's flat in Upper Parliament Street, where Bel was lying on her luridly patterned settee wearing black satin lounging pyjamas and reading *She*. She looked up and grinned widely, the deeply etched laughter lines around her eyes and mouth adding yet more char-acter to her already animated face. 'You look as if you've just been for a turn in one of your machines,' she said.

'I feel as if I have.' Flo threw herself into an armchair with a sigh. Bel's flat wasn't relaxing, more like a fair-ground with its bright walls and ceilings, and curtains that could do serious damage to the eyes. Still, it was nice to sit in a comfortable chair at last. 'I want you to promise me something, Bel,' she said.

'What, luv?'

'If I die before you, make sure I'm buried, not cre-mated. I want a few bits of me left to rise to heaven when the Day of Judgement comes.'

'Rightio, Flo,' Bel said laconically. 'I don't give a stuff what they do with me. Once I'm dead, they can throw me in the Mersey for all I care, or feed me to the lions at Chester Zoo.'

'Another thing, Bel. I've taken out an insurance policy to cover the cost of me funeral. It's in the first-aid box in the cupboard by the fireplace, the right-hand side. I'd put it in the bureau with all me papers, but you'd never find it. I can never find anything meself.'

'That's because you keep every single bit of paper that drops through your letterbox,' Bel snorted.

'It's a legacy from Stella Fritz. I always kept me bills in case she accused me of not paying the 'leccy, or something. Now I can't get out of the habit. Anyroad, when I'm looking for something, it's nice reading through me old letters. I've still got the ones you sent during the war. You can have them back if you like.' She didn't say, because Bel would have been disgusted, that it was quite interesting to look at old bills, see how much prices had gone up.

Bel grimaced. 'Thanks, but no thanks.'

'One more thing. Under no circumstances must our Martha come to me funeral. I'm not having it, d'you hear?'

'I hear, Flo, but why all this morbid talk about death and funerals?'

'I took the policy out years ago. It was this morning at the crematorium that I decided I'd sooner be buried.'

'Flo!' Bel's face was a tragedy. 'I'd completely forgotten about Ian's funeral. Was it awful, luv? How's your Sally taking it? Did the dress fit all right?'

'The dress looked simply divine,' Flo said tiredly. The expression had become a joke between them. 'As for the other, it was awful, yes. Sally's taken it hard, and so's Jock.'

'Shall we do something exciting tomorrer night, Sat'day, like go somewhere dead extravagant for a meal? It might cheer you up.'

'Sorry, Bel, but I'm going on retreat in the morning.'

Bel groaned. 'You're a miserable bugger, Flo Clancy. What do you do on these retreats, anyroad?'

'Pray,' Flo said virtuously.

'They're a waste of time – a waste of life!'

'I don't see you doing anything earth-shattering.'

'I've got an important job.'

'So've I.'

'I get taken out to dinner.'

'Mr Fritz takes me out to dinner sometimes.'

'He takes us both, so that's not counted.' Bel sat on the edge of the settee and rested her chin in her hands. She said, thoughtfully, 'Actually, Flo, it's well past the time you and Fritz got something going together.'

Flo laughed. 'I'm happy as I am, thanks all the same. Anyroad, it's well past the time you found yourself another husband.'

Bel ignored this. 'These damn retreats, I can't think of anything more boring and miserable than praying non-stop for two whole days.'

'Oh, I dunno,' said Flo. 'The thing is, I always come back feeling spiritually uplifted and enriched.'

2

'I can't understand it,' Sally said distractedly. 'It's as if Ian was the glue that kept us together.' She ran her fingers through her short, greying hair. 'But when did me and Jock need anything to keep us together? I love him, and I know he loves me. Remember the day we met him and his mate, Flo, on the New Brighton ferry?'

'I'll never forget that day, luv.' It was the last time she had seen Tommy O'Mara.

Her sister's marriage was falling apart. Grace didn't help. She accused her mam and dad of always having cold-shouldered her, of making her feel second best. 'Then me and Jock have a go at each other,' Sally moaned. 'I tell him it's his fault Grace feels the way she does, and he says it's mine.'

The only good thing to come out of the whole sad business was that the two sisters had become close again.

Sally frequently turned up at the launderette just as Flo was closing, and they would walk back to William Square, arm in arm. Jock went to a social club in Kirkby almost every night – 'As if all he wants is to have a good time with his mates. I think I remind him too much of what we went through with Ian. He won't come with me to church.'

'I don't know what advice to give, Sal,' Flo said truthfully. She thought her sister spent far too much time in church, but preferred not to say so. 'Perhaps it's just a stage he's going through. He needs to let off steam. Jock's a good man at heart.'

'It's not advice I need,' Sally sniffed, 'just someone to talk to. Our Martha's come up with enough advice to write a book, from giving our Grace a good hiding to wiping the floor with Jock.'

'Both of which would do more harm than good.'

'That's what I said. Mind you, her Kate's been a great help. She often comes round to see me.' Suddenly Sally seemed to find a mole on the back of her hand enormously interesting. Without meeting her sister's eyes, she mumbled, 'I can't understand how our Martha ended up with such a lovely daughter, and we were landed with Grace. Oh!' she cried tearfully. 'Forget I said that. I love my girl, but I don't half wish she were different.'

'I wish all sorts of things were different, Sal.' Flo sighed. 'You must bring Kate round to see me sometime. I'd like to get to know her.'

She had never intended it to be this way, but it had all started the day she first saw Tommy O'Mara through a mist of steam in Fritz's laundry: Flo's life seemed to be divided into little boxes, each one carefully marked 'Secret'.

Martha and Sally knew this about her, Mr Fritz knew that. Hugh O'Mara thought he was her friend. No one knew about the servicemen during the war. There were her bogus 'retreats'. Bel, who thought she knew everything there was to know, knew virtually nothing, only that for a short time before the war she'd gone out with Tommy O'Mara.

Flo often worried that one day something might be said that would lift the lid off a box, give away one of her secrets, expose one of her lies.

It nearly happened the day Sally came to the flat, bringing Kate Colquitt with her. Bel was there, and they'd just watched *Roman Holiday* on television – Bel still went weak at the knees over Gregory Peck.

'This is Kate Colquitt, our Martha's girl,' Sally said.

Flo could have sworn that Bel's ears twitched. She still longed to know why Flo and Martha never spoke. 'Martha's girl, eh! Pleased to meet you, Kate. How's your mam keeping these days?'

'Very well, thank you.' The girl had a sweet, high-pitched voice.

'Why didn't you bring her with you?' Bel enquired cunningly. Flo threw her a murderous glance. Bel caught the look and winked.

Kate merely replied, 'Me mam doesn't know I've come.' She turned to Flo, green eyes shining in her lovely fresh face. 'I've always wanted to meet you, Auntie Flo. I saw you at Ian's funeral. I was going to introduce meself, but when I looked for you you'd gone.'

'Please call me Flo. "Auntie" makes me feel a bit peculiar.'

'Okay.' She followed her aunt into the kitchen when Flo went to make a pot of tea, chatting volubly. 'I like your flat, it's the gear. I'd love a place of me own, but me mam's dead set against it. She says I'm too young. How old were you when you came here, Flo?'

'Twenty.'

'There! Next month I'll be twenty-two. So I'm not too young, am I?' She looked at Flo, wide-eyed and artless.

'I was a very old twenty,' Flo muttered. An incredibly

old twenty compared to this girl, who was too innocent for this world. She looked as vulnerable and defenceless as a flower by the wayside.

'There are times,' Kate sighed, 'when I'd love to be by meself. Y'know, read a book and stuff, watch the telly.'

Flo imagined her mother, Martha the Manipulator, never allowing her daughter a minute's peace. 'Why do you need a red bow in your hair when you're only going to see Josie Driver?' 'I'd sooner you didn't go out with a Protestant, Sal.' 'You've always got your head buried in a book, Flo Clancy.' And then there was Norman, which meant that Kate had two overbearing people to cope with, wanting her to do things their way. Sally said that he had moved to Kirkby and he was round at the house almost every night.

'Are you having a party on your birthday?' Flo asked brightly, as she arranged the cups and saucers on a tray.

'Just a few friends. You can come if you like.'

'Ta, luv, but I don't think that's such a good idea.' She picked up the tray. 'D'you mind bringing that plate of biscuits with you, save me coming back?'

'What happened between you and me mam, Flo?' Kate enquired earnestly. 'Auntie Sally says I'm not to mention I've been to see you. It must be something awful bad.'

Flo chuckled. 'That's something you need to ask your mam, luv.' One thing she knew for certain was that the girl wouldn't get a truthful answer.

They went into the living room. 'You took your time,' Bel said. 'I'm parched for a cuppa.'

'I remember you used to wait for Hugh O'Mara outside St Theresa's,' Kate went on, 'though I didn't know you were me auntie then.'

Bel's head jerked upwards and she looked at Flo, her face full of questions.

The very second Sally and Kate left, Bel burst out, 'Hugh O'Mara! Who's Hugh O'Mara? Is he related to Tommy? I didn't know he had a kid.'

'Why should you?'

'I thought you'd have said.'

Flo explained that Hugh had been born after Tommy died. It was hateful giving credit to Nancy for something she'd done herself, but too much time had passed for Bel to know the truth. Flo couldn't have stood the gasps of incredulity, the astounded comments. Bel *would* have crawled through the snow to get back her baby. Bel would have stood on the rooftops screaming to the world that her baby had been stolen, then demolished Nancy's front door with a battering ram once she had discovered where he was. The realisation that another woman wouldn't have taken it as meekly as she had made Flo feel uneasy. It was a bit late to regret what a coward she'd been, too easily influenced by the wishes of her family.

'That's all very well,' Bel hooted, when Flo finished her careful explanation, 'but what the hell were you doing waiting for the lad outside St Theresa's?'

I should have been a spy, Flo thought. I would have been brilliant at lying meself out of the most dangerous situations. She said that a woman at the laundry had had a son in the same class as Hugh. 'They were friends. I used to go by St Theresa's on Fridays on me way from the bank. Peggy asked me to make sure Jimmy was going straight home. That's how I met Hugh. He was a nice lad, quite different from his dad. I still see him,' she added casually. 'If he's passing the launderette, he might drop in.'

'Why didn't you tell me this before?' Bel said, outraged out of all proportion.

'I didn't think you'd be interested.'

'Why, Flo Clancy, you know I'm interested in *everything!*'

'Well, you know now, don't you?' Flo snapped.

It was a whole year before Jock tired of the social club and Sally stopped going quite so often to church. The old harmony was restored. It helped when Grace got engaged to a nice young man called Keith, who worked in a bank, and became absorbed in plans for her wedding eighteen months off at Easter 1966. 'Jock's pulling out all the stops. It's going to be a grand affair,' Sally announced. 'He thinks if we spend all our savings she'll realise we love her just as much as we did Ian.'

Sally continued coming to William Square, sometimes bringing Kate Colquitt with her. Flo and Kate got on like a house on fire. 'You should have had kids, Flo,' said Bel, who usually managed to be there when visitors came. 'You would have made a wonderful mother.'

It was a bitterly cold January afternoon, a month after her twenty-third birthday, when Kate turned up alone at the launderette. 'I hope you don't mind. I finish work at four.' She made a nervous face. 'Norman's off with a terrible cold and he's moved in with us for a while so me mam can look after him. I don't feel like going home just yet. I can't stand it when both of them get on to me.'

'I don't mind a bit, luv.' Flo sat the girl in her cubby-hole and made her some tea. Once she'd warmed up, she'd let her loose among her ladies, who'd soon make her forget her troubles. 'What do they get on to you about?' she asked.

Kate raised her shoulders and heaved a great sigh. 'Norman wants us to get married and me mam thinks it's a grand idea. He's so sweet. I can't remember a time when he hasn't been around, yet . . . oh, I dunno. It's worse now Grace is engaged – she's four years younger than me. Mam keeps saying I'll be left on the shelf, but I'm not sure if I care. I've started training to be a State Registered Nurse, and I'd like to finish before I settle down. In fact, sometimes I think I wouldn't mind staying single like you, Flo.'

She made herself useful, helping to untangle washing that had knotted together in the spin-driers, and getting on famously with the customers. She was still there when Flo was about to turn the Open sign to Closed, and Hugh O'Mara came in wearing the leather coat that had taken three months to save for, and which Nancy strongly disapproved of him wearing for work.

'Hugh!' Kate cried, her face lighting up with pleasure. 'I haven't seen you in ages.'

He appeared equally pleased to find her there. They sat on a bench, heads together, engrossed in conversation, and when the time came for Flo to lock up, the pair wandered off happily, arm in arm. A few days later, Kate turned up again, then Hugh arrived as if it had been prearranged. The same thing happened the next week and the next, until Flo got used to Tuesday and Friday being the days when Kate came to help untangle the washing, was joined by Hugh, and they would go off together into the night. She watched, entranced, as the looks they gave each other became more and more intimate. She realised they were falling in love, and couldn't have approved more. Her son would never find a prettier, nicer, more suitable wife than Kate Colquitt. She felt sure that even Nancy would be pleased when she was told. So far, everyone except Flo was being kept in the dark.

As the months crept by they were still in the dark. It was obvious to everyone in the launderette, including Mr Fritz, that the young couple were mad about each other, but Kate was too scared to tell her mam. 'She never liked Hugh much. She said there was something not quite right about his background.' She asked Flo how people got married in Gretna Green.

'I've no idea, luv,' Flo confessed, exasperated. She badly wanted to interfere, to tell them to get a move on, but held her tongue.

'Martha suspects Kate's got a secret boyfriend,' Sally remarked one day. Apparently there were nights when Kate didn't get home till all hours and refused to say where she'd been. Poor Norman Cameron was doing his nut.

Flo wondered if Kate was more scared of Norman than of her mam. 'He'd kill any man who laid a finger on her,'

Sally had said once. Perhaps she was scared for Hugh. Or maybe she was enjoying the clandestine nature of the affair, just as Flo had enjoyed her illicit meetings with Hugh's father all those years ago.

Secrecy must have run in both families, the O'Maras and the Clancys, because Kate and Hugh continued to see each other for over a year before everyone found out and all hell broke loose.

Flo had been out of bed barely five minutes when there was a pounding on the door. She opened it, still in her dressing-gown, and Sally came storming in, her normally placid face red with rage.

'Why aren't you at work?' Flo said, in surprise. Sally had been working full-time at Peterssen's the confectioner's to help with the wedding expenses, which were turning out to be horrendous. She wondered why her sister was so angry. Had Jock gone off the rails again? Grace was getting married on Saturday – perhaps she'd called it off or, even worse, perhaps Keith had.

Either Sally didn't hear the question or she ignored it. 'You knew, didn't you?' she said, loudly and accusingly.

'Knew what?' Flo stammered.

'About Kate and Hugh, soft girl. Nancy O'Mara passed the launderette on the bus last night and she saw them come out kissing and canoodling, so you must have known.'

'So what if I did?'

'You're a bloody idiot, Flo Clancy, you truly are. They're *cousins*!'

'I know darn well they're cousins. What's wrong with that?'

'They're *Catholic* cousins. The Church forbids that sort of thing between cousins.' Sally was staring at her sister belligerently, as if Flo had committed the worst possible crime. 'I hope they're not planning on getting married or anything daft like that.'

'They are, actually, once Kate plucks up the courage to

tell her mam. It's not illegal. As they don't know they're related, under the circumstances it never entered me head that anyone would care.'

'Holy Mary, Mother of God.' Sally groaned. 'Not care! You never heard anything like the commotion that went on in our Martha's last night. 'Stead of going home, Nancy went straight to Kirkby, then Martha sent for me. We had to turn Norman Cameron away as we didn't want him listening to private family business. Me and Nancy had left before Kate came home. Christ knows what Martha said to the girl. And what's Nancy supposed to tell Hugh?' She groaned again. 'Why the hell didn't you do something to stop it, Flo?'

Flo gave a little sarcastic laugh. 'Such as?'

'I don't know, do I?'

'I suppose,' Flo said slowly, conscious of her own anger grating in her voice, 'I could have said "Sorry, Hugh, but you're not to have any romantic notions about Kate Colquitt, because the truth is, I'm your mam, not Nancy, which means you're cousins." That might have stopped it, and I'm sure everyone would have been dead pleased, particularly Martha and Nancy.'

Sally's rage subsided. 'I'm sorry, luv. Our Martha got me all worked up. I hardly slept a wink all night, but I shouldn't have blamed you.' She looked curiously at her sister. 'Did you ever think about telling him when he got older?'

Flo had thought about it a million times. 'Yes, but I decided it wouldn't be fair. It might do the poor lad's head in, knowing the truth after all this time. He'd feel betrayed. All the deceit, all the lies. He might never want to see either me or Nancy again, and he'd be the one who'd suffer most.'

Sally shivered suddenly. 'It's cold in here.'

'I'm used to it. I'll turn the fire on.'

'What are we going to do, Flo, about Kate and Hugh?'

'Leave them alone, do nothing. Let them get wed with everyone's blessing.'

'Come off it, Flo. You must be out of your mind,' Sally said resignedly.

'I've never felt saner.' Flo's voice was cold. 'You, Martha and Nancy are nothing but a bunch of hypocrites. You pride yourselves on being great Catholics, yet you're quite happy to let me son be lied to all his life. Martha and Nancy caused this mess and I don't see why Hugh and Kate should suffer. Anyroad, marriage isn't out of the question. Perhaps they can get a dispensation?' She couldn't understand the need some people had to interfere in other people's lives. The young couple had fallen in love in all innocence, and they were perfect for each other. She was desperate for them to be left alone, not be parted over some silly rule that couldn't even be explained to them. Kate was a nice girl, but she was weak. Once Martha got to work on her, Flo couldn't imagine her holding out.

'I suggested a dispensation,' Sally said tiredly, 'but Martha and Nancy nearly hit the roof. How would they explain the situation for one thing? It's not just the parish priest who gets involved, it can go up as far as the bishop. And it means Hugh and Kate would have to know the truth.'

'But, Sal,' Flo tried to convey her desperation to her sister, 'we're the only ones who know they're cousins. It's not against the law of the land. If all of us kept our traps shut, Hugh and Kate could get married tomorrer.'

To her relief, Sally looked more than half convinced. 'There might be something in what you say,' she conceded. 'I'll go straight to Kirkby and see our Martha.'

Over the next few days, Flo tried to ring Sally several times from the telephone in the launderette, but either there was no reply or Jock said she was out somewhere, busy with arrangements for Grace's wedding. There was no sign, either, of Hugh or Kate. She prayed that Hugh wouldn't be annoyed or get into trouble if she rang him at work, but when she did, she was told he hadn't been in all week. Desperation turned to frustration when she realised there was nothing she could do. She thought of going to Martha's, or to Clement Street to see Nancy, but she didn't trust herself not to blurt out the truth if there was a row.

She had bought a new outfit for Grace's wedding: a pale blue and pink check frock with a white Peter Pan collar, a white silk beret and gloves, and high-heeled linen shoes. On the day, she went through the motions, chatting to the guests, agreeing that the bride looked like a film star in her raw silk dress. She did her best to get Sally on one side and pump her for information, but found it impossible and came to the conclusion that her sister was avoiding her. She wanted to know why Martha wasn't there and what on earth had happened to Kate, who was supposed to be a bridesmaid.

The ceremony had been over for twenty-four hours, the newly wedded couple had already landed safely in Tenerife to start their fortnight's honeymoon when Sally came to William Square to tell Flo that, at the same time as Grace had been joined in holy matrimony to Keith, in another church in another part of Liverpool, Norman Cameron had taken Kate Colquitt to be his wife. It had been a hastily arranged ceremony, with an emergency licence, attended by only a few friends. The bride wore a borrowed dress. They were spending two days in Rhyl for their honeymoon

'Martha made me promise not to tell you,' Sally said. 'She thought you might turn up and make a fuss.'

'Since when did I ever make a fuss?' Flo asked bitterly. 'I let her tread all over me. I let her ruin me life, just as she's ruined Kate's.' She thought of Hugh, who must have felt betrayed when he heard the news.

'You're exaggerating, Flo. Norman has loved Kate all his life. Now his dreams have come true and they're married. He'll make the best husband in the world.'

Perhaps Norman's dreams had been nightmares, because the stories that reached Flo in the months and years that followed scarcely told of a man who loved his wife.

Kate Colquitt, now Cameron, had become pregnant straight away. Late the following November she gave birth to a daughter, Millicent. Flo hadn't set eyes on Kate since the girl had walked out of the launderette on Hugh's arm just before Easter. She felt hurt at first, until a dismayed Sally informed her that Norman hardly let his new wife out of doors. 'She can go to the local shops and to church, but no further. I can't think why, but he doesn't trust her. Perhaps he knows about Hugh O'Mara, but Kate was single then so what does it matter?'

On impulse, Flo decided to go and see her niece at the maternity hospital. Afternoon visiting was from two till three so she arranged for the woman who did the morning shift at the launderette to hang on until she got back. 'I'm off to see me niece in hospital,' she said proudly. 'She's just had a baby, a little girl.'

'Would you like to see the baby first?' the nurse enquired, when Flo asked where she could find Mrs Kathleen Cameron.

'That'd be nice.'

The hospital bustled with visitors, mainly women at this time of day. 'That's her, second row back, second cot from the end.' The nurse's voice dropped to a whisper: 'I wouldn't want anyone else to hear, but she's one of the prettiest babies we've ever had.'

Flo was left alone to stare through the nursery window at the rows of babies. Some were howling furiously, their little faces red and screwed up in rage. A few were awake but quiet, their small bodies squirming against the tightly wrapped blankets. The rest, Millicent Cameron among them, were fast asleep.

'Aah!' Flo breathed. She was perfect, with long lashes quivering on her waxen cheeks, and a little pink rosebud mouth. Hugh had probably looked like that. She wondered if he'd also had such a head of hair: masses of little curls, like delicate ribbons. I never even knew how much he weighed, she thought. She pressed her forehead against the glass in order to see better. 'I wish you all the

313

luck in the world, Millie Cameron,' she whispered. 'And I tell you this much, luv, I don't half wish you were mine.'

She left the nursery and went to the ward, but when she looked through the glass panel in the door, Martha was sitting beside Kate's bed. Flo sighed and turned away. On the way out, she took another long look at her new great-niece. She felt tears running warmly down her cheeks, sighed, wiped them away with her sleeve and went home.

Almost two decades passed before she saw Kate Cameron and her daughter again.

The girl came into the launderette and looked challengingly at Flo. She had jet black wavy hair, wide brown eyes, and enough makeup on her coarse, attractive face to last most women a week. She seemed to be wearing only half a skirt, and a sweater several sizes too small so it strained against her large, bouncing breasts. A cigarette protruded from the corner of her red, greasy mouth, and she spoke out of the other corner like Humphrey Bogart. 'Are you the one who's a friend of Hugh O'Mara?' she demanded in a deep, sultry voice.

Flo blinked. 'Yes.'

'He said I could leave a message with you. If he comes in, tell him I'll meet him outside Yates's Wine Lodge at half past eight.'

'Rightio. What name shall I say?'

'Carmel McNulty.' The girl turned, flicked ash on the floor, and strode out, hips swaying, long legs enticing in their black, fishnet tights.

Flo's ladies were all eyes and ears. 'Was that Carmel McNulty?' one enquired eagerly.

'Apparently so,' Flo conceded.

'I hope that nice Hugh chap isn't going out with her. She's no better than she ought to be, that girl.'

Everyone seemed to know or have heard of Carmel NcNulty.

'Didn't her last feller end up in Walton jail?'

'She was a hard-faced bitch even when she was a little 'un.'

'I'd give my lads the back of me hand if any of 'em dared to look twice at Carmel McNulty.'

Flo listened, appalled. In the year since Kate had got married, Hugh had never mentioned her name, or been seen with another girl. Surely he didn't have designs on Carmel McNulty. Maybe she had designs on him. Hugh was a catch – one of the best-looking men in all Liverpool, with his own car and a good, steady job. Perhaps she was prejudiced, but Flo couldn't understand why there wasn't a whole line of women queuing to snap him up.

Having demolished Carmel McNulty, Flo's ladies began to put her back together again. 'Mind you, Carmel's got her hands full with her mam. How many kids has Tossie got?'

'Twenty?' someone suggested.

'Twenty!' Flo squeaked.

'Nah, I think it was eighteen at the last count.'

'Carmel's the eldest and she's had a babby to look after ever since she wasn't much more than a babby herself.'

'She still looks after 'em. I saw her only the other Sunday pushing a pramload of kids down Brownlow Hill.'

'You can't blame her wanting a good time after all that. How old is she now?'

'Nineteen.'

Six weeks later Hugh O'Mara and Carmel McNulty were married. The bride held her bouquet over her already swelling stomach. Flo went to the church and watched through the railings. It was more like a school outing than a wedding, as hordes of large and small McNultys chased each other around the churchyard.

Nancy O'Mara hadn't changed much: she still wore her black hair in the same enormous bun and the same peculiar clothes, a long flowing red dress and a black velvet bolero. She looked as if at any minute she might produce castanets and start dancing, except that her face was set like yellow concrete in an expression of disgust. According to a rather sullen Hugh, she loathed Carmel and Carmel loathed her. Nancy had only come to the wedding because of what people would say if she didn't.'

'It serves you right,' Flo murmured. 'If it weren't for you and our Martha, Hugh would be married to Kate by now and everyone would be happy, apart from Norman Cameron.' Instead, Kate was stuck with a man who kept her a prisoner, and Hugh was marrying a woman he didn't love. There was nothing wrong with Carmel: once she'd got to know her, Flo liked the girl. She was big-hearted, generous to a fault, and as tough as old boots. But she wasn't Hugh's type. Flo clutched the railings with both hands. Her son was doing his best to look as if he was enjoying his wedding day, but his mam could tell he was as miserable as sin.

Flo went through the backyard of the terraced house in Mulliner Street and let herself into the untidy kitchen. She shouted, 'Is he ready for his walk yet, Carmel?'

Carmel appeared in slacks and one of Hugh's old shirts, a cigarette between her lips. She looked exhausted. 'The little bugger kept us awake half the night laughing! I'll be glad to be shut of him for a few hours, I really will.'

A small boy burst into the kitchen and flung his arms around Flo's legs. 'Can we go to the Mystery? Can we play ball? Can I have a lolly? Can I walk and not sit in me pushchair?'

Smiling, Flo loosened the arms around her legs and picked the child up. 'You're a weight, young man!'

Tom O'Mara was over-active and inordinately precocious for a three-year-old. Even as a baby, he had hardly slept. He didn't cry, but demanded attention with loud noises, which got louder and louder if he was ignored. As he grew older, he would rattle the bars of his cot and fling the bedding on the floor. Lately, he'd begun to sit up in bed in the early hours of the morning chanting nursery rhymes or singing, and now, apparently, laughing. He could already read a little, count up to a hundred and tell the time. Carmel said she'd never come across a child quite like him. 'I feel like knocking bloody hell out of the little bugger, but you can't very well hit a kid for being happy!'

When relations between Carmel and her mother-in-law broke down completely and Nancy was barred from Mulliner Street, Flo grasped the opportunity and offered to take her grandson out in the mornings.

'Would you, Flo?' Carmel said gratefully. 'Honest, I don't know where Hugh found a friend like you. I wish you were me mother-in-law, I really do.'

It was June, not exactly hot, but quite warm. Flo played football with Tom until her limbs could no longer move. She lay on the grass and declared herself a goal post. 'You can kick the ball at me, but don't expect to have it kicked back. I'm worn out.'

Tom sat on her stomach. He was a handsome little chap with the same devil-may-care expression on his face as his grandad. 'Are you old?'

'Is fifty-one old? I'm not sure.'

'Dad's old.'

'No, he's not, luv. He's nineteen years younger than me.'

'Mam says he's old.'

Things were not well with the O'Maras. In the evenings, after being stuck in the house all day with a child who would crack the patience of a saint, Carmel was anxious for a break, a bit of excitement. Hugh, who worked hard and was rarely home before seven, preferred to stay in and watch television. Flo had offered to babysit and did occasionally at weekends, but in the main the couple stayed put, much to Carmel's chagrin. She declared loudly and aggressively that she was bored out of her skull and might as well be married to an old-age pensioner.

Flo couldn't help but sympathise. Hugh was growing old before his time. He already had a stoop, his hair was thinning, his gentle face was that of a man weighed down by the cares of the world. He was unhappy. Flo could see it in his dead, green eyes. He didn't seem to care when Carmel started going out alone. She was going clubbing, she announced. Hugh was welcome to come with her if he wanted, otherwise he would just have to like it or lump it.

After the launderette had closed, Flo often went to Mulliner Street to sit with her son. She had never thought she would have the freedom to be alone with Hugh, Nancy out of the picture. Even so, she would have preferred the circumstances to be different. They didn't talk much. He sat with his eyes fixed on the television, but she could tell he wasn't really watching.

'Do you see much of Kate nowadays?' he asked one night.

'No, luv. I haven't seen her in years.'

'I wonder how she is.'

She didn't dare repeat the things Sally told her – Hugh was miserable enough. 'She's had another baby, a little girl called Trudy,' was all she said.

Another night he said, 'Why did you wait for me outside St Theresa's that day, Flo? I've often wondered.'

'I wanted to meet you. I knew your dad, remember?'

'That's right. What was he like? Mam never talked about him much, except that he died on that submarine.'

'The *Thetis*. He was an ould divil, your dad. Full of himself, dead conceited. Women were after him like flies.' Perhaps she should have come up with a more positive, more flattering description, but at least she hadn't told him his dad had lied through his teeth.

Hugh allowed himself the glimmer of a smile. 'Not like me.'

'No, I'm pleased to say.' She didn't like the way he

always talked about the past, as if he'd given up on the future. Usually, Tom could be heard upstairs, where he'd been put to bed hours ago, making aeroplane or car noises, but Hugh seemed unaware of his delightful son and his attractive wife – who might be as common as muck but was basically a good girl, anxious to be a good wife. Carmel was only twenty-three: she needed a husband who did more than just bring home a regular wage. If only Hugh would take her out now and then, she'd be happy, but he didn't seem to care.

In the Mystery, Tom bounced several times on her stomach. 'Strewth, luv,' Flo gasped. 'Are you out to kill me?'

'Can we go to your house for a cuppa tea?'

'There isn't time, Tom. It'd make me late for work.' Sometimes when it was raining she took him to William Square and read him books, which he adored. 'I'll get you an ice lolly, then take you back to your mam.'

He gave her stomach a final, painful bounce. 'Rightio, Flo.'

When she returned the kitchen was still in a state. It was unlike Carmel not to tidy up – she usually kept the house spotless. Flo went into the living room and could hear voices upstairs, one a man's. 'Carmel,' she shouted.

It was several minutes before Carmel came running down. She'd changed into a mini-skirted Crimplene frock. Her lipstick was smudged.

Flo frowned. 'Is Hugh home?'

The girl looked at her boldly. 'No.'

'I see.'

'I doubt if you do, Flo. If you were married to that drip Hugh O'Mara you might see then.'

'It's none of me business, is it, girl?' Flo considered herself the last person on earth entitled to criticise another woman's morals, but her heart ached for her unhappy, lacklustre son.

Tom had turned five and been at school only a matter of weeks when Carmel walked out for good. 'She's gone to live in Brighton with some chap she met in a club,' Hugh said wearily. 'She said she would have taken Tom but her new feller doesn't want to be landed with a kid. "Flo will look after him," she said.'

'I'll be happy to.' It would never have come to this if I'd been allowed to keep me baby, Flo thought sadly.

'There won't be any need,' Hugh said, in his expressionless voice. 'I'm moving back in with me mam. She'll take care of Tom. She's not seen much of him 'cept when I took him round.'

Flo turned away, her lips twisted bitterly. She supposed that that was the last she would see of her grandson, but on the day that the family moved to Clement Street to live with Nancy, Tom O'Mara burst into the launderette after school. He was everything his father had never been: untidy, uninhibited, full of beans. 'Hiya, Flo,' he sang.

'What are you doing here?' she gasped. He'd come half a mile out of his way to get there. She noticed he had a skull and crossbones drawn upside down on both knees. 'Mrs O'Mara will be worried stiff wondering where you've got to.'

'You mean me gran? Don't like her. Me mam always said she was an ould cow. Can I have a cuppa tea, Flo?' He settled on a bench and allowed himself to be made a fuss of by Flo's ladies.

'How on earth could Carmel McNulty bring herself to walk out on such a little angel?'

'He's the spitting image of Hugh.'

'He's the spitting image of Carmel.'

From then on, Tom never failed to turn up for a cup of tea after school. Nancy couldn't control him and Flo didn't even try.

3

Mr Fritz was seventy-five, the same age as the century, and becoming frail. His limbs were swollen and twisted

with arthritis, and it was heartbreaking to see him struggle up and down the basement steps with his stick. Even
worse, more important parts of his body had ceased to
work. He and Flo went to the Isle of Man rarely nowadays, and then only to lie in each other's arms.

'I'm sorry, Flo,' he would say mournfully, 'I'm like
one of my old washing-machines. I need reconditioning.
A new motor wouldn't do me any harm.'

'Don't be silly, luv. I'm not exactly in tip-top condition meself,' Flo would answer. In fact, she was as fit as a
fiddle and missed making love.

Increasingly his family came over from Ireland to see
him. Flo found it difficult to recognise the hard-eyed
middle-aged men and women as the children she'd once
played with, taken for walks and to the pictures. Their
attitude towards her was unfriendly and suspicious. She
sensed that they were worried she might have undue
influence over the man with whom she'd shared a house
for so long, a house that was now worth many thousands
of pounds, added to which there were the six launderettes. All of a sudden, the little Fritzes seemed to regard
their father's welfare of great importance.

'Harry would like me to live with him in Dublin,' Mr
Fritz said, the night after Ben and Harry had been to stay
for the weekend. 'And I had a letter from Aileen the
other day. She never married, you know, and she wants
me to live with her!' He chuckled happily. 'It's nice to
know my children want to look after me in my old age,
don't you think, Flo?'

'Yes, luv,' Flo said warmly. She felt frightened, convinced that it was their inheritance his children were
concerned with.

'I told Harry that, if I went, I'd want nothing to do
with Stella.' Flo went cold. He was actually considering
Harry's offer. 'He said they hardly see her nowadays.
She's still on the same farm and the toilet facilities are
barely civilised, which is why none of them go to visit.'

It turned out he just wanted to spend a long holiday in

Dublin, to get to know his children properly again. 'I would never leave you, Flo,' he said. 'Not for good.'

While he was away, the launderettes could virtually run themselves, but for the second time in her life, Flo was left in charge of Mr Fritz's business. This time though, an agent would collect the money each day and bank it. Flo would be sent a cheque to pay the staff, with the power to hire and fire should the need arise. Herbie Smith, a reliable plumber, had promised to be on call in case any of the machines broke down.

Harry came over from Ireland to fetch his father, and Flo longed to remind this cold, unpleasant man that he'd once had a crush on her. Mr Fritz made his painful way down the steps towards the taxi that would take them to the Irish boat. He gave Flo a chaste kiss on the cheek. 'I'll be back in three months. Keep an eye on upstairs for me.'

'Of course, luv. I've done it before, haven't I?' Flo had no idea why she should want to cry, but cry she did.

'So you have, my dear Flo.' There were tears in his own rheumy eyes. 'The day I came home from the camp and found you here will always remain one of my fondest memories, though not as precious as our weekends together.' He grasped both her hands in his. 'You'll write, won't you? Has Harry given you the address in Dublin?'

'I'll write every week,' Flo vowed. Harry was looking at them darkly, as if all the family's suspicions had been confirmed. 'C'mon, Dad,' he said, making no attempt to keep the impatience out of his voice. Flo felt even more frightened for Mr Fritz, the man she had loved since she was thirteen, not romantically, not passionately, but as the dearest of friends. 'I'll miss you,' she sobbed. 'The place won't seem the same.'

'It's not for long, Flo. The three months will go by in a flash.'

He'd been gone less than a fortnight when Flo heard noises coming from upstairs as if furniture was being moved around. She ran outside. The front door was open and two men were struggling down the steps with the big pine dresser from the kitchen. A removal van was parked further along the square.

'What's happening?' she cried.

'We're taking the good stuff to auction and leaving the rubbish behind,' she was told brusquely.

Flo returned to the basement, knowing that her worst fears had been realised. Mr Fritz would never again live in William Square.

Soon afterwards, a gang of workmen descended on the house. Each floor was being converted into a separate flat, and Flo feared for herself. She'd always insisted on paying rent, but it was a nominal sum. What if the little Fritzes put up the rent so that it was beyond her means? What if they threw her out? She couldn't imagine living anywhere else, where she might have to share a kitchen and lavatory with other tenants. Flo had grown used to her subterranean existence, where she happily ignored the real world. The years were marked for her not by the election of various governments, Labour or Conservatives, the Cuban crisis or the assassination of an American president, but by films and music, *Gone with the Wind, Singing in the Rain, The Sound of Music*: Paul Newman, Marlon Brando, the Beatles . . .

'Mr Fritz would never throw you out!' Bel scoffed.

'I'm not sure if he's got much say in things any more,' said Flo.

'You can always live with me.'

'That's very kind of you, Bel, but I couldn't stand you bellowing down me ear all day long. And it's not just the flat I'm worried about, what about me job?' Each week, she sent her rent, along with a little report: a woman had left and she'd had to take on someone new, a machine had needed servicing and she enclosed Herbie Smith's bill. The address Harry had given her turned out to be a firm of accountants, and although she frequently enclosed a letter for Mr Fritz, there'd been no reply so far, and she wondered if her letters were being passed on.

Four families moved in upstairs, but Flo heard nothing about her own situation. 'Perhaps the little Fritzes are playing games with me,' she said to Bel. 'Lulling me into a sense of false security, like.' She might come home one day to find the locks changed and her furniture dumped on the pavement.

Bel made one of her famous faces. 'Don't talk daft. Y'know, what you need is to get away for a while, leave all your troubles behind. I've been thinking, why don't we go on holiday? A woman at work is going to Spain for two whole weeks on a charter flight, I think it's called. It's ever so cheap and she said there's still a few places left.'

'Spain! I've never been abroad.'

'Neither have I since I left the forces, but that's no reason not to go now. We might cop a couple of fellers out there.'

The small swimming pool shone like a dazzling sapphire in the light of the huge amber moon, and the navy sky was powdered lavishly with glittering stars. Less than fifty feet away, the waters of the Mediterranean shimmered and rustled softly and couples were clearly visible lying clasped in each other's arms on the narrow strip of Costa Brava sand. Somewhere a guitarist was strumming a vaguely familiar tune, and people were still in the pool, although it was past midnight. There was laughter, voices, the clink of glasses from the outside bar.

Flo, on the balcony of their room on the second floor of the hotel, refilled her glass from the jug of sangria and wondered if you could buy it in Liverpool. Wine was so cheap that she and Bel were convinced they would never be sober if they lived in Spain.

They'd been lucky to get a room with a view like this. The guests on the other side of the building could see only more and more of the hotels that cluttered the entire length of coast.

Someone opened a door by the pool and a blast of music filled the air: The Who, singing, 'I can See For Miles . . .' 'Miles and miles and miles,' Flo sang, until the door closed and all she could hear was the guitarist again. Every night at the Old Tyme Dance while she was being led sedately around the floor to the strains of 'When Irish Eyes Are Smiling', or 'Goodnight, Eileen', she thought enviously of the youngsters in the other ballroom leaping around madly to the sound of Dire Straits or ABBA.

Bel hadn't bothered to inform her that the group they were travelling with were old-age pensioners. Flo had been horrified when they got on the plane and she found herself surrounded by people with hearing aids and walking sticks and not a single head of hair in sight that wasn't grey.

To her further consternation, there were actually a few wolf-whistles – in this company, two women in their mid-fifties must seem like teenagers: Bel still managed to look incredibly glamorous, though her lovely red hair was in reality lovely grey hair that had required a tint for years.

There were still five more days of the holiday to go, and Flo supposed she'd had quite a good time. During the day, they wandered round Lloret del Mar, admiring the palm trees and the sparkling blue sea. They bought little trinkets in the gift shops. She got Bel a pretty mosaic bracelet, and Bel bought her a set of three little brass plaques that had taken Flo's fancy. Then they had found a bar that stocked every liqueur in existence and were sampling them one by one. Flo had sent cards to everyone she could think of, including Mr Fritz, though she had no faith that he would get it. Why had he never written as he'd promised? It was six months since he'd left William Square and she worried about him all the time. If she didn't hear soon, she resolved to go over to Ireland in search of him, even though she didn't have a proper address.

Evenings, they went dancing. Flo wrinkled her nose: she hated being taken in a pair of gnarled, sunburnt arms for the Gay Gordons or the Military Two-step or, somewhat daringly, a rumba, played to a slow, plodding beat in case it overtaxed a few dicky hearts. Mr Fritz was old, but in her eyes he had always remained the same lovely little man with brown fuzzy hair and twinkling eyes she'd first met in the laundry. The other night one sly old bugger in fancy shorts had had the nerve to get fresh during the last waltz.

'You're no spring chicken yourself,' Bel snorted, when Flo complained.

'I wouldn't mind dancing with fellers me own age,' Flo said haughtily. Bel had taken up with Eddie Eddison, a widower in his seventies, who came from Maynard Street, though it seemed daft to come all the way to Spain to click with a feller who lived only two streets away in Liverpool.

Most nights when Bel wasn't looking, Flo slipped away. She enjoyed sitting on the balcony, staring at the sky, listening to the sounds by the pool, drinking wine. When she got home, she might do something with her backyard, paint the walls a nice colour, buy some plants and a table and chairs, turn it into one of them patio things. It would be pleasant to sit outside in the good weather. The flat could get stuffy when it was hot.

That's if the flat remained hers. Oh, Lord, Bel would be cross if she knew she was worrying about the flat again. Flo rested her arms on the balcony and stared down at the pool. Even at this hour children were still up. Two little boys, one about Tom O'Mara's age, were splashing water at each other in the shallow end. If only she could have brought Tom with her. He would have had the time of his life. Instead of dancing with men old enough to be her father, or sitting alone on a balcony, she could have been down at the pool with Tom. It seemed a normal, everyday thing to do, to bring your grandson on holiday, but the things that normal, everyday people did seemed to have passed her by.

Flo sat back in her chair and sighed. Another few days and they could go home. She couldn't wait, though she wouldn't let Bel know she was homesick. She would laugh and smile, and look cheerful, pretend to be having a great time, make the best of things as she always had.

Out of the corner of her eye, she glimpsed a star shoot across the sky. It disappeared into the infinite darkness – or was it just her imagination that she could see the faintest, barely discernible burst of yellow, which meant that millions and millions of miles away there'd been an almighty explosion?

The idea made her shudder, and she remembered being told as a child that God had created the world in seven days. 'But did He create the universe as well, Dad? Did He create the sun and the moon and the stars at the same time?' She couldn't remember what his answer had been.

It was ages since she'd thought about Dad. Living in Burnett Street had been perfect when he was alive and Martha had yet to assume the role of Being In Charge. Flo had never planned on getting married, but had just known that one day she would and that she would have children, two at least. Then, as if the shooting star had struck its target, Flo felt as if every muscle in her body had instantly wasted, as if every bone had turned to jelly. All that was left was her heart, which pounded like a hammer in her cavernous chest.

She'd spent her entire adult life in the way she was spending this holiday! Making the best of things, pretending to enjoy herself. *Waiting for it to end!*

'Oh, Lord!' The awful feeling passed as quickly as it had come, but in the mad scramble of thoughts that followed she knew that she should have made the best of things in a more practical way, by marrying Gerard Davies, for instance, or almost any one of those other young servicemen. It was no use blaming Martha. It was Flo's own fault that she'd wasted her life.

The basement flat felt unusually chilly when she arrived home from Spain to find three letters waiting for her on the mat. She went through them on her way to the kitchen to put the kettle on, aching for a cup of tea made with ordinary leaves instead of those silly teabags. Two were bills, but she stopped in her tracks when she saw the name and address of a solicitor in Castle Street on the third. She'd never had a letter from a solicitor before, and her hands were trembling as she tore it open, convinced that the little Fritzes were demanding formally that she quit the flat.

The heading was enough to make her burst into tears. 'Re: Fritz Erik Hofmannsthal (deceased).'

He was dead! *Mr Fritz was dead* – and not one of his children had bothered to let her know. Flo forgot the tea and poured a glass of sherry instead. Her imagination ran riot as she thought of all the different ways he might have died, none of them pleasant. She'd like to bet he'd wanted to return to William Square and be with her, but his children hadn't let him. Lovely, long-cherished memories flicked through her brain: the laundry on Tuesdays when he'd brought cream cakes, the day Stella had taken the photograph of him and his girls outside – the family had just come back from Anglesey and seemed so happy. How strange and cruel life could be that it should all have turned so sour. She recalled their first weekend in the Isle of Man, two old friends comfortably together at last.

It was a long time before she could bring herself to read the letter, to learn that dear Mr Fritz had bequeathed her the leasehold of the basement flat, as well as the launderette in Smithdown Road. The letter finished, 'We would be obliged if you would telephone for an appointment so that arrangements can be made for various papers to be signed.'

'Mr Hofmannsthal's children are seeking to question the validity of his will,' the solicitor informed her. He was younger than expected, not the least bit pompous, and from his build and his broken nose, looked like a rugby player or a boxer. 'But as same was dictated in my presence ten years ago while my client was in full possession of his senses, there is no question of it not being valid.'

'I don't think the little Fritzes liked me very much,' Flo said, in a small voice. 'Least, not since they stopped being little.'

'They like you even less now, which isn't surprising. You're very much the fly in the ointment. They want the house in William Square put on the market, but it won't fetch anything like it would have done had the basement been included.' The solicitor smiled, as if this pleased him enormously.

'I'm sorry,' Flo said weakly.

'Good heavens, Miss Clancy!' he exploded. 'Sorry is the very last thing you should be. It's what my client, Fritz Hofmannsthal, wanted, and I'm sure he had the best reason in the world for doing so.'

Flo felt herself go pink, wondering what Mr Fritz might have told him. 'Do I still have to look after the other launderettes?' she enquired.

The solicitor was so outraged to discover that she'd been 'acting as manager', as he put it, for six whole months without even so much as a thank-you from the little Fritzes, that he suggested putting in a claim against the estate for 'services rendered'. 'We'll demand ten pounds a week for the period involved, and probably end up with five. Will that suit you?'

Flo was about to say she didn't want a penny, but changed her mind. Even if she gave away the money, it was better than the little Fritzes having it. 'Five pounds a week would be fine,' she said.

The whole thing went into another of Flo's invisible

boxes marked 'Secret'. If people found out, they would wonder why Mr Fritz had remembered her so generously. She owned her own property. She owned her own business. But no one would ever know.

In his day Edward Eddison had been a professional magician and had appeared halfway down the bill in theatres all over the country. When he married Bel Szerb in a register office two months after their holiday in Spain, he produced two white doves from his sleeve, which fluttered around the room, much to the annoyance of the registrar who disapproved of confetti, let alone live birds.

Bel, gorgeous in lavender tulle and a feathered hat, screamed with laughter when a bird settled happily on her head.

Flo, still shaken by the strange, unsettling thoughts she'd had in Spain and the loss of Mr Fritz, felt depressed when the ceremony was over, and Bel and Eddie departed to Bournemouth on their honeymoon. The newly-weds intended to live in Eddie's house in Maynard Street, and Bel planned on doing the place up from top to bottom. Flo tried to cheer herself up by decorating her own flat. She painted the walls white and the big wooden beams across the middle of the room black. The plaques Bel had bought her in Spain went well against the glossy surface, and when she mentioned this to her ladies, they presented her with several more. She painted the little yard a pretty rose pink, bought garden furniture and plant-holders, but when it came to new furniture for inside, she couldn't bring herself to part with a thing. After all, Mr Fritz and Jimmy Cromer had struggled downstairs with the settee and chair out of Stella's sitting room, as well as the big sideboard, which was probably an antique – if the little Fritzes had known it would probably have gone for auction, along with the lovely oak wardrobe and chest-of-drawers in the bedroom. As for the brass bed, she'd no intention of changing it for one of those padded-base things like they'd had in Spain – it had been like sleeping on wooden planks. She even felt quite fond of the little rag rug in front of the fire, which had been there when she arrived. She made do with buying pictures for the walls and armfuls of silk flowers to arrange in vases, and a nest of round tables to put the vases on. The big table she folded against the wall because she rarely used it. Nowadays, she ate on the settee in front of the television. Last Christmas, Bel had bought her a coffee table for this very purpose, an ugly thing, Flo thought secretly, with legs like clumps of giant onions.

The only light that glimmered through this dark period was her grandson Tom, seven years old and a continual thorn in the side of Nancy O'Mara, just like his grandad. Tom came and went as he pleased, no matter what Nancy told him. Hugh, of whom Flo saw little these days, appeared to have given up on his son and took no interest. On Sundays, Flo would return from Mass to find Tom sitting on the steps outside her flat, ready to spend the day with her. She took him to matinée performances at the cinema. Once she got used to the idea that she was her own boss and could take time off whenever she pleased, she and Tom sometimes went to football matches to see Everton or Liverpool play.

Tom was at Flo's place too often to be kept hidden in one of her secret boxes, so Bel got used to finding him there, though she thought it most peculiar. 'You're obsessed with the O'Maras, Flo,' she hissed. 'Tommy, Hugh, now little Tom.'

Gradually the dark period passed. It was a relief when the unpleasant middle-aged couple on the ground floor moved out, and a beautiful black girl, still a teenager, with two small children, moved in. But Flo was shocked to the core when she discovered that Charmian was one of the women who took up position along the railings of the square each night. Even so, it was hard not to say, 'Good morning,' or 'Isn't it a lovely day?' or 'We could do with some rain, couldn't we?' when they came face to face. The two became rather wary friends, although Charmian continually felt the need to defend her doubtful and precarious lifestyle. 'Me husband walked out on me. No one'll give me a job with two kids under school age. How else am I supposed to feed 'em and pay the rent?' she demanded aggressively, the first time she came down to the basement flat.

'Don't go on at me, luv,' Flo said mildly. 'It's your life. I haven't uttered a word of criticism, have I?'

'I can see it in your eyes. You're disgusted.'

'No, I'm not, luv. The disgust is in your own eyes. I think you're ashamed, else you wouldn't go on about it so much.'

Charmian stormed out, but returned the following night to say, 'You're right, but I don't know another way to keep me head above water.'

Flo said nothing. As the months rolled by, she listened patiently while Charmian struggled loudly and vocally with her conscience. When the woman who worked the morning shift in the launderette gave in her notice, Flo casually mentioned it to her upstairs neighbour. 'There'll be a job going the Monday after next, eight till two. The pay isn't bad, enough for the rent and to keep two kids without too much of a struggle.'

Charmian glared at her. 'Is that a hint?'

'No, luv, it's an offer.' Flo shrugged. 'It's up to you if you take it.'

'What about the owner? He mightn't want an ex-pro working in his bloody launderette.'

The girl scowled, but she hated what she was doing and Flo could tell that she was tempted. 'The owner will go on my recommendation.'

'And you'd recommend me when you know . . .' Two large tears rolled down the satiny cheeks. 'Oh, Flo!'

4

Eddie Eddison didn't last long. He died a happy man in the arms of his glamorous wife only eighteen months after their wedding. Bel was left with a hefty weekly pension, a gold Cortina saloon, and immediately began to take driving lessons.

Charmian gave up her job when she married the emergency plumber, Herbie Smith, who moved into the ground-floor flat with his ready-made family. Unlike his dad, Tom O'Mara didn't desert his friend Flo when he started comprehensive school. He was a cocky little bugger, full of confidence and sure of his place in the world. It didn't bother him being seen going to the pictures on Sunday afternoons with a middle-aged woman, or two middle-aged women if Bel decided to come. Bel had transferred her affections from Gregory Peck to Sean Connery.

1983

When his dad died Tom was fifteen, and the cockiness, the confidence, turned out to be nothing but a sham.

The firm in Anfield swore that the accident had been caused by negligence on the part of their workman, Hugh O'Mara. The house he was rewiring was dripping with damp: he'd been a fool to try fitting a plug in a socket that was hanging off the wall, the existing wiring having been installed half a century before. Knowing O'Mara, he'd probably had only half his mind on the job. His heart hadn't been in it for years. He was usually in either a trance or a daydream, the boss was never sure. Anyroad, the stupid sod had been thrown across the room, killed instantly.

Flo didn't go to the funeral. She couldn't have stood it if Nancy, the Welsh witch, had behaved as she had outside the gates of Cammell Laird's, weeping and wailing and making an exhibition of herself. At least she'd had a claim on Tommy, but she'd none on Hugh.

It was as if Hugh had already been dead a long time, Flo thought, strangely unmoved, as if she had already mourned his loss. Tom, though, was distraught. He came into the launderette after the funeral, his face red and swollen as if he'd been crying for days. Flo took him into her cubicle out of the way of her ladies' curious eyes.

'No one wants me, Flo,' he wept. 'Me mam walked out, me dad went and died on me, and Gran doesn't like me.'

He was almost as tall as her. Flo's heart ached as she stroked his bleak, tearstained face. If only her own history could have been rewritten, how would things have turned out then? 'I like you, luv,' she whispered.

'Promise not to die, Flo. Promise not to go away like everybody else.' He buried his face in her shoulder.

'We've all got to die sometime, luv. But I won't go away, I promise that much. I'll always be here for you.'

Tom took a long time to recover from the loss of his dad. When he did, there was a callousness about him that saddened Flo, a chill in his green eyes that hadn't been there before. He left school before he could sit his O levels and moved out of his gran's house to doss down in the homes of various friends, sleeping occasionally on Flo's settee if he was desperate. He got a job helping out at St John's market. 'I'm going to start a stall meself one day,' he boasted. 'There's no way I'm working for someone else all me life, not like me dad.'

He brought her presents sometimes: a portable wireless for the kitchen, expensive perfume, a lovely leather handbag. She accepted them with a show of gratitude, although she was worried sick that they were stolen. He even offered to get her a colour telly at half the list price.

'No ta, luv.' She would have loved a colour telly, but felt it might encourage the criminal tendencies she was convinced he had.

★

Bel was doing her utmost to persuade her friend to retire in May, when she turned sixty-five. 'You've worked non-stop since you were thirteen, Flo,' she said coaxingly. 'That's fifty-two long years now. It's time to put your feet up, like me.'

Tact had never been one of Bel's stronger virtues: the reason behind her solicitude for Flo's welfare was obvious. 'You only want me to retire so you'll have company during the day.'

'True,' Bel conceded. 'But that doesn't mean it's not a good idea.'

The launderette provided a good, steady income, and Flo had no intention of giving up, not while she remained fit and well, though she got tired if she was on her feet for too long. Her ladies had changed over the years, but they were still the irrepressible, good-humoured Scousers she loved. Nowadays not all were poor: they went on holiday to places like Majorca and Torremolinos and brought brasses back for Flo's walls.

When the letter came from the property firm in London offering to buy her out for twenty-five thousand pounds, her first instinct was to refuse. The firm was acting for a client who wished to turn the entire block into a supermarket. But the offer had come as a boon to Flo's neighbours. Hardly anyone ordered coal at a coal office, these days, when they could phone from home. Who'd buy wallpaper and paint from a little shop that had to charge the full price when it could be got for much less from a big do-it-yourself store? The watch-repairer, the picture-framer, the cobbler all reported that business was at an all-time low. Flo couldn't bring herself to turn down the offer and spoil things for those who were desperate to take it.

There were thousands of pounds in the bank now and not much to spend it on. Flo went to see the solicitor in Castle Street and made a will. She'd never thought she'd have property and money to leave behind, but she knew who she wanted to have it. She put the copy at the bottom of the papers in the bureau – one of these days, she must clear everything out. There was stuff in there she'd sooner people didn't know about when she died.

She bought the coveted colour television, a microwave oven, because they seemed useful, and a nice modern music centre, hoping that the man in Rushworth and Draper's didn't think a woman of her age foolish when she chose a dozen or so records: the Beatles, Neil Diamond, Tony Bennett. She didn't *feel* old, but later the same day, when she was wandering around Lewis's department store, she saw an elderly woman, who looked familiar with rather nice silver hair, coming towards her. As they got closer, she realised she was walking towards a mirror and that the woman was herself. She *was* old! What's more, she looked it.

When Bel was told she laughed. 'Of course you're old, girl. We all grow old if we don't die young. The thing is to get the best you can out of life till it's time to draw your last breath. Let's do something dead exciting this weekend, like drive to Blackpool. Or how about London for a change?' She was fearless in the car and would have driven as far as the moon if there'd been a road.

'Oh, Bel,' Flo said shakily, always grateful for her friend's unfailing cheerfulness and good humour. 'I'm ever so glad I went to Birkenhead that morning and met you.'

Bel squeezed her hand affectionately. 'Me too, girl. At least one good thing came out of that business with Tommy O'Mara, eh?'

'Where did we go wrong, Flo?' Sally cried. She asked Flo the same question every time they met.

Flo always gave the same reply. 'Don't ask me, luv.'

Ten years before, Grace, Keith and their two sons had upped roots and gone to live in Australia. Sally and Jock only occasionally received a letter from their daughter, and Grace ignored their pleas to come and visit. Jock was becoming surlier in his old age, Sally more and more unhappy. One of these days, she said bitterly, she was convinced she would die of a broken heart.

'I could easily have done the same when me little boy was taken,' Flo said. She thought of Bel with her three husbands and three lost babies. In her opinion, Sally was giving up far too easily. 'You and Jock have still got each other, as well as your health and strength. You should go out more, go on holiday. It's never too late to have a good time.'

'It is for some people. You're different, Flo. You're made of iron. You keep smiling no matter what.'

Flo couldn't remember when she'd last seen her sister smile. It was impossible to connect this listless, elderly woman with the happy, brown-haired girl from Burnett Street.

Sally went on, 'I remember when we were at school, everyone used to remark on me sister with the lovely smile.'

'Why don't you come to the pictures with me and Bel one night?' Flo urged. 'Or round to William Square one Sunday when Charmian usually pops down for a sherry and a natter.'

'What's the use?'

Grace didn't bother to cross the world to be with her father when her mother died. Sally's heart gave up one night when she was asleep in bed, but perhaps it really had broken.

Bel went with Flo to the funeral on a dreary day in March. It was windy, dry, sunless. Grey clouds chased each other across a paler grey sky. Jock held up remarkably well throughout the Requiem Mass. When Flo had gone to see him, he said that he intended moving to Aberdeen to live with his brother, and she could tell that he was looking forward to returning to the city of his birth. It was as if he and Sally had dragged each other down in their misery, frozen in their grief, unable to come to terms with the loss of Ian, and Grace's indifference. Flo had expected that Sally's death would be the last straw for Jock; instead, it seemed to have released him from a state of perpetual mourning.

It was obvious that Martha, stiff with self-importance, was relishing her role of Being in Charge. Jock, a bit put out, said that she'd taken over the funeral arrangements, had ordered the coffin, the flowers, seen the priest. In the cemetery, in the wind, beneath the racing clouds, Flo saw the gleam in her sister's eyes behind the thick-lensed glasses that she remembered well, as if this was a military operation and she'd like to tell everyone where to stand. When the coffin was lowered into the grave, Jock suddenly put up his hand to shield his eyes and Martha poked him sharply in the ribs. It wasn't done for a man to cry, not even at his wife's funeral. That gesture put paid to the vague thoughts Flo had had of exchanging a few polite words with her sister.

The Camerons were there, Norman handsome and scowling – but, oh, Kate had changed so much, her lovely hair chopped short, her once slim figure swollen and shapeless. There was a battered look on her anxious face, no bruises, bumps or scars, but the same look some of Flo's ladies had, which told of a hard life with many crosses to bear. Yet her eyes remained bright, as if she retained a hope that things would get better one day – or perhaps the light in her eyes was for her children, who would have made any mother proud. Millicent, whom Flo had last glimpsed in the hospital, only a few days' old, had grown into a graceful, slender young woman, with none of her mother's vulnerability apparent in her lovely, strong-willed face. She was with her husband, as was Trudy, whose wedding had been only a few weeks before. Trudy was pretty, but she lacked her sister's grace and air of determination. However, it was the son, Declan, who took Flo's breath away. A slight, delicate lad of ten, it could have been her own little boy she was staring at across the open grave. The Clancys might well be pale-skinned, pale-haired and thin-boned, but they had powerful genes that thrust their way forcefully through each generation. There was no sign of Albert Colquitt in Kate, no indication that Norman Cameron was the father of these three fragile, will o'-the-wisp children. There was another girl, Flo knew, Alison, who had something wrong with her and was in a home in Skem.

'Aren't we going for refreshments?' Bel was disappointed when the mourners turned to leave and Flo made her way towards the gold Cortina.

'I'm not prepared to eat a bite that's been prepared by our Martha,' Flo snapped. 'And don't look at me like that, Bel Eddison, because there's not a chance in hell I'll tell you why. If you're hungry, we'll stop at a pub. I wouldn't mind a good stiff drink meself.'

Sally had gone, to become a memory like Mam and Dad, Mr Fritz and Hugh. Each time someone close to her died, it was as if a chapter in her life had come to an end. One day, Flo too would die and the book would close for ever. She sighed. She definitely needed that drink.

September, 1996

Flo pressed her fingers against her throbbing temples, but the pressure seemed only to emphasise the nagging pain. She knew she should have been to the doctor long ago with these awful headaches but, as she said to Bel, 'If there's summat seriously wrong, I'd sooner not know.' There were times when the pain became unbearable, and all she wanted to do was scream: it felt as if an iron band was being screwed tighter and tighter around her scalp. A glass of sherry made it worse, two glasses made it better, and with three she felt so light-headed that the pain disappeared. Getting drunk seemed preferable to having her head cut open and someone poking around inside, turning her into a vegetable. Peter, the nice young lad from next door who reminded her so much of Mr Fritz, got rid of the bottles for her because she felt too embarrassed to put them out for the binmen.

A concerned Bel had persuaded her to have her eyes tested, but the optician said she had excellent sight for a woman of her age, though he prescribed glasses for reading.

Mam, Flo remembered, had been terrified of letting a doctor near her with a knife. The girls used to get upset, worried that she'd die. But Mam had only been in her forties. Flo was seventy-six, nobody's wife, nobody's daughter, with no children to care if she lived or died. Bel would miss her terribly, Charmian less so, what with a husband, two kids and three grandchildren to look after since Minola had gone back to school. Tom O'Mara didn't need her so much now that he was married with a family, two lovely little girls, though he still came to William Square regularly, at least once a week, often bearing food from the Chinese takeaway around the corner and a bottle of wine. She never asked how he made the money he was so obviously flush with. After years spent living on his wits, involved in ventures that were barely this side of legal, he was now something to do with a club that he adamantly refused to talk about. Flo suspected she was probably the only person on earth who knew the real Tom O'Mara, the man who loved and fussed over her tenderly, and brought her little presents. Outside the four walls of her flat, she'd like to bet that Tom was an entirely different person – even his wife and children might not know how soft and gentle he could be. Bel, who couldn't stand him, had to concede it was decent of him to put Nancy in a posh nursing-home in Southport when her mind went haywire and she could remember nothing since the war.

Music filled the basement flat, reaching every nook and corner, wrapping around her like a magic blanket woven from the dearest of memories. And shadows from the lamp Tom had brought from abroad passed slowly over the walls, the figures lifesize. When Flo felt especially dizzy, the figures seemed real, alive. He had brought the record, too, not long ago. 'Close your eyes,' he said teasingly, when he came in. 'I've got you a prezzie, a surprise.'

So Flo had closed her eyes, and suddenly the strains of 'Dancing in the Dark' came from the speakers at each end of the room. Her eyes had snapped open and for several seconds she felt muddled. She'd told no one that this was the tune she and Tommy had danced to in the Mystery more than half a century ago. 'What made you buy that, luv?' she asked querulously.

'You've been humming it non-stop for months. I thought you'd like to hear it sung by an expert. That's Bing Crosby, that is, the one who sings "White Christmas."'

'I know who Bing Crosby is. It's lovely, Tom. Ta very much.'

At first she didn't play the record much, scared of raking up the painful past, but lately, as her head got worse and she couldn't read, not even with her new glasses, she played it more and more often. It was soothing, better than a book, to remember her own romantic affair, more passionate and tragic than anything she'd ever read. She saw herself dancing under the trees with her lost lover, making love, whispering what was to be their final goodbye.

Bel had told her she should exercise more, not sit like a lump in front of the telly getting sozzled every day. 'I ride for miles every morning on me bike in the bathroom,' she hooted loudly, through her ghastly new dentures, which were much too big and made her look like an elderly Esther Rantzen.

'I'm seventy-six, Bel,' Flo said indignantly. 'I'm entitled to be a sozzled lump at my age.' What would she have done without Bel? Without Charmian and Tom, Mr Fritz, Sally, even Hugh, her son, for a while? She'd been lucky to have so many people to love and love her back.

'What time is it?' She looked at the clock. Just gone six. But was that night or morning? What month was it?

What year? It was frightening when she couldn't remember things, when she forgot to go to bed, forgot to eat, forgot to watch one of her favourite programmes on the telly. Once she'd nearly gone out in her nightie. One of these days she'd forget who she was. It wasn't that she was losing her mind like Nancy. She smiled. No, the trouble was, she was either in terrible pain or as drunk as a lord.

She went over to the window and lifted the curtain, but still couldn't tell if it was dawn or dusk. A thick mist hung in the air, suspended a few feet from the pavement. There were noises in the square, but there always were, no matter what the time; a car drove away, she could hear people talking, someone walked past and she could see less of them than usual because their knees were shrouded in mist. She heard the clink of milk bottles. It must be morning, which meant she'd been sitting up all night.

The record, which she'd played countless times, came to an end yet again. Oddly, the ensuing silence felt louder than the music. It was a buzz, as if she was surrounded by a million bees. As she listened to the silence, Flo's mind drained of everything and became completely blank. She sat on the chest in front of the window and wondered what was she doing in this strange room full of shadows. There was too much furniture, too many ornaments, too many flowers. She didn't like it. A memory returned, crawling like a worm into her head: she lived in Burnett Street with Mam and Dad.

'But what am I doing here?' she asked of the strange room and the shadowy figures passing overhead. There was no answer. Had she been visiting someone? Whose house was this?

'Is anyone there?' Still no answer. Flo pressed her hands together distractedly, trying to make up her mind what was the best thing to do. Get away from this place, obviously, go home. Even better, go into work early, get on with the pressing left over from yesterday. It would give Mr Fritz a nice surprise when he came in.

She saw a coat hanging behind the door that looked

faintly familiar. She put it on and went outside. A man was running towards her dressed in a funny red outfit, just like Father Christmas. 'Mr Fritz!' She smiled.

The man reached her. 'It's Peter Maxwell, Flo, from next door. I've been for a run. But what are you doing out so early, luv? It's awful damp. You'll get a chill.'

'I've got to go somewhere,' she said vaguely.

'Would you like me to come with you?' The man was looking at her worriedly.

'No, ta,' she told him pleasantly.

She set off into the wet mist at a fast pace, along Upper Parliament Street and into Smithdown Road, passing closed shops and empty shops, new buildings and old, Clement Street and Mulliner Street, names that seemed familiar, though she couldn't remember why. She looked for the dress shop, which had that lovely lilac frock in the window – she'd seen it only yesterday and intended to buy it. Later, in the dinner hour, she might well come back and get it. But she couldn't see the shop anywhere. The fog didn't help – perhaps that was why no trams were running – she could scarcely see across the road. Worse, when she turned into Gainsborough Road, there was no sign of the laundry. A brick building stood in the place where the old wooden shed should be, a clinic, with notices in the window advertising a playgroup, ante-natal classes, a mother-and-toddler group.

'Oh, Lord!' Flo groaned. The fog seemed to have entered her head. It lifted briefly when she read the notices and wondered how she had got to Gainsborough Road. Why was her heart racing? Why did her legs feel so weak? She didn't realise she'd walked for miles with the energy of a young girl. The fog drifted in again, smothering the pain and everything that was real.

'I'll go and see Mam and Dad.' She made her way towards Burnett Street. The fog in her head cleared for a second when she stood outside the three terraced properties at the end of the street and remembered that they'd been built on the spot where the Clancys' and two

343

neighbouring houses used to be. She stood for a moment, staring up at the tiled roofs, the small windows. The door of the middle house opened and a man in a donkey jacket and greasy overalls came out.

'Are you after something, missus?' he demanded irritably, when he found an elderly woman standing virtually on his doorstep.

'I used to live here,' said Flo.

'You couldn't have.' He scowled. 'Me and the missus were the first to move in when the place was built forty years ago.'

The fog had descended again, enveloping her brain. 'There used to be a bay window and steps up to the door.' She put a trembling hand to her forehead. 'Did it get bombed? Is that what happened?'

'Look, luv,' the man's gruff voice became kind, 'you seem a bit confused, like. Would you like to come inside and me missus'll make you a cup of tea, then take you home? You live round here, do you?'

'I thought I lived here.' Flo wanted to cry. She said fretfully, 'Is the Mystery still there?'

'Of course it is, luv, but this isn't a good time to go walking in the park.'

But Flo was already on her way, nineteen years old, with a red ribbon in her hair, about to meet Tommy O'Mara outside the gates for the first time. She felt as if she was walking towards her destiny, and that afterwards nothing would be the same again.

He wasn't there. He was probably inside waiting under one of the trees, which were shrouded in a veil of mist. The wet grass quickly soaked through her shoes as she made her way towards them. A whiff of reality returned when she noticed the road leading from gate to gate, and the sports arena glimmering palely through the haze, things that hadn't been there before.

It was 1996, not 1939. 'Flo Clancy,' she breathed, 'you're making a right fool of yourself this morning.' She'd better catch the bus home while she had the sense to do it. But she hadn't brought a handbag, she had no money. She wept aloud. 'I feel too weary to walk all that way back.'

She plodded back towards the gates. It wouldn't be a bad idea to take the red ribbon out of her hair. It must look dead stupid on an ould woman. She blinked when she found there was no ribbon there. Martha must have snatched it off before she left the house.

Poor Martha! Flo had never before had such a feeling of sympathy for the sister who'd never had much happiness in her life, if any. 'It's time to forgive and forget, luv.' Sally must have said that a hundred times over the years.

'I'll go and see her tomorrer,' Flo vowed. 'I'll take her a bunch of flowers.' At that moment, she couldn't precisely remember where Martha lived, but it would come. The fog inside her head kept lifting and falling, she kept drifting backwards and forwards in time, and the present was becoming confused with the past. She was leaving through the gates when she heard a shout. 'Flo!'

Flo turned. Her face melted into a smile, the dimples deepened in her wrinkled face, she could feel the brightness shining from her eyes as she watched Tommy O'Mara emerge from the white mist that swirled and floated in and around the Mystery and come towards her. She stood stock-still, waiting for him, waiting for him to take her in his arms.

She waved. Oh, he was a divil of a man, with his swaggering walk, a red hanky tied carelessly around his neck, an old tweed cap perched jauntily on the back of his brown curls. She had never stopped loving him. She never would.

'Flo, girl,' he called again.

'Tommy!' Flo held out her arms to welcome her handsome lover, who had never told a lie, had meant everything he'd said, who would have married her one day if he hadn't gone down with the *Thetis*. They would have lived happily ever after with their child. Then, from somewhere within the hazy clouds, she heard the orchestra of her dream a lifetime ago, playing 'Dancing in the Dark'. Her tired old body was swaying, this way and that, to the music that swelled and quivered in the smoky, dew-spangled morning.

She didn't hear the lorry backing slowly through the fog and the gates of the Mystery. It hit her full square, flinging her forward, and the phantom figure of Tommy O'Mara was the last thing Flo saw before she died.

The lorry drove away, the driver unaware that he'd hit anyone.

It was a young lad on his way home from his paper round who found the body. He stared at the old woman lying face down on the path. Was she dead, or had she just fainted?

He knelt down and gingerly turned the old girl over by the shoulder. She was dead all right, he could tell, but, Jaysus, never in all his life before had he seen such a brilliant smile.

Millie

I

The church hall was an Aladdin's cave of treasures; stalls
with handmade jewellery, tie-dyed T-shirts, embroidered waistcoats, patchwork cushions, pottery, paintings,
intricately moulded candles far too elegant to burn. But
I'm sure I wasn't prejudiced in thinking our Trudy's stall
was the most outstanding of all – and the cheapest.

Colin had added a shelf to the back of a pasting table so
that the glassware could be exhibited on two levels.
Nightlights flickered in painted wineglasses and tumblers
that had been placed between the taller bottles so that the
flames glittered through the jewel-coloured glass, the
patterns outlined lavishly in gold or silver. The stall was
alive with every imaginable hue – 'Like a rainbow on fire,'
I said, and sighed with satisfaction when everything was
done. I'd come early to help Trudy set up.

Trudy was shaking, as if she was about to take the
starring role in her first play. 'What if I don't sell a single
thing?'

'Don't be daft. I've got my eye on at least five bottles
for Christmas presents.'

'I can't take money off me sister.'

'What nonsense! There's no room for sentiment now
you're a businesswoman, Trude.'

'Oh, Mill!' Trudy glanced left and right at the other
stallholders, most of whom had finished setting up and
were waiting impatiently for the doors to open at eleven
o'clock. 'I feel dead conspicuous.'

'You look perfectly okay to me. Would you like a cup
of tea?'

'I'd love one. But don't stay away long, Sis,' she called nervously, as I went towards the room behind the stage where tea and coffee were being served. 'I can't do this on me own.'

It turned out to be a day when the Camerons came of age, I thought afterwards, when we appeared to be just like any other family. James came at exactly half past eleven, as promised. Declan was already there, deeply interested in the process of tie-dying. Mum arrived at midday, her face red and bothered. Beads of perspiration glistened on her brow, although the November day was cold. I went to meet her. 'Your dad turned dead nasty when he realised I was going out,' she panted. 'He insisted I made his dinner first. I've put it in a low oven for when he comes home from the pub, but I daren't think what it'll be like by then.' She dropped her handbag, bent to retrieve it, then dropped the car keys and her gloves. 'How's our Trudy getting on?'

'Her bottles are selling like hot cakes. Half have already gone. She's not asking nearly enough.' Trudy hadn't even noticed I was no longer there. Flushed with confidence, she was coping with her busy stall on her own. I clutched my mother's arm. 'Mum, could you come back to Flo's with me when this is over? There's something I want to show you.'

'What on earth can that be, luv?'

'You won't know till you've seen it, will you?'

She shook her head. 'I couldn't possibly, Millicent. Your dad was in a terrible mood. It'd be best if I went straight home.'

'In that case I'll come over tonight and fetch you,' I said firmly. 'There's something you've got to see.'

James had already been introduced to Trudy. It was time he met my mother. How could I ever have felt ashamed, I wondered, with a lump in my throat, of this warm-hearted, kind woman, whose face shone with pleasure as she said, 'I'm ever so pleased to meet you, James, luv. Does your mam call you Jim or Jimmy?'

When Colin arrived with Melanie and Jake after dinner, Trudy's stall was almost empty. Starry-eyed and triumphant, she'd taken over two hundred pounds. 'I can't believe people are actually willing to pay for me bottles. Just imagine, they'll be on window-sills all over Liverpool.' She promised to paint more for me over the next few days. Mum was in her element. She wandered around, saying, 'I see you've bought one of me daughter's bottles. Aren't they lovely?' If people were inclined to stop and chat, she'd tell them about her other daughter. 'That's her over there,' I heard her say more than once. 'That's our Millicent. She works for an estate agent in Liverpool town centre. And that's me son, the lad in the brown jersey. He's going to college next year.'

To everyone's astonishment, Gran turned up and bought the last of Trudy's bottles. 'I couldn't very well not come, could I?' she grunted sourly. 'Someone gave me a lift. I hope our Kate came in the car so she can take me home.'

I studied my grandmother carefully. This was the woman who'd given Flo's baby to Nancy O'Mara. Oh, how I'd love to find out exactly what had happened. But this wasn't the right time — would there ever be a right time to raise such an emotive subject?

We all went into the room behind the stage for a cup of tea. Trudy folded up her stall and joined us, which meant that there were three Camerons, four Daleys, Martha Colquitt and James — who were, inexplicably, having an animated conversation about football. The only person missing was my father, which probably accounted for the jubilant atmosphere.

'I never thought I'd witness this,' Colin whispered to me.

'Witness what?'

'Well, it's almost a case of Happy Families, isn't it? It's the way you'd expect any normal family to behave. Everyone's had a great day, including the kids.'

When it was time to leave, I arranged to pick up Mum

at seven o'clock and take her to Flo's flat. My father would have gone out again by then.

'I wish you'd tell me what it's all about,' she said.

'What is it all about?' James asked later. We'd driven into town in our separate cars and met up in a restaurant for a meal. 'I'd hoped we'd spend the rest of the day together.'

I ignored the last comment. 'It's something truly amazing and wonderful,' I said happily. 'Auntie Flo's left her flat and all her money, nearly twenty-four thousand pounds, to Mum. I only found a copy of the will last night. I want her to be at Flo's when she reads it for herself.'

When I drew up outside, the house in Kirkby was in darkness. Surprised, I went round to the back. The kitchen door was unlocked, which meant that someone must be in. 'Mum?' I shouted. 'Declan? Is anybody home? It's me.'

A faint noise came from upstairs, a whimper. Alarmed, I switched on the light on the stairs and went up. 'Mum?' I called.

'In here, luv.' The voice, little more than a whisper, came from the front bedroom. I pushed open the door and reached for the light switch.

'Don't turn the light on, Millicent.'

I ignored her. In the dim glow of the low wattage bulb, I saw my mother half sitting, half lying in bed. Her right eye was swollen, her lip split and bleeding. She had bruises on both arms. She looked utterly wretched, but despite everything, there was still that indefatigable look in her eyes, as though she was the most resilient victim in the world, who would survive whatever came her way. I was convinced that if a tank rolled over her, she would pick herself up and carry on as if nothing had happened.

'Mum! Oh, Mum, what's he done to you?' Rage enveloped me like a cloak and I could scarcely speak. If my father had been there, I think I could easily have killed him.

'Close the curtains, luv. I don't want people seeing in.'

I drew them with an angry flourish, and sat on the bed. Mum winced. 'It's not as bad as it looks,' she said. 'I tried to ring you, stop you coming, but all I got was your machine.'

'I've been in town with James.' I forced myself to speak calmly.

'Mrs Bradley dabbed some TCP on it, and she bathed me eye an' all. I'm just a tiny bit tipsy too. She gave me this great big glass of brandy. She wanted to call the police, but I wouldn't let her.' Over the years, Mrs Bradley had frequently threatened to report Norman Cameron, but Mum had always stopped her. 'I told her this was the first time he'd hit me in years, which is the God's honest truth.'

'What brought it on, Mum?'

She shrugged, then winced again. 'His dinner was ruined. I knew it would be, stuck in the oven all that time.'

'You mean this . . .' I gestured towards the black eye, the split lip, the bruises — '. . . is solely due to a ruined dinner?'

'Only partly. I was out an awful long time, Millicent, nearly four hours. And, oh, it was a lovely afternoon.' Her eyes brightened when she thought about the day that had gone. 'I really enjoyed meself, what with our Trudy doing so well, Colin and the kids being there, your gran turning up, you and Declan. James is ever such a nice chap, I really liked him.' She managed a laugh. 'I even bought meself a pair of earrings to wear at your wedding — little red flowered ones to go with me best coat.'

'Oh, Mum!' I lightly touched her fading hair.

She sighed. 'He could never stand me being happy. I daren't ever come in with a smile on me face that I got from somewhere else, it always riled him. It makes him feel shut out, and he hates that. Today I just didn't think.

I suppose I expected him to be pleased about Trudy and everything. 'Stead, he just lashed out at me. He'd been getting more and more worked up the longer I stayed out.'

'He's always been a miserable bugger,' I said acidly.

There was a long silence. Mum seemed to have drifted off into a world of her own. A motorbike growled to a halt outside. I got up and looked through the curtains. A girl from a house opposite came out, got on to the pillion, and the bike shot away. I stayed at the window, though there was no longer anything to see apart from the orange street lights, the still houses, the occasional car driving by. A group of boys wandered past, kicking a football to each other. Then my mother spoke in a soft, far-away voice: 'I remember once, I was only a titch, two or three. We'd been out for the day, your gran and me. It was late when we got back. Did I ever tell you we lived with Elsa Cameron for a long time? Anyroad, Elsa was out, and we heard noises coming from the cupboard under the stairs, terrible sobs. The poor little lad had been shut in there in the dark for hours. You never saw anything like his eyes, all feverish and bright, as if he'd have gone mad if he'd been left there much longer. He was only six.'

'Who are you talking about, Mum?' I asked perplexed.

'Why, your dad, luv. After that, your gran never left him alone with Elsa again. She had that illness, they call it purple depression or something now. She should never have been allowed to keep a child.'

I felt myself grow cold. I recalled the photo in Flo's flat of the grim-looking woman with the beautiful baby on her knee, the baby that had become my father. I tried to visualise the monster who had conducted a reign of terror throughout our childhood as a terrified little boy of six. It was hard. 'Why have you never told us this before, Mum?' I asked shakily.

'Your dad made me swear never to breathe a word to another soul. I suppose he felt ashamed. I'd be obliged if you didn't mention to him that I'd told you.'

'It might have helped us to understand.' It only might have.

'I suppose things would have been different if I hadn't let him down,' she said, half to herself.

'In what way, Mum?'

Her face went blank, as if she'd said too much. 'Oh, it doesn't matter, luv. It's a long time ago now. Do you fancy a cup of tea? I'm dying for one meself. I haven't had one since I came home.'

'I'll make one straight away. Where's Declan?'

'He's not back yet. He went off with the couple who made them funny-coloured T-shirts.'

While I made the tea my mind was in a whirl. I had no idea what to think. No matter what had happened to my father, it was impossible to excuse the things he'd done. It wasn't Mum's fault, or his children's, that his own mother had suffered from puerperal depression. Why take it out on us?

When I returned to the bedroom with the tea, Mum said, 'What's the big surprise for me at Flo's? Or are you still not prepared to tell me unless I'm actually there?'

'I'd forgotten all about it!' I took hold of both Mum's hands. 'Prepare yourself for a shock. Flo's left you her flat and all her worldly wealth. Twenty-three thousand, seven hundred and fifty-two pounds and elevenpence to be precise.'

I didn't leave until my father came home. The back door opened, I kissed Mum goodbye, and went downstairs. He was coming through the kitchen, unsteady on his feet, eyes blurred.

'If you lay a finger on my mother again,' I said, in a grating voice that made my ears tingle, 'so help me, I'll kill you.' He looked at me vacantly, as if he wasn't sure where the strange voice had come from. 'Do you understand?' I persisted.

He nodded. I paused, my hand on the front door, feeling oddly perturbed by the look of naked misery on

353

his face, which I probably wouldn't have noticed before. Then he said something that didn't make sense, but nevertheless made my stomach curl.

'It's all your fault.'

I was scratching through my mind, trying to think of a response, when I realised he was drunk, talking rubbish. I shook myself and left.

I'd tried to talk Mum into leaving there and then. Flo's flat was ready to move into. Wasn't it fortunate I hadn't touched a thing? The place was exactly as Flo had left it.

'There's no hurry, luv,' she said. 'Your poor dad'll be feeling dead sorry about things for a week or two. I'd sooner tell him, face to face, when I'm ready to go. I owe him that much, and I won't be scared, not now I've got money and somewhere to live. It makes me feel strong.' She still looked stunned, as if she couldn't get over the news of her good fortune. 'I remember saying to Flo how much I liked her flat when I first went there. I can't believe it's mine,' had been her initial reaction.

'Don't tell Dad about the money yet,' I warned. 'If he got his hands on it, every penny would go in no time on the lottery and the horses.'

'I may look a fool, Millicent, I've probably been a fool for most of me life, but I'm not that stupid.'

'Come and have a proper look round in the morning,' I said excitedly. 'I'll take the day off work. I've still got two days' holiday left, I was leaving them till Christmas.' My mind was working overtime, sorting out my mother's life. 'You need only stay at Flo's for a few months, then you can sell it and buy a similar place in Oxford.'

'Mmm, I suppose I could,' Mum said, in a dreamy, rather vague way that made me wonder if she could ever bring herself to leave Kirkby when it came right down to it.

'Do you still love him?' I demanded sharply.

'No, Millicent. I never loved him. The trouble is, you

might find this hard to believe, but he loves me, he always has. I'm not sure how he'll manage with me not here.' She laughed girlishly when she saw me frown 'Don't worry, I'm going. I'd already planned to, hadn't I? It's thirty years last Easter since we were married, so I've done mé stint. You and Trudy have got your own lives, Declan will be off soon. Now, Alison comes first.'

'And you? What about you?' I was doing my best to hide my impatience. 'Isn't it time you put yourself first?'

'I'll be doing that when there's just me and Alison.'

Later, when I parked the car in William Square, I thought sadly that this would be one of the last nights I would spend there. But the place was staying in the family, at least for a while. Even if that hadn't been the case, I could still come back to see Bel and Charmian. As I went down the steps to the basement room, I saw that the light was on and my heart lifted eagerly. I opened the door. Tom O'Mara was sitting on the settee watching television, his feet resting on the coffee table. Everything that had been good or bad about the day that would shortly end was forgotten.

'Hi,' he said. Our eyes met. 'You're late.'

'No, you're early.'

'Whatever.' He stood up and took me in his arms and we locked together in a long, lingering kiss. I couldn't wait for us to make love, I couldn't wait a minute longer. Neither could he. He picked me up and, still kissing, carried me into the bedroom.

Later, when it was over, Tom fell asleep, but I had never felt more wide awake, as if little electric currents were passing endlessly around my head. The affair had to end some time. He would never get divorced, and I didn't want him to. Perhaps, now that I was moving back to Blundellsands, it was time to call a halt. But could I bring myself to turn him away? Would he let me? Had I the will to resist if he flatly refused to be turned away?

My restless brain refused to stop working. Would

Mum be safe in Toxteth, even if it wasn't going to be for ever? It hadn't crossed my mind till now. I thought of the few people I knew who already lived here: Charmian and Herbie and their children, Bel, Peter Maxwell, nice, respectable, honest people, like Flo. Anyway, Mum would be safer anywhere in the world, including Toxteth, than with her husband.

When I got up in the morning, I must clear the bureau of the things that gave away Flo's secrets. I'd keep the love letters, the photo of the little boy who looked so much like Declan, and the drawing he'd done of 'MY FREND FLO'. No wonder Tom had felt so drawn towards her. He was her grandson. I recalled how indifferent he'd been with Nancy.

'Don't worry, Flo,' I whispered. 'Everything's safe with me.'

At half past nine next morning, I asked Charmian if I could use her phone – I never remembered to bring my mobile to William Square – and called Stock Masterton to say I wasn't coming in. Oliver answered. 'Diana's back,' he hissed. 'She's ruling the roost already.'

I groaned. 'I'm not looking forward to tomorrow.'

Next, I called the solicitor in Castle Street who'd dealt with Flo's affairs and made an appointment for late that afternoon.

Downstairs again, the bureau looked pathetically empty, the papers I wanted to keep already stowed in the boot of the car, the rest thrown away. I dusted everywhere, swept the yard, pulled the last few dead leaves off the plants, had a word with the same black cat that had watched me before. Then I cleaned the kitchen and the bathroom, although they'd scarcely been used, but I wanted everywhere to look perfect for when Mum came. The flat looked different today, not just cleaner but more impersonal. I didn't feel quite so much at home.

I'd barely finished when there was a knock on the door. It was too early for Mum. Perhaps it was Charmian inviting me upstairs for a coffee. I rather hoped so. Charmian had been thrilled to learn that my mother was moving in below. I was sure they'd get on well together.

'Gran!' I remarked in astonishment, when I opened the door. 'Come in.'

'Your mam phoned with the news this morning,' Martha Colquitt said grumpily, as she crunched into the living room in the crêpe-soled, fur-lined boots that were almost as old as I was. She wore a camel coat, and a jersey hat shaped like a turban with a pearl brooch in the middle. The room instantly began to reek of mothballs and liniment. 'I had an appointment at the women's hospital, so I thought I'd come and look the place over.'

'What's wrong? I mean, why did you have to go to hospital?' None of us Cameron children had much affection for our grandmother, but it was impossible to imagine life without her bad-tempered presence.

Gran was predictably bad-tempered with her reply. 'I dunno what's wrong, do I?' she barked. 'They took X-rays and did tests. I have to wait for the results till I know what's wrong.' Her voice softened. 'So this is where she lived, our Flo. I always wondered what it looked like.' She walked into the room. 'This is her all over. She liked things to be pretty.'

I watched her closely. I'd never seen her face so gentle, almost tender, as she surveyed her sister's room. 'Take your coat off, Gran,' I said. 'Would you like a coffee?'

'I never touch coffee, you should know that by now. I'll have tea. And I'll not take me coat off, thanks all the same. I'm not stopping long.'

'I'm afraid there's only powdered milk.'

Gran shrugged. 'I suppose that'll have to do, won't it?' Her head was cocked on one side, she was almost smiling as she watched Flo's lamp turn round. 'I'm dying for a ciggie and it tastes better with a cup of tea.'

When I came back, she was examining the drawing on the wall over the mantelpiece, which I'd meant to take down.

'What does this say?' She peered at it closely, her nose almost touching the wall. 'I can't see in these glasses, and I left me reading ones at home. I could never get along with them bi-focals.'

'It says, "MY FREND FLO". It was done by someone called Hugh O'Mara.'

Gran took a step back, but continued to stare at the drawing. I would have given anything to know what was going on inside her head. A faint hum came from upstairs, Charmian was vacuuming the carpets. One of Minola's children gave a little shriek. Gran was still looking at the drawing, as if she'd forgotten I was there. I licked my lips, which suddenly felt dry. I didn't want to upset her, but I *had* to know.

'He was Flo's son, wasn't he, Gran? She had him by a man called Tommy O'Mara who died on the *Thetis*. He probably never knew she was pregnant.' I licked my lips again before plunging on. 'You gave him away to Tommy's wife, Nancy.'

'What in God's name are you talking about, girl?' She spun round, wobbling slightly when her clumsy boots became tangled with each other. I felt myself shrivel before the angry eyes behind the thick lenses. 'What the hell do you know about it?'

'I know because Nancy told me.'

'Nancy!' The yellow lips split in a hoarse, unbelieving laugh. 'Don't talk rubbish, girl. Nancy's dead.'

'No, she isn't, Gran. I met her the other week. She's in a nursing-home in Southport. She said . . .' I screwed up my eyes and tried to remember word for word what Nancy had said. I visualised the old liver-spotted face, the hot dark eyes, the long fingers clawing at my arm. 'She said, "Your Martha gave him to me fair and square. You're not getting him back. I'll kill him first." Her's mind's gone,' I finished. 'She thought I was Flo.'

Gran's face crumpled and she started to cry, an alarming and uncomfortable sight. She stumbled back into a chair and lit a cigarette with shaking hands.

'Gran!' I put the tea down, ran across the room and knelt at her feet. 'I didn't mean to upset you.' I was angry with myself for being too curious, too uncaring, yet I knew I wouldn't have hesitated to do the same thing again.

'It's all right, Millicent. Where's that tea?' There was a loud sniff, a quick removal of spectacles to wipe her eyes, a conscious effort to pull herself together. She looked embarrassed, unused to revealing any emotion except anger. Her hands were still shaking as she took the tea, though she'd recovered enough to grimace disapprovingly at the mug. She said, 'I never regretted what I did. It's hard for you young 'uns to realise the disgrace it was in those days for a baby to be born on the wrong side of the blanket. The whole family would have suffered.' Her face was hard again, her tone fierce. This was the grandmother I had known all my life. 'Nancy kept her head down and Hugh well hidden for a good six months. We never dreamed Flo would recognise the baby after all that time.'

She wasn't sorry! Despite everything that had happened, losing her sister for a lifetime, she still wasn't sorry. Frowning, she jabbed the air with her cigarette. 'I can't understand this business with you and Nancy. Who told you about her? Who took you to see her in Southport?'

I sank back until I was sitting cross-legged on the floor, the heat from the gas-fire hot on my shoulders. 'Tom O'Mara did. He's Nancy's grandson – or Flo's grandson. I'm not sure how to describe him.'

'Tom O'Mara!' Gran's eyes narrowed. She stared, her gaze so penetrating, so intensely suspicious, that I knew straight away she'd guessed what was going on. I felt my cheeks burn.

At the same time, to my surprise, her face turned parchment white. Her bottom lip quivered. She looked a hundred years old. She put the half-full mug on the floor, the cigarette fell in, sizzled briefly and floated on the top, but she didn't seem to notice. She immediately lit another. 'I reckon there's a curse on the Clancys and the O'Maras,' she said. Her voice was dull, listless, almost funereal. It scared me.

'What do you mean?'

'Well, first there was Flo and Tommy.' She took a long, hard drag on the cigarette, and the end glowed bright red. 'Then our Kate and Hugh. Would you believe they actually wanted to get married?' She gave a little strained laugh, and nodded at me incredulously.

'Why couldn't they get married?' I ventured. *I'd nearly had Hugh O'Mara for a father!*

'Because they were cousins, of course,' Gran explained, as if to a child. 'It's not allowed – least, it wasn't then. Fortunately, Norman stepped in like the good lad he always was, even though he knew he was accepting soiled goods. Poor Norman . . . Until then, he'd worshipped the ground your mam walked on. He would have made the best husband in the world if she hadn't spoiled things.'

'I don't know what you're talking about, Gran.'

'I'm talking about your mam being up the stick when she married Norman Cameron.' She still spoke in the same flat, dull voice, which seemed at odds with the rather coarse expression. 'We told her Hugh O'Mara had done a bunk once he knew she was pregnant, else we'd never have got her up the aisle.'

'Who's we?' I said weakly.

'Me and Nancy. As if we could have asked for a dispensation, like our Sally suggested. Imagine telling the Church authorities about our Flo's dirty little secret.' She almost choked on the last words.

Upstairs the vacuuming had stopped. I heard the front door open and Charmian come out with the children. I felt totally mixed up. My brain, which had been working so well the night before, could no longer take anything in. What was this leading up to?

'If Mum was pregnant when she married my father,' I said slowly, 'then what happened to the baby?'

'I'm looking at her.'

'Me?'

'Yes, Millicent, you.' Gran's eyes had shrunk, skull-like, deep into their sockets. She took another long puff on her cigarette, and blew the smoke out in an equally long sigh. 'You know what that means, don't you?'

I felt myself tingle all over. 'Hugh O'Mara was my father?'

'That's right. It means something else an' all. Jesus, Mary and Joseph!' She groaned. 'It was bad enough with our Kate! I bet the devil's laughing up his sleeve at the moment.' She leaned forward, her eyes boring into mine. 'Think, Millicent, think what it means.'

So I thought very hard and eventually came up with the answer. 'It means that Tom is my brother, my half-brother,' I breathed.

2

'Millie,' Diana said importantly, 'Will you come here a minute, please?'

'Yes, miss.' I abandoned the photocopier and stood in front of Diana's desk, my hands clasped meekly behind my back. June grinned and Elliot stifled a giggle.

Diana looked at me suspiciously, not sure if she was being made fun of. She flourished a sheet of paper. 'This property you went to see last week, the one in Banks. On the particulars you describe the upstairs as having a recess with a window. You quite clearly don't know that this is what's called an oriel window. Would you change it, please, before we run the details off?'

The first thing I'd done when I was promoted was buy a book on architecture so that I could accurately describe any unusual aspects of a building. 'I'm afraid you've got it wrong, Diana,' I said sweetly. 'An oriel is a recess in the projection of a building. There's no projection on the house in Banks, just a recess.'

Diana waved the paper again. 'I beg to differ. I think I know what an oriel window is by now.'

'Millie's right,' Oliver said, from across the room. 'I doubt if I could have described it better myself.' The man sitting next to him at the same desk, nodded. Barry Green had only started the day before. He was taking over as assistant manager when Oliver transferred to Woolton on 1 January. 'I second that,' Barry said, with a charming smile.

'Even I knew that,' June chortled.

'Oh!' Diana got up and flounced into George's office. She slammed the door, and everyone glanced at each other in patient resignation when we heard the sound of her raised, complaining voice.

'Actually,' June said, 'I've never heard of an oriel window. I just wanted to get up Madam's nose.'

'I must say,' Barry Green remarked, 'that I'm glad the horrendous Miss Riddick won't be here much longer. I don't know what's got into George but he's well and truly smitten.' Barry Green had given George his first job thirty years ago, and they had remained friends ever since. His vast experience as an estate agent hadn't prevented him from being made redundant when the chain he worked for had been taken over by a building society. He reminded me of actors in the old black-and-white British films I sometimes watched on television. In his sixties, with bountiful silver hair, perfectly coiffured, he wore a light grey suit with a slight sheen, and an eggshell blue bow-tie. His diction, like his hair, was perfect, as was his moustache, two neat, silvery fish. He looked the embodiment of a 1930s ladies' man, but appearances were deceptive. Barry had a wife, Tess, four children and eight grandchildren, whose various achievements he let slip into the conversation whenever he found the opportunity. One son was an architect, his two daughters had given up dazzling careers when they started their families, several grandchildren were already at university, including the one who could walk at eight months and play the piano when she was three. He rarely mentioned his youngest son, who was abroad, but no one asked what he was up to in case Barry launched into another long, adulatory explanation.

There was nothing subtle about the change of atmosphere in Stock Masterton since Diana had returned yesterday. I wondered if it was just my imagination that I was being picked on more than the others. If I hadn't been so preoccupied with my own life, it might have mattered more. Diana wasn't rude, merely loudly and forcefully officious. She kept telling people what to do when they already knew, offering advice when it wasn't needed. She was having an affair with the boss and wanted everyone to know how much her stock had risen.

'What did you mean,' I said to Barry, 'about Diana not being here much longer?' Maybe she was leaving to marry George.

'Because she's coming to Woolton with me.' Oliver sighed. 'George only told me yesterday. She's got a title, assistant manager. I'm not sure if I can stand it.'

'Your bad luck is our good fortune,' I said cheerfully. With Diana out of the way, perhaps I could get back on good terms with George.

This seemed unlikely when Diana appeared, saying, 'George would like a word with you, Millie.'

'I'd be obliged,' George said coldly, when I went in, 'if in future you'd refrain from upsetting Diana in front of the entire office. Everyone makes mistakes from time to time. It doesn't help to have them exposed in public.'

I made one of the faces I'd caught off Bel. 'Isn't this all a bit juvenile, George, like telling tales at school?'

'It's not long since the poor girl's father died. She's feeling very vulnerable at the moment.'

'So am I,' I said curtly. I'd scarcely slept for two nights in a row and was already sick to death of the situation at work. I knew I was only sinking to Diana's level when I said, 'It was Diana who pointed out my mistake first –

what she thought was a mistake. I put her right, that's all. As she did it in front of the entire office, Oliver and Barry merely backed me up.'

'Oh, is that what really happened?' George looked nonplussed.

'Yes, George, it is.'

'I'm sorry, I must have got the wrong end of the stick.' He became quite friendly and asked how I was getting on with the flat in William Square.

'It's a long story, George. Perhaps I could tell it to you one day over lunch?' I'd only tell him the least important bits.

'Great idea, Millie. We'll do that, eh?'

Diana was scowling at me through the glass partition. I resisted the urge to stick out my tongue, and reckoned there was no chance of having lunch with George once she got back to work on him. She seemed to be pursuing a private vendetta against me.

When I came out, June shouted, 'There's just been a phone call, Millie. Some woman particularly asked for you. She says her boss, a Mr Thomas, has a property to sell as soon as poss in Clement Street off Smithdown Road, number eighteen. It belonged to a relative. He wants a valuation. I looked in the diary and told her you'd be there at two o'clock.'

'I think I'll go,' Diana stretched her arms. 'I feel like some fresh air.'

'They asked for Millie,' June said pointedly.

'This is an estate agent's, not a hairdresser's,' Diana snapped. 'It doesn't matter who goes.'

Oliver said sweetly, ''Yes, it does, Diana. It might be a former client who would prefer Millie rather than an-other member of staff.' He winked at me. 'Will you be all right on your own? Take Darren, if you'd feel safer.'

'I doubt if I'll come to any harm in Clement Street, it's too built-up.' Female staff weren't usually sent to deal with properties if a man on his own was involved.

It felt odd to drive past William Square and think of

Flo's flat, as familiar now as the back of my hand, waiting for my mother to move in on Friday. Yesterday, she'd astounded me by announcing that when the time came for Alison to leave Skelmersdale, she'd have her in William Square instead of going to Oxford.

'Is that wise, Mum?' I said worriedly. 'You realise it's a red-light area. That girl outside is a prostitute. And it can be very violent.'

'I don't know what's wise or not, luv. Our Alison's always had plenty of care and attention, but she's never had much love. The change is bound to upset her, whether she goes to Oxford or comes to me, so I'd like to give it a chance.' Kate's eyes glistened. 'We'll sleep together in the same bed and I'll hold her in me arms if she'll let me. As to the prostitutes, they're only working girls who've fallen on hard times. They won't harm our Alison. The violence I'll just have to take a chance on. After all, I can always move, can't I?'

I regarded her doubtfully. 'I hope you're not making a terrible mistake. What will you live on?'

'I'll eke out the money Flo left so it lasts as long as possible. In a few years, I'll be due for me pension. I might get a carer's allowance for looking after Alison. Don't worry, luv,' she said serenely, 'I'll be all right. I haven't felt so happy in ages.'

Perhaps the last time she'd been happy was with Hugh O'Mara. Even now, the next day, I found it difficult to grasp what Gran had told me.

I turned into Clement Street, found a place to park, took a photograph of number eighteen, then knocked at the door. The street was comprised of small terraced properties, the front doors opening on to the pavement. The house in question had been relatively well maintained, though the downstairs window-sill could have done with a fresh coat of paint. I noticed the step hadn't been cleaned in a while.

The door opened, 'Hello, Millie,' said Tom O'Mara. Yesterday, I'd written to him, then fled back to

Blundellsands when I came out of the solicitor's with my mother, so there would have been no one in when he turned up at Flo's last night. I'd thought long and hard about what to write. In the end, I'd merely stated the facts baldly, without embellishment or comment. I didn't put 'Dear Tom', or who the letter was from, just a few necessary words that explained everything. He would know who'd sent it. I'd posted it to the club because I didn't know his address.

Tom turned and went down the narrow hallway into a room at the rear of the house. He was dressed in all black: leather jacket, jeans, T-shirt. I took a deep breath and followed, closing the door behind me. The room was furnished sixties style, with a lime green carpet, orange curtains, a melamine table, two grey plastic easy chairs, one each side of the elaborate tiled fireplace, which had little insets for knick-knacks. Everything was shabby and well used, and there were no ornaments, or other signs that the place was inhabited.

'This is where me gran used to live,' Tom said. His jacket creaked silkily as he sat in one of the chairs and stretched out his long legs. He wore expensive boots with a zip in the side, and looked out of place in the small dark room with its cheap furniture. I sat in the other chair. 'I bought it years ago as an investment. I got tenants in when Nancy went to Southport. Now they've moved I thought I'd sell. They say the price of property has started to go up.'

'When did you decide to sell?'

'This morning, when I heard from you. It made a good excuse. I got a woman from the club to ring the place you work. I had to see you again.'

'Why?'

'I dunno.' He shrugged elegantly. 'To see what it felt like, maybe, knowing you were me sister, knowing it was over.' He looked at me curiously. 'Didn't you want to see me?'

'Oh, I don't know, Tom. I've no idea what to think.' I

felt slightly uncomfortable, but not embarrassed or ashamed. I'd pooh-poohed Gran's gruesome claim that the family was cursed, that the devil was involved, and the world was about to end because a half-sister and brother who'd known nothing about their relationship had slept with each other. 'We didn't know, Gran. It wasn't our fault. If it hadn't been for all the secrets . . .' It was irritating to know that I was now accumulating secrets of my own, things I couldn't tell my mother or Trudy or Declan. 'Don't repeat a word of this to your mam,' Gran pleaded. 'I'd be obliged if you wouldn't mention to your dad that I told you,' Mum had said the other night, about something or other I couldn't remember right now.

'You can go back to that boyfriend of yours,' Tom remarked drily. 'What's his name?'

'James.'

He looked amused. 'James and Millie. They go well together. What's Millie short for, anyroad? I always meant to ask.'

'Millicent.'

There was silence. Then Tom said something that made my stomach lurch. 'Will you come upstairs with me?' He nodded at the door. 'There's a bed.'

'*No!*' Despite my vehemently expressed horror, somewhere within the furthest reaches of my mind, I remembered what we'd been to each other and did my best not to imagine what it would be like now.

'I just wondered,' Tom said lightly. 'It's not that I want to, bloody hell, no. The whole idea makes me feel dead peculiar. I'm just trying to get things sorted in me head.'

'It's all over, Tom.' I could hardly speak.

'Christ, Millie, I know that. I'm not suggesting otherwise.' He smiled. Over the short time I'd known him, he'd rarely smiled. Whenever he did, I'd always thought him even more extraordinarily attractive than he already was, more desirable. I had that same feeling again, and it made me slightly nauseous. He went on, 'I wish we'd found out we were related before we . . .' he stopped, unwilling to say the words. 'It would have been great, knowing I had a sister.'

'And knowing Flo was your gran.' And my gran, I realised with a shock.

'Aye.' He nodded. 'That would have been great an' all.'

I refused to meet his eyes, worried about what I might see there. It seemed sensible to get away as quickly as possible. I took my notebook out of my bag and said briskly, 'Is it really your intention to put the house on the market?'

'I'd like to get rid of it, yes.'

'Then I'd better take some details.' I stood, smoothed my skirt, conscious of Tom watching my every move. I didn't look at him. 'I'll start upstairs.'

Quickly, I measured the rooms, made a note of the cupboards, the state of decoration, the small modern bathroom at the rear. Downstairs again, I took a quick look in the lounge, which was the same size as the front bedroom and had a black iron fireplace with a flower-painted tile surround, which could be sold for a bomb if it was taken out. There was an ugly brocade three-piece with brass pillars supporting the arms – I must tell Tom to get rid of the furniture.

In the hall, I paused for a moment. Tommy O'Mara had lived here, walked in and out of the same rooms, up and down the same stairs, sat in the same spot where I'd sat only a few minutes ago when I talked to his grandson. One day, a long time ago, Martha Colquitt, my other gran, had probably come to this house bringing Flo's baby with her, the baby who'd turned out to be my father. I stood very still, and in my mind's eye, I could actually see the things happening like in an old, faded film, as if they were genuine memories, as if I'd lived through them, taken part. It was an eerie feeling, but not unpleasant.

When I went into the living room, Tom O'Mara had

gone. He'd left the key to Flo's flat on top of my handbag. He must have slipped out of the back when I was upstairs, and I was glad that my main emotion was relief, mixed with all sorts of other feelings that I preferred not to delve into. A car started up some way down the street and I didn't even consider looking through the net curtains to see if it was him. In one sense, I felt numb. In another, I felt entirely the opposite. I knew I would never make love with another man the way I had with Tommy O'Mara – Tom! The thing that had drawn us together was a crime, yet it would be impossible to forget.

When I returned to the office, Diana was cock-a-hoop. She'd just shown the Naughtons round a property in Childwall, and they were anxious to buy.

'How many places did you show them, Millie – ten, a dozen? I only took them once and they fell in love with it straight away,' she crowed.

'I'm sure they were more influenced by the house than the agent,' I said mildly. Right now, I couldn't give a damn about the Naughtons, or Diana.

After my parents' thirty brutal, wretched years of marriage, I expected there would be something equally brutal about its end: a fight, a huge scene, lots of screaming and yelling. I even visualised my father physically refusing to let Mum go. In other words, I was dreading Friday. Several times during the week, I asked Mum, 'What time are you leaving?'

'For goodness sake, Millicent, I don't know. It's not high noon or anything. I'll pack me suitcase during the day, and once I've had me tea I'll tell him I'm off before he has time to brood over it.'

'It can't possibly be that simple, Mum.'

'He can't stop me, can he? He can't guard over me for ever.' She bit her lip thoughtfully. 'I'll leave him a casserole in the fridge for the weekend.' She smiled at me radiantly. Over the last few days, the anxious lines around her eyes and mouth had smoothed away. I had never known her look so happy.

'I'll come straight from work and give you a lift,' I offered.

'There's no need, Millicent. I'll catch the bus. I won't have much to carry – a suitcase, that's all.'

I didn't argue, but on Friday, as soon as I finished work, I drove straight to Kirkby. Trudy had obviously had the same idea. When I drew up the Cortina was parked outside the house.

My mother was kneeling on the kitchen floor playing with Scotty, who was lying on his back, wriggling in ecstasy as his tummy was tickled. 'I'll really miss this little chap,' she said tearfully, when I went in. 'I'd take him with me if there was a garden. But never mind, he'll be company for your dad.'

'Where is he?' I asked.

'In the front room.'

'Does he know?'

'Yes. He's taken it hard, I knew he would. He pleaded with me to stay. He promised to turn over a new leaf.'

'Really!' I said sarcastically.

Mum laughed. 'Yes, really.'

'Do you believe him?'

'Not for a minute, luv. I don't think he could, no matter how much he might want to.'

Trudy came into the room with a plastic bag. 'You'd forgotten your toothbrush, Mum.' She grinned at me. 'Hi, Sis. She's hardly taking a thing, just a few clothes, that's all.'

'I don't want to leave your dad with the house all bare. It'll be nice to start afresh with Flo's stuff. I must say,' Mum nodded at the ancient stove, 'I'll be glad to see the back of that ould thing.'

'Flo's is even older,' I said.

'Yes, but she's got a microwave, hasn't she? I've always wanted a microwave. Now, Trudy,' she turned to my sister, 'I want you to promise that you'll bring Melanie and Jake to see their grandad from time to time. He loves them kids, and it would be cruel to deprive him of their company.'

Trudy rubbed the scar on her left eyebrow and muttered, 'I'm not promising anything, Mum. We'll just have to see.'

'Well,' Mum said cheerfully, 'it's time I was off.'

The moment had come. Trudy and I looked at each other, and I saw my own incredulous excitement reflected in her green eyes as we followed Mum into the hall, where she paused at the door of the lounge. The television was on, a travel programme showing an exotic location with palm trees, sun and sand. To my surprise, Declan was sitting on the settee reading a newspaper. My father – the man I'd always thought was my father – was smoking, apparently quite calm, but there was something tight about his shoulders, and he seemed to hold the smoke in for too long before he blew it out again.

'I'm going now, Norman,' Mum said. She spoke as casually as if she were going to the shops. I sensed a subtle shifting of power.

Her husband shrugged. 'Please yerself,' he said.

'Your clean shirts are in the airing cupboard, and there's a meat casserole in the fridge. It should last at least two days.'

Declan got up. 'I'll come out and say tara, Mam.'

'Heavens, lad! I'll be seeing you tomorrer. You promised to come to dinner, didn't you? There's no need for taras.'

'Yes, there is, Mam. Today's special.'

Trudy picked up the suitcase and we trooped outside. Dry-eyed and slightly breathless, Mum paused under the orange street lights, looking back, her brow furrowed in bewilderment, at the house of silent screams and hidden tears, as if either that, or the future she was about to embark on, was nothing but a dream. Trudy put the case into the boot of the Cortina, Mum gave a queenly wave, and the car drove away.

It was as easy as that.

Declan and I were left standing at the gate, with me feeling inordinately deflated by this turn of events. I'd expected to take my mother to William Square, help her settle in, show her where everything was, gradually hand the place over. But now I felt excluded, unnecessary. All of a sudden it hurt badly, imagining other people going through Flo's things, sitting in Flo's place, watching her lamp swirl round, playing her favourite record.

Scotty came out and licked my shoe. I picked him up and buried my face in his rough, curly coat to hide the tears that trickled down my cheeks. I'd never felt so much at home anywhere as I'd done at Flo's. From the very first time I'd gone there, the flat had seemed mine. I knew I was being stupid, but it was almost as if I'd entered my aunt's body, become Flo, experienced the various highs and lows of her life. I'd discovered something about myself during the short time I'd spent there, though I wasn't sure what it was. I only knew I felt differently about things, as if Flo had somehow got through to me that I would survive. Never once, in all the nights I'd slept there, had I dreamed the old dream, heard the slithering footsteps on the stairs, wished I were invisible.

I sighed. I could follow the Cortina, still help Mum settle in, but I knew I was being daft, feeling so possessive about a basement flat that had belonged to a woman I'd never even spoken to.

'What's the matter, Sis?' Declan said softly.

'I feel a bit sad, that's all.'

Declan misunderstood. 'Mam will be all right, you'll see.'

'I know she will, Dec.' I put Scotty down and gave his beard a final rub, wondering if I would ever see the little dog again. 'Will he be all right?'

'Scotty's the only member of the family Dad's never laid a finger on.' Declan grinned.

'And what about you? You can always sleep on the sofa in my place until you find somewhere of your own.' I'd welcome his company at the moment. The thought of returning, alone, to Blundellsands and the flat I'd been so proud of was infinitely depressing.

'Thanks, Millie, but I think I'll stay with me dad.'

I stared at him, open-mouthed. 'But I thought you couldn't wait to get away?'

'Yes, but he needs me, least he needs someone, and I suppose I'll do.'

'Oh, Dec!' I touched his thin face. My heart felt troubled at the idea of my gentle brother staying in Kirkby with Norman Cameron.

'He can't be all bad,' Declan said, with such kind reasonableness, considering all that had happened, that I felt even worse. 'I know he loves us. Something must have happened to make him the way he is.'

I thought of the little boy locked in a cupboard. 'Perhaps something did.' I watched Scotty sniffing the rose bushes in the front garden. One day, I might come back. Perhaps we could talk. Perhaps.

A taxi drew up outside the house next door and hooted its horn. The Bradleys came out, dressed in their ball-room-dancing gear.

'Has your mam gone?' Mrs Bradley shouted.

'A few minutes ago,' I replied.

'About time, too. I'm going to see her next week.' Mr Bradley helped to scoop the layers of net skirt into the taxi. As it drove away, I said, 'I suppose I'd better go, it's cold out here.' I kissed Declan's cheek. 'Take care, Dec. I won't stop worrying about you, I know I won't.'

'There's no need to worry, Mill. Nowadays, me and Dad understand each other in our own peculiar way. He accepts me for what I am.'

I paused in the act of unlocking the car. 'And what's that, Dec?'

Beneath the glare of the street lights, Declan flushed. 'I reckon you already know, Sis.' He closed the gate. 'Do you mind?'

'Christ Almighty, Dec!' I exploded. 'Of course I don't

mind. It would only make me love you more, except I love you to death already.'

'Ta, Sis.' He picked Scotty up and waved a shaggy paw. 'See you, Mill.'

I started up the car and watched through the mirror as my brother, still hugging Scotty, went back into the house. A door had opened for my mother, at the same time as one had closed for Declan.

3

Every morning, I woke up with the feeling that I'd lost something infinitely precious. I had no idea what it was that I'd lost, only that it had left a chasm in my life that would never be refilled. There was an ache in my heart, and the sense of loss remained with me for hours.

My flat, my home, seemed unfamiliar, like that of a stranger. I stared, mystified, at various objects: the shell-shaped soap dish in the bathroom, a gaudy tea-towel, the yellow filing basket on the desk, and had no idea where they'd come from. Were they mine? I couldn't remember buying them. Nor could I remember where particular things were kept. It was as if I'd been away for years, having to open cupboards and drawers to search for the bread knife or a duster. There was food in the fridge that was weeks old: wilted lettuce, soggy apples, a carton of potato salad that I was scared to take the lid off. The cheese was covered in mould.

The only place where I felt comfortable and at ease was the balcony. Most nights I sat outside wearing my warmest coat, watching the branches of the bare trees as they waved, like the long nails of a witch, against the dark sky. I listened to the creatures of the night rustling in and out of the bushes below. There were hedgehogs, two, never seen during the day. The light from the living room was cast sharply across the untidy grass and straggly plants – no one tended the garden in winter – and under the light I read the book that Tom O'Mara had given me about the *Thetis*. I read about the bungling and ineptitude of those at the top, the heroism and desperation of the ordinary seamen as they tried to rescue the men who were trapped, so near and yet so far.

How would it have been, I wondered, if Tommy O'Mara hadn't died? How differently would things have turned out for Flo?

I felt very old, like someone who knew that the best years of their life were over and was patiently sitting out the rest. Having a birthday didn't help. I turned thirty, and became obsessed with wondering how the next ten years would turn out. What would I be doing when I was forty? Would I be married, have children? Where would I be living? Where would I be working? Would Mum still be living in William Square with Alison?

Which was stupid. I told myself how stupid I was being a hundred times a day, and made sure no one guessed how dispirited I felt. When I went with James to the theatre one night, I sat in the bar in the interval while he went to fetch the drinks. He came back, saying, 'Are you all right, darling? I looked across and your face was terribly sad.'

'I'm fine,' I said confidently.

'Are you sure? Is it over between you and that Tom chap? I've kept longing to ask. Is that why you're sad?'

'I said I wasn't sad, James, though it is over between me and Tom.'

He looked relieved. 'I'm glad there's no one else.'

'I never said that!' His face collapsed in hurt. I knew I was being horrid, but the last thing I wanted was to offer him encouragement. The strangest thing had happened with James, and I didn't know how to deal with it.

He'd promised not to pressurise me and he hadn't, but in the few times I'd seen him since we'd broken up, then come together again, he wanted to know every little thing about me, every detail. It was as if now that he could no longer have my body he was determined to possess my mind. Perhaps some people were willing to divulge their every thought, their every wish, but I wasn't one of them.

It was hard to escape from such overpowering, almost suffocating love, his tremendous need, which some women might have envied. It was also hard to reject, as if I was giving away something uniquely precious by refusing him. Such love might never come my way again. He appeared to worship the ground I walked on.

Where had I heard those words said before only recently? The bell rang once to indicate that the interval was nearly over and I finished off my drink. Back in the theatre I remembered. They were the words Gran had used to describe how Norman Cameron had felt about my mother . . .

The curtain rose, but as far as I was concerned the actors' efforts were wasted. I had no idea what had happened in the first act. Perhaps you could love someone too much, so much that you resented all the things they did without you, resented them even being happy if you weren't the reason why they smiled.

It wasn't strictly true to hint that there was someone else, but tomorrow night I was meeting Peter Maxwell. He was going to show me where the tall, wild forests had once been in Toxteth, which King John had turned into a royal park and where he had hunted deer and wild boar.

'It's incredible!' I breathed, the following evening, as we strolled through the icy drizzle along Upper Parliament Street and into Smithdown Road. I closed my eyes and tried to imagine I was stepping through a thick forest and the drizzle was the dew dripping from the trees at dawn.

'The area's mentioned in the Domesday Book,' he said proudly.

I forgot how cold the night was as he explained, with mounting enthusiasm, that Lodge Lane was called after one of the King's hunting lodges, that the ancient manor of Smethedon was where the name Smithdown came from. The descriptions, the words he used seemed incongruous, as we passed the narrow built-up streets and endless shops. Traffic fizzed by in the wet; cars, buses, lorries, headlights fixed on the noxious fumes spewing out from the vehicles in front, and reflected in the watery surface. We seemed to be walking through a toxic yellow fog, as Peter talked about Dingle Dell, Knot's Hole, sandstone-cliff creeks, glens, farms, a game reserve. He even quoted a poem – 'The Nymph of the Dingle'.

'It's fascinating, Peter,' I said, when he paused for breath. His black bushy hair and beard glistened in the damp, as if they'd been touched with frost.

'I've not nearly finished, but this isn't a good night. Perhaps we could come one Sunday. I can show you other places. Did you know that less than two centuries ago Bootle was a spa? There used to be watermills, springs, sandhills and fields of flowers?'

I confessed I'd had no idea. He asked if I'd like a drink, and when I said yes he steered me into the nearest pub. 'Will it be safe in here?' I asked nervously.

'I doubt it,' he said soberly, though I noticed his eyes were twinkling. 'We're probably taking our lives in our hands.'

The pub was old-fashioned, Victorian, with sparkling brasses and a gold-tinted mirror behind the bar. The few customers looked very ordinary and not in the least threatening.

'Well, we seemed to have survived so far,' Peter said, apparently amazed. 'What would you like to drink?'

I poked him in the ribs with my elbow. 'Stop making fun of me. I'd like half a cider, please.'

A few minutes later he returned with the drinks. 'Sorry I was so long, but the barman offered me five thousand quid to carry out a contract-killing. See those old girls over there?' He pointed to two elderly women sitting in a corner. 'One's a Mafia godfather in disguise, the other is the chief importer of heroin in the northwest. The cops have been after her for years. She's the one he wanted me to kill.' He took his donkey jacket off and threw it on a vacant chair. Underneath, he wore a polo-necked jersey, which had several loose threads. He regarded me solemnly. 'I refused, of course, so I doubt if we'll get out of here alive.'

By now, I was doubled up with laughter. 'I'm sorry, but I always feel a bit fearful around here.'

'It sounds priggish, but the worst thing to fear is fear itself. Taking the worst possible scenario, no one's safe anywhere.'

'I like being with you, it's rather soothing.' I smiled, feeling unusually contented.

He stroked his beard and looked thoughtful. 'To be "soothing" is not my ultimate aim when I'm with a beautiful young woman, but it'll do.'

I welcomed the fact that he was so easy to be with, relaxing, particularly after the intensity of James, and the total preoccupation Tom O'Mara and I had had with each other. There was a hint of flirtatiousness between us, which meant nothing. He reminded me about the Christmas concert at his school next week. 'You promised you'd come.'

'I hadn't forgotten.' It would soon be Christmas and I hadn't bought a single present. I must remind Trudy about the bottles she'd promised to paint, and remembered that one had been for Diana. After the way things had gone, I wasn't sure whether to give it to her or not.

For the next half-hour, we chatted about nothing in particular. We'd been in the same year at school, which meant that Peter had also recently had his thirtieth birthday, and we discussed how incredibly old we felt. 'It's quite different from turning twenty. Twenty's exciting, like the start of a big adventure. Come thirty, the excitement's over,' he remarked, with a grin.

'Don't say that. You make thirty sound very dull.'

'I didn't mean it to sound dull, just less exciting. By thirty you more or less know where you are. Would you like another drink?'

378

'No thanks. I thought I'd pop in and see my mother. I left my car in William Square.'

'I've already met your mum. She seems exceptionally nice.' He reached for his jacket. 'Come on. If we make a sudden rush for the exit, we might get out of here all in one piece.'

It was only natural that Mum should have the keys to Flo's flat. Even so, I felt slightly miffed at having to knock to be let in. Fiona, who was draped outside in her usual spot, condescended to give me a curt nod.

'Hello, luv!' Mum's face split into a delighted smile when she opened the door. 'You're out late. It's gone ten.'

Peter Maxwell leaned over the railings. 'Hi, there, Kate. 'Night, Millie. See you next week.'

'Goodnight, Peter.'

'Have you been out with him?' Mum sounded slightly shocked as she closed the door.

'He's very nice.'

'Oh, he's a lovely young feller. I knew his mam in Kirkby. She's a horrible woman, not a bit like Peter. No, I just thought you and James were back together for good, like.'

'We're back together. I doubt very much if it's for good.'

Mum shook her head in despair. 'I can't keep up with you, Millicent.' Then, eyes shining, she demanded, 'What do you think of me new carpet?'

In the two weeks since I had left and my mother had taken over, much in the flat had changed. Too much, I thought darkly, but kept my opinion to myself. It was none of my business, but as far as I was concerned Flo's flat had been perfect. I wouldn't have altered it one iota. But now the silk flowers had gone because they gathered dust, as well as the little round tables and the brasses on the beams. Colin had fitted deadlocks on the windows, a heater on the bathroom ceiling and, with Declan's help, was going to wallpaper the place throughout. 'Something fitting,' Mum announced excitedly, 'little rosebuds, violets, sprigs of flowers.' She would have liked a new three-piece, but needed to conserve the money and was buying stretch covers instead. 'I don't like that dark velour stuff. It's dead miserable.' Next week, British Telecom were coming to install a phone.

I regarded the maroon fitted carpet. 'It looks smart.' I far preferred the faded old linoleum. 'What's happened to the rag rug?'

'I chucked it, luv. It was only a homemade thing.'

Trudy came out of the bedroom, struggling with a cardboard box full of clothes. 'Hello, Sis. I didn't know you were here. I'm just sorting out the wardrobe. Phew!' She plonked the box down and wiped her forehead with the back of her hand. 'I'll take this lot to Oxfam tomorrow, Mum. Hey, Mill, what do you think of this? I thought I'd keep it. It's not at all old-fashioned.' She held up the pink and blue check frock with a Peter Pan collar. 'I'm sure it'll fit.'

'It's lovely, Trude.' It had fitted me perfectly. George had said it made me look sweet and demure.

'Help yourself to anything that takes your fancy, Millicent,' Mum said generously.

'There's nothing I want, Mum.' I felt all choked up. It was horrible to see Flo's things being thrown away, given to Oxfam. I didn't even want Trudy to have the check frock. Then I thought of something I did want – wanted desperately. 'Actually, Mum, I'd like that lamp, the swirly one.' I looked at the television, but the lamp wasn't there, and I felt a thrust of pure, cold anger. If it had been chucked away I'd track it down, buy it back from Oxfam . . .

'I'm afraid your gran's already nabbed it,' Mum said apologetically. 'I wish I'd known, luv. You should have said before.'

If I'd known she was going to tear the place apart, I would have. I knew I was being unreasonable, and felt even more unreasonable when I refused a cup of tea. 'I only came for a minute to say hello. I think I'll have an early night.'

I'd never felt less like an early night. Outside, I thought about calling on Charmian, but the ground-floor flat was in darkness – Herbie had to get up at the crack of dawn for work. Peter Maxwell's light was on, but did I know him well enough to call at this hour? He might think I was being presumptuous, a bit pushy.

Fiona, in a short fur coat, thigh-length boots, and no other visible sign of clothing, was staring at me suspiciously, as if I'd set myself up in competition. I got into the car and drove round to Maynard Street. It was weeks since I'd seen Bel, though she'd been to William Square to renew her acquaintance with Mum.

'She'll probably think me an idiot.' I didn't even switch the engine off when I parked as near as I could to Bel's house, but drove off immediately. On my way to Blundellsands, I slipped a tape into the deck and turned up Freddie Mercury's powerful voice as loud as it would go to drown my brain and stop me from thinking how much I would have liked someone to talk to. It didn't work, so I turned it down and talked to myself instead. 'I must pull myself together, keep telling myself there is Life After Flo. Tomorrow I'll take a proper lunch break, buy some Christmas presents. I'll get jewellery for Mum, gold earrings or a chain.' By the time I got home I was still musing on what to get Declan, feeling more cheerful. My flat was slowly beginning to feel my own again, though it still seemed oddly empty when I went in.

Mum's decorating splurge was catching. I didn't want to change the colour of my own living-room walls, but a wide frieze would look nice, or stencilled flowers. I decided I'd take a look at patterns at the weekend.

Next day after lunch, I was showing June the gold chain with a K for Kate that I'd bought for Mum, and the red-velvet knee-length dress with short sleeves I'd got as a

Christmas present for myself, when George called, 'Can I have a word with you, Millie?'

'Sit down,' he said shortly, when I entered his office. This was always a bad sign, and I wondered what I'd done wrong now. He cleared his throat. 'I've been having a long talk with . . . with someone about your position in the firm. It was pointed out that you have no qualifications for the job you do. Darren and Elliot both have degrees, and even June has three A levels.' He regarded me sternly, as if all this was new to him and he'd been misled.

'You knew that when you took me on, George. You knew it when you promoted me.' I tried to keep my voice steady. 'I've always carried out my work satisfactorily. No one has ever complained.'

George acknowledged this with a cursory nod. 'That's true, Millie, but it was also pointed out that there are a lot of people around, highly qualified people, who might do the work even better. Yet by employing you, I am, in effect, denying one of these people a position with Stock Masterton.' He leaned forward, frowning earnestly. 'Look at that business with the Naughtons, for example. You must have shown them around a dozen properties, but Diana had only to take them once and a deal was clinched on the spot.'

I clenched my fists, feeling the nails digging painfully into my palms. My heart thumped crazily. 'Are you giving me the sack, George?' I'd never find another equivalent job if I was sacked.

He looked slightly uncomfortable. 'No, no, of course not. We, that is, I, thought it would be a good idea if you went to Woolton with Oliver and Diana.'

'I don't understand,' I stammered. 'If I'm useless here, I'll be just as useless in Woolton.'

'No one's said you're useless, Millie. Oh dear!' He put his hand to his chest. 'I feel a panic attack coming. Lately, I've been having them quite frequently. No, we . . . I think you should be our receptionist. After all, that's what you were originally taken on as.'

It was so unfair. I'd never asked to be promoted, it had been all his idea. I blinked back hot tears of anger. No way would I let him see me cry. I knew I'd be burning my boats, but didn't care. I said, 'I'm afraid that isn't acceptable, George. I'd sooner leave. I'll finish at the end of the month.'

It hadn't gone quite the way he wanted – the way he knew Diana wanted. He rubbed his chest, frowning. 'Then you'd be breaking your contract. One month's notice is required, dated the first of the month.'

'In that case,' I said coolly, though I felt anything but cool, 'I'll leave at the end of January.' I got up and went to the door. 'I'll let you have my resignation in writing this afternoon.'

It was worse, far more shocking, than having discovered all those closely kept family secrets. I'd been dumbfounded to learn that my father wasn't who I'd thought he was. But I'd rejected Norman Cameron a long time ago, and the news didn't matter now – in fact, it was welcome. As for Tom O'Mara, I had thought I would never forget, but already it was hard to remember the way we'd felt about each other. There was just relief that it was all over, though I knew I would worry about him, watch for his name and any mention of Minerva's in the paper, hope that he wouldn't come to harm in the vicious world he lived in. After all, he was my brother.

But the business with my job – trivial in comparison to the rest – was different, directed against me personally. I felt as if someone had just delivered a mammoth blow, knocking all the stuffing out of me. I realised that my job had given me a sense of identity, a feeling of achievement, and without it I was nothing. I hadn't, after all, done better than the other girls in my class, the ones who'd seemed so much smarter than me. I was the backward child again, the girl who could hardly read, so hopeless that I hadn't been entered for a single O level.

Later, when I tried to type a letter of resignation, my fingers no longer seemed capable of accepting messages from my brain. I'd thought George was my friend. I'd tried to help Diana. Why had they turned against me? I felt betrayed.

In the window, through the glass around the boards showing the houses Stock Masterton had for sale, I watched the people passing, their bodies crouched protectively as they fought their way through the gale that howled up Castle Street from the Mersey. I longed to go down to the Pier Head, hold on to the railings, let the wind blow me any way it wanted.

There was a photo of Nancy's house on one of the boards in the window, between the house in Banks which didn't have an oriel window, and a manor house with ten acres of grounds priced at half a million, which George dealt with exclusively. I'd asked Oliver if he would please send someone else to Clement Street if a prospective purchaser wanted to view. 'I know the chap who's selling it slightly. I'd sooner not go,' I said. I still felt the same when the keys for the property arrived through the post, which meant that no one would be there. Unlike Flo's flat, Nancy's house, the place where she'd lived with Tommy O'Mara, where the father I'd never known had been raised, would go to strangers, who would know nothing about the drama that had taken place. People rarely thought about previous owners when they bought a house, no matter how old it was. As far as they were concerned, its history began when they themselves moved in.

Across the office, Darren and Elliot were having a deskbound lunch, eating sandwiches and giggling over something in *Viz*. I felt envious of their gloriously trouble-free lives. June was on the telephone, Barry's carefully combed silver head was bent over a heap of files. Oliver was out with a client. In his office, George, who usually made his presence loudly felt, was strangely quiet. At the next desk, Diana was singing a little tune as she typed into her computer. Was there a note of triumph in her voice? She must know why George had called me in, be aware of my humiliation. Was it worth making a fuss, I wondered, causing a row, telling Diana exactly what I thought in front of everyone? No, it wasn't, I decided. George seemed slightly ashamed of what he'd done. If I left quietly, at least I'd get a good reference, possibly a glowing one if he felt contrite enough.

Oliver returned, his face flushed by the wind. He hung up the keys. 'Whew!' he exclaimed. 'That was a proper shambles. Mum and Dad insisted on viewing the loft, so I went up with them, then one of the kids pushed the ladder up and the damn thing got stuck halfway. I thought I'd be there all afternoon. I managed to do a Tarzan and swing myself down.'

Diana said, 'I was beginning to wonder why you were taking so long.'

'Were you now! I didn't realise you kept an eye on my movements.' Oliver took his coat off, then put it on again. 'I think a beer and a snack in the Wig and Pen is called for after that misadventure. Come on, Millie, I'll treat you.'

I looked up, surprised. Oliver had never made such an offer before. 'I've already been to lunch.'

At the same time, Diana said quickly, 'She's already had lunch, Oliver.'

Oliver poked his head inside George's office. 'I'm off for a quick bevy, George, and taking Millie with me. Okay?'

George didn't look up. 'Okay,' he mumbled.

'Okay, Diana?' Oliver raised his eyebrows questioningly.

'It's none of my business, is it?'

'Too right it isn't.'

'What was all that about?' I asked, when we were outside. The wind gripped me immediately, powerfully, blowing my hair up into a fan around my head. The air was sharp and clean and refreshingly salty. I twisted my face to and fro, trying to breathe in as much as I could, until I felt almost light-headed.

Oliver's usually good-natured face twisted into a scowl. 'I loathe that bloody woman. I can't abide the thought of working with her. I want her to know that when we move I'm the one in charge. She thinks I'm a wimp who can't take decisions, but she doesn't realise how much George regards Stock Masterton as his baby. Take a major decision over his head and he goes ballistic. She'll find that out for herself soon enough if she starts throwing her weight around.'

When we turned into Dale Street the wind lessened fractionally. Oliver's scowl disappeared and he said kindly, 'Enough of my hang-ups. It's you I'm worried about. You look as if you've been crying, which is why I asked you out.'

I clapped my hands to my cheeks, which felt both hot and cold. 'I haven't been crying, but I'm dead upset. Is it so obvious?'

'Yes. I don't want to pry. Don't tell me if it's something private.'

We arrived at the Wig and Pen, where the midday rush was over and only a few tables were occupied. Oliver brought me a whisky and a chicken sandwich, and I told him what had happened. 'I feel gutted,' I finished. I could have said more, much more, but kept myself to a few short words.

Oliver shook his head unbelievingly. 'Darren and Elliot may well have degrees, but neither has an ounce of charm. As for Diana, she positively alienates the clients. She's in completely the wrong profession, which George knows only too well. He's talked about letting her go more than once.' He shook his head again. 'I don't understand the sudden turnaround. Mind you, the poor man has been an emotional wreck since his wife walked out with the children. He's easy prey for any woman who sets her cap at him.'

'But why does Diana hate me so much?' I wailed.

'That's easy to explain.' Oliver smiled and patted my hand. 'George was smitten with you right from the start.

386

I think I can safely say that your promotion had more to do with your legs than your capabilities, not that you didn't make a good fist of the job once you had it,' he added hastily, when he saw my dismayed expression. 'I wasn't the only one to notice, Diana did, too. She's jealous of you, Millie. She wants you out of George's way.'

'I knew George liked me, that's all,' I muttered. 'You see an awful lot, Oliver.' I felt a bit better. I'd been demoted because of another person's weakness, not my own, though it didn't change the fact I was about to give up my job.

On the way back to the office, Oliver said, 'By the way, you mentioned the Naughtons. Mr Naughton rang this morning to say they've withdrawn from the house in Childwall. They parked outside for several nights. Apparently, there's several teenagers next door, belting music out till all hours, which they find totally unacceptable – it would seem the neighbours they have now are darn near perfect.'

Despite everything, I couldn't help laughing. The talk with Oliver had done me good. I even felt a tiny bit flattered. Diana might well have had the upper hand at the moment but, incredibly, it was me who had the power. If I wanted I could ruin everything. I was no good at flirting, but I knew how it was done, I could learn. I didn't know I'd ever had George, but I could easily get him back. It was a challenge I might once have welcomed but, thinking about it now, it seemed rather demeaning.

'About the Naughtons,' I remarked, 'it's time someone suggested they stay put. They're already in their ideal house, and they'll never find another like it.'

'Someone already has – me. Mr Naughton said he'd never wanted to move, it was all his wife's idea. He's going to try to talk her out of it. If he's successful, every estate agent on Merseyside will breathe a big sigh of relief.'

There was no tortuous Christmas dinner in Kirkby this year to bring back memories of the bleak dinners that had gone before. Norman Cameron had always nursed a decidedly unfestive spirit throughout the holiday, grim and bitter, his dark eyes searching for any signs of un-welcome gaiety from his children, rationing our time spent in front of the television or with our presents. For the first time, with a glimmer of understanding, I won-dered if his own childhood Christmases had been so dark that he could see no other way, though I wasn't con-vinced I would ever have the Christian charity to forgive.

This year, we had dinner at Flo's without Norman. The dining table was pulled out as far as it would go, so big that only a sheet would cover it. It was set for eight, and there was already a trifle laid out, mince pies, an iced cake from Charmian, the plates intertwined with tinsel. Night-lights in delicately painted wine glasses were wait-ing to be lit when the meal began. Mum asked Trudy if she would bring her cutlery because there wasn't enough, so Trudy bought her a set for Christmas. It wasn't an expensive set, the handles were bright red plastic, but they looked perfect on the table with the red paper napkins.

There was a real tree in the window, the coloured lights shaped like pears, and new decorations strung from wall to wall. The flat – no longer Flo's with its carpet, new curtains and pink-and-white-flowered wall-paper – was warm with the smell of roasting turkey and Christmas pudding. Melanie and Jake were persuaded that it was too cold to eat on the wooden table in the yard. 'You can have a drink out there afterwards,' Trudy told them, 'as long as you get well wrapped up first.'

Bel was there. She'd always had dinner with Flo on Christmas Day, ever since she'd come out of the forces, she'd hinted, and she wasn't looking forward to eating alone for the first time in her life. 'Mr Fritz always came. Later I used to bring Edward, and Charmian would come down with her little ones. When she married Herbie, me and Flo used to have our dinner upstairs.' She turned up on the day in her leopardskin fur coat, a silver lamé suit and high-heeled silver boots, her hair a magnificent halo of russet waves and curls, and her lovely old face as shrivelled as one of the nuts in the bowl on the sideboard. The first thing she did was grab my hand. 'I've not seen much of you lately, girl. I thought we were friends.'

'I nearly called one night, but it was awfully late,' I explained. 'I wanted someone to talk to, but I was worried you'd think I was stupid.'

'Jaysus, Millie. You're talking to the stupidest woman in the world. I always welcome company, no matter what the hour. What was it you wanted to talk about?'

'I can't remember now. I think I was missing Flo.'

'You never met her, but you miss her. Now, that really is stupid.' Bel's beautiful eyes were wise. 'Mind you, luv, I understand, I'll never stop missing Flo.' The violet eyes searched the room. 'Where's your gran, by the way? There's something I've always wanted to ask Martha Colquitt.'

'She's at an old-age pensioners' do in Kirkby.' Gran needed an operation, only minor, but her own prognosis was gloomy – she was convinced she'd die: 'Me mam swore she'd never let a surgeon near her with a knife,' she'd said. 'I don't trust them doctors.'

I gave Bel her present, an unusual oval-shaped bottle that Trudy had painted various shades of blue and green. Bel gave me an intricately patterned mosaic bracelet. 'It's not new, Flo bought it me in Spain. I thought you'd like it as a memento.'

'Oh, thank you,' I breathed. I fastened the bracelet on to my wrist. 'I'll treasure it all my life.'

Mum presided over the table. I could scarcely take my eyes off my new mother, and every now and then noticed the others glancing at her curiously, as if they, too, found it hard to believe that this Kate Cameron had been lurking behind the old one for so many years. She already looked thinner. Charmian had trimmed and silver-tinted her hair the day before, and the thick, straight fringe and feathery cut took years off her. For the first time in ages, she was wearing makeup, and had bought a new dress – the last new one had been for Trudy's wedding ten years ago. It was plain dark green, emphasising the colour of her sparkling eyes. She already had my present, the gold chain with K for Kate, around her neck. Mum was reborn, confident, relaxed, with her children all around her, except for Alison who was coming to tea that afternoon. 'As an experiment, like, to see how she gets on. See if she takes to the place.' It would be best if not too many people were around in case it frightened her. I was going to Southport to have tea with James's family, the Daleys to Colin's parents in Norris Green. Bel had been invited upstairs. Only Declan would be there to see if his sister felt at home in William Square.

Declan seemed perfectly content living in Kirkby with his father. They saw little of each other, Norman either at work or in the pub, and Declan deeply involved with helping the couple he'd met at the craft fair with their tie-dyed T-shirts. His own first attempts had been highly professional, and Melanie and Jake had been given one each as a present. Next September, he was starting a course in fabric design.

'What about that young feller from next door?' Bel said suddenly. 'Flo always had him in for a drink on Christmas Day.'

I offered to fetch Peter Maxwell. It was a still, windless day, without a patch of blue in the sombre grey sky. The leathery leaves on the trees in the central garden shone dully, still wet with dew. Cars lined the square, but otherwise it was empty, no sign of Fiona or the other girls, who must be having a rare day off. Gran had once mentioned that Flo had spent her first Christmas in the flat entirely alone: Mrs Fritz had gone to Ireland. I wondered what it had looked like then, with only a few cars and a single family living in each house.

Peter was getting ready to have Christmas dinner with a colleague from school. There was just time for a drink with the Camerons.

'Did you enjoy the play?' he asked, as he walked around the plain room with its clean-cut furniture, so different from next door, turning off lights and testing locks.

'It was very cleverly written and well acted,' I said tactfully. It had been awful and I hoped he hadn't any ambition to become a playwright. 'I found it hard to talk to the other teachers, though. I kept expecting to get marks out of ten whenever I answered a question.'

'They liked you. Quite a few said next day what a cracking girl you were.' He took his coat off the rack, and dark eyes glinted at me mischievously. 'They wanted to know when we were getting married.'

'What did you say?'

'What do you think I said?'

I stuck my finger under my chin and thought hard. 'Never?'

Peter laughed. 'Precisely! There's no spark, is there, Millie? I wish there were because I like you very much. We know things about each other that would be hard to tell other people.' He looked at me quizzically. 'Could you pretend I'm a woman so we could be best friends?'

'Oh, Peter!' He was right, there was no spark. If we went out together for long enough we might get married because it seemed the comfortable thing to do, but it wasn't what I wanted – and neither did he. 'You'd need to do something about your beard before I could remotely regard you as a woman, but there's nothing wrong with having a man for a best friend.'

He kissed my forehead, as if to seal our friendship. 'Friends it is, then. Now, where's that drink? Has your mum got beer? I'm not a wine person.'

★

I was convinced that nowhere on earth could a family have enjoyed their Christmas dinner more than the Camerons. It was nothing to do with the food, though for the first time in months I ate a proper, three-course meal, and the skirt of my red-velvet dress felt tight when I'd finished. It was to do with a shared sense that the nightmare had ended. It had already faded, a little, for Trudy and me, but now it was well and truly over for Mum. As for Declan, he was coping. The only awkward moment came when Melanie, pulling a cracker with her father, said in surprise, 'Where's Grandad?'

'He couldn't come, luv,' Mum said firmly. She looked anxiously at Declan 'He's all right, isn't he?'

'Fine, Mam. He'll have found a pub that's open all day. That's where he'd have been, anyroad.'

'I suppose so.' A shadow almost cast itself over Mum's face, but she blinked it away. 'I'll go round in a day or so, give the house a bit of a clean, like, take him some rations.'

Later, when Trudy and I were washing the dishes, Trudy said, a touch bitterly, 'What a pity she couldn't have brought herself to do this years ago. Think of all the misery it would have saved.'

'It was the money and the flat that gave her the courage, Trude.'

'I'd never have stood it for a minute. I'd have been off the first time he laid a finger on me, and once he'd touched me kids . . .' Trudy shook her head. It was beyond her comprehension.

I reached for a fresh tea-towel – the one I was using was sopping wet. 'We're a different generation, but there's an even newer generation of kids roaming the streets of London and other cities who've run away from violent homes. Why didn't we run away, Trude? He nearly killed you once, but you still stayed. You waited for Colin to rescue you, like I waited for Gary.'

Trudy stared at me blankly. 'I think I felt paralysed,' she whispered.

'Maybe Mum did, too.' One day soon, despite my promise, I resolved to tell Trudy and Declan about the little boy locked in the cupboard. They had a right to know, and could be left to make their own judgement.

Melanie and Jake were aching to sit in the yard. Colin put their coats on, Kate supplied a glass of lemonade and a plate of mince pies and, giggling, they perched themselves on the bench in front of the wooden table. I watched through the window, bemused. It seemed such an uncomfortable thing to do on a cold day in December, and I marvelled at the children's ability to turn it into a great adventure. Colin and Trudy came indoors, shivering. 'Perhaps we could get some garden furniture?' Trudy suggested. They began to discuss the best sort to buy, wood or plastic. They would have preferred wrought-iron, but it was too expensive.

It was just such mundane, ordinary decisions that made the world go round, I thought wryly. Freed from the tensions and the dreary atmosphere of our old house, I became aware of the easy-going intimacy between Colin and my sister, the way they smiled at each other for no reason in particular, as if they were passing on an unspoken message or reading one another's thoughts. I noticed the way they seemed to form a unit with their children, a little world of their own. I thought how satisfying it must be to have little human beings completely dependent upon you, loving you without question, the most important person in their lives. To my surprise, I felt envious of my sister.

Though I could have what she had, I thought later at the Athertons', I could have it easily, straight away. I could be a wife, possibly a mother, by next Christmas. All I had to do was say yes to James. I'd no longer have to worry about my job. I could share in some of this . . .

The difference between my mother's Christmas table and the Athertons' couldn't have been greater. Cut-glass decanters, crystal glasses, heavy silver cutlery with embossed handles, beautifully laundered napkins in silver rings were laid with geometrical precision on a vast expanse of rich, gleaming mahogany, with a rather formal display of upright chrysanthemums in the centre. The dining room was about half as big again as Flo's entire flat, with only a fraction of the furniture. The curtains were ivory satin, drawn carefully to hang in smooth, symmetrical folds.

Mrs Atherton had kissed me coolly on the cheek. 'It's ages since we've seen you, dear. What have you been doing to my son?'

'Nothing that I know of,' I replied, startled. Had James told her about our problems? Or Mrs Atherton might have guessed. After all, she was his mother.

Anna, James's sister, was up from London with her husband and two children. I'd never met her before and found it hard to believe that she'd been an anarchist at university. Her husband, Jonathan, was a dealer in the City, a hearty, fresh-faced man with neat brown hair and designer spectacles. The children, boys, were equally neat, in white shirts, grey pullovers and shorts. They were well behaved and said little, even when their parents encouraged them to talk. I found myself yearning for Melanie and Jake's bright faces, their inability to keep quiet no matter how many times they were told. I longed to discuss garden furniture and tie-dyed T-shirts. Instead, I was forced to listen to Jonathan's talk of bull markets and bear markets, shorts, longs and mediums, stocks and shares. He'd recently netted a cool hundred thou profit on a highly risky venture in Indonesia that everyone else had been too afraid to touch. Anna, blonde hair swinging, pretty face glowing with admiration, leaned over and stroked his chin. 'You're so clever, darling!' she cooed.

Throughout the meal, James kept his eyes glued on me so firmly that I felt uncomfortable. Afterwards we went into the vast, chintzy living room, where he sat on the arm of my chair, towering over me. I felt as if I'd been stamped with his personal seal of ownership.

Jonathan gave his rather unfortunate high-pitched giggle and said to James, 'Understand you've given up flirting with left-wing politics, brother-in-law. Are you still marching with those wretched dockers?'

'I haven't for some time,' James admitted.

So far, Mr Atherton hadn't opened his mouth except to eat; his eyes were always far away, thinking of other things, probably business. He spoke now, with contempt in his voice: 'Lazy buggers, don't know which side their bread's buttered. It's about time they got back to work.'

I had no idea if I was pro-establishment or anti, or if my politics were left or right, I only knew it made my blood boil to hear the dockers being called 'lazy buggers' by a man smoking a fat cigar who owned three garages. I wished I knew some hard facts and figures that I could quote in the dockers' defence, but I knew nothing about the dispute other than it was happening. I jumped up. 'Excuse me.'

In the eau-di-Nil tiled bathroom with its matching carpet and fittings, I stared unseeingly at my reflection in the mirror and realised, with a sense of overwhelming relief, that I was wasting James's time. I felt alien from his family. If I loved him, I would have taken them on and done my best, but I didn't love him and never would. 'I'm glad I came,' I whispered. 'It's helped me make up my mind once and for all.'

When I came out, James was hovering on the landing, and I felt a stab of anger. I wanted to say something coarse and brutal: 'Would you like to have come in to watch me pee?'

He stared at me and I felt repelled by the abject adoration in his eyes. 'You look lovely in that dress,' he said huskily. 'You suit red.' He tried to take me in his arms, nuzzle my hair, but I pushed him away. He patted his pocket, 'I've a present for you, a ring.'

'I don't want it!'

'But, Millie . . .' His lips twisted in an arc of misery. 'Is it this other chap you've been seeing?'

'I haven't been seeing another chap – least I have, but he's just a friend. There's no one, James. No one!' I emphasised the last word, my voice unnaturally shrill, to impress upon him that I was announcing I was free – and he was free to forget me and find someone else.

We began to argue. He refused to believe I meant what I said. Anna must have heard the raised voices. She came out into the hall downstairs. 'Are you two all right?' Her laugh tinkled up the stairs. 'Oh, you're just having a little domestic.' She made a show of pretending to creep back into the room.

James's eyes were glassy, his face was swollen, red. I didn't know this man. Falling in love with me had changed him for the worse. 'It can't be over,' he insisted doggedly.

'It is, James.' I was worried that he was about to hit me. His fists were clenching and unclenching, as if he was itching to use them and it could only be on me. Then I did something that surprised me later when I thought about it. I flung my arms around his neck and hugged him tightly. 'James, I'm bad for you,' I whispered urgently. 'Can't you see? There's something not quite right about the way you love me.' I stroked his neck. 'One of these days, you'll meet someone else who you'll love in a quite different way, and everything will be wonderful for you both.' I pulled away. 'Goodbye, darling,' I said softly.

He remained silent, his eyes no longer glassy, but full of misery and shock. I thought, I wasn't sure, that there was also a trace of comprehension that I could be right.

I flew down the stairs, opened the door of the living room, and said breathlessly, 'I'm awfully sorry, I have to go. Thank you so much for the meal. It was lovely. No, no, please don't get up,' I implored, when Mrs Atherton began to get to her feet. 'I'll see myself out.'

It was past nine when I got back to Blundellsands. The first thing I did was ring my mother. Alison had been very quiet but not too disturbed by the strange surroundings. 'She didn't flick her fingers, the way she does when she's upset,' Mum said gratefully.

Relieved, I hung up my red dress carefully and ran a bath. Afterwards I watched a Woody Allen film on television, then went to bed with a book and a glass of warm milk, feeling contented and relaxed.

Just after midnight the telephone rang. I prayed it wouldn't be James, pleading for a second chance or a third, or whatever it would be by now, but when I picked up the extension by the bed, Peter Maxwell said cheerfully, 'Hi! I've just got in and thought I'd give you a ring. Did you have a nice day?'

'Nice and not so nice. I finished with a boyfriend. It wasn't very pleasant.'

'The hunk from the party?'

'That's right.'

'I didn't realise you were still seeing him. He's definitely not your type.'

'Are you going to be the arbiter of who's my type from now on?' I smiled at the receiver.

'It's what friends are for. I shall always ask for your opinion on any future girlfriends.'

'It shall be given with pleasure,' I said graciously. We chatted idly, and he was about to ring off when I remembered something. 'By the way, knowing it won't be taken the wrong way and you'll think I'm after your body or your money, would you like to come to a drinks party tomorrow afternoon?'

'Sorry, but I'm taking a group of first-years to a panto-mime. Will you be at Charmian's on New Year's Eve?'

I said I would, and we promised each other the first dance.

The drinks party was being held at Barry Green's. He had casually offered an invitation to the whole office. 'We've been having one on Boxing Day for more than thirty years. The world and his wife usually come. Any time between noon and four, you're all welcome.'

Elliot and Darren had wrinkled their noses: a drinks party sounded much too tame. June would be away. Oliver welcomed the idea of escaping from his kids for a few hours. 'I love them, but it's usually hell on earth at home over Christmas.' George, who always went anyway, would be there with Diana, bringing his children who were over from France. I had intended taking James, but now I would have to go alone.

The Greens' house in Waterloo, only a mile from my flat, was semi-detached and spacious, the furniture and carpets shabby and worn. The Christmas decorations looked well used, as if the same things were hung in the same place year after year. Everywhere had a comfortable, lived-in look, very different from the Athertons' Ideal Home. By the time I got there it was already crowded. Barry's wife, Tess, let me in. She was a pretty woman with a tumble of grey curls and a wide, smiling mouth, wearing an emerald-green jumpsuit. She took my coat and ordered me to mingle. 'I'll do the hostess bit later and we'll have a proper talk. Right now, I'm busy with the food.'

I found Oliver and his alarmingly aggressive wife, Jennifer, waved to George, who was standing in a corner with two rather sullen teenagers, clutching his chest as if in the throes of a panic attack. There was no sign of Diana. Barry came up with a tray of drinks. 'Food's in the kitchen, help yourselves, won't you?' He'd abandoned the usual bow-tie for a Paisley cravat under a canary-yellow pullover.

Over the holiday, Jennifer had been pressing Oliver remorselessly to start his own estate agency. 'Then he won't get pissed around rotten by whoever George happens to be screwing at the moment. I told him, "Millie will go in with you."' She gave me a painful but encouraging dig. 'You would, wouldn't you, Millie? You could be his assistant.'

'Willingly,' I said, with a smile. Oliver groaned.

Over the next few hours, I well and truly mingled.

Several guests were estate agents, and we gravely discussed the state of the market. Was it up or down? One man gave me his card. 'If you should ever think of changing your job . . .' Barry introduced me to his children: Roger, the architect, an earnest man in jeans and an Arran sweater, Emma and Sadie, who would take the world by storm for a second time as soon as their children were old enough and they could resume their careers.

'Where's your other son?' I asked. 'Is he still abroad?'

Barry's perfectly groomed moustache quivered slightly. 'According to his mother, Sam won't be gracing us with his presence until New Year's Eve.'

Later, I forced myself to approach George. He eyed me appreciatively in my red dress before introducing me to his children, Annabel and Bill. 'Have you had a nice holiday?' I asked them.

They both shrugged. 'Okay.'

'I haven't a clue what teenagers get up to nowadays.' George sighed and looked harassed. 'I think they've been rather bored.' Bill rolled his eyes to confirm that this was definitely the case.

'Why don't you take them to the Cavern?' I suggested.

'Oh, Dad, would you?' Annabel pleaded. 'The girls at school will turn green if I tell them I've been to the Cavern.'

'Aren't I a bit old?' George said plaintively.

'You can just hover in the background,' I said. 'By the way, where's Diana? I thought she'd be here.'

George shrugged vaguely. 'She spent Christmas at her place. I haven't seen her in a few days.'

'Diana's horrible!' Bill burst out. 'You'll never guess what she did. She actually drew up a timetable of things for us to do – the pantomime, McDonald's, card games, charades, and idiotic films to watch on telly. She seemed to think we were children!'

Tactfully I wandered off. People had begun to leave. For the first time, I was aware of being the only youngish woman without a partner, and felt conspicuous as the crowd thinned, though I told myself I shouldn't care. I went upstairs to look for my coat. It was with a pile of others in what appeared to be Barry and Tess's untidy bedroom. I was putting it on when Tess came in, wearing her rather impish smile. 'Ah, there you are, Millie! I've been so rude. I always like to have a little chat with guests who've come for the first time, get to know them, as it were.' She sat on the bed and patted the space next to her. 'Sit down a minute.'

Under Tess's friendly questioning, I revealed all sorts of things about myself I wouldn't normally: about Diana, being demoted, James, and the awful tea at the Athertons' the day before.

'Never mind, love,' Tess said comfortingly. 'Things always turn out for the best in the long run, or so I've always found. Oh, well,' she levered herself off the bed, 'I'd better go downstairs and be the good hostess. I always feel a sense of relief when it's over, but sad too that it will be another year before I see some of our friends again. The children always found them a bit of a giggle, but they wouldn't miss their mum and dad's Boxing Day party.'

'Except Sam,' I reminded her.

'Ah, yes, Sam. He's in Mexico.' I was surprised when Tess looked at me rather speculatively, then said, 'Let me show you our Sam.' She opened the drawer in a bedside cupboard and took out a sheaf of newspaper cuttings. 'Barry doesn't know I've kept these. He's rather ashamed of Sam.' She handed me a cutting. 'That's him, in the *Daily Express*.'

A wiry young man with crew-cut hair was standing on a wall, baring his chest defiantly to the world. He held a banner aloft proclaiming, AXE THE TAX. Several policemen were reaching up in a vain attempt to grab his feet. 'He was sentenced to three months in prison or a thousand-pound fine for that,' Tess said proudly. 'Barry paid the fine and he was released, much to Sam's disgust. They rub one another up the wrong way, yet secretly they think the world of each other.'

There was a photo of Sam at the gates of Greenham Common with his then girlfriend, several of him protesting during the miners' strike. 'He hasn't been in court for years,' Tess said, slightly disappointed. 'Our three elder children are very conformist, but Sam takes after me. I used to go on CND marches when I was a girl – Barry disapproved of that, too.'

'What's he doing in Mexico? Has he gone to start a war?' I wasn't sure if I approved of Sam or not, but I admired his independent spirit.

'Oh, no. He's a record producer. He spends three or four months of the year travelling the world, taping folk songs, tribal music, that sort of thing. Then he comes home and turns them into proper recordings. He's got a studio in the attic. Much to his dad's amazement he's doing very well.' Suddenly she changed the subject, rather drastically, I thought. 'I expect your mum worries about you, still single at your age?'

'She does, yes.'

Tess hadn't changed the subject, after all. 'I worry terribly about Sam. He's thirty-three and I wish he'd establish some roots, start a family, have something more worthwhile to come home to than boring old Mum and Dad.'

A woman came in to collect her coat and Tess put the cuttings away. I thanked her for a lovely time and went home.

Over the final days of the year, I felt like two different people. There was only a skeleton staff at work and I had several half-days off, during which time I stencilled flowers on the corners of the living room and cleaned the flat from top to bottom, whistling tunelessly, happy. But when I stopped for a break, my mood would darken and I would feel restless, haunted by a sense of failure and hopelessness. There'd been a time, not long ago, when

I'd considered myself the only Cameron with an aim in life and any hope of a bright, successful future, but now I was the one with nothing to look forward to. Empty years loomed ahead, a vast, yawning abyss.

Mum had got a job in an office and would start the following week. 'Only making the tea, running a few errands.' She'd giggled merrily. 'I'll be the office junior. It's just temporary, till Alison comes.'

Trudy was gearing up for when Melanie started school in January or painting bottles for the stall she intended having every week. Should I get a hobby? I wondered. I rang Declan several times, worried that Norman would answer and whether I should engage him in conversation if he did, but there was never any reply. I badly missed Flo's flat, where I'd been quite happy to do nothing but watch the swirling lamp and listen to music. For want of something to do, on Sunday morning, I went to Mass at the Cathedral with my mother. I felt no spiritual reawakening or miraculous re-conversion in the remarkable circular building with its brilliant blue stained-glass windows, but on the way back to Flo's, I thought I might go again. Then something happened that I'd always dreaded.

Two boys were coming towards us. I hardly took them in, aware only that they were about fourteen and relatively well dressed. As they passed, one leaped at Mum and snatched the chain with K for Kate from around her neck.

Mum screamed, the boys ran only a short distance, then turned. The one who'd snatched the chain dangled it at us tauntingly, before they skipped away, laughing, almost dancing in their triumph.

'It could have happened anywhere,' Mum said later, when we were back at Flo's and she'd calmed down after I'd made us tea. 'It's not just Liverpool. It could have happened anywhere in the world.'

Something funny was going on between George and

Diana – or perhaps there was nothing going on at all. Everyone managed to glean little pieces of information and put them together to make a whole. It appeared that George had suggested Diana return home when it became obvious that she and the children weren't getting on, but had made no suggestion that she come back now that the children had gone. She'd spent Christmas alone in the house where she'd lived with her father. Even Oliver had to concede he felt sorry for the haggard little woman who stumbled round the office as if she were drunk, ignored by George. It wasn't that George was being deliberately cruel, he was taken up with the new office, which was opening in a few days' time. He appeared to have forgotten that Diana existed.

Like Oliver, I was sorry for Diana. If I'd been gutted by my demotion, she must have been feeling as if the bottom had dropped out of her world. But I was terrified that I was seeing myself in another five or ten years' time. Might I one day find myself waiting for a kind word from a man I'd been hoping would rescue me from a life of loneliness?

'Is this the girl who's just dumped a guy who runs an Aston Martin speaking?' Peter Maxwell chuckled when I phoned him. 'Men are terrified of loneliness, not just women. Sit back, have a good time, and see what happens. Don't wait for things, don't expect them, they won't come any sooner. It's like that song Flo used to play all the time. We're all dancing in the dark.'

'You're very clever,' I said admiringly. We rang off, deciding that if we were still single at forty we would live next door to each other.

I thought of James, who was going through the same experience as Diana, and wondered if I'd been too cruel, too abrupt. If he hadn't followed me to the bathroom, I would have told him tactfully in a more appropriate place. I recalled the way he'd been outside the nightclub – it seemed like years ago, but it was only a few months – when he'd said he was sick of selling cars to idiots like himself. He wanted to do something more worthwhile with his life. And the time by the Pier Head when he told me how much he loved me. He'd joined the Socialist Workers' Party to prove he wasn't shallow. We'd got on well until he decided he was in love with me; from then on, he began to fall apart. I felt sure that one day James would marry someone who didn't play such havoc with his emotions. They would have several children, and he would be back in the Conservative Party, still running his father's garage – perhaps all three – having forgotten he'd ever wanted to do anything else.

On New Year's Eve, I woke up with that aching feeling of loss again, a haunting sensation that something was missing from my life. I'd never been able to identify what it was, but in the darkness of my bedroom on the final day of the year, the knowledge came washing over me so forcefully that my body froze.

I was mourning the father I'd never known!

After a while, I made myself get up, convinced I might freeze altogether, die, if I stayed in bed any longer. I felt heavy and lethargic as I made myself a cup of tea. After I'd drunk it, I fetched the photo of my father, the one I'd found at Flo's, and stared at the sober little five-year-old, the only child not smiling. How would it have been if he'd married Mum? Would there have been a Trudy, a Declan, an Alison? If so, they would be different from the ones I knew now, and Tom O'Mara would never have existed. I remembered reading that if a time traveller went back to the beginning of time and destroyed a blade of grass, it could change the entire course of history.

It was all becoming too deep for me. Anyway, if I thought about it long enough it would be easy to cry and never stop. I took a long shower, made myself a decent breakfast for a change, then went to work, feeling only slightly better.

Stock Masterton was in turmoil. The Woolton office

had been decorated and furnished; it was ready to move into the following day. To celebrate the opening, clients would be offered refreshments and a glass of wine. There were adverts in the local press, though no mention of the food and drink, otherwise there would be a deluge of people who had no intention of buying or selling a house.

Every file had been copied, duplicates made of the wall charts. The contents of Oliver and Diana's desks were transferred. People kept rushing in, collecting papers and rushing out again. I sat behind my desk, feeling dazed. I hadn't the faintest idea what was happening to me. Should I transfer my things to Woolton or not? George seemed to have forgotten that I was to have been the receptionist, just as he'd forgotten that Diana lived and breathed. I'd typed out my notice weeks ago and put it on his desk, but it had never been acknowledged. Yesterday he'd asked me to make an appointment early in January with a firm who were erecting a small estate in Seaforth and wanted Stock Masterton to handle the sales side.

'An appointment for you?' I enquired.

'No, for yourself, of course,' George replied testily. There was mention of someone called Sandra in the new office, but no one seemed sure what job she was to do.

Oliver was no help. He complained that he was being kept in the dark and was at loggerheads with George, though George hadn't noticed, and Jennifer, Oliver's wife, was touring commercial property agents, presenting him with sheafs of offices to rent when he got home. 'She's approached her father for a loan,' he said soon after I arrived. 'I told her that Diana's like a pricked balloon, but she said, "You never know, the whole thing might start up again." Would you come in with me, Millie?' he said plaintively. 'I don't think I could do it on my own.'

'I'd be glad to,' I told him, for the umpteenth time. Even if my job turned out to be safe, after all, I didn't think I could bring myself to trust George again.

To add further to my confusion Barry Green came up

later in the morning and looked at me searchingly, as if he'd never seen me before, then gave a little 'Humph' of what sounded like approval. 'Tess has suggested I invite you round to dinner one night next week,' he said jovially. 'She said to please give her a ring if you'd like to come.'

I said I would, and meant it. I'd liked Tess enormously, and everything else about the Green household. I was thrilled to be asked to dinner.

Oliver took off again for Woolton. George was in his office, noisily slamming drawers and talking to himself. Everyone else was either at lunch or in Woolton, except for Darren, who had taken a client to view Nancy O'Mara's old house in Clement Street. I'd seriously thought of buying the place myself, cutting my mortgage by a third. After about half a minute, I realised it would be wrong, like going back instead of forward.

I leaned on my desk and thought about Flo, who would always remain a mystery, even though I knew so much about her. Had she been happy in the flat in William Square with her memories of Tommy O'Mara? Flo, with her secret lover, her secret child, the weekends spent with Mr Fritz on the Isle of Man.

George appeared, clutching his forehead dramatically, and announced that he was off to the Wig and Pen to have a pint and a panic attack. June had already left for lunch.

There'd been numerous times in the past when I'd been in the office alone, but when George slammed the door, it was like being shut in a place I'd never been before. I looked around uneasily, as if adjusting to strange new surroundings. There were decorations, very tasteful: a silver tree with 'presents' – a dozen empty boxes wrapped in red and green foil – and silver bells pinned to the walls. The fluorescent lights seemed to be hum-ming much too loudly. Outside, people hurried past, loaded with carrier bags, and I remembered that the sales were on. The sound of the endless traffic was oddly muted, and I had a sensation of being in a different dimension, and while I could see the people, they couldn't see me. The light, bouncing off one of the silver bells on the wall behind, was reflected in turn on to the screen of the computer, and all I could see was the dark shadow of my head surrounded by a bright, blurred halo. I stared at the screen, hypnotised, and the shadows seemed to shift and change until I thought I could see a face, but it wasn't mine. The eyes were very old, set in deep, black hollows, the mouth was . . .

The phone on my desk rang stridently. I jumped and grabbed the receiver, glad to escape from the face on the screen. It was Declan.

'Could you come to Mam's early tonight?' he said eagerly. The Camerons and the Daleys had been invited to Charmian and Herbie's New Year's Eve party.

'Why?'

'You'll never guess what our Trudy's bought!' Declan paused for effect. 'Champagne! I've never had champagne before. We're going to drink to the future, before we go upstairs. Oh, and there'll be a special guest – Scotty!'

I laughed, delighted, and promised to be there by eight. When I rang off, there was no longer a face on the computer, merely the dazzling reflection of a silver bell, and the office appeared quite normal. A man tapped on the window and made the thumbs-up sign. He could see me, I was real. I smiled at him and he opened the door.

'You should bottle that smile and sell it, luv,' he said. 'You'd make a fortune.'

I knew then that I'd come through. My mind cleared, and I was myself again, but better than the self I'd been before. The future no longer seemed bleak and hopeless, but bright and full of promise. Never again would I dream about slithering footsteps on the stairs or wake up with a feeling that something was missing from my life. I stretched my arms as wide as they would go, scarcely able to contain the sensation of total happiness.

There was wine on Elliot's desk. I went over and

poured myself a glass just as the door opened and a boy came in, not very tall, with an engaging face burned dark brown by the sun. He looked so ridiculous I had to smile. A long mac swirled around his muddy, wrinkled boots, but the comical thing about him was his hat: a brown felt beehive with a wide turned-up brim and a brightly patterned band.

'Hi!' He grinned, and lines of merriment crinkled beneath his eyes and around his mouth. I realised that this wasn't a boy but a man. I recognised the young rebel in the photographs Tess Green had showed me on Boxing Day, as well as her impish smile.

I returned to my desk. 'If you're looking for your father, I'm afraid he's out, I'm not sure where.'

'Shit,' he said amiably. 'Will he be long?'

'I'm not sure about that, either.'

'How come you know who I am?'

'Your mum showed me your photograph.'

He grinned again. 'Did she now?'

The atmosphere in the office had changed yet again. There was a tingling in the air, a crackle of excitement.

'So, you're just back from Mexico,' I said.

'That's right, early this morning. Dad had left for work by then, and Mum suggested I come and make my peace. I'd promised to be home for Christmas, you see, but got delayed. Dad gets worked up about these things, not like Mum. I had to borrow his matinée-idol mac. I mislaid my coat somewhere on the journey.' He gestured vaguely. 'He'll be annoyed.'

I could feel my lips twitching and longed to laugh. 'It's a pity you didn't mislay your hat instead.'

He removed the beehive and regarded it dispassionately. His hair was yellow, like wild straw. 'All the men wear them in Mexico.'

'This is Liverpool,' I reminded him.

'So it is.' He threw the hat to me like a frisbee. I caught it and put it on. 'It suits you. Keep it, not to wear, to hang on the wall.'

'Thanks. Help yourself to a drink while you're waiting.'

He poured a glass of wine and perched on the edge of his father's desk. I noticed his eyes were very blue, his face neither ugly nor handsome. It was an interesting face, open and expressive, and I could tell he had a great sense of humour. 'You obviously know loads about me,' he said, 'but I bet you'll be astounded to learn I also know a lot about you. You're Millie Cameron, you live in Blundellsands, have just dumped a boyfriend called James, and are in a bit of a tizzy over your job.'

'What on earth possessed your mum to tell you that?' I wasn't sure whether to be annoyed or not.

'Because – you'll be horrified to hear this – she really fancies you for a daughter–in–law. She started pinning my ear back about it the minute I arrived home. That's the real reason she asked me to come, not to see Dad but to see you.'

I released the laughter I'd been trying to contain ever since he came in. 'That's a mad idea.'

'I just thought I'd warn you, because I understand you've been invited to dinner next week, when Mum will really get to work on you.'

'Will you be there?'

'She'll handcuff me to the chair if I refuse. What about you? Will you come?'

'Under the circumstances,' I said gravely, 'I'll have to give the matter some thought.'

I removed the Mexican hat, which suddenly felt too heavy, and laid it carefully on the desk. The door opened and Oliver came in, followed by a sullen Diana.

'Do you fancy lunch?' Sam Green said. 'We can laugh ourselves silly over my mother.' Our eyes met fleetingly and I felt something pass between us. I had no idea if it meant something or not.

I reached for my bag. 'Why not?'

And why not go to dinner at the Greens next week. If the truth be known, I quite liked Sam Green, and fancied

Tess for a mother-in-law. Nothing might come of it, but so what? As Peter Maxwell said, we were all dancing in the dark.

MAUREEN LEE

MAUREEN LEE IS ONE OF THE BEST-LOVED SAGA WRITERS AROUND. All her novels are set in Liverpool and the world she evokes is always peopled with characters you'll never forget. Her familiarity with Liverpool and its people brings the terraced streets and tight-knit communities vividly to life in her books. Maureen is a born story-teller and her many fans love her for her powerful tales of love and life, tragedy and joy in Liverpool.

The Girl from Bootle

Born into a working-class family in Bootle, Liverpool, Maureen Lee spent her early years in a terraced house near the docks – an area that was relentlessly bombed during the Second World War. As a child she was bombed out of the house in Bootle and the family were forced to move.

Maureen left her convent school at 15 and wanted to become an actress. However, her shocked mother, who said that it was 'as bad as selling your body on the streets', put her foot down and Maureen had to give up her dreams and go to secretarial college instead.

As a child, Maureen was bombed out of her terraced house in Bootle

Family Life

A regular theme in her books is the fact that apparently happy homes often conceal pain and resentment and she sometimes draws on her own early life for inspiration. 'My mother always seemed to disapprove of me – she never said "well done" to me. My brother was the favourite,' Maureen says.

> I know she would never have approved of my books

As she and her brother grew up they grew apart. 'We just see things differently in every way,' says Maureen. This, and a falling out during the difficult time when her mother was dying, led to an estrangement that has lasted 24 years. 'Despite the fact that I didn't see eye-to-eye with my mum, I loved her very much. I deserted my family and lived in her flat in Liverpool after she went into hospital for the final time. My brother, who she thought the world of, never went near. Towards the end when she was fading she kept asking where he was. To comfort her, I had to pretend that he'd been to see her the day before, which was awful. I found it hard to get past that.'

Freedom – Moving on to a Family of Her Own

Maureen is well known for writing with realism about subjects like motherhood: 'I had a painful time giving birth to my children – the middle one was born in the back of a two-door car. So I know things don't always go as planned.'

My middle son was born in the back of a car

The twists and turns of Maureen's life have been as interesting as the plots of her books. When she met her husband, Richard, he was getting divorced, and despite falling instantly in love and getting engaged after only two weeks, the pair couldn't marry. Keen that Maureen should escape her strict family home, they moved to London and lived together before marrying. 'Had she known, my mother would never have forgiven me. She never knew that Richard had been married before.' The Lees had to pretend they were married even to their landlord. Of course, they did marry as soon as possible and have had a very happy family life.

Success at Last

Despite leaving school at fifteen, Maureen was determined to succeed as a writer. Like Kitty in *Kitty and Her Sisters* and Millie in *Dancing in the Dark*, she went to night school and ended up getting two A levels. 'I think it's good to "better yourself". It gives you confidence,' she says. After her sons grew up she had the time to pursue her dream, but it took several years and a lot of disappointment before she was successful. 'I was *determined* to succeed. My husband was one hundred per cent supportive. I wrote

'I think it's good to "better yourself". It gives you confidence'

lots of articles and short stories. I also started a saga which was eventually called *Stepping Stones*. Then Orion commissioned me to finish it, it was published – and you know the rest.'

What are your memories of your early years in Bootle?

Of being poor, but not poverty-stricken. Of women wearing shawls instead of coats. Of knowing everybody in the street. Of crowds gathering outside houses in the case of a funeral or a wedding, or if an ambulance came to collect a patient, who was carried out in a red blanket. I longed to be such a patient, but when I had diptheria and an ambulance came for me, I was too sick to be aware of the crowds. There were street parties, swings on lamp-posts, hardly any traffic, loads of children playing in the street, dogs without leads. Even though we didn't have much money, Christmas as a child was fun. I'm sure we appreciated our few presents more than children do now.

What was it like being young in Liverpool in the 1950s?

The late fifties were a wonderful time for my friends and me. We had so many places to go: numerous dance halls, The Philharmonic Hall, The Cavern Club, theatres, including The Playhouse where you could buy tickets for ninepence. We were crushed together on benches at the very back. As a teenager I loved the theatre – I was in a dramatic society. I also used to make my own clothes, which meant I could have the latest fashions in just the right sizes, which I loved. Sometimes we'd go on boat trips across the water to New Brighton or on the train to Southport. We'd go for the day and visit the fairground and then go to the dance hall in the evening.

We clicked instantly and got engaged two weeks later

I met Richard at a dance when he asked my friend Margaret up. When she came back she said 'Oh, he was nice.' And then somebody else asked her to dance – she was very glamorous, with blonde hair – still is, as it happens. So Richard asked me to dance because she had gone! We clicked instantly and got engaged two weeks later. I'm not impulsive generally, but I just knew that he was the one.

*Do you consider yourself independent
and adventurous like Annemarie in*
The Leaving of Liverpool *or Kitty* in Kitty
and her Sisters?

In some ways. In the late fifties, when I was 16,
Margaret and I hitchhiked to the Continent. It
was really, really exciting. We got a lift from
London to Dover on the back of a lorry. We sat
on top of stacks of beer crates – we didn't half
get cold! We ended up sleeping on the side of the
road in Calais because we hadn't found a hotel.
We travelled on to Switzerland and got jobs
in the United Nations in Geneva as secretaries.
It was a great way to see the world. I've no
idea what inspired us to go. I think we just
wanted some adventure, like lots of my heroines.

*Your books often look at the difficult side
of family relationships. What experiences
do you draw on when you write about
that?*

I didn't always find it easy to get on with my
mother because she held very rigid views. She
was terribly ashamed when I went to Europe.
She said 'If you leave this house you're not

coming back!' But when we got to Switzerland we got fantastic wages at the United Nations – about four times as much as we got at home. When I wrote and told her she suddenly forgave me and went around telling everybody, 'Our Maureen's working at the United Nations in Geneva.'

> 'If you leave this house you're not coming back!'

She was very much the kind of woman who worried what the neighbours would think. When we moved to Kirby, our neighbours were a bit posher than us and at first she even hung our curtains round the wrong way, so it was the neighbours who would see the pattern and we just had the inside to look at. It seems unbelievable now, but it wasn't unusual then – my mother-in-law was even worse. When she bought a new three-piece she covered every bit of it with odd bits of curtaining so it wouldn't wear out – it looked horrible.

My mother-in-law was a strange woman. She hated the world and everyone in it. We had a wary sort of relationship. She gave Richard's brother an awful life – she was very controlling and he never left home. She died in the early nineties and for the next few years my kind, gentle brother-in-law had a relationship with a wonderful woman who ran an animal sanctuary. People tend to keep their family problems private but you don't have to look further than your immediate neighbours to see how things really are and I try to reflect that in my books.

You don't have to look further than your immediate neighbours to see how things really are

Is there anything you'd change about your life?

I don't feel nostalgic for my youth, but I do feel nostalgic for the years when I was a young mum. I didn't anticipate how I'd feel when the boys left home. I just couldn't believe they'd gone and I still miss them being around although I'm very happy that they're happy.

Are friendships important to you?

Vastly important. I always stay with Margaret when I visit Liverpool and we email each other two or three times a week. Old friends are the best sort as you have shared with them the ups and downs of your life. I have other friends in Liverpool that I have known all my adult life. I have also made many new ones who send me things that they think will be useful when I write my books.

Have you ever shared an experience with one of your characters?

Richard's son from his first marriage recently got in touch with us. It was quite a shock as he's been in Australia for most of his life and we've never known him. He turned out to be a charming person with a lovely family. I've written about long-lost family members returning in *Kitty and Her Sisters* and *The Leaving of Liverpool* so it was strange for me to find my life reflecting the plot of one of my books.

Q & A

....

Describe an average writing day for you.

Wake up, Richard brings me tea in bed and I watch breakfast television for a bit. Go downstairs at around 8 a.m. with the intention of doing housework. Sit and argue with Richard about politics until it's midday and time to go to my shed and start writing. Come in from time to time to make drinks and do the crossword. If I'm stuck, we might drive to Sainsbury's for a coffee and read all the newspapers we refuse to have in the house. Back in my shed, I stay till about half seven and return to the house in time to see *EastEnders*.

Don't miss Maureen's bestselling novels:

Mother of Pearl

1939. Amy was just eighteen when she met Barney and they fell deeply in love. Their romantic, passionate marriage was a match made in heaven – and then war came. Barney volunteered to fight, and when he returned to Liverpool after VE Day, everything began to change. But what was it that made Amy kill her adored husband – and what happened to their five-year-old daughter, Pearl?

1971. Amy has been released from prison. But her freedom changes the lives of everyone – not least Pearl. Now twenty-five, she was brought up in a very happy home by her aunt, and has no idea of the terrible secret hidden in her past. As the truth unravels, both Amy and Pearl are caught up in the shocking fall-out of one family's tragedy.

£6.99
ISBN: 978-0-7528-9381-5

Sign up now to discover more about other authors you may enjoy

CherryPicks

Sign up now to our Cherry Picks Newsletter
to receive all the latest news about our
women's fiction authors, new books
and hot competitions, plus the latest author
events in your area.

Simply go to
www.orionbooks.co.uk/cherrypicks

To access all this for free:
Like Cherry Picks on ▪️ Follow Cherry Picks on ▪️